Sergio Olguín was born in Buenos Aires in 1967. His first work of fiction, *Lanús*, was published in 2002. It was followed by a number of successful novels, including *Oscura monótona sangre* (*Dark Monotonous Blood*), which won the Tusquets Prize in 2009. His books have been translated into English, German, French and Italian. *The Foreign Girls*, following on from the success of *The Fragility of Bodies*, is the second in a crime series featuring journalist Veronica Rosenthal. Sergio Olguín is also a scriptwriter and has been the editor of a number of cultural publications.

THE FOREIGN GIRLS

Sergio Olguín

Translated by Miranda France

BITTER LEMON PRESS
LONDON

BITTER LEMON PRESS

First published in the United Kingdom in 2021 by
Bitter Lemon Press, 47 Wilmington Square, London WC1X 2ET

www.bitterlemonpress.com

First published in Spanish as *Las extranjeras*
by Suma de Letras (Penguin Random House Grupo Editorial Argentina), 2014

Bitter Lemon Press gratefully acknowledges the financial
assistance of the Arts Council of England

Work published within the framework of "Sur" Translation Support Program
of the Ministry of Foreign Affairs and Worship of the Argentine Republic

Obra editada en el marco del Programa "Sur" de Apoyo a las Traducciones
del Ministerio de Relaciones Exteriores y Culto de la República Argentina

A CIP record for this book is available from the British Library

PB ISBN 978–1–913394–387
eBook USC ISBN 978-1-913394-394
eBook ROW ISBN 978-1-913394-462

Typeset by Tetragon, London
Printed and bound by the CPI Group (UK) Ltd, Croydon, CR0 4YY

To Mónica Hasenberg and Brenno Quaretti

To Eduardo Arechaga

These insurgent, underground groups, the mara wars, the mafias, the wars police wage against the poor and non-whites, are the new forms of state authoritarianism. These situations depend on the control of bodies, above all women's bodies, which have always been largely identified with territory. And when territory is appropriated, it is marked. The marks of the new domination are placed on it. I always say that the first colony was a woman's body.

RITA SEGATO,
INTERVIEW BY ROXANA SANDÁ
IN *PÁGINA/12*, 17 JULY 2009

One goes in straightforward ways,
One in a circle roams:
Waits for a girl of his gone days,
Or for returning home.

But I do go – and woe is there –
By a way nor straight, nor broad,
But into never and nowhere,
Like trains – off the railroad.

ANNA AKHMATOVA,
"ONE GOES IN STRAIGHTFORWARD WAYS"
(TRANSLATED BY YEVGENY BONVER;
FIRST PUBLISHED IN *POETRY LOVERS' PAGE*, 2008)

We are all hiding something sinister. Even the most normal among us.

GUSTAVO ESCANLAR, *LA ALEMANA*

Contents

Prologue

FROM: Verónica Rosenthal
TO: Paula Locatti
RE: Radio Silence

Dear Paula,

This is going to be one long email, my friend. Apologies for not replying to your previous messages nor to your request, so elegantly expressed, that I "stop sending fucking automatic replies". Originally I intended not to answer any emails during my vacation and anyone who wrote to me was meant to get a message saying I wouldn't be responding until I got home. But what has just happened to me is shocking, to put it mildly. I need to share it with someone. With you, I mean. You're the only person I can tell something like this. I thought of ringing you, even of asking you to come, because I didn't want to be alone. But I also can't behave like a teenager fretting about her first time. That's why I decided not to call but to write instead. On the phone I might beg you to come. And, to be honest, there's other stuff I want to tell you, things I could never bring myself to say in person, not even to you. Written communication can betray our thoughts, but oral so often leads to a slip of the tongue, and I want to avoid that. There's a slip in the last sentence, in fact, but I'll let it go.

As I was saying, what I write here is for your eyes only. Nobody else must find out what I am going to tell you. Nobody. None of the girls, none of your other friends. It's too personal for me to want to share it. Come to think of it, delete this email after you've read it.

I told you that I was going to start my trip in Jujuy, then go down from there to Tucumán. Well, I didn't do that in the end. A few days before I set off, my sister Leticia reminded me about the weekend home that belongs to my cousin Severo (actually, he's the son of one of my father's cousins). He's not only a Rosenthal but also part of 'our' legal family: a commercial judge in Tucumán. I think he'd love to work in my dad's practice, but Aarón has always kept him at arm's length. He's forty-something, married to a spoiled bitch and father to four children. Anyway, Severo has a weekend cottage on the Cerro San Javier, and whenever he comes to Buenos Aires he insists that we borrow it. I checked and the house was available for the time I needed it, so I decided to change my route: to start in Tucumán, stay a week in Cousin Severo's house and then go on to Salta and Jujuy. I thought it wouldn't be a bad thing to spend a quiet week there, resting and clearing my mind after the very shitty summer I'd had.

So I arrived at the airport in San Miguel de Tucumán, picked up the car I'd rented and swung by the courts to see my cousin and collect the keys to the house. I spent half an hour in his office exchanging family news (his eldest son starts law this year – another one, for God's sake). I graciously declined his invitation to lunch and, with barely suppressed horror, another invitation to have dinner at his house with the wife and some of the four children. He gave me a little map with directions (even though I had rented a GPS with the car – although God knows why, since you can get anywhere just by asking) and a sheet of paper with useful telephone numbers and the Wi-Fi code. He told me that a boy came to clean the pool once a week and there was a gardener too, but that they came very early and had their own keys to the shed, that I wouldn't even know they were there (and he was right, I've never seen their faces). He offered to send me 'the girl' who lives in their house in the city, but I declined this invitation.

If you saw my cousin's house you'd go berserk. It's hidden away behind a little wood on the hillside. A typically nineties construction, Californian style: huge windows, Italian furniture, BKF butterfly chairs (uncomfortable), a Michael Thonet rocking chair which, if it isn't an original, certainly looks the part, a spectacular view (even from the toilets), a Jacuzzi in almost all the bathtubs, a sauna, a well-equipped gym, huge grounds (looking a bit sparse now that autumn's on its way), a heated swimming pool, a changing room, a gazebo which is in itself practically another house and lots, lots more. Plus full cupboards, a wine cellar and more CDs and DVDs than you could possibly ever need. Never mind a week, it's the kind of paradise to hide away in for a year.

And that's what I've been doing. Reading, spending time in the pool, watching movies. Even though there's Wi-Fi I haven't gone online; I haven't watched the news or read the papers. If there had been a coup, a tsunami in Japan or World War Three had broken out, I would be none the wiser.

It feels like a kind of professional and life detox. After spending the summer covering for other people at the magazine who were on leave, writing pieces no one was interested in, and feeling no appetite to get my teeth into a proper story, I needed this: to be far from the relentless noise of the city – no friends, no guys, no family. Nothing. It's the first time since Lucio died that I've been able to spend time alone with myself. And I've needed it. The summer was hard. I don't need to tell you that.

A few days ago I decided to go out for a bit. It was still light when I set off in the car with no particular destination. The mountain road in this area is really beautiful, so I was driving along, taking in the view without worrying about anything. After a thousand twists and turns, the road came to a kind of seaside town, like a cool resort: a few pubs, boutiques with hippie clothes, groups of shouting teenagers. The usual.

I stopped at a bar that looked promising and had a parking spot right beside it. Inside there weren't many people. I sat down at a table near the bar and asked for a Jim Beam. It seems my order caused a stir because, when the glass of bourbon arrived, I noticed some guys on a nearby table were staring at me – them and the barman too. I focussed on my maps and guidebooks. I wasn't there to flirt with the locals.

Soon after that, two girls arrived. I didn't actually see them come in and go up to the bar. It was their voices I noticed first. Or rather the voice of one of them who, in very good Spanish but with a foreign accent, asked the barman where they could buy "una cuerda".

I think it was the word cuerda that got my attention, and I immediately imagined that these two women were looking for rope to tie up some man, not thinking that cuerda can also mean "string". The barman must have thought something similar, because he asked them "Una cuerda?" in a surprised tone of voice. The foreign girl clarified: "Una cuerda para la guitarra".

The barman said if they were looking for a music shop they should go to the provincial capital, San Miguel de Tucumán. The other girl asked if they could call a taxi to take them there from the bar. And I, who had been listening as though I were part of the conversation, offered to take them myself.

I don't tend to have such quick reactions. And I still don't know what prompted me to make the offer: whether I was starting to get bored sitting there, or I wanted to talk to someone after so many days alone, or that the fact they were foreign girls prompted a sudden urge to be a good ambassador for my country. Anyway, the girls were happy to accept the offer.

As for what happened next, I'll be brief. I realize now that the reason I included so many unimportant details in what I wrote before was to put off the most important part, the only thing I really want to tell you. That I need to tell you.

Petra, Frida and I quickly bonded in the way that people who meet while travelling often do. We talked about our lives over empanadas in a restaurant on the edge of town. Petra is Italian, sings and plays the guitar. The other girl, Frida, is Norwegian and spent a year living in Argentina. That was when they got to know each other. And then they made a plan to meet up again to travel together in northern Argentina, Bolivia and Peru.

They both speak perfect Spanish. Frida has a slight Castilian accent because she studied in Madrid. Petra, on the other hand, sounds really Argentinian. She lived in Milan with a guy from Mendoza for more than a year and after that she was in a relationship with someone from Córdoba. Nothing like pillow talk to improve your accent.

On more than one occasion we raised our glasses to all the idiot men who have ruined our lives. My Italian and Norwegian friends would have been right at home on a night out with you and me in Buenos Aires.

We decided to travel on together, at least until we reached the city of Salta (they want to spend a few days there, but I'd rather press on to Jujuy). Yesterday I went to pick them up so they can move into my cousin's place. There's plenty of room.

The girls are a lot less prudish than me. They sunbathe topless and don't mind walking naked out of their rooms. I've tried to follow suit, at least by going topless next to the pool. They're two lovely, cheerful girls, a few (but not many) years younger than me.

I've realized from one or two things they said that there is, or was, something between them.

Last night we got drunk on some whisky that my cousin is definitely going to miss. Don't ask me how – or how far – things went, but Frida and I ended up in what you might call a confusing situation.

There it is, I've said it.

It was nice, unnerving, exhilarating.

I don't want any jokes, or winks, or sarcasm from you. Is that possible? Or for you to cling to the edge of the mattress if we end up sharing a bed when we go to the hot springs at Gualeguaychú.

I'm writing all this from my bed (alone, obviously). Midday. I woke up with a crashing hangover. But even so, I remember absolutely everything that happened last night. I still haven't left the room. There's too much silence in the house. Ah well.

Kisses,

Vero

*

FROM: Verónica Rosenthal
TO: Paula Locatti
RE: Kolynos and the party

Hi Pau,

Thanks. I expected nothing less from you. But your thing doesn't count. Nothing one does as a virgin can be taken seriously. If I told you about the stuff I got up to back then, you'd be appalled.

I'm in Cafayate now. All on my own.

After the last email I wrote you, I showered, got dressed and went into the kitchen. Petra and Frida were there. They were making coffee and didn't seem to be in a much better state than I was. I mean, they were obviously hung-over too. None of us mentioned the disconcerting experience we'd had a few hours previously. During our last days at the house there were a few histrionics from Frida, too boring to go into details. Nothing worth sharing.

Eventually, we decided to go to the north of Tucumán province. They wanted to head for Amaicha del Valle, but I was keen to stop first at Yacanto del Valle, a little town much closer than that, which I'd been told I should see. We agreed to stay there for two or three nights.

In Yacanto we stayed in a charming hotel run by a couple from Buenos Aires. The girls stayed in one room and I was in the other.

Yacanto is a boutique town. All very cool and fake. Apart from the main square and the eighteenth-century church, everything else is like a kind of stage set put together by city types from Buenos Aires and San Miguel de Tucumán. There are vegetarian restaurants, clothes shops (more expensive even than the ones in Palermo), antique shops; there's even a contemporary art gallery – whose owner is related to my cousin's wife and from a traditional Salta family, like her.

I took the girls to the gallery and we met him there. He's called Ramiro. I already knew a bit about him from my sister, who met him on a trip she made with her husband and the kids. Leti practically drooled when she told me about Ramiro. Knowing my brother-in-law, and Leti's taste (in all things),

I was prepared for the worst. But on this occasion my elder sister wasn't completely wrong.

Ramiro. Roughly my age or possibly a couple of years older, a bit taller than me, broad shoulders, lantern jaw, blue eyes, Kolynos smile, very short hair that left his nape dangerously exposed (bare napes should be banned). And single. This information he offered himself, two minutes into our conversation.

Kolynos behaved like a gentleman. He showed us round his gallery. Nothing too earthy, no indigenous art: there were pieces by artists from the Di Tella Foundation, a Plate, a Ferrari, a couple of Jacobys and work from the eighties and nineties (Kuitca, Alfredo Prior, Kenneth Kemble). The guy has good taste and clearly likes showing it off.

I already know what you're thinking: run a mile from exhibitionists! You'd equate his artworks, the big house where he has his gallery and his Japanese pickup with the kind of man who flashes at the entrance of a girls' school. But the only time that ever happened to me I had a good look. I was shocked, but I still looked.

Evidently some methods of seduction don't work with foreign girls – or perhaps contemporary Argentine art is the problem – because Petra and Frida seemed bored as they listened to Ramiro. I tried to arrange something for that night because I didn't feel like only being with the girls. Ramiro said he was busy, that he had a lot on. It came across a bit like an excuse. I know what you're going to say: he sounds like a dick.

Kolynos asked for my phone number, asked if I used WhatsApp – obviously, I said no – and looked at me as though I'd landed from another planet. "I'm an old-fashioned girl," I added, with a quiet pride.

I could already see myself spending the evening eating tamales with Petra and Frida, then going to get drunk in their room or mine. But get this: an hour after we left the gallery, Kolynos called me. He said that there was a party that night at a house on the outskirts of Yacanto, and did the three of us want to go. Obviously I said we did, without even running it by the girls.

Petra and Frida were both happy when I said we'd been invited to a party. I'd almost say I was mildly offended that they were so keen to spend the night with someone other than me. And so…

That evening Ramiro came to fetch the three of us in his pickup and off we went. Why didn't we walk, since it was only six or seven blocks away? More exhibitionism. It's true that the house was on the outskirts of town, but that's because Yacanto is only five blocks long.

We arrived. A big-ass country house with music blaring out and people dancing and holding glasses. It looked like a beer ad.

To start with the girls stuck by me, something I wasn't thrilled about. Kolynos was very gallant. We danced, we chatted, we strolled around the garden. All very proper.

He introduced me to the owner of the property, a certain Nicolás. Also single. I marvelled at the size of his house and the idiot started boasting about the huge estate that surrounded it. As Mili would say: good game, terrible result.

We were still with Nicolás when a group of offensively young twenty-somethings turned up. One was a dreamboat – bronzed, sub-twenty-five. You'd have loved him. "My little brother, Nahuel," Kolynos said by way of introduction. Well, that was a surprise. Immediately I thought of Leti, who had recommended the older brother without mentioning the younger one. Either she hadn't met him, or she considered me far too old for such a morsel. Anyway, full disclosure: Nahuelito barely registered me and didn't have much time for his brother either. He started talking to Nicolás and we moved away from the group.

At one point it seemed to me that Petra was annoyed about how Frida was treating me, or about something, anyway. For some reason the Italian kept freaking out at Ramiro or any other man who came her way (and a lot did).

A lot of alcohol later, I ran into Frida coming out of the bathroom (was she waiting for me?) and she told me that she wasn't enjoying the party at all. I asked where Petra was and she pointed at the dance floor. That was when I realized that these two were a couple of drama queens who got off on making each other jealous and wanted to stick me in the middle. She didn't like Ramiro either, she said. I laughed and she got annoyed. I made it clear that I was planning to leave with Ramiro and that she should go and have fun with other people. Before she had a chance to answer, I was already walking away.

Soon afterwards, Ramiro took me upstairs. He kissed me and suggested we go to his house. I told him that I was with the girls and couldn't leave them alone. He said that I shouldn't worry, that they could walk back to the hotel if they couldn't find anyone to take them back, but that he suspected they wouldn't be leaving alone. They could even sleep over here, at the house.

Long story short, I went home with Señor Kolynos. We had a good time. The next morning I felt a bit awkward. Not about him, but about the girls. I felt as though I had betrayed them. A stupid reaction, because the last thing I needed was to be giving them chapter and verse on everything I did or didn't do. I got angry with myself. I went to the hotel, packed my case, paid the bill and left. I was going to leave a note for the girls but that felt like giving explanations, something I wanted to avoid.

At 8 a.m. I set off for Cafayate. I've just arrived. I'm in a really pretty hotel. The owner, yet again, comes from Buenos Aires. Have I really travelled eight hundred miles to meet people from Buenos Aires?

This place is beautiful. I'm going to enjoy the provincial peace. I'm sorry about leaving the girls, but I needed some space. I'll write them an email. Perhaps we can meet up in Salta, or in Jujuy itself. Yes, I know, I'm impossible to please. It's only half a day since I saw them and already I miss them. I'm going to wait for them here.

Kolynos? He was a summer storm. Not even that. I don't think we'll see each other again.

V.

*

FROM: Verónica Rosenthal
TO: Paula Locatti
RE: Re: Kolynos and the party

The girls are dead. Petra and Frida. They killed them, raped them, treated them like animals. It was after the party. I'm to blame for all of it, everything that happened to them. If I hadn't left them there, they'd be alive. Yesterday the bodies were found lying in some undergrowth. Why the fuck did I leave them alone? I'm going back to Yacanto del Valle. I'm going to find out who the bastards were. I swear if I find them first I'll kill them. I'll tear them apart.

1 *New Moon*

I

Flying made her sleepy. Any time she had to take a long flight, she slept for a large part of the journey and only woke up to eat or go to the bathroom. People must think she took sleeping pills, but it was just the way she was. She couldn't even stay awake on a two-hour flight like the one she was on now to Tucumán. Only the shudder of the plane as it touched down at Benjamín Matienzo airport made her open her eyes. Verónica stretched and looked out of the window at the other planes on the ground, the trailers stacked with suitcases and the airport workers moving around.

After collecting her luggage, she went to the car rental office. She had reserved a Volkswagen Gol to take her as far as Jujuy. A small and practical car. In Buenos Aires she made do with borrowing her sister Leticia's car every now and then, because she didn't like driving in the city, but the prospect of a journey through Argentina's north without having to rely on buses and timetables, taking back roads and stopping whenever she liked, was appealing enough to persuade her to hire a car.

The rental company employee asked her name.

"Verónica. Verónica Rosenthal."

Together they walked to the parking lot. The employee made a note in the file of a couple of scratches on the bodywork, showed her where the spare wheel was and how to remove it, reminded her that she must return the car with a full tank and finally handed over the keys and relevant documents.

Verónica switched on the GPS she had rented along with the car and entered the address of her cousin Severo's house in the centre of San Miguel de Tucumán. She lowered the window and felt the breeze on her face, in her tousled hair. A kind of peace swept through her body.

She hadn't felt like this for a long time. During the last few difficult months there had been only one objective: to get through the day. She had been like a patient in a coma, except that she walked, she talked, she got on with her job. She didn't want anything, seek out anything, need anything. She tried not even thinking. How long could she have gone on like that?

Verónica's colleagues at the magazine, her family and friends would have had no hesitation in describing her as a successful journalist. When she had started working in journalism it had been with the dream of exposing corruption, injustice, lies. She had been not quite twenty with everything ahead of her, both in her own life and in the wider world. If someone had told her then that at the age of thirty she would take down a criminal gang that gambled on the lives of poor children, she would have been proud. That was exactly the kind of journalism she wanted to do. And she had done it. She had put a bunch of men behind bars who were responsible for the death and mutilation of boys. She had exposed and eliminated a gambling racket that nobody had investigated before her. No kid would ever again stand on a train track waiting for ten thousand tons of metal to come thundering towards him. But she had also paid a price she had never imagined: Lucio, the man she loved, had been killed, a victim of the same mafia.

She had published her article while her grief over Lucio's death was still raw. The repercussions were such that, in the days following the publication of her piece in *Nuestro Tiempo,* she had been expected to appear on various television and radio programmes. She had given the requisite answers to her colleagues' questions, smiled at the end of every interview and thanked them for inviting her on. How could she have told them the truth? How could she put into words the anguish of knowing that one of her informants, Rafael, had so nearly been murdered? What would have happened if one of those condescending colleagues had asked what she had done to save the lives of Rafael and the doorman of the building where she lived? She could have answered: *It wasn't easy. I had to commandeer a work colleague's car to get there in time. I found four professional assassins about to slay Rafael and Marcelo and had no option but to drive into them. Run over all four of them.*

The journalist would have considered this with an expression of utmost compassion. They would have asked how she had felt at the moment she crushed the assassins.

Relief, knowing that two people I loved weren't going to die at the hands of those brutes.

But nobody would ask those questions, nor did she want them to. She preferred the generous silence her boss and her colleagues had brought to the reporting of her article. The fearful silence of her father and sisters. The complicit silence of her friends. The critical silence of Federico.

She had spent the summer going between the newsroom and home, home and the newsroom. Knowing that her colleagues with children preferred to take their vacations in January and February, she had asked for leave in March. She spent much of the summer helping Patricia, her editor, writing twice as many lifestyle pieces as usual, filling pages. The bosses would be happy.

For some time Verónica had been thinking of making a trip to the north of Argentina. She had been to Jujuy with her family as a child but didn't remember much about it. It was her sister Leticia who had said she ought to go to their cousin Severo's weekend house. Strictly speaking, Severo Rosenthal was the son of a cousin of their father's who had moved to Tucumán decades earlier. Severo had studied law at the Universidad Católica Argentina in Buenos Aires, and during those years her parents had treated him like a son: he often went to eat at the Rosenthal home; some nights he even stayed over. Verónica would have been not yet ten at the time.

After he graduated, Severo worked for a time at Aarón Rosenthal's law firm, but soon afterwards he returned to Tucumán. Supposedly he was going back to the provinces to do what he eventually did: forge a career in the provincial courts. But when Aarón talked about his cousin's son he often said that he had "got rid of him" because he was "slow on the uptake". Whatever the truth, Severo was now a commercial judge. He had married, had children. And along with these accomplishments he had acquired a spectacular weekend house that was every now and then at the disposal of the Buenos Aires Rosenthals, perhaps to repay them for the many meals they had shared with Severo in his student days.

When Leticia found out that Verónica was planning a trip to Tucumán, Salta and Jujuy she urged her to spend a few days in that house. She also gave her two other instructions.

The first was "Steer clear of the Witch." That was how she referred to Severo's wife, Cristina Hileret Posadas, who was from a traditional northern family. The Rosenthal sisters had never liked her, not that they considered Severo a great catch or anything. But to fall into the clutches of someone so bitter, bilious and pessimistic, whose only redeeming feature was having family money, struck them as a terrible fate – even for Severo.

Her second piece of advice was this: "You should definitely visit Yacanto del Valle. The town is really pretty. Plus the Witch has a cousin who lives there, and he's hot."

For the first time in many years, Verónica was considering following her older sister's advice.

II

She wasn't used to driving on mountain roads, so she couldn't enjoy the views as she climbed the road that led to her cousin's house in Cerro San Javier. And even though her cousin had given her the GPS coordinates as well as a map with directions, she was convinced she was going to get lost. But here she was: in front of the gate to The Eyes of San Miguel, as the property was called, a name that Verónica found unnerving, to say the least. That a Rosenthal should give his house the name of a Christian saint was already controversial. She understood the choice better when she parked the car and walked round to the property's back entrance. From that vantage point there was a spectacular view of the city of San Miguel de Tucumán, nestled in a valley in the distance. Closer were the hills of the San Javier sierra, dotted with big houses similar to her cousin's.

She took off her sandals and sat on the edge of the swimming pool with her feet in the water. For a while she took in the view, feeling the afternoon sun draw a light sweat onto her elephant-grey Tommy Hilfiger T-shirt. There was still heat in these end-of-summer days.

With wet feet, Verónica walked from the garden to the back door of the house. She opened the door and disconnected the alarm. Despite having assured Severo that she would put it on every time she left the house, she didn't plan to reconnect it until the last day. She hated alarms in houses, cars or on telephones.

She took her suitcase and bag out of the car and dropped them on the living-room floor. The house smelt of hardwood, cinnamon and spices. Verónica was amazed by the living area with its inviting Italian armchairs and wall-mounted fifty-inch television. A shelving unit covered all of one wall but wasn't stuffed with books: spaces had been left for artistic objects. Some pieces of furniture seemed to have been bought in antique shops. A Tudor-style cupboard, two BKF chairs, a Louis XV sideboard, a Thonet rocking chair. The eclectic mix of antique and contemporary pieces worked well in this house with its picture windows, with its fireplace in one of the few walls that didn't have a window onto the garden. Was the Witch responsible for the decor? Were these pieces inherited from her family in Jujuy and Salta? Could she have bought them from some neighbour in need of ready cash? Stolen them? When it came to the Witch, anything was possible.

The kitchen was stunning, with an extraordinary variety of appliances Verónica had never even known existed. The island with its lapacho-wood counter was larger than the table in her place in Villa Crespo. The kitchen alone was bigger than her apartment.

There was more food in the larder than you'd find in a bunker designed for surviving a nuclear attack. And there were two fridges. One of them was all freezer, in fact, and packed with frozen food. Cousin Severo had gone out of his way to save her the trouble of visiting a supermarket.

Verónica looked around the rest of the house, trying to decide which bedroom she was going to sleep in. She crossed a room with a pool table, a drinks cabinet and a cupboard containing a box of cigars. The room smelled of good tobacco.

Finally she settled on a room with a double bed and an en-suite bathroom boasting a Jacuzzi and more enormous windows. It particularly amused her that she could sit on the lavatory, pissing or shitting while contemplating the horizon. It seemed like the strangest thing ever – but she liked it.

III

There was Wi-Fi in the house, but Verónica barely used it. The automatic reply set up on her account was the perfect alibi not to keep on top of emails. She didn't really feel like surfing the internet, either. She'd rather read, or watch movies. She had brought some books with her (Laure Adler's biography of Marguerite Duras, Murakami's *1Q84* and Ernest Hemingway's *Complete Short Stories*). She had begun *1Q84* with great enthusiasm, but had been losing interest and finally decided to abandon the novel after finding the language used in erotic scenes too medicalized. Perhaps the problem was with the translator, rather than the Japanese author.

Her cousin Severo's library had stopped expanding sometime in the 1970s but was very good all the same. He had an almost complete collection of Emecé's Great Novelists series. She was surprised to find *Informe Bajo Llave* by Marta Lynch, an author she had never thought of reading. She found the novel, with its story of a writer in love with a military man during the dictatorship, both dark and passionate. She had also selected a Ken Follett novel and Graham Greene's *Dr Fischer of Geneva* for her vacation reading.

The DVD collection contained many movies Verónica had never seen. Unlike most of her friends, she wasn't a cinephile, but she liked going to the cinema and watching the odd movie on television. She wasn't partial to any particular era or style of movie, so her cousin's giant screen was able to tempt her with such offerings as *All About Eve*, that classic story of ambition and treachery. It was the first time she had seen a whole Bette Davis movie, and Verónica thought her the most wonderful actress ever to appear on screen. She also watched *All That Jazz* (the alphabetical organization of the DVDs guided her choices), *GoodFellas*, *Ginger & Fred*, *In the Name of the Father* and *2001: A Space Odyssey*.

She never got up before eleven, and then the first thing Verónica did every morning was make herself coffee with the Nespresso machine. That said, she usually suffered a brief episode of insomnia at around 7 a.m. She woke up feeling anxious, as though some forgotten nightmare had left shards in her brain. Perhaps it was simply that she wasn't used to the birds' dawn chorus. She got up, had a piss, smoked a cigarette and read her Duras biography by the light of the bedside lamp (she didn't want to open the curtains yet). Half an hour later she was fast asleep again, and those extra three hours of sleep were restorative.

Verónica would take her coffee and cigarette to the veranda, along with whatever book she was reading, and stay there until after noon. Then she connected her iPod to the music system speakers, made a sandwich or a salad, opened a beer and put on the television. No news bulletins or gossip programmes. Verónica preferred those reality shows where couples swapped their homes, a chef explored the gastronomic possibilities of insects from Burundi, a badly behaved dog was retrained, a woman with a crane hijacked a car or a policeman transformed himself into a rock star.

It was always past three by the time she swapped her T-shirt and underwear for a bikini and headed off for the pool. Even though the house was distant from its neighbours and the pool shielded from view, she didn't dare swim naked. Around the pool, there were some exceptionally comfortable loungers for lying on and drifting off to sleep. She couldn't read in the sun – had never liked it. Every so often, then, she went to sit in one of the armchairs on the veranda and read more of her book. When it started getting dark she filled a thermos with hot water and made herself a maté. She defrosted some bread, took a jar of dulce de leche out of the fridge and carried the whole lot back to the recliners on the deck. Normally she wouldn't have allowed herself bread with dulce de leche, but this was a vacation. No sugar in the maté – she liked it bitter.

Verónica could easily spend a couple of hours there. After eating the bread, and when there was no more water in the thermos, she gazed off into the distance. That was the best moment for her. She let her mind empty, stared at the horizon, the distant houses, the mountain greenery. She listened to the sound of birds and parrots as the air filled with a sweet perfume. A light breeze gave her goosebumps. There was nothing in her head. All thoughts, feelings, fears and anxiety completely disappeared. If she had been dead and a part of nature, a jumble of cells scattered through this landscape, she would have felt no different.

It was usually dark by the time Verónica went back into the house. She had a hot shower (she couldn't stand to wash with cold water, even in summer), dried her hair, which had not been cut for nearly six months, and put on pants and the T-shirt she slept in. With the television or her iPod on in the background, she uncorked a bottle of wine first, then heated up a pizza, put some absolutely delicious frozen Tucumanian empanadas in the oven, or boiled some German sausages, which she ate with sauerkraut from a jar. When her supper was ready, she put it on a tray to eat in front of the television, with that night's choice of movie.

She never drank more than half a bottle of wine. In the study where the spirits were kept, she had searched unsuccessfully for a bottle of Jim Beam. There wasn't any – no Jim Beam Black and no Jim Beam White. But cousin Severo had a nice selection of British whiskies.

This is no time for dogmatism, Verónica told herself, picking up a bottle of Johnnie Walker Black Label. *Between Scotch and nothing, I prefer Scotch.*

She finished the movie drinking whisky and smoking, then, half asleep, made her way to her room. Sometimes she would read for a bit longer, other times she would collapse straight into the unmade bed. Right away she would fall asleep and keep sleeping until insomnia struck again at seven o'clock the following morning.

That was how Verónica spent the first five days. On the afternoon of the sixth she got bored and decided to leave the house. Coincidentally, her stash of cigarettes was running low.

IV

It was the first time Verónica had got properly dressed since arriving in Tucumán. Her jeans felt rough against her skin. She had very quickly got used to life in the great outdoors. She thought of putting on a shirt she had bought shortly before leaving which had struck her as perfect for the trip but, looking at herself now in the mirror, it seemed very formal. Instead she opted for a DKNY T-shirt in pastel colours and put a light blue jacket over it. The weather was getting cooler.

Instead of taking the road by which she had come from San Miguel de Tucumán, Verónica decided to keep driving up through the hills. She had noticed that the route was almost circular and that, if she kept following it, she would arrive at the provincial capital. The aim was to find a bar before she reached the centre of town. She drove along, enjoying the mountain road, absorbing as much as she could of the view without taking her eyes off the winding road, its ups and downs. As the road finally levelled out and became straighter, she passed a neighbourhood of weekend homes. In the distance she saw a sign advertising a bar called Lugh, which seemed to have the vibe of an Irish pub. The availability of a free parking space right in front of it was enough to persuade her to stop outside, although, on closer inspection, it looked less like a happening pub and more like a typical small-town bar.

There weren't many people in Lugh and very few of the tables were occupied. There was a couple, a group of four men, and a family of two adults and two pre-teens who were sitting at one of the tables outside. She asked the waitress for a double Jim Beam Black and a still mineral water on the side. For a moment she sensed that the four men, who were sitting alone at a table at the other end of the bar, were watching her. The barman also watched her as he poured the bourbon. Verónica pretended not to notice, turning her attention instead to the map of Argentina's north-east she had brought with her. It was time to relinquish the sepulchral peace of her cousin's house and continue north. She would pass through Yacanto del Valle, meet that relative of her cousin-in-law; he'd be a charming guy, she'd fall in love with him and spend the rest of her life in the little town.

Admittedly the plan had some flaws: she wanted to reach Humahuaca and couldn't let a man detain her en route.

Perhaps she could take him along with her, though. Settle down together in some other little town. But even if this guy turned out to be a perfect combination of Clive Owen, Rocco Siffredi, nineties Arno Klasfeld and Leonard Cohen at any point in his life, it wouldn't be enough to tempt her away from Villa Crespo, her beloved neighbourhood in Buenos Aires. So she might as well quickly abandon the fantasy of staying in Yacanto del Valle.

Verónica had already finished the water and drunk half the bourbon when two girls entered the bar. Absorbed in the map, she didn't notice them come in, only becoming aware of them when one of them asked, in Spanish with inflections of German or Russian or something similar, "Good afternoon, where can we get some rope?"

You could tell straight away that they were foreign, especially the blonde, who had a Nordic look and was wearing military-style trousers with lots of pockets, a black vest and lace-up boots. The other one could have passed for Argentine with her slightly curly black hair, bone-coloured shorts, flat strappy sandals and a loose T-shirt with some writing on it that Verónica couldn't make out.

The question sounded absurd. What did two foreign girls want with a length of rope? She stared at them with the same expression as the barman.

"It's for a guitar," the blonde girl clarified.

The barman told them that they would have to go to the city. He looked in a telephone directory for the address of a specialist shop and mentioned that it was about to close. The dark-haired girl asked if they could call a taxi from the bar. Verónica listened to the whole exchange and thought nothing of offering to take them herself.

Frida and Petra had come into her life a few seconds earlier, when Frida first spoke. Now she was the one entering into the destiny of the Norwegian and Italian girls. They looked at each other and all three felt a connection. They exchanged smiles, never suspecting that they were already moving towards a tragedy. Days later, Verónica would keep revisiting, tirelessly, each moment they had spent together, and would alight on various things that she wished she could change, but she would never regret speaking to them in that lost wayside bar.

By the time they arrived in San Miguel de Tucumán some minutes later, they had already told each other a bit about themselves. Frida was a sociologist with a doctorate titled "Migrations and Social Change in the Suburbs of Buenos Aires between 1950 and 1990". Her studies had brought her to Argentina on various occasions. Petra was a music teacher and an amateur singer-songwriter. Petra and Frida had first met in Córdoba two years previously. At that time Petra was living in San Marcos Sierra and about to separate from her Córdoban boyfriend. Frida had moved to Buenos Aires to work on the final part of her thesis. Petra made several trips to the capital to visit Frida, who returned to Oslo a few months afterwards. Petra went to visit her there. Together they had travelled through the Norwegian fjords, then Sweden and Denmark. They had visited other parts of the European continent too. But Petra didn't want to stay there. Her new corner of the world was Córdoba: "I'm an orphan, I have no siblings, no aunts or uncles. And the mountains of Córdoba remind me of Piedmont, which is where my paternal grandparents were from. I feel at home in the San Marcos Sierra."

While travelling through the Norwegian fjords, Frida and Petra had promised each other to visit the ruins of the Incan Empire. They would start in the north of Argentina, travel through Bolivia and then on to Peru. They were at the start of that adventure now.

Verónica briefly described her work and home life. When the other two pressed her on her love life, she told them only that she had been dating a married man and that it was over now.

"Good thing too. Married men are the worst."

She didn't tell them that Lucio had been killed or about the circumstances of his death. Nor any of what she had been through at the end of the previous year. Why would they want to know? When it came down to it, Verónica was exactly as she must have appeared to them: a friendly girl.

They arrived at the music shop just before it closed, then decided to get something to eat. A colleague of Verónica's from the magazine had recommended a wine bar where they served the best Tucumanian empanadas and tamales to die for. The GPS said it wasn't far, so they headed for Lo de Raúl, a traditional bar full of families. That night there was no show. From the loudspeakers came the voice of folk legend Atahualpa Yupanqui:

I went to Taco-Yaco
To buy a Spanish steed
And I came back with a little bay
A snoring, skinny low breed

They ordered empanadas, tamales, *humita* and red wine. Deciding against the house wine, they asked for a bottle of Finca Las Moras. Over coffee they polished off a second bottle.

Petra told them how she had broken up with her Argentinian boyfriend, also a music teacher, prompting Frida to observe, as though she were writing a sociology paper about the local male, "All Argentine men are liars. I don't know a single man in this country who hasn't lied to his wife at least once."

"Not to sound overly patriotic or anything, but I don't think lying is exclusive to Argentinians."

"Or to men," Petra added.

"Sorry, girls, no. I've met men from all over and none of them is like the Argentine male. He reels you in, he gives you a lovely present, all beautifully wrapped and with a ribbon on top. And inside is a big fat lie. Greek mythology talks about the sirens. In this country they should talk about the Argentine male: deceptive, charming – I won't deny it – but incapable of honesty. Even the Uruguayans are better!"

"Hey, that's going too far."

Verónica wanted to know if her knowledge was based on some specific romantic disappointment.

"Well, obviously I went out with some Argentinians. A European woman on her own in Argentina is going to end up in the bed of a local male at some point. They talk to you, they whisper sweet nothings. They work so hard to seduce you, as though their lives depend on it."

"They put their backs into it."

"Their backs?"

"They make an effort."

"Right – they put their backs into it. And you fall for it like a sailor on the Aegean in Homeric Greece. You end up in their bed. And it takes a while for you to realize that they aren't men, they're more like mermen."

"What, fish?"

"No, I mean like sirens. A lot of singing, no substance."

"You're exaggerating."

"Just look around the table: you used to go out with a married man. Petra got cheated on by her little music maker. I've had men tell me they'd move to Norway for me."

"And why not?"

"Nobody in their right mind wants to go and live in Norway! It's all talk. They think they're Borges. But at least Borges really did have a passion for Nordic countries."

The bar had a patio with no tables, which smokers could use without having to go out into the street. Petra and Verónica went there for a cigarette and Frida accompanied them so as not to wait alone inside. It was a moonless night, quite cold. There were vines on a trellis above the patio from which a few bunches of grapes still hung. The attenuated sound of music and chatter reached them from inside the bar. The women smoked in silence and Frida looked around at the trees and the vines as though searching for something.

"I always feel that nature's hiding something."

"Men lie, nature hides. Nothing's safe."

"No, no. I mean that it's hiding something supernatural. I'm an animist. I believe that there are spirits in the branches, in those vine leaves. We're surrounded by ethereal beings."

"Ah, *la piccola* Frida and her childhood full of Viking legends," said Petra, going over to her friend and smoothing her hair as though they were mother and daughter.

Frida let her do it, like a good girl, then moved her hand to Petra's face and stroked her cheek. A brief but unmistakable gesture. It was dark and Verónica couldn't see how they were looking at each other, but she intuited there was something more than friendship between the two women.

Back at the table, they decided not to drink any more – since Verónica had to drive – and ordered coffee. While they were waiting for the bill, the girls suggested that she join them on their journey to Bolivia and Peru. Verónica thought this over for a moment: it wasn't a bad idea, although she would prefer to stick to her original plan and not go further north than Jujuy, but they could at least travel that far together.

She accepted and immediately invited them to stay at her cousin's house, an idea that delighted them both.

She dropped them off at the door of their hotel and they agreed that she would return to pick them up the following day, before lunch. Then Verónica returned alone to Severo's house. The road was completely dark. She could see only what was illuminated by her car's headlights. The alcohol was beginning to disperse through her body. She felt strange. All the same, she arrived safely at the house in Cerro San Javier and stayed outside in the garden for a little while. A year ago Verónica would never have invited two strangers to come and stay in her house. But the last few months had taught her that worthwhile things were often to be found somewhere unexpected. When it came down to it, if she had chosen to be a journalist it was because she felt a particular kind of adrenaline when confronted with something unknown. To seek out the unknown was to know it. And she was a full-time journalist, even on vacation.

V

"*Klar som et egg*," said Frida, appearing in the living room in a bikini. Verónica looked to Petra for a translation, but the Italian shrugged her shoulders. "I'm as ready as an egg," Frida said, in Spanish. Verónica and Petra stared at her expectantly. "As ready as an egg to go outside. That's what we say in Norway." And without waiting for them she went down to the decked area by the pool. Petra and Verónica followed her.

They had arrived at the house less than an hour ago, carting their rucksacks and a guitar. Verónica had given them a little tour of the house and the girls had seemed enthralled by every discovery: the spectacular view of the garden, the larder, the drinks corner, the pool table, the bedrooms with en suites, the Jacuzzi in every bathroom. Verónica had invited them to take their pick of bedrooms (and was careful not to say anything else). She was surprised when they opted for separate rooms. They left their luggage there and went to the veranda. Verónica brought out three open Corona beers. They sat and looked out over the landscape, smoking and drinking.

"This is much more amazing than I'd imagined," said Petra.

"Exactly how I felt when I arrived a week ago."

"Is your cousin single?"

"He's married and very boring."

"Shame."

They finished the beers and decided to get changed and go and sunbathe.

When Verónica came out of her room, Petra was in the living area looking at the CDs and sound system. She was wearing a pink, orange and yellow bikini that accentuated her brown skin.

"Which part of Italy are you from?"

"I was born in Turin, but my father's family was from Villadossola and my mother came from Sicily. My parents met at university. They were both psychologists against shutting people away in asylums, believing in the principle of no one being truly 'normal': *Da vicino nessuno è normale.* They were two amazing people. They died when I was twenty. An accident on the Milan–Turin freeway."

"How awful."

"Yes, it was. I was studying at the Conservatory. I thought of giving it all up. But then I changed my mind. I got my degree and left Italy. I don't think I could live there again. Too much sadness."

Frida appeared, said something in Norwegian and the three of them went outside to lie in the sun. Each settled onto her lounger. Petra and Frida both took off their bikini tops. Verónica stared at them.

Petra smiled back. "You'll get tan lines."

"It's just that I feel like someone's watching us."

"So what if they are?"

Verónica felt a bit foolish. Or worse: prudish. She took off her top and dropped it down by the lounger.

Verónica watched Frida put sunscreen on her hands then, rather than rub it into her own body, walk over to Petra and start to spread the lotion over her back. Petra murmured something Verónica couldn't hear. Verónica decided it was better to lie back and not keep ogling them like a voyeur.

"You should put some cream on."

"Yes, I should."

"Turn over and I'll do your back."

Verónica did as she was instructed.

"I'll warm it in my hands first so it doesn't feel too cold."

She felt Frida's hands sweeping over her back. Softly, from her shoulders to her waist. It was what she had been needing: to be touched. She closed her eyes. Some horrible music was playing in the distance, perhaps that summer's hits. Closer, she could hear cicadas and her own breathing. She didn't want this moment to end. She wanted to go to sleep feeling Frida's hands on her skin. In this sleepy state, she heard Frida's voice.

"Right, time for one of you to do some work."

Verónica turned her head and saw Frida lie face down on her lounger and Petra pick up the bottle of sunscreen. She closed her eyes again and seemed to hear Petra's hands sliding over Frida's back.

VI

That evening she received an unexpected call. Apart from her sisters, nobody had been in touch with Verónica since she arrived in Tucumán. So the sound of her phone ringing took her by surprise. She didn't even remember where she had left it. When she found it, she saw Federico's name on the screen.

And at that moment, it stopped ringing. It was strange for Federico to call her. He knew that she was on vacation – she had told him by email a few weeks before setting off. They didn't often write to each other anyway. Although they had spent last New Year's Eve together, with members of her family, Verónica had gone to spend the night at her father's house. Her sisters were also going, with their husbands and children, along with some of her father's friends. And of course they had invited Federico, the most promising lawyer at the Rosenthal law firm, a junior partner, the son that Aarón Rosenthal had never had and the man everyone, including her father, sisters and even nieces and nephews (who, egged on by their mothers, called him "uncle") wanted to see her marry. Her sisters knew that there had once been something between them and that it hadn't come to anything, a detail that seemed not to strike them as important. Her father must have made Federico a partner on professional merit; even so, Verónica suspected that her father's gesture was something like an advance on the dowry he would hand to Federico if he ever managed to trap her and whisk her off into a mixed marriage. Because, as long as they could see her married, it didn't matter too much to her father and sisters that Federico was a goy. Her father hadn't given up hope that his star lawyer might have Jewish ancestry. He had said as much to Verónica at one of their lunches at Hermann ("Córdova is a Jewish *converso* surname") and added, with that smile so typical of the Rosenthals when they knew themselves to be in the right, "I've done my homework."

In truth, Federico Córdova's parents were from Argentina and his grandparents – from Seville and Galicia – were as Catholic as the Macarena and the Virgen del Monte. Both sets of grandparents had made the same immigrant journey. They had arrived in Argentina with nothing and built a life for themselves and their children. One of Federico's uncles had risen to the rank of judge in La Plata. He was the one who had offered to organize an internship for Federico at one of the capital's courts or at the law firm that belonged to his friend: Doctor Aarón Rosenthal, an eminence in the legal world. Federico had opted for Rosenthal and Associates.

It was the best decision of his life because it meant he'd met her, Federico told Verónica after the first time they'd fucked – right afterwards, in fact, because, in contrast to what many people say about men, Federico loved post-coital chat. And while Federico told her his story, and that of his parents, uncles and aunts and of his immigrant grandparents, Verónica was thinking that this had been a mistake, that sleeping with Federico was practically incest. Because ever since they had first met at her father's firm, they had enjoyed a friendly camaraderie; they were more like siblings than friends. And if she had led him on … well, it wouldn't be wrong for her to do that. At the end of the day he wasn't actually her brother.

Such were the contradictions that plagued her for months before she finally decided to fuck him. And while he was still talking, she was thinking that she needed a whisky and a spaceship to beam her out of the motel and back to her parents' house (she was still living at home).

It was a long time before they had fucked again. That next time hadn't seemed so incestuous to her but, noticing how in love he was, she felt obliged to say what she believed everyone should say when they know they won't be faithful to someone who loves them: that there were, and would continue to be, other men in her life. Federico thanked her for her honesty, and they didn't go out together again. He had remained very present in her life, though.

Federico never asked her for anything, never showed her any weakness. And that annoyed Verónica. It seemed that the only time he was prepared to reveal himself emotionally was in bed. And given that he never asked her for anything, why had he called her?

The phone rang again. Federico's name reappeared on the screen. She answered straightaway.

"Federico Córdova?"

"Dr Córdova to you."

"Like that, is it?"

"Or Lil Daddy, if you like."

"I've only got one Daddy and he's sitting ten feet away from you."

"More like twenty, to be precise."

"Has something happened?"

"No, nothing. I just wanted to know how the vacation's going."

"Well. I'm at Severo's house."

"Are you going to stay there much longer?"

"I don't know, a couple of days. Why?"

"Just curious."

"Come on, Fede. Why do you want to know?"

"Don't panic – I'm not thinking of joining you. My mother doesn't let me out of Buenos Aires on my own. Are you going to Salta afterwards?"

"No. I'm heading to Yacanto del Valle. From there I think I'll go to Cafayate."

"And are you on your own?"

"Fede, if I didn't know you, I'd think that you were monitoring me or that my dad's asked you to make sure I'm eating properly."

"And are you?"

"Is there anything else, sweetheart? Make it quick, because I've got a couple of friends waiting for me."

"Ah, that's great you've got company. It's boring travelling alone. I'm sending you a kiss."

Verónica hung up feeling that Federico wanted to talk to her about something but had decided not to for some reason. Could something have happened to her father? No, it wouldn't be that: her sisters would have told her. Might Federico and old Rosenthal have fallen out? Impossible. Some other woman was messing him around and making him sad? Who knew…? It couldn't be anything too serious. She might as well return to the pool.

VII

They spent most of the day in the sun, getting in the water every so often or going to the kitchen for drinks and snacks. The only time they left the pool area was at lunch, when they ate a salad of chicken, lettuce, carrot, sweetcorn and tomato in the cool shade of the veranda. As evening fell, they went to their rooms to shower and get changed. Verónica took the opportunity to lie on her bed for a bit and read the Marta Lynch novel she hadn't yet finished. Then she had a shower with warm water that felt boiling. Despite using sunscreen, her body seemed sensitive to the heat. She stepped out of the shower, dried herself and looked for her Méthode Jeanne

Piaubert moisturizer. For a moment she remembered Frida's hands putting cream on her back. She thought that she shouldn't spend so much time alone.

It was dark by the time she went through to the living room. Frida had opened a bottle of white wine and was working her way through a block of provolone. Petra was sitting in an armchair, tuning her guitar. Verónica brought out a jar of anchovy-filled olives, a liver sausage with herbs, blue cheese and some crackers. Thinking the Roquefort might taste best with pasta, she set off to find butter, whisky, Tabasco sauce and a dish. She mixed a couple of ounces of butter with the Roquefort, a splash of whisky and a few drops of hot sauce, then put it all in the microwave and twenty seconds later, with a bit of forking, it had turned into a serviceable pasta sauce. Frida was still grappling with the provolone.

They sat around the coffee table, Frida and Petra in the armchairs and Verónica on the sofa with her feet up. What did they talk about? Everything and nothing – and perhaps that was the best proof that in twenty-four hours they had built a friendship: they could glide over any subject, leave an idea half-finished or jump to another story without the need to finish the last or spend an hour analysing some anecdote. If, days later, someone had asked Verónica what they had talked about that night and during the subsequent days, she would have struggled to supply a precise answer.

At some point in the evening, Petra picked up the guitar and sang some of her own compositions. Her music was like her character: ironic, funny, sometimes dramatic or overblown. Verónica observed as much to her.

"I'm an Italian who'd like to be Argentinian. What would you expect me to be like?"

"I don't know. Like Mina Mazzini?"

"I never liked Mina very much. I prefer Iva Zanicchi." Petra started singing: "*Prendi questa mano, zingara / Dimmi pure che destino avrò / Parla del mio amore / Io non ho paura.*"

Petra accompanied herself on the guitar, although at times she scarcely touched it. Her voice was her favoured instrument.

"*Mi hai detto 'non scordarti di me' / Il cielo già portava l'autunno / L'estate se ne andava con te / Ed io, io t'ho visto andar via senza di me / Portavi la mia vita con te / Fra noi è finita così.*"

Frida had gone to fetch another bottle of wine, and when she returned she sat on the sofa next to Verónica. As Petra finished the song, Frida raised her glass to Verónica.

"Let's toast our songbird."

Frida was slightly drunk and, for a moment, Verónica thought that she was annoyed to see Petra at the centre of attention. Or to see her, Verónica, paying more attention to Petra. As they clinked glasses, Verónica wished she could think of something to say specifically to Frida, but nothing came to mind. She closed her eyes and, as if the absence of one sense sharpened the others, she smelled Frida's sweetish perfume. Eighteenth-century English gardens must have smelled like this when heroines fainted of love. Without opening her eyes, she asked:

"What perfume do you use?"

"Flowerbomb, by Viktor & Rolf."

"It smells like you've escaped from a Jane Austen novel."

"To escape you have to run. Are you saying I smell of sweat?"

She felt Frida's hand stroking her cheek. The perfume exploded in her face. She kept her eyes closed.

"No. I'm no perfume expert, but your hand smells of flowers."

"I smell of ancient history."

Frida's fingers stroked her chin. Verónica could have sat for hours enjoying the caresses on her face. That girl. She opened her eyes. Frida was smiling at her, amused. Petra was no longer in her chair or anywhere in the living room. Frida took her hand away but kept looking at Verónica, observing her in the way that a mother looks at a child who's woken up after many hours asleep.

"And Petra?"

Frida gestured towards the garden. "I think she's gone out to smoke."

"I need a cigarette too."

It was hard to see Petra standing in the darkness, far from the lights of the house. She was smoking and looking at the sky. Verónica asked her for a cigarette.

"I love these moonless nights," Petra said. "*Guarda le stelle*– they're like gemstones on a velvet mantle."

"Maybe. I'm not a big fan of nature."

"I'm going to show you something that has nothing to do with nature. Concentrate on the sky. Let me see... Look over that way. Where the swimming pool is, above the light coming from that house in the distance. What can you see?"

"In the sky? Stars."

"Look harder, city girl. There's a star that's moving to the right."

"A moving star? Hang on, yes. A star's moving!" She almost shouted it. "It's the first time I've seen a shooting star go so slowly."

"It's not a shooting star. It's a satellite. Perhaps one belonging to NASA, or the European Union. Perhaps a spy satellite. But tell me it isn't poignant to see that little light lost in the immensity of the cosmos."

"Are there others like that?"

"If you stayed out here a while, you'd see several other satellites."

"I don't think I'm patient enough."

"Patience makes us wise."

"I'm not patient, I'm curious."

"And curiosity killed the cat. We'd better go back inside – Frida will be getting bored."

But when they went inside, Frida wasn't in the living room any more. After another glass of wine each they concluded that she must have gone to bed. Petra cleared their plates from the coffee table and Verónica put away the leftovers. Finally on her own, she poured herself one last glass of wine; she would have preferred whisky, but didn't have the energy to go and get it. She wondered why Frida had gone to bed without saying anything to them. And also if it had been a coincidence that Petra had gone out to the garden when Frida was stroking her face.

Suddenly there was a blow against the door to the garden, as if someone outside had thrown something at it. Verónica jumped. She waited a few seconds but didn't hear anything else unusual. Then she got up from the armchair and walked towards the window, holding her glass like a defensive weapon. The outside light was on and she could see nothing out of the ordinary, except for something on the ground. A small animal was lying there. She opened the door and from the doorstep could see it a bit better. It was a mouse or a cavy, or something similar. The animal was dead and streaked with blood, as though it had escaped from a predator. Not a clean escape, though. Had it crashed into the door? Swallowing her fear of rats and similar creatures, she approached the animal, prodding it with the toe of her shoe to make sure it was dead. She crouched down and studied it more closely. The area around the neck was ravaged. The blood was still sticky and smelt vile, but Verónica didn't flinch. One leg seemed to have been yanked out of place, exposing a reddish bone. Without thinking, she put her free hand on the animal's back. The body was still warm and soft. From the darkness, among the shrubs, came a noise. Verónica quickly stood up and tried to see if anything was there, but she could make nothing out. It must have been whatever predator had caught and killed this rodent. For a second, Verónica imagined the beast was going to launch itself at her. Could it be a puma, a fox, a wild dog? She stood and waited, alert to an attack that never arrived. Then she walked slowly backwards, without taking her eyes off the black denseness beyond the garden. Entering the house, she closed the door, still watching, but the quiet now was absolute. Seen from this distance, the rodent's body was no longer repulsive. It was a stain, easy to forget. But she had seen it up close. And details are hard to forget.

2 *Unfinished Business*

I

They were arguing about the Argentina team: who should and shouldn't be in it, strategies for playing at home and away, whether the coach should be changed or given another year. He didn't actually know the two occupants of the front seats, just the one sitting beside him: Martínez. Chancha, or Snorter Martínez. Officer Martínez. Speaking for himself, Three wasn't very interested in soccer. He preferred horses, poker, the lottery. So he spent the journey looking out at the city, not something he had seen much of in the last few months. He liked seeing how the other drivers gave way to their patrol car. That was the best thing about travelling in a police vehicle. Once they'd had a siren like the ones used by unmarked police cars, but it had attracted too much attention. They had to stop using it on orders of Doctor Zero.

Usually they didn't take him in the patrol car, but in a van with any other prisoner who needed to go to hospital. This time, though, since he was the only one with a physio appointment, they were taking him by car. For five months now he had been having physiotherapy, as well as kinesiology and pain therapy. He had begun the treatment after they removed the plaster casts for the multiple fractures to his right arm and leg, and when the lacerations and internal injuries ceased to be a risk. The first months had been very hard.

There was no lessening of the pain, even with painkillers, and his joints were stiff. He felt like a mummy, but without bandages (although he'd had those too, along with the casts, since leaving intensive care). He was much better now. His leg was responding correctly, despite a slight but noticeable limp, and his arm shook a little when he wanted to keep it firm. That didn't worry him too much, though, because the right arm was the important one. He had never learned how to fire a gun with his left hand.

They arrived at the hospital and, as usual, drove round to the back, to the area reserved for ambulances and employees. The police sitting in the front of the car made some quip about the nurses and he smiled at them. Only two of them got out – he and Officer Martínez, who put a coat over his hands to hide the cuffs from view. Chancha had been accompanying him here for months and knew exactly where to take him. The reports described Three as a model prisoner. His behaviour on these trips had always been exemplary. Other prisoners required an escort of two or three police officers. He was a gentleman by comparison.

They arrived on the second floor and went into the room where Three was scheduled to see the physiotherapist, a female doctor, old, bad-tempered and smelling of cigarettes. It was still early. Their timings were spot on. They had deliberately arrived ten minutes before the appointment. Martínez closed the door so the two of them were alone in the brightly lit, antiseptic hospital room. He removed Three's handcuffs and gestured for him to open and close his hands to increase blood flow and flexibility.

Calmly, Martínez told him, "You've got five minutes. Take the stairs on the left down to the ground floor. Walk out of the main entrance. Don't rush, or dawdle, or do anything to attract attention. The policeman on duty at the door won't even look at you. Hold your head high but don't make eye contact with anyone. You might run into some of the doctors who treated you."

"Chancha, I know what to do."

Martínez walked out of the room, leaving Three alone. He waited a minute, put on the jacket and left. No sign of police in the corridor. He walked to the staircase that led down to the ground floor. It wouldn't be the first or last time a prisoner had escaped from a hospital. That's what the police authorities would say when the judge furiously demanded an explanation. It might not even get that far if the judge was also getting his cut from Doctor Zero, in which case he would simply instruct the clerk of the court to follow the relevant procedures, sending search and arrest warrants to all the country's branches, which would then make little effort to find him.

He reached the ground floor without a hitch and continued, through a throng of people trying to be seen, towards the front door. Outside, the March sun hit him full in the face. It was hot. He removed his jacket, taking his time, as though he had all day to enjoy being outside. It was six months since Three had last walked along a street, and his first thought was the same one that had occupied him all that time. A fixed idea, a mantra that had sustained him through those long months in prison while he waited to recover physically and for Doctor Zero to get him out – because he never doubted that Doctor Zero would get him out of prison. That fixed idea, that recurring thought, was to commit a murder. He was going to kill Verónica Rosenthal.

II

The simplest cases can become complicated. He had always known that. He didn't trust straightforward jobs; in fact, they annoyed him. He preferred complicated assignments: a businessman with a security detail, a well-armed police chief, some narco traitor loaded up with guns. For that reason, when Doctor Zero had asked the four of them (One, Two, Four and him) to go and beat up one guy, a skinny runt, it struck him as way more force than the job required. Any one of the four of them could have taken him out alone. Then everything got crazily fucked up. Some Chinese dude turned up to defend the skinny guy, humiliating them with his karate moves. They got their revenge on the Chink soon enough, then they had to go and find the other one, the skinny motherfucker who was hiding in the journalist's apartment. This time not just to rough him up but to put him six feet under.

All four of them went over there and when they were about to finish off the job on the sidewalk outside the building, the journalist chick turned up and drove over them all in her car. Twice. One and Four were killed instantly. Two died two days later. He was the only one to survive. By a whisker, but still, he was alive. And ready to take revenge on that bitch.

When he reached the corner there was a car, with Five at the wheel. He got into the passenger seat and put on his seat belt. Five put his foot down and sped away from the hospital.

"All good with Chancha?"

"He's a fool."

It was all they said on that journey to San Fernando. Three had no idea where they were heading, but he knew there was no point asking. Five took him to a bar beside a river. At that time in the morning the terrace was still full of people having breakfast, except for one table, whose occupant was drinking a glass of wine. Doctor Zero. It wasn't often you saw him. Usually everything was done by phone. He thought the doctor must want to give him some long instruction, or deliver a warning, or a dressing-down.

Doctor Zero gestured to Three to come over. When Three arrived at his table, he pointed at the chair opposite. Five had stayed at another table, on his own.

"Have you had breakfast?"

"At the prison."

Doctor Zero drank some wine but didn't seem about to call the waiter over to order anything for Three, who was sitting rigidly upright like a dog waiting for instruction.

"I have a job for you."

"I'm at your orders."

Doctor Zero wiped his lips with a paper napkin. He crumpled it into a ball and a breeze sent it tumbling to the ground.

"Simple and quick. But you need your brain in gear."

Three said nothing.

"Are you still thinking about neutralizing the journalist?"

Three nodded while watching the river sweeping serenely along the banks.

"Don't nod like a pansy. Say 'yes'."

"Yes, Doctor."

"You need to know you're on your own for that one."

"I know that."

"If you fail for any reason, I'm not going to help you."

"All I need is some time to do it."

"Get this little job out of the way, then take some leave."

There was a long silence. Doctor Zero scrutinized him, concerned.

"A professional kills for money. Revenge is a luxury reserved for people who can afford to pay someone else to do the killing. You don't have the money it would take to hire someone else like you. This isn't a joke, it's a warning: don't start thinking that the person capable of killing this girl isn't a professional but a guy blinded by his lust for revenge. Because then you're screwed."

III

Five drove him to the apartment where he'd be staying for the time being. It was where Calle Brasil crosses Matheu, in one of those run-down buildings subdivided into many units. The building was located just a few blocks from the old Caseros prison, an irony not lost on Three, who had done time there at the end of the 1990s, not long before it closed down.

He couldn't go back to his old apartment because a prosecutor or judge might just turn up there accompanied by police. But Doctor Zero's people had made sure his belongings were brought to the new place. Clothes, shoes, what little crockery he had, a CD player he didn't use, an electric shaver, a fake ID that might be useful for some transactions but which would never pass muster with the police. Not much more. And the apartment was partly furnished: a table, two chairs, a mattress, a pillow, some blankets. They had also left him a bag containing maté, coffee, crackers, toilet paper, soap and a bottle of Bols gin. He opened the bottle and took a swig from it.

Five had also given him a mobile with the number written on the back. There was a missed call on it, from Five, in case Three needed to contact him or Doctor Zero. He went out for a walk even though he wasn't sure how far he could go without attracting attention. Feeling hungry and thirsty, he decided to walk to Calle San Juan and found a pizzeria where he ordered a small mozzarella pizza and half a bottle of Moscato. Now that he was free again he would have to go back to taking care of himself. He had started getting fat in prison. The exercises he was doing there weren't the same as intensive training in the gym. The television in the pizzeria was tuned to a news channel, but there was nothing about a prisoner having escaped during a hospital transfer. Three returned to the building complex that housed his apartment. Nobody paid him any attention. A new neighbour wasn't noteworthy. He plugged in the CD player to see if the radio worked, then threw himself down on the mattress with the bottle of gin beside him.

The next morning Three went early to El Turco Elías' gym on Flores Sur. El Turco greeted him with a hug. He was in a safe space: the police never went to the gym except to deliver Christmas greetings. El Turco also worked for Doctor Zero, keeping an eye out for promising thuggishness among the boys who went there to pump iron or to take part in more rigorous training.

They sat down in the gym bar and El Turco ordered Three a protein shake he brought in specially from the United States: it nourished while at the same time burning fat and building muscle. Then he took him through to the offices. At the back was a room that seemed built to withstand a nuclear attack. There was a safe in it, where Three kept his savings and something else: a Glock 39 and four six-bullet loaders, .45 GAP calibre. But El Turco Elías had taken him there to give him two envelopes from Doctor Zero. One contained money: payment for the work he was going to do the following day. In the other was a gun, a 9 mm Sig Sauer with silencer, photos and details of the target. He put everything into the safe and went to the main gym room to start his routine. At midday, Five and Six turned up. They all went to the grill on the corner and ate sweetbreads with fries. Five explained the job to him. All very straightforward.

After lunch, Five stayed with him to do weights. Three took a shower after his routine and then put his savings, the Glock, the loaders, the Sig Sauer and information about the target in his gym bag. Five offered to drive him to the apartment and left him on the corner of San Juan and Matheu.

They agreed Five would come by to pick him up at half past eight in the morning.

Three put the bag in the bottom of the closet and covered it with an old bedspread. As he had slept well the previous night and the exercise had filled him with energy, he decided to go out to a whisky bar on Avenida Garay, a little before Calle Boedo. He had been there a couple of times, but nobody knew him. Three picked out a girl with dyed blonde hair, small tits and a nice ass. She was wearing hot pants and a top that exposed her stomach. She was called Luli. They went to one of the rooms at the back of the building. He spent fifty minutes with her and came twice. Between one screw and the next, she told him all about her life, but Three wasn't all that interested in the girl's story. When he went, he left her a hundred-peso tip.

He walked back to the apartment. Brought out the weapons. He cleaned the Glock and put it away again. He counted the money. He thought that he shouldn't have taken out all his savings. Even though he had a job the next day, he couldn't stop thinking about his revenge plan.

When Three woke up at six o'clock in the morning, he drank a few matés and ate a few crackers. At eight o'clock he went downstairs. The same type of Audi that One and Two used to drive was parked across the road. Inside, Five was smoking with the window down.

They had to get to Calle Moreno, in La Tablada, before ten o'clock and wait a few yards from a lottery kiosk called San Cono. At quarter past nine they were there. It was still early, so they drove around the area for a while. At quarter to ten they were back on Calle Moreno. They parked about thirty yards away, on the other side of the road.

At exactly ten o'clock they saw the owner of the kiosk walk past, unaware he was being watched. He arrived at the kiosk, lifted up the shutter and went inside. Five and Three got out of the Audi and headed for the kiosk. When he saw them walk in, the owner knew straightaway that these guys hadn't come to pick a lucky lottery number or place a bet on the horses.

"Lads, I'm just opening. There's nothing in the till."

Three took out his gun and stepped closer.

"If Tito sent you, I can explain —"

The first shot hit him in the forehead. Three finished him off with two shots to the chest. Thanks to the silencer, the bullets made more noise as they ripped into the tissue of the man's body than when they were discharged. His body lay splayed behind the counter. As the lottery seller had grasped just before they killed him, the men weren't there to rob him, but now they needed to simulate a robbery. They opened the till, which contained only a few pesos in change, and took the owner's phone and his wallet. Job done, in under thirty seconds. They strolled back to the car then drove away. Once they were on Route 3, Five called Doctor Zero to let him know everything had gone as planned.

Three gave the weapon they had used to Five, who also kept hold of the stolen items and the photos of the target. He would be responsible for ensuring there was no trace left of compromising evidence. Neither of the men knew who the Tito named by the dead man was, but he must be the one who had paid for their services.

Even though it was early for lunch, on the way back they stopped at a grill beside the road. They ate tenderloin sandwiches and drank a bottle of Vasco Viejo, the best wine on offer. Then Five dropped him off at the gym and Three did a workout. When he finally left the gym that evening it was with the thought that now he could start putting into action the plan he had been hatching since he was first admitted to hospital.

IV

Three dreamed of being a champion wrestler. He had started boxing at the Huracán club, but he lacked technique and couldn't move his waist and arms quickly enough. The boys who had been boxing there for a while used to beat the crap out of him. But one of the trainers thought he might be suited to kick-boxing because he had strength, stamina and the flexibility to kick with a raised leg. He took Three to El Turco Elías' gym, where kick-boxing champions were made. And he was really good. He won a few contests, until one day he damaged his meniscus and had to take something like three months off and when he went back he just wasn't the same any more. He was too cautious, fearful even, when delivering kicks. It was around that time he and another kid started stealing car radios, or whatever they could find in parked cars. Once he got caught breaking a van window. He was taken to the police station and his only thought was to ring the gym. El Turco Elías went to get him out. He didn't say anything to him, didn't scold him or give him a sermon or anything like that. A month later El Turco got him work as a bouncer in a disco.

Now Three's nights consisted of ejecting troublemakers, roughing up the odd prick, watching out for the people dealing drugs on the dance floor and making sure nobody bothered them. It was good work because he got laid a lot, took uncut drugs and made good money. After two years working there, El Turco Elías took him to Doctor Zero. He had to change his habits and, even though he had never stopped his daily training at the gym, he had to work on his fitness. Fewer drugs, no messing around with girls, better focus. The first few jobs for Doctor Zero didn't involve any kind of weapon. Just fists. Then he had to learn to use a gun. It was three months before they sent him on a hit job. And that time he was just accompanying the man who was going to do the shooting.

Six months in, Three killed his first man. The instructions that day would be similar to those in subsequent jobs: he would arrive with one other, or with two others, and suddenly, without a word, they would shoot the target. Killing quickly became a routine like any other, like going to the gym or a strip club. It didn't produce any particular feeling in him, and perhaps for that reason he had always done his job perfectly. He had no weaknesses, and so Doctor Zero began to entrust him with more important jobs. He was one of Doctor Zero's four favourites. Four professional hitmen who never failed. Until they failed. If there was one thing he didn't understand about that whole saga, it was that the Doctor wasn't as angry as Three was. At the end of the day, Doctor Zero had lost three indispensable men. But the Doctor seemed not to believe in vengeance. He had other men to call on. Whereas Three wasn't going to let his months in hospital and prison be the end of the story.

Since that first job, the procedure had been the same: to go to the designated address and do what they had been asked to do. Without questions, clarifications or any information beyond what was required to beat someone up, or to kill him. The intelligence work preceding the action was taken care of by other people, who were also Doctor Zero's people but with whom he had no direct dealings. Now that he found himself planning a revenge killing, he had no idea how to approach this groundwork, since he had never had to do it: learning the target's habits, familiarizing himself with her life, her relationships, everything needed to establish the ideal moment to get close enough to kill her.

In prison Three had got to know El Gallo Miranda, who was serving time for attacking an armoured van and killing a security guard in the same operation. El Gallo had links with the police and with gangs who specialized in big heists, and got the kind of treatment in prison that a businessman would expect in a five-star hotel. Three got friendly with El Gallo, who offered to work with him when he got out, but Three turned him down because he already had a job and wasn't planning to leave it. El Gallo liked that Three was loyal to his old boss and offered to help him whenever he needed it.

"When I get out, I'm going to need someone to get some information for me."

El Gallo invited him to share a maté. They were in his cell, where he usually had meetings and conducted all kinds of business. Three accepted the maté but turned down the crackers with dulce de leche which an assistant of El Gallo's had prepared and arranged on a plate.

"Someone to do intelligence? For you?"

"To find out someone's movements, what they're doing, where they go, all that stuff."

"And this is for you."

"Yes, for me."

El Gallo chewed thoughtfully on a cracker. Three passed him the maté gourd.

"There are a couple of lads. They do good work. I've used them a few times and they never let me down. They're called Nick and Bono. If you need to get into a bank's system or to find out who an army general's fucking, they're not for you. It's quite a basic service and for that reason they don't charge as though they were stealing Obama's sex tape."

He wiped his hands on a napkin and scrolled through the contacts on his phone, then wrote down a number on a clean napkin and passed it to Three.

"Phone Nick. Tell him I told you to call. Is it going to be soon?"

"I hope so."

"Best of luck then. Oh, and don't be put off by the way they look. They know their stuff."

Now that he'd carried out the job Doctor Zero had assigned him, Three decided to get in touch with this Nick guy. He called him from a phone booth, but nobody answered. Half an hour later he called again and there was still no reply. Nearly an hour later, Nick's phone was still ringing without anyone picking up. Three went back to the apartment thinking El Gallo must have given him the wrong number, either deliberately or by accident. But he woke up at dawn suddenly certain that his call hadn't been answered because he had made it from an anonymous number. Using the protection of a public phone might work for him, but not for Nick. The next morning he called from his mobile phone and got through straightaway.

"Nick?"

"He's not here. Who's calling?"

"El Gallo Miranda gave me this number."

"I'll call you back in five minutes."

Before he had a chance to say anything else, the line went dead. Three hadn't even got as far as giving his name. Less than five minutes later, the phone rang. The voice at the other end was the same, but the tone sounded much more friendly.

"Hello, boss. El Gallo sends his regards."

"Hello, I need to speak to Nick."

"Go to the bar on Rivadavia and Misiones at three o'clock this afternoon."

"How will I recognize him?"

"I'm Nick and I'm easy to spot: ginger, with a lot of freckles and tortoiseshell-framed glasses. I'm six foot two, although if I'm sitting down perhaps you won't notice. I'll be there with my colleague, who has no distinguishing features whatsoever."

El Gallo Miranda had been right to warn him about Nick and Bono's appearance. When Three arrived, they were sitting at a table away from the windows. The redhead was easy to pick out while Bono, as Nick had said, was almost completely nondescript: dark brown hair, neither tall nor short, not fat or thin. They both looked like university students playing at spies, or teenagers who spend too many hours watching porn on the computer. Nick was wearing a multicoloured shirt that was tight on him. Bono, meanwhile, wore a baggy black T-shirt with a picture of Che Guevara on it. They were drinking freshly squeezed orange juice. Three walked over to them and introduced himself. They looked at him the way you might look at a madman bursting in on a private conversation, eyeing him suspiciously and letting a few seconds elapse before Nick gave him a friendly smile.

"Three. That's what Doctor Zero calls you," he said, motioning at him to sit down.

If they wanted to surprise him, they had succeeded.

"Have you been investigating me?"

"It's routine. And a bad habit picked up from work. If Doctor Zero ever needs our services, we're at his disposal."

The waiter arrived and Three ordered a coffee. He noticed that Bono paid him no attention and seemed to be playing on a computer screen or some sort of device. Every now and then he said something to Nick in English or another language. Three would have thought he was a foreigner if not for the fact that, in a moment of frustration, he suddenly exclaimed "*Qué boludo!*" without taking his eyes off the screen.

"What do you need, Three?" Nick asked him, in the bland tone of a sales assistant.

Three said that he needed to know everything possible about the movements of a journalist called Verónica Rosenthal. He told Nick what he knew already, which wasn't much, the fruit of research he had done while recovering from his injuries. Three had seen the journalist's name in *Nuestro Tiempo* magazine. He had discovered that she lived in the apartment where he had been with his colleagues, seconds before they were run over. He didn't know much more.

"That's plenty. That's all we need. Now to the matter of our fee."

He mentioned a figure that struck Three as high: a quarter of all his savings. But he wasn't going to haggle over the price, nor did he plan to look for anyone else to do this work that he couldn't do. Nick made it clear the budget included comprehensive information about the woman but not hacking into emails or social media, or phone-tapping. If he needed any of that, they could arrange it, but it would cost him more and they would need more time. Three said that what they were offering him was enough. He paid them 10 per cent on the spot (which was all the money he had on him) and Nick agreed to ring him very soon with news. Within the next forty-eight hours, in fact.

Around noon the next day Nick called and asked him to come to a pizzeria on Corrientes and Anchoa. They had got to work faster than he was expecting.

"Before anything else, you should know this: Verónica Rosenthal has a powerful father. He runs the law firm Rosenthal and Associates and he's the kind of lawyer I wouldn't want to have across the aisle from me at the Tribunales law courts. That said, Verónica Rosenthal isn't in Buenos Aires. She's gone on vacation. She won't be back for two weeks, give or take. On top of the statutory annual leave for journalists, she's taken five days of compassionate leave. She's travelling in the interior. We can wait for her to come back and get back into a routine here, in Buenos Aires. Or we can try to track her down in the interior."

It occurred to Three that Verónica had more protection in Buenos Aires, and for that reason it would be better to go and find her wherever she was.

"I'd rather know where she is now."

"We also found out something else important. The building where she lives has no security camera, but there is a doorman who's there all day watching people come and go. We think we can get into the girl's apartment in the early hours. We're going to go there at two o'clock tomorrow morning. Come with us if you like."

It sounded like a good idea. He would go with them to Verónica Rosenthal's apartment. He would see how the woman who had tried to kill him lived.

They met on Avenida Córdoba, on the corner of Calle Palestina. Nick was driving, Bono dozing with his head against the door. They left the car about a hundred yards away from the building. Nick had told him not to bring a gun or any weapon, but Three had come with his Glock anyway. They walked down the empty street. When they reached the building, Nick and he stood to one side while Bono, wearing gloves, managed to open the door in thirty seconds. They took the elevator up to the second floor. This was the risky part: a neighbour could get into the elevator and ask them what they were doing. If that happened they would have to neutralize the neighbour and his family and then continue their investigation. Plus they would have to take some things away to leave the impression of a break-in, although it was likely the journalist would suspect this was no run-of-the-mill burglary.

Bono opened the apartment door quickly and silently. It wouldn't be necessary to stage anything here. On the contrary; they would have to leave everything as it was. Nick put on his gloves and offered a pair to Three.

The apartment was beautifully ordered. The blinds were down, so they turned on the lights without a second thought. Nick threw his jacket down on the ground against the front door so no light would be seen from the corridor. Then he switched on the computer.

"Wouldn't it be great if she'd left her mailbox open."

Three looked over the apartment, starting with the immaculate kitchen. Everything was in its place. There wasn't so much as a used teaspoon or cup left out on the counter. He opened the fridge and found only a block of membrillo quince jelly, a few cans of beer, some soft drinks, a bottle of water, mayonnaise, a tub of mustard, a jar of pickles and another, unopened, of olives. He went back into the living room, where Nick was at work on the computer while Bono looked through the CDs and books.

"Unfortunately she didn't leave her email open. I see it's a Gmail account. I'm trying to get in now."

Three left him to work and went to the bedroom. Bed made, not even a speck of dust on the television set. There were some family photos on the walls. He went over to look at them more closely: Verónica as a girl with the woman who must be her mother, Verónica with two other women her age. There were also photos of children, of an older man. In the months Three had spent in prison he had been able to familiarize himself with Verónica's face and physique. He had seen her in videos being interviewed about her journalism. He had found photos of her, too.

He knew you must never get distracted by ideas that have nothing to do with work. His task was to find Verónica Rosenthal and kill her. He mustn't think about anything else. Whether she was pretty or ugly, strong or weak, these things were irrelevant. Even so, Three felt a certain thrill being in this woman's room. He opened the closet and saw her clothes neatly ordered, opened a drawer and found her underwear. He didn't want to rummage through it or take anything away. He closed the closet doors and went to the bathroom. He opened the cabinet, saw the array of bottles, shampoos, creams, soaps.

Something on the floor beside the bidet caught his attention. Some multicoloured item of clothing. He picked it up off the floor: it was a thong. Three took it in both hands and stretched it out, imagining Verónica with this underwear on. He felt himself getting an erection. He sniffed the thong, trying to imagine the smell of Verónica's body. Why, considering how tidy she had left the place, had she left her dirty underwear on the bathroom floor? He thought of throwing it back on the floor where he had found it but didn't. Instead, he tucked the thong into one of his jacket pockets. Verónica wouldn't miss it. Come to that, she would never return to this apartment anyway if he managed to find her first.

When he came out of the bathroom, Nick was still busy on the computer.

"OK, I can give you a picture of the situation so far. The mail isn't open, but the last thirty days' browsing history is here. I'm making a backup of her computer's cache, but I've already run into some interesting things. Before she left she bought a return ticket to Tucumán. We have the PDF with the reservation issued by the website. So we know which flight she's coming back on in sixteen days. She looked at hotels in different parts of northern Argentina. She didn't make reservations in any of them, but she did check the availability on different dates. The strange thing is that she didn't look for a hotel in San Miguel de Tucumán, which might mean she already knew in which hotel or other place she was going to stay. The first place she looked up is Yacanto del Valle. After that she looked at places to stay in Cafayate, Salta, San

Salvador de Jujuy, Purmamarca, Humahuaca and La Quiaca. She also rented a car in Tucumán, which has to be returned to the airport the day she returns."

"And can we find out where she is now, or where she'll be tomorrow?"

"Since she hasn't booked any hotels, it's hard to know whether she's sticking to the itinerary she came up with when she was looking into availability. By the looks of things, she should be in Yacanto del Valle. Or perhaps in Cafayate, if she moved on earlier. I don't think she's still in San Miguel de Tucumán."

"Is she travelling alone, or with someone?"

"The flight and internet searches are all for one person. I'm going to take everything away and I'll make a summary of dates, hotels, possible routes. Anything that might be useful to you. Found anything over there, Bono?"

"Addresses of bookshops and music shops she goes to regularly. She quite often travels on line B of the Underground, and she uses the tickets as bookmarks. She speaks, or at least reads, English and French. She gets free books from publishers... She smokes and drinks coffee. She's a bit clumsy."

"We're bound to have more information once we've analysed the data from her computer. Did you find anything, Three?"

"Just that she's very tidy."

"It's not an inconsequential detail. That kind of woman makes no false steps."

V

There wasn't much more in the report Nick handed him in the McDonald's on Avenida Caseros and Entre Ríos the next day, except for the names of several hotels, some of which were in the same town. Nick also gave him the subject of all the emails she had opened in the previous month, but without their contents, so what would have been most useful to him was missing. The strangest revelation in Nick's report was that every so often Verónica visited a website where people posted pornographic stories, and another belonging to Club Atlético Atlanta. She must have a boyfriend or relation who was into soccer.

Three paid him what was still owing and Nick told him to keep in touch and to call if he needed any help while he was up north. They wouldn't charge a peso more.

"It's part of our customer service, Three."

"That's my name when I'm working for Doctor Zero. Now I'm working for myself. The name's Danilo."

And Danilo walked out of McDonald's, leaving Nick and Bono to their burgers with fries and their Coke Zeros.

He couldn't afford to lose time. Ideally, he would have flown to Tucumán, but it was impossible to travel by plane carrying a gun and ammunition and using his real name. He thought of getting a car, but driving more than eight hundred miles didn't appeal, and there was always the possibility some provincial police officer would know about the arrest warrant surely hanging over his head. There was no option but to go by bus.

Three went back to the apartment and put everything he needed into a bag. He took out the thong and smelled it again. It reminded him of her. He felt like one of those dogs that are given an item of clothing to smell so they can follow the scent. He thought the thong could be a kind of amulet and threw it into the bag on top of his things. Its cheerful colours were like a scandalous stain on his dark clothes.

He went to the bus station in Retiro and tried to find the bus that took the least time to get to San Miguel de Tucumán.

There was one that could do the journey in fourteen hours, between 8.30 at night and 10.30 in the morning. He could sleep in the bus and arrive refreshed. Then he would work out how to get to Yacanto del Valle on local transport. If he didn't find Verónica in that town, he would travel on to Cafayate. He was confident of finding her quickly, but he knew patience would prove a necessary virtue in the coming days.

3 *Scandinavian Blonde*

I

Sunbathing topless with the girls by the pool late one morning, Verónica had a sensation of déjà vu. They had spent the day before like this and presumably the next day would be the same, unless autumn suddenly descended and it started getting cold, or rainy. So she suggested to the others, as they ate their lunchtime salad on the veranda, that it would be a good idea to continue with their trip. Leave in two or three days, perhaps. Petra and Frida agreed. They wanted to go to Amaicha del Valle, Verónica to Yacanto del Valle. There wasn't much difference between one town and the other, but there was a guy in Yacanto Verónica was keen to meet.

That compelling logic was enough to convince the others. Verónica told them what little she knew about the man: that he came from a wealthy family in Salta, like the wife of her cousin, who owned this house. That he was an art dealer – he owned a gallery in Yacanto – and that he was, at least according to the most recent reports, a bachelor.

"And it's universally acknowledged that a millionaire bachelor must be in need of a good wife."

Frida and Petra looked at her, puzzled.

"Are you husband-hunting?" Petra asked.

"No, girls, just paraphrasing Jane Austen. Relax."

The last thing Verónica wanted was a husband, but the thought of going somewhere for the sole purpose of meeting a man amused her. It was almost like a game, another tourist attraction ticked off. And when they asked her what she had seen on her trip she could say: "I saw the Yungas, the red rock formations of Cafayate, the Quebrada de Humahuaca valley and a promising marriage candidate."

The final part of the night began like a carbon copy of the previous one: she and Petra smoking and staring at the sky in search of spy satellites. Even if they weren't shooting stars, Verónica would have liked to make a wish or two. That black, moonless sky over the dark landscape made her anxious, though. She didn't like it.

This time when they returned to the living room, Frida was still there and was opening a bottle of red wine. They had been planning to go out for dinner but changed their minds at the last minute. There were some pizzas in the freezer that would do the trick.

Verónica connected her iPod to the speakers and put a playlist on shuffle. The first song to come on was "Vambora", by Adriana Calcanhotto. Petra brought out one of the pizzas, half of which was destined to languish, forgotten, on the coffee table. Verónica lit a cigarette with no intention of going outside to smoke it. The girls were still drinking, but she was tired of red wine. She went to the study to fetch her cousin's bottle of Black Label Johnnie Walker and some whisky glasses, but poured out only one, for herself. The music playing was familiar to her, even though it wasn't coming from her iPod. Without saying anything, Frida had connected her own device. Verónica knew the song, but not this version. She asked what it was.

"It's 'Bobby Brown (Goes Down)', by a French singer called Swann."

Verónica took a long draught of whisky. Frida and Petra started talking about a Swede they had met in the Norwegian fjords. A guy in his thirties, chubby, friendly, a bit shy, who they had chatted to on various occasions during their boat trip. They couldn't agree on whether he had been called Svan or Stieg.

"Svan tried to kiss me at one point," Petra recalled.

"Stieg."

"I rebuffed him, nicely, and he gave me a look of pure hatred, only for a second, but…"

"I always got the feeling he was giving us funny looks."

"That's what you said afterwards, but up until that moment we'd thought he was a nice guy."

"Whatever – the next morning the boat came into port at Bergen and from the breakfast room we saw all these strange movements on the dock. Loads of police cars."

"There was a commotion on the boat too. People were going out on deck, so we got up and followed them. My heart almost stopped when I saw they were taking Svan away in handcuffs, surrounded by police."

"Stieg. Afterwards, we found out the same guy had killed a girl on another trip a year earlier. The police hadn't been able to find the person who did it until that moment."

"We were so lucky. I still don't know what stopped him showing up in our berth. The other girl had been killed in hers during the night, and in the morning he'd thrown her body into the sea."

Verónica listened to the story as though it were part of the music. She poured herself another whisky. Frida and Petra were still drinking wine and telling her about their travels. Listening to their voices, Verónica felt herself to be in a kind of rapture, her body stretched out on the sofa with Petra opposite, on the other side of the table, and Frida beside her. Sitting up to take another drink, she realized the glass was already empty. She felt dizzy but decided to pour herself another measure anyway. After taking a sip she lay back, leaving the glass on the floor. She closed her eyes.

Now Frida and Petra were talking about some wonderful, mysterious girl, whose eyes spoke of sadness, who had secrets she told no one – not even them, who, being both so close and so distant, would be the perfect confidantes. A person should never be as weighed down by pain or sadness as she was. What could she do to end the pain that was so deep-rooted in her? It was a few seconds or even minutes before Verónica realized this wasn't a dialogue but just Frida talking. And she understood that Frida's words were directed at her. She should open her eyes. But she didn't. And she wasn't surprised when the air filled with Flowerbomb and Frida's lips pressed against her mouth. Not even a kiss. Just lips touching. The gesture would become a kiss only if she reacted. And she did. She moved her lips, felt Frida's mouth, the warm breath, the perfumed skin. Verónica opened her eyes. She wasn't going to let this be like a dream, like a wave that carried her along without her doing anything. She moved slightly away and took Frida's face between her hands. Only now did she see her friend's eyes were grey, or perhaps a muted green. Nordic eyes. Eyes like that had loved Vikings and Valkyries, and now they were looking at her. Verónica didn't want Frida to think she had any doubts as she looked in her eyes. She pulled Frida's face towards her and kissed her again.

One of Frida's hands, resting on her knees, began to move up to her inner thigh. It stopped at the edge of her shorts. Verónica glanced over at Petra, but she was no longer sitting in the armchair opposite. Had she gone out to smoke, like last night? Was she in another part of the living room, watching them? Frida's fingers caressed her thighs and ran over the trim of her underwear. Then she took her hand away, unbuttoned Verónica's shorts and, with her help, took them off. Frida caressed her legs, stomach, breasts. Verónica didn't know what to do. She had never experienced anything like this before. She was enjoying the kissing, touching, Frida's perfume; she loved feeling the girl's soft skin, but she wasn't particularly interested in her tits or in moving her hand down to her pussy, as Frida was doing now, having put her hand inside her underwear and started gently stroking her, very slowly, almost distractedly, in the same way she pleasured herself alone. Now Verónica did want to know if Frida was as turned on as she was. She caressed the other girl's nipples and Frida let out a strange-sounding moan. As if moans were different in different languages and this was the Norwegian version. Verónica wanted to know if Frida was as wet as she was. She moved her hand under the miniskirt which was now pulled almost right up, stroked Frida's lower stomach and moved her hand down until she felt the damp warmth of her body. At that moment Verónica started to come. She squeezed Frida's hand between her legs and didn't let it go until her orgasm was finished. She felt her body grow limp then, as if all the alcohol she had consumed that night were sweeping over her. Frida kissed her lips again and Verónica closed her eyes. If she didn't open them soon, she was going to fall asleep. And she didn't open them.

II

When she woke up a few hours later she was on her own. The lights were all turned off, apart from one lamp in a corner of the living room. The house was quiet. From outside came the sound of crickets. Her body felt like a dead weight. Her hand still smelled of Frida. Sitting up on the sofa, she found her discarded shorts underfoot. She picked them up and summoned the energy to get up and go to her room, where she fell face down on the bed and went back to sleep. Around midday, as the crickets made way for the cicadas, she woke up again.

What a night, Vero, she told herself. She had done a lot of wild things in her life, but never this. She hadn't even been one of those adolescents who made out with her friends amid fits of giggles. She had always been very clear that she liked men, and didn't feel that had changed. But had it? How well did she know herself at that moment? Best not to dwell on it and instead start the new day. And yet she hesitated to come out of her room. How should she act? What should she say? Where had Petra been all that time? What would happen if Frida came up to her, touched her again? Should they talk about what had happened last night? Questions, questions. Verónica needed advice. She could call her friend Paula, but that felt like something a teenager would do. It would help her understand more clearly what had happened. For the first time in ages she turned on her laptop and wrote a long email to Paula, giving her a brief rundown of what had happened in the days leading up to and including last night. She wasn't very explicit about last night's events, but she made her confusion clear.

After sending the email she showered and gathered herself to leave the room. She could hear someone splashing in the pool. In the kitchen, Petra was making coffee and offered her one. She admired Verónica's T-shirt, a violet one from GAP that her sister Daniela had brought back from Miami. Petra asked her about her sisters. From the way she acted, she seemed to know nothing about what had happened the night before. They walked to the pool together and there was Frida, swimming. When she noticed them there, she stopped and said hello cheerfully. She stepped out of the water, briefly dried herself and lay down face up on a lounger next to the one Verónica had selected for herself.

"Are you OK?" Frida asked her.

"Fine. A bit hung-over."

"You should never mix wine and whisky."

"How about you?"

"No hangover at all. Must be because I didn't mix my drinks."

The afternoon progressed like any other: they went from the sun to the veranda, and from there to the kitchen in search of something to eat and drink. After her initial awkwardness, Verónica started to feel more at ease. This indifference about what had happened suited her. She even began to enjoy observing Frida and Petra as they went back and forth. She found them different, attractive. So was she someone who liked women now? Had she always liked them? Or was it just the company of these two girls that she found erotic? Whatever the answer, she felt good.

She tried picturing the same situation with two guys: to be lying in a bikini – or rather, topless – sunbathing while the guys came and went, swam, brought coffee in a thermos. She wouldn't be able to feel relaxed or comfortable, not even about the fantasy of hooking up with them both. She would feel like she was sending out sexual signals all the time. With Frida and Petra, however, it was different. Everything was much more natural, less laden with subtext. They were all there having a good time. Period. There was no need to worry about anything else.

As dusk fell, Verónica went to her room. She took a shower and put on moisturizer. Her skin was a little tender after all the time spent in the sun. She ought to have used more protection. She had waited too long for Frida to offer to rub it into her body, but Petra was the one who noticed she'd been lying in the sun for a long time without any cream on. It had been good to feel Petra's hands on her. They were soft like Frida's, though perhaps less charged with unnerving energy.

She put on a short, light sleeveless dress that she didn't often wear in Buenos Aires but which felt ideal for this evening after a day of sun. Emerging into the living room, she met Petra, who was more done up than usual and seemed ready to go out. For a moment Verónica thought the girls had arranged a night on the town, not something she was really in the mood for.

"Have we got plans?" Verónica probed.

"I have," Petra replied. Frida was fiddling with the sound system. As she attached her MP3 player, she added, "A date. A boy I met on the bus to Tucumán. He lives in Villa Nougués."

"And she literally means a *boy*," said Frida.

"He's over the age of consent," said Petra, directing herself at Verónica. "I didn't want to give him my number because I'm terrified of stalkers, but he wrote me such a charming email that I thought, well, what's another notch on the bedpost?"

"Sing him the song," said Frida, a reference Verónica didn't understand.

The taxi Petra had ordered was already at the front door. She gave each of them a kiss and went on her way. Verónica and Frida were left standing in the room, like characters in a bad play. A serious male voice growled from the speakers.

"I want to go to the beach," said Frida.

"What?"

"Iggy Pop. Do you like him?"

"I liked him when he was more of a rocker."

No, these weren't lines from a bad play. This was a cowboy movie. When the good guy squares up to the villain and they get each other's measure, exchanging words but all the while thinking ahead to the moment when they'll pull out their guns and fire. It was a shoot-out, but Verónica wasn't sure which of them was the good guy and which the villain.

"I saw some salmon in the freezer. I could make sandwiches."

"I'm not hungry yet."

"Do you want a *caña*?"

"A what?"

"A little beer. It's what they say in Spain."

"Sometimes I think I'd understand you better if you spoke Norwegian."

"*Tror ikke det.*"

Frida went to the kitchen to get some bottles of Corona. Verónica considered going with her, but she didn't want to look clingy. Instead she went to sit on the sofa. Frida appeared with two bottles and passed her one, before taking the armchair opposite. Evidently she wanted to keep her distance, passing up the opportunity to get friendly with Verónica again. Either Frida was very polite, or she didn't fancy her any more. The first possibility could be remedied, but the second would mean that any attempt Verónica made at seduction would fall on stony ground. How many times had she been all over some guy one moment and then not wanted anything to do with him the next? And even though it had never happened the other way round (the man fleeing after a few kisses), it was still possible Frida wanted to step back or have nothing more to do with her, sex-wise. Perhaps Verónica had been gauche when they were making out the previous night. Perhaps Frida had expected more, or something different, from her. Women are impossible to understand, she thought. Frida was drinking her beer in little sips and watching her. Scrutinizing her. OK, so now they were back in the bad theatre play with two armchairs and background music.

"A penny for your thoughts," said Verónica after downing some Corona to contrast with the little birdlike sips Frida was taking from her bottle.

"A what?"

Verónica repeated the phrase in English.

"Oh, I wasn't thinking anything in particular. I was enjoying the beer and the view."

That settled it: Frida was the movie villain. She was playing with her like the cowardly cat plays with the poor mouse in that tango by Carlos Gardel. Had Petra really gone out because she had a date, or to leave them alone? Had Frida asked her to go? Had she wanted to be alone with Verónica? What for – to drink beer?

"I like that Liberty print dress. I love flowers."

Verónica looked down at her own dress, trying to arrive at a conclusion. A man would have told her he liked the way her short dress showed off her bare thighs. Men were definitely better.

"I have a dress a bit like that. Only with sleeves," she said, and, as if she had just had a brilliant idea, she added, "You have to see it, it's very similar. Come, and I'll show you."

Without waiting for an answer, Frida set down her nearly empty bottle and went towards her bedroom. Verónica had no choice but to follow her. It was the first time she had gone into Frida's room, and she noticed there were clothes lying all over the place. She had imagined a Norwegian girl would be more tidy. Frida went over to the wardrobe, opened it and stood looking at the clothes. Verónica had stopped just inside the door.

"Come to think of it, I left that dress in Norway."

"It's going to be difficult for me to see it, then."

"Never mind, lovely. Take it off."

"What?"

"Take off the Liberty. I want to see what you've got underneath."

Verónica wanted to make some remark that made her look witty, or at least funny. Say, for example, "Ah! That old dress-left-behind-in-Norway trick," but all she managed was a nervous laugh. Just hearing that laugh was enough to make her hate herself.

"Seriously, take it off."

Verónica pulled her dress over her head and let it fall to one side. Underneath she was wearing matching white underwear, a simple cotton set, the white accentuating the tan she had picked up in the last few days. Frida walked towards her, looking at her with the expression of someone about to give a verdict on the quality of her clothes, or the shape of her tits, or the wisdom of her haircut. But she did none of those things. She stretched out her arms, placed her hands on Verónica's hips and slipped her fingers between the elastic of her underwear and her body. Gently she eased the garment down to knee level, where it fell the rest of the way unaided. She had knelt down to do this and was now gazing at Verónica's pubic area. She seemed to be carrying out a connoisseur's evaluation. Lifting her head, she said, looking at Verónica:

"I like the way you don't wax everything. It makes me want to touch you even more." And she lightly ran the tips of her fingers upward until they reached Verónica's navel.

Verónica put her hands on Frida's shoulders and made her stand up. As she kicked off the underwear, she pushed Frida gently but firmly against the wall.

"I like you a lot, but I'm no good at playing the part of innocent little girl. Either you take off your clothes too, or I'll put mine back on and go and get drunk in the garden."

"Verónica, you bad girl. Then take my clothes off for me."

"Funny how you seem to be getting more fluent."

Verónica unbuttoned the shorts Frida was wearing and took them off together with the scanty bikini bottom she had on underneath. She made her raise her arms so she could take off her T-shirt and, while she had her arms up, kissed her. She sent the T-shirt spinning through the air while Frida did the same with her own top half. Verónica's bra flew to a far corner of the room. In a vortex of kisses they fell onto the bed. At that moment Verónica wasn't thinking that this was her first time with a girl. Instinct was her perfect guide. She wasn't a disciple, or a young virgin in need of sexual education. Her hands sought out Frida's pussy with the same enthusiasm they would a cock. The pleasure of discovering another person's body, of being able to touch it, satisfy it, wasn't very different. Frida kissed her mouth, her tits, and she felt that skin sliding over a body was the most spectacular thing that could happen to a person. Frida had gone down, leaving a trail of saliva that went from her navel to her clitoris and then her ass. If she did that for a few more seconds, Verónica would come. She tugged her hair to bring her up and now Frida's tongue was exploring her mouth with the same dedication. Frida's body rubbed against her. Her right hand took Verónica's left and guided it to penetrate her. Frida moved rhythmically, making her caress the labia before going inside her again. Verónica's face was buried in Frida's neck. She liked her smell. She would have inhaled her whole body if it had not been that the movement of their two bodies had fallen into an even rhythm that had them reaching climax at the same time, both with a smile. There must have been at least one in her life, but she couldn't recall a single man who had smiled when he came.

III

She woke up at first light. Frida was sleeping deeply. Verónica breathed in the smell of her again. It had been an incredible night. She wondered how it would be when they woke up in the morning. She didn't like the idea of waking up next to Frida and talking about inanities. Or rather: she was scared to think that Frida might not like waking up next to her and having to talk about everyday things. Better to go now, in the afterglow of their kisses, their caresses. Yes, better to go. She picked up her clothes, or at least the few items she could find in the dark, and went to her room. There was no sound in the house. Was Petra back? Could she have heard them?

Verónica went to her bathroom and looked at herself in the mirror: her hair was all over the place, her expression was dazed, as if she had smoked a joint, and there was a bruise under her left breast. She smiled to think that Frida was unlikely to have fared any better. She drank a glass of water, went for a piss and climbed into bed.

At midday she got up. She put on shorts and a T-shirt and went to the kitchen. Petra and Frida were already there having coffee. Petra poured her a cup and they all sat around the table. There was no word or gesture from Frida to hint at what had taken place between them. But this time such behaviour didn't surprise Verónica, so she concentrated on enjoying her coffee and the musical lilt of Petra's voice as she talked them through the events of the previous night. She had gone to meet the boy at the house of his parents, who were away in Buenos Aires.

"There's nothing like young men. They're tireless. He barely let me sleep. At dawn I had to ask him to call me a taxi because I had nothing left to give."

"So what plans have you made with this teenager? Are you going to take him to the zoo, or to a museum?"

"He's not really a teenager. He'll be twenty in two weeks. I haven't made any plans – how could I? I told him I was travelling onwards with my friends, that we were bound to see each other again in the future."

"So are you thinking of seeing him again?"

"I don't think so, but he seemed smitten and I felt bad. It's been a long time since a man looked at me with such love."

"A man ... a boy, you mean."

"Whatever. He insisted on taking my mobile number and I said it would be better if he wrote to me, that I don't like talking on the phone."

The day spun out its usual routine of pool, food and sun worshipping. Verónica observed everything as though taking part in a game, as if she knew Frida was waiting for her to react. She wasn't willing to give her that pleasure, despite being willing to give her every other pleasure that came to mind. As she dozed on the lounger, Verónica thought that she'd had a very good time with Frida the previous night but that, save for the minor details, it hadn't been all that different from being with a man. And this difference was nothing to do with the presence or absence of a cock, but with a certain intimacy that she could share with a woman but had never managed to achieve with a man. That was what she had most liked about Frida. That feeling of a shared essence. There was no artifice between them like when she was with a guy. The word honesty came to mind. She wondered if perhaps it was a more honest experience – but that word didn't seem quite right either. It wasn't a question of honesty but of comprehension. A woman would always understand another woman better.

For dinner they ate oven fries with hamburgers made by Petra and drank beer before moving on to vodka and whisky.

They listened to music, went out to the garden to gaze at the night sky and at some point Frida said she was going to bed because she was very drunk, she had had too much. Petra and she were alone again. Verónica asked if she really believed the boy was in love with her.

"At that age it's all love and sex. And I sometimes feel a bit old for both those things."

They also went to bed soon afterwards. The next morning Verónica woke up feeling annoyed that she didn't know what Frida was playing at, so the first thing she said when she saw the girls in the living room was that they would leave for Yacanto del Valle the next day. They both agreed.

Perhaps as a result of this announcement, Frida seemed much more affectionate, at one point walking over to Verónica to give her a shoulder rub. When they crossed paths in the kitchen, she gave her a quick kiss on the lips as she took drinks to the living room. A couple of times she shot her complicit looks, and Verónica imagined they would be together again that night. So she was surprised when Frida and Petra both agreed that they would like to have dinner out that evening. She had expected that they would all eat together in the living room, as on the previous nights, especially since this was their last day in the house. Although she put up mild resistance, Verónica didn't want to push the idea of staying in. Instead she went off to her room in a bad mood and struggled to concentrate on Hemingway's stories. Then she had a shower and put on moisturizer and clean clothes. Jeans and a shirt.

As they were about to leave, she asked if either of them could drive so that she didn't have to be the one watching what she drank again. If not, they could order a taxi. Frida and Petra looked at her with surprise: they both drove and didn't mind not drinking. It was decided that Verónica would drive on the way there and Petra on the way back. They ate in a restaurant that had looked nice from outside, but the food wasn't great and the wine was very expensive. Petra drank only one glass. At about midnight they returned to the house and Petra opened a bottle of wine in the kitchen. Frida wanted a vodka and went to the study where the drinks were. Verónica followed her there.

"I'm impressed by how well stocked your cousin's house is," said Frida, as she hesitated between a bottle of Absolut and another of Finlandia. Verónica watched her from the doorway.

"Frida."

"Yes?" Still hesitating between the bottles, Frida answered without turning round.

"I was going to say 'we need to talk' and now that sounds pathetic, even to me."

Frida turned round with the bottle of Absolut in her hand and, putting on a serious voice, said, "Verónica, we need to talk."

"See? It sounds stupid."

"Shall I bring a bottle of whisky for you?"

Verónica nodded and walked towards Frida, who now had a bottle in each hand. Verónica kissed her. Not a very long kiss. Frida had no chance to put the bottles down or make any kind of gesture.

"Looks like you don't want to talk after all," she said, and laughed.

"It's the first time I've ever tried to kiss a girl. Don't make it difficult for me."

Frida put the bottles down on a cabinet. "You are a beautiful soul."

"I already know that. Now explain to me what we're doing."

"Enjoying ourselves, having a good time."

"And Petra?"

"I imagine she's having a good time too."

"Are you two a couple?"

"No, we aren't. And neither are you and I."

"I know we're not. But I want to know if you two are having the same sort of good time we did the other night. If today or tomorrow it's my turn with her, or if we all have a good time together, like playing cards or something."

"Petra prefers men. I like women. That doesn't mean we don't get on, or that we haven't had good times together, to keep using this metaphor we've adopted. All three of us together? It could happen. Petra likes you. She thinks you're great. Although I know my limitations: I like one person at a time."

"And the day before yesterday it was my turn."

"Is that a reproach? Next you'll be telling me you were drunk."

"I was a bit drunk, but that had nothing to do with it. I'm not used to this kind of thing and it's —"

"Yes, I know, it's the first time you've had to ask a woman to explain what's going on. Think of it this way: it's just the same as asking a man. Awkward."

Frida laughed again and put her hand on Verónica's face. Then she kissed her. "Shall I take you to the living room and get you drunk?"

If the question contained the promise of something more interesting, the reality was going to bring any such illusion crashing down to earth. They drank (wine, vodka and whisky, Petra, Frida and Verónica, respectively), they chatted, they listened to music. After an hour, Frida stood up and said she was going to bed, since they would be leaving early the next morning. Petra went soon afterwards and Verónica thought of following her to see if the Italian went to her room or Frida's, but decided this would be a petulant gesture. She stayed in the living room on her own. She wasn't tired yet. Verónica thought about the next day. They would go to Yacanto del Valle, she would meet the man of her dreams, she would spend the rest of her time off there or she'd continue on her trip with the guy in tow and the experience with Frida would just be something that had happened on vacation. Frida would send emails asking to see her again and Verónica would have to explain that they could have a drink some time, but that she shouldn't get her hopes up. I'm rapidly turning into a massive jerk, she told herself.

Suddenly she remembered the dead rodent she had seen a few nights ago. What had happened to it? She hadn't seen it the morning after finding it. Could the girls have picked it up and thrown it in the garbage? If so, it was strange neither of them had said anything. The animal's appearance was too alarming not to mention. There was always the possibility that the disembowelled animal had never existed. That it had been a figment of her imagination. A dream, a nightmare, a message she had yet to decipher. As she walked out of the door leading to the garden, she felt as though she might find the animal's body tossed on to the veranda. But there was nothing there. Just the chirping of crickets, a few stars above, the rustling of branches and the sensation that someone (a human, an animal, a divine being from another world?) was watching her from the shadows. Fearfully, she retreated.

4 *A Party*

I

Before setting off for Yacanto del Valle, Verónica checked her email. It was the second time she had turned on her laptop while on vacation, and that already felt excessive. There was a reason why she refused to upgrade her mobile phone for one that allowed her to check her inbox; she didn't want to be thinking about emails or feeling the pressure to reply instantly. She glanced at the inbox: among the spam, press releases and the odd work-related message was exactly what she was looking for – an email from Paula. She wanted to know her friend's thoughts on what had happened with Frida. To her relief, Paula had suppressed the scandalized tone that came to her so easily and instead told her about her own teenage fling with a friend at secondary school. She gave plenty of details, most of which Verónica would have preferred her to leave out – but then her friend was like that, an enemy of ellipsis. Paula also urged her to do whatever she wanted and not give a shit what anyone thought. *What happens on the Bolivian border stays on the Bolivian border*, she wrote, betraying a dismal ignorance of geography along with the best kind of female solidarity. Verónica thought of writing back instantly to tell her what had happened the day before, but she didn't want to come across as a bewildered and confused ingénue. She would write to her the next day instead, and collapse what had happened with the girls into a minor episode in her wanderings through the north.

Cousin Severo had told her not to bother tidying up too much. After she left, he would send the maid over to clean the place. Verónica preferred to leave everything as tidy as possible. She got up at eight o'clock and an hour later had the house more or less shipshape. The girls appeared then with their rucksacks and the guitar. Petra insisted they take some selfies and photos in the house and garden, with the panoramic view as a backdrop.

They filled up the tank and had breakfast at a service station before heading south on Route 38. They were going to take the scenic road through the Calchaquí Valley and expected to reach the city of Tafí del Valle in time for lunch. Over breakfast they looked at the map again. They had to go to Acheral and join Route 307 there. It was a glorious day, not a cloud in the sky. Frida and Petra were wearing sunglasses. All three had on their shortest shorts, and the sight of so many female legs together brightened the weary expressions of the men at the service station. The three women made no comment.

Frida was sitting beside her and Petra was in the back. As Verónica rejoined the freeway (a denomination that seemed too grand for this potholed road), Frida connected her MP3 player to the USB port in the car stereo.

"What are we listening to?"

"'La Fille du Lido'. It's by a singer called Inna Modja. She's from Bamako."

"From where?"

"The capital of Mali, in Africa. She sings in French and English. She also sings in Fula, her native language."

They found the right road without difficulty. The view that opened up before them was dazzling, the route winding through mountains and jungle-like forests. At one point they pulled off the road to enjoy the landscape and take some photographs with Petra's camera. Verónica kept a few paces back.

"Don't you like photos?" Petra asked her.

"I love them," she replied.

"But you never take them, not even with your phone."

"I don't think my phone can take them, and I didn't bring a camera."

"I think you don't want to take away any memories," said Frida teasingly.

"It's possible. I don't rule that out."

"I'll email you ours. Stand together so I can take one." Petra focussed the lens on Verónica and Frida joined her, putting an arm around her shoulders. Verónica, motionless, smiled at the camera.

"Can you relax a bit?" Frida asked, and tickled her. Verónica tried to fight her off but couldn't help laughing or stop Frida from hugging her tighter.

Arriving in Tafí del Valle well before lunchtime, they set out to explore the city. They found a clothes shop all of them loved, where Frida bought a little cotton cardigan which she quaintly referred to as a *rebeca* in her European Spanish. Petra bought some artisanal slippers that were more pretty than practical and Verónica a multicoloured waistcoat she thought was beautiful but which she would doubtless end up giving to one of her sisters, once the vacation fever had passed.

Lunch was in a little tavern, where the soft drinks came in litre bottles. All three of them ordered Wiener schnitzel with fries. They were hungry and not in a hurry. After coffee they wandered a bit more but found only a few lost tourists. The locals were all having a siesta. It was quite a while before they continued on their journey. This time Frida drove and the landscape was less striking.

They arrived in Yacanto del Valle at about 5 p.m. and drove around the town. It comprised six or seven blocks with a typical square at its heart, around which were a church and various shops: an ice-cream parlour, bars, clothes and antiques shops and even a veterinary surgery. Verónica had identified a hotel on the internet that looked quite pretty, called La Posada de Don Humberto. It was a rambling old house that had been converted into a hotel for tourists. High season was finished and, perhaps for that reason, there were rooms available.

La Posada de Don Humberto was run by its owners, a loquacious gay couple from Buenos Aires. In a matter of minutes the girls learned that they had come to live in Yacanto del Valle five years ago and that they were not related to Humberto Correa, a rich landowner who'd had the house built at the end of the nineteenth century when he left the home on his estancia and moved into town.

"I'd like a single room. How about you two?" Verónica asked.

"A double is fine for us," Frida replied.

Verónica was given a double room to herself anyway. As the girls walked to their rooms, they agreed to meet back at the hotel entrance after a few minutes' rest. Their plan was to have a coffee in some little bar and then go on to the art gallery recommended by Verónica's sister.

"What's the name of the eligible bachelor?" Petra enquired as she sipped her cappuccino in the bar.

"Ramiro. Ramiro Elizalde."

II

"Is Ramiro Elizalde here?" Verónica asked a cleaner in the empty gallery. They had arrived either too early or too late for art.

The gallery was called Arde, a play on words alluding to the Tucumán Arde protest art movement. Tucuman Is Burning, a campaign born in Rosario and Buenos Aires in 1968, had set out to denounce the social inequalities in Tucumanian society at that time. Arde was housed in an old building similar to their hotel, except that the exhibition rooms had been refurbished along the lines of a New York art gallery. The resulting contrast with the little town of Yacanto was like an odd piece of performance art, perhaps unintended by the owner, who appeared at that moment. He was wearing worn-out jeans, sneakers and a lilac-coloured Lacoste polo shirt. His hair was too short and tidy, a style that didn't flatter him but didn't look bad either. As for the rest of him, he was a little taller than Verónica and could still conceal his gut. He didn't have a limp or any discernible tics, and his smile boasted all the teeth a human could possibly have. He could have starred in a toothpaste ad. If he didn't turn out to be gay or married, you might say this man was a rare catch.

"Ramiro? I'm Verónica Rosenthal."

"Verónica. Leticia's sister. Your reputation precedes you. I got two emails saying you'd be coming some time around now. One from your little sister and the other from my cousin Cristina."

"They obviously wanted to warn you about me."

"That seemed to be the gist of it – not that they succeeded."

What had her idiot sister and Cousin Severo's bitch wife written about her?

Verónica introduced him to the girls and explained that they were travelling together. Ramiro invited them into his office. Verónica examined the paintings on display as they walked.

"Do you only show contemporary Argentinian art?"

"I mainly have works from the sixties, seventies and eighties, actually. If something good turns up, I don't care what year it's from."

"I thought I saw a León Ferrari."

"I've got a few Ferraris. If you like I'll give you a tour of Arde's three rooms later."

Ramiro had a large office divided into two parts, his desk in one and a more relaxed area with armchairs and a coffee table in the other. They sat in red leather pop art chairs, very seventies, like all the other furniture in the room. Ramiro asked them what they would like to drink. He phoned his secretary to request coffee, orange juice and water. "Oh, and if there's anything left over from lunch, bring that too," he added, explaining to them: "We also use the space for book launches. There was one today and we have some sandwiches left over. Which is rare because usually nothing's left over, not even paper napkins."

Like a good host, Ramiro asked all the right questions, even showing a great interest in Frida's social studies and Petra's music. That meant sharing the limelight with Petra and Frida, something Verónica wasn't entirely happy about: they were prettier than her, after all, and had the charm of being foreign. For a moment she regretted bringing them to the gallery, but then realized that was absurd. It wasn't as if she had gone there looking for a boyfriend.

After they had polished off the sandwiches, juice and coffee, and before the conversation dried up, Ramiro offered to show them round the gallery.

"Have you been doing this long?"

"The gallery's been here for seven years. I opened it when I moved to Yacanto. My family's from Salta and I started buying artworks there, ten years ago. My dad had a good collection of Argentine art, and when I moved here I brought some of his canvases as an advance on my inheritance. And there's always some acquaintance or friend of a friend who wants to get rid of these strange pieces because they prefer more traditional art."

They went to the first room, which was also the biggest.

"I try to buy everything available by the artists who showed at Di Tella or who started coming to public attention in the seventies. So you're going to see a lot of works that aren't paintings but more like installations or sculptures, like these ones by Marta Minujín. I've also got these suits by Delia Cancela and Pablo Mesejean, which I acquired in London. There are some pieces by Edgardo Giménez, and those shoes with a double platform are by Dalila Puzzovio, the wife of Charlie Squirru, who made these two pieces. And here's my favourite, *Intimacies of a Timid Man,* by Jorge de la Vega."

"Is everything for sale?"

"Not everything. In fact, some day I'm hoping to have a permanent collection. I put a few works up for sale that don't particularly interest me, so I can acquire others."

They moved on to the next room, where works by Pablo Suárez were displayed alongside ones by Rómulo Macció and Marcia Schvartz. Verónica's eye was caught by one of the Schvartz paintings, because she had seen it on the cover of a book she had never finished reading.

"Do you like Schvartz? This is *Portrait of Cacho.* A work from the early eighties. Come on, let's go to the next room. There are some paintings by Alfredo Prior and Kenneth Kemble I think will surprise you."

The tour concluded, Ramiro asked what their plans were.

"Nothing special," Verónica said quickly. "Any suggestions?"

"Today's a bit busy, but we could get together tomorrow. I can give you a tour of the area. Give me your number."

The next day? He was going to let her escape so easily? He was letting them all escape. There must be something wrong with the guy. Or perhaps he felt flustered having so many women around him. Whatever the reason, they might as well meet up tomorrow to discover the telluric secrets of Yacanto del Valle.

The three friends walked across the square. Before returning to the hotel they visited the church and then stopped to look in a few shop windows. Frida and Petra seemed happy. Verónica, on the other hand, was beginning to feel antsy. What was their plan? Would they get together for a round of strip poker in one of their rooms? Would Frida start leading her on again? She wasn't sure she could bear that, and she had no idea how she would react.

Her mood changed a couple of hours later when she got a call from Ramiro.

"There's a party tonight that's going to be really good. Would you all like to come?"

"We love parties. Where is it?"

"Just on the edge of town. I can come and get you around eleven o'clock. What do you think?"

"Perfect."

Verónica hadn't asked the others if they felt like that kind of outing, but she was confident of persuading them. A party. It was all they needed that night.

III

She tended not to wear dresses but a year ago, in a María Cher sale, she had bought a short, white fitted dress that had never been worn and was now languishing at the bottom of her suitcase. It wasn't too creased and she could wear it with some white flats she had bought at the same time. Come to think of it, she hadn't been to a party for ages. That was what came of hooking up with a married man. You don't feel like going to a party on your own and having everyone look at you as if you're missing a leg.

She got out her evening bag. The strap was detachable to make it a clutch. She applied a little foundation and some lipstick, put on sunglasses, looked at herself in the mirror and was happy with what she saw. It was already nearly eleven o'clock. She went to get the girls from their room. Frida was adjusting the belt on her flowery dress. Petra was still in the shower.

"Nice dress. I love the colours," Verónica said.

Frida came over and kissed her on the mouth. Still standing close, she whispered, "And I love the colour of your lips."

"I thought you were over that."

"You think too much." Frida's right hand stroked her ass over her dress then went under it and touched the edge of her underwear. Verónica didn't move or put up any resistance.

"I thought you weren't going to wear any underwear to make things easier for that guy," Frida said, as her fingers delved under the G-string.

"You think too much."

"*Touchée.*"

"I'm the one who's being *touchée*, wouldn't you say?"

Frida removed her hand and stepped away without dropping her gaze. Petra came out of the shower naked and drying her hair.

"Hey, you two look so beautiful. I'm going to lower the tone in my jeans."

"Tight jeans beat bare legs," said Verónica.

"Men are so basic." Frida was still looking at her.

"Women too."

Just then Verónica's phone rang. It was Ramiro, who was already at the door of the hotel. In ten minutes Petra was ready, and the three went out together.

He was standing waiting for them beside his 4 × 4, a shining silver Hilux that didn't appear to have spent much time out in the country mud. Ramiro had put on a shirt with rolled-up sleeves. He greeted them pleasantly but made no comment on their appearance. He was either shy or very used to driving girls like them around in his pickup. Petra sat in the front and chatted breathlessly to Ramiro. She even smoothed down the collar on his shirt.

It was a short drive. At the end of town the street became an asphalt road and, less than a hundred yards further on, there was a gate. This was no simple country gate but seemed to be the entrance to a club or something similar. There was a security booth with two guards, who hurried forward to block their way. Ramiro waved at them and drove on in the direction of some lights that could be seen in the distance. Two hundred yards further on, fields gave way to a parking area for vans and sports cars. From here you could hear the sound of music and a DJ who obviously thought he was in Ibiza.

Rising in front of them was a three-storey house in a minimalist style. They walked around it to the back and found the hub of the party. A human tide was jumping, dancing, drinking from cans of beer or from large glasses of some concoction prepared at the bar by two bartenders who mixed drinks with more speed than skill. These two were also in charge of serving champagne. The partygoers could help themselves to beers and white wine from enormous vats of ice and water. The red wine was on a table surrounded by glasses and plates of snacks.

Verónica saw Petra take Ramiro's hand and lead him to the middle of the dance floor. Was this an excuse to leave her alone with Frida, or did she actually like Ramiro? Frida suggested they go and get drinks. The bar was thronged with people, so they went to pick up beers first then joined the queue of people waiting for cocktails.

"I want to say something to you before I get drunk," said Frida, who had already drunk quite a bit during dinner in the restaurant at the hotel. "I don't like that guy at all."

"Ramiro?"

"Not at all. And before you say something silly, let me be clear this has nothing to do with jealousy. And I love men. Some of them. But this Ramiro is bad news."

"On what do you base that?"

"Instinct, a hunch, call it what you like."

A boy who was also fighting to get served pointed at their beers. "Not fair," he protested.

"In love and war everything is fair," said Frida.

"So are you in love or at war?" the boy shot back, but he got no answer.

Finally they arrived at the bar. Frida asked for a mojito and Verónica a double whisky. The whisky wasn't good, but it could have been worse. The boy was with a friend now and came over to chat them up. They weren't bad-looking lads. Frida said she wanted to dance, so the four of them headed to the dance floor. After a while the girls delicately detached themselves from their companions and returned to the drinks area.

"No way I'm getting back in that chaotic queue," said Verónica as she saw Ramiro and Petra coming towards them, Petra wiggling her ass in her tight jeans.

Verónica complained about the drinks situation and Ramiro looked at her with surprise. "My dear, whatever you want you shall have."

He went inside the house and returned minutes later

with a bottle of ten-year-old Chivas Regal and another of Herradura Añejo tequila.

"Come, I want to introduce you to Nicolás Menéndez Berti, the owner of this house," Ramiro said to her, and Verónica liked the way he addressed this to her alone rather than to the three of them.

They went towards a group standing by the pool. Even from a distance it was clear who the owner of the house was: he was the centre of attention for everyone around him. Ramiro walked over and embraced him. He said something that Verónica couldn't quite catch and the owner of the house turned towards her.

"It's a pleasure to meet you, Verónica. I'm Nicolás."

"Congratulations on the party. What a beautiful house you have."

"Yes, it's pretty, but the land is even better."

"Which land?"

"The house sits on the edge of an estate of 2,500 acres. You should see it."

"I bet."

"Are your European friends having a good time?"

He seemed older than Ramiro and was a little shorter and more solidly built, like a recently retired rugby player. He obviously liked imposing his physical presence, getting noticed. Seven centuries ago he would have been sitting on a throne observing how his subjects entertained themselves. Something else caught Verónica's attention: Nicolás was the only one who didn't have a glass in his hand.

"How dreadful that the owner of the house hasn't got a drink," she said. It was a technique she had developed: whenever she had a difficult interview, she disguised the questions she thought might be contentious, or which the interviewee might answer with a lie, as an innocent aside.

"I don't drink alcohol, and alcohol-free drinks are boring," he answered.

Their group was joined by a trio of youths who must have been about twenty-five, perhaps younger. One of the men kissed Ramiro on the cheek. Ramiro introduced him to Verónica: "This is my younger brother, Nahuel."

The younger brother kissed Verónica with the indifference of one who knows he is handsome and observed, then moved away from them with Nicolás. Verónica was beginning to tire of these patrician, beautiful and wealthy youths. Ramiro wanted to take her back to the dance floor, but she felt the pull of that bottle of whisky. Back at the drinks area, they found Frida on her own, guarding the bottles. Verónica asked her where Petra was. Frida pointed at the dance floor. "She went off with that guy." They poured themselves another glass of whisky.

Verónica wanted to go to the bathroom. She had to fend off a couple of creeps who were determined to drag her onto the dance floor as she crossed part of the garden to get to the toilet facilities, which came with changing rooms and showers. Verónica could imagine that beyond the garden there might be a soccer pitch and tennis courts to provide amusement for the bored young people during the day. She came out of the toilet thinking about how irritating she found people like Nicolás and bumped into Frida, who was waiting for her at the door.

Taking her arm, Frida moved her to one side. "What are we doing, Verónica?"

"In what sense?" Verónica asked, without irony.

"This party, us here. We should leave."

"You and I? The three of us?"

"All three. I really don't like this place."

"You don't like Ramiro, and now you don't like the party."

Frida stepped towards Verónica, who took a step back.

"I can't stand women who lead men on. Or women, either."

"You really don't get it, Verónica."

"What I get is that these last two days I've been at the mercy of what you do or don't do. All it took for you to lose it was a man coming onto the scene."

"They're two different things. You're confusing things, mixing things up. All we want is to share this journey and make it the best it can possibly be for all three of us. What's happening here with all these people who are out of their heads, with guys who won't take no for an answer, is something else. Can't you see there are loads more men here than women?"

"Look, Frida, we're all three of us grown up. If you don't like the party, leave. If Petra wants to go with you, fine. If tomorrow you want to set sail for China, that's your right. And the same applies to me."

"I thought you were sharper than that."

Verónica considered answering back but she was too angry. She simply said "Bye, Frida" and walked away, leaving the Norwegian alone. Walking quickly, she stamped across the ground as though delivering hammer blows. She didn't feel like going back to Ramiro, so she went off to one side, to be alone for a while. What Frida had said was right: the guys here were unbearable. There was something else, too, and now she saw it: the age difference. Most of the men here were in the thirty-to-forty bracket. The girls, on the other hand, seemed mainly to be in their twenties. Come to think of it, Frida and Petra were in their twenties too. She was the only thirty-something at the party, or one of just a handful.

Hoping to escape the men who continually approached her (couldn't they bear to see a woman on her own? Why did they think women must always have a male beside them?), she went back to the place she had last seen Ramiro but didn't find him there. Finally, he appeared from inside the house.

"Come, I want to show you something," he said and took her hand, steering her back towards the house. Although there were a few people indoors, it was clear the party was outside and that only a privileged few had access to this enormous room, perhaps only Nicolás's close friends.

Ramiro took her up to the first floor. Verónica suspected this was a ruse to get her into one of the bedrooms. There was nobody on this floor, further feeding her suspicions. Ramiro opened a door and they entered a room in darkness. He switched on the light, revealing a master bedroom.

"Wow, that's beautiful."

The painting was about three feet high. At first she could make out only colours, but if she looked more closely she could see the body of a reclining woman, like Goya's *La Maja Desnuda.* A surrealist version of the naked Maja.

"It's a Chab."

"A what?"

"A Víctor Chab, quite recent. I love it. Nico beat me to it and bought it in Buenos Aires. I offered him twice what he paid, but the little shit doesn't want to sell."

"Nico collects art too?"

"I got him started. He's got the makings of a nice little gallery."

They stood looking at the painting for a few minutes. Then Ramiro kissed her. They spent almost as long kissing as they had spent admiring Chab's Venus. Verónica still thought this was all a ploy to get her onto the bed. So she decided to take the initiative and began pushing him gently towards it.

"Not here. Let's go to my house," Ramiro said.

"I can't. I'm with the girls."

"Are you their nanny? If so, I should let you know that one's escaped. I'm pretty sure I saw the Italian coming into the house with a guy. If you like we can look in all the rooms so you can tell her we're leaving."

"How will they get back?"

"Someone will take them. Worst-case scenario they'll have to walk, but it's only half a mile back to the hotel."

There was no point staying there any longer. Was she going to look for the girls and take them back to the hotel? Throw herself at Frida? She decided to go with Ramiro. She'd talk to Frida the next day.

Verónica waited for Ramiro to go and say goodbye to the host. No doubt he'd gone to brag that he was taking her back to his place. Verónica didn't mind about that. She lit a cigarette and Ramiro appeared just as she was tossing the butt onto the ground. In the interim she saw neither Frida nor Petra, nor did she care that she hadn't seen them.

IV

A few years previously, Verónica had worked on a magazine targeted at female readers. One of those publications that, with their articles on cooking, fashion and sex, deliberately place women a step below men. And everything is aimed at the upper-class (or aspiring to be) white heterosexual woman. One of the articles she'd had to write was about the sexual fantasies of women while they fucked. That required consulting sexologists, psychologists and the odd celebrity with erotic cachet. Since it was an article that had to be written urgently and she was short of time, and since the subject matter didn't seem all that serious to her, she did something she had always considered a grave sin in journalism: she made up quotes. She interviewed the current hot celebrity, but the specialists were all characters she dreamed up. And the fantasies that these experts on the subject explained to her, in lurid detail, were also the fruit of her imagination. She sent the article to her editor, one of the few male editors still working on this kind of publication, with two results:

One: her article was rejected. Apparently her imagination was not similar enough to that of the rich, white heterosexual women who read the magazine.

Two: the editor asked her out to dinner. An invitation she turned down perhaps a little too firmly, because she never had a piece published in that magazine again. They didn't even pay her a cancellation fee for the article.

Sometime later there was a third consequence: she opened up a user account on a pornographic website in order to write stories and so channel her fervid imagination. But the few stories she had written always covered the same territory: sadomasochistic relations between a man and a woman.

Among the many fantasies Verónica had included in that article was that of getting turned on by thinking of a woman while fucking a man. Something that hadn't happened in her case before but was within the realm of possibility. What she had never imagined was that the thought would recur so often for her. She kissed Ramiro and thought of Frida's mouth. Ramiro caressed her and she remembered the other girl's tongue between her legs. When Ramiro penetrated her, she imagined Frida's fingers inside her. She came thinking of Frida, semi-naked, putting sunscreen on Petra down by the pool.

When, later, they started all over again with kissing, Verónica made an effort to concentrate on Ramiro, on his body, which he clearly worked on in the gym, on his weight-lifting biceps, but it was useless. She couldn't get Frida out of her mind.

Perhaps Ramiro had intuited some of this, because while they were in the kitchen making coffee he asked what the deal was with Frida.

"What do you mean by 'the deal'?"

"I don't know. Just that she seemed a bit unfriendly. Whereas Petra's really nice. It's so weird that they hardly knew each other and then started travelling together."

"It's not that weird. But it's true that the trip has become a bit more complicated in the last few days."

Ramiro poured coffee for her and offered a sweetener. Verónica reminded him that she took it unsweetened.

"Of course. I noticed that yesterday. And you don't drink orange juice."

"Well, I didn't drink it yesterday. I'm not that set in my ways."

"Coming back to the girls, I don't think you need that kind of complication in your life, do you? You can stay here in Yacanto and let them go on without you."

She answered with a smile and they went back to bed. A couple of hours later, Verónica had reached a conclusion: she needed some distance from Frida. She couldn't carry on behaving like a teenager with a crush on the girl who sat next to her at school. She needed a few days alone, without the girls. But she also didn't feel like having to explain herself, and she definitely didn't want to stay on in Yacanto del Valle. Ramiro was sleeping peacefully, without snoring. A point in his favour. She got dressed, realizing that she had a slight headache. Hesitating over whether or not to wake him, she walked to his side of the bed and passed her hand over his forehead. Ramiro opened his eyes.

"I'm off. I'm going to carry on north. On my own."

"When will I see you again?"

"Let's write to each other. I'll come through Yacanto on the way back for sure. My return flight leaves from Tucumán."

She had no plan, at least at that moment, to see Ramiro again.

Back at the Posada de Don Humberto, the night receptionist was still on duty. She asked him to prepare her bill. In her room, she took two aspirin, showered, put on comfortable jeans and a T-shirt. Everything else went in the suitcase. For a moment she thought of leaving Frida and Petra a letter at the reception desk, then decided it would be better to get going and write to them from her next destination: Cafayate. They were sure to be heading that way, or perhaps they would stop sooner, in Amaicha del Valle. In any case, all the northbound buses went through Yacanto, so they wouldn't have any trouble getting transport. When she went downstairs to pay her bill, Mariano – one of the owners – was already behind the desk.

"Tell me what you didn't like about our house that you should leave so soon."

"It's not that. I love the hotel. I just need to travel onwards."

"Are the other girls staying?"

"I think they're leaving sometime this morning, but I'm not sure."

From the moment she left her room until the moment she was in her car, turning onto the provincial highway, Verónica feared bumping into the girls and having to explain herself. She would have felt like a thief, skulking away in the night. But now she was on the road. Verónica thought she'd put on some music. Frida's MP3 player was still connected to the car stereo, and she should have gone back to return it to her. She didn't, though. Instead she put on the music Frida had been listening to. The voice of a woman singing in Portuguese, and then a man, drifted from the speaker. Without taking her eyes off the road, she looked to see who was singing: they were called Ana Carolina and Seu Jorge. The subject seemed very sad:

Os passos vão pelas ruas
Ninguém reparou na lua
A vida sempre continua
Eu não sei parar de te olhar
Eu não sei parar de te olhar
Não vou parar de te olhar
Eu não me canso de olhar

Footsteps go along the streets
No one notices the moon
Life always goes on
I can't stop looking at you
I can't stop looking at you
I will not stop looking at you
I never tire of looking

And even though Verónica knew *olhar* meant "look" in Portuguese, to her it sounded like the Spanish *llorar*, "weep", as if Seu Jorge were singing "I will never stop weeping."

5 *The Others*

I

If there was one thing that annoyed him, it was being compared to a policeman. Or called an old snooper or, worse, the residents' slave. The doorman in a residential block wasn't any of those things. His work was more like that of a psychologist or a psychiatrist. He had to maintain the mental health of the building – no easy task given how unhinged the occupants were. He had to transmit calm to them, make them feel that all those things worrying them (a persistent drip, the neighbour screaming next door, the beggars outside, the rising cost of cleaning) were not going to disrupt their lives. And he was a specialist in that, even if they didn't realize it.

Verónica was different, though. Ever since arriving at the building on the same day (she to live, he to work), coincidence had defined their relationship. And, just as a doctor or a psychologist has a favourite patient, there was no doubt his pet neighbour was the single girl on the second floor. He liked protecting her, making her feel safe in this building full of psychotic women, despicable men and diabolical children. He sorted out any problem that might arise in the apartment, from fixing the flush button on the lavatory to repairing a short circuit in the light under the kitchen cabinet. And she reciprocated with a special affection, betokened by a bottle of good wine on the anniversary of the day they both moved into the building and a generous tip at the end of the year, which she always handed to his wife because he refused to accept any money.

He worried about what she got up to outside the building. Not with men, because he had seen her change boyfriends and lovers regularly, apparently without much drama. But with her work as a journalist. His feeling was that Verónica lived in constant danger. And he'd had an opportunity to confirm that fear: she had kept a witness in the investigation she was conducting hidden in her apartment and four hitmen had come to kill him. That day Verónica – who wasn't at home – had managed to call him, Marcelo, the doorman, just in time to task him with saving the young man. And he had. Not very cleanly, it's true, because he made the witness jump from the second floor – with all the risk that entailed – and he himself had been shot and nearly killed in the process. But then she had saved his life and the young man's by driving over the four assassins. It had been the most terrifying experience of his life and he wouldn't recommend it to anyone. From that moment he had been even more worried about Verónica. What new investigation was she involved in? What trouble would she get into next? Would he be able to help her again?

To these questions one more should be added: did Marcelo have the hots for Verónica? Yes, of course, but he wasn't about to do something stupid with one of the neighbours like he had back in the days when he was young and single. These days he was happy just to fantasize about them during sex with his wife. More than once he had imagined himself with Verónica. But as soon as he came, everything went back to how it was: his wife in their bed and Verónica on the second floor. Nothing better than clear-cut relationships.

He was happy when he heard that Verónica was going on vacation. At least while she was having fun she couldn't get into trouble. She told him she was going to travel through the north-east, that first she would stay at a cousin's house in Tucumán and then cross three provinces before reaching La Quiaca.

With Verónica away, he could concentrate on other matters relating to the building. Various residents had complained about the lack of security, which for them manifested itself in the presence of *cartoneros*, poor people who rummaged through the garbage looking for cardboard they could sell by the kilo; a group of adolescents who hung around on the corner; and supposedly an exhibitionist, whom only the madwoman in 5B had ever reported seeing. Marcelo had proposed installing security cameras.

The residents, for all that they were very worried about security, weren't prepared to spend money on cameras. He had explained the paradox to a red-headed lad who came to offer a surveillance service with monitored cameras at a very good price. Marcelo had asked him to leave his telephone number and the company's details to pass on to the residents' committee, but the redhead had given out his last card at a building round the corner. He didn't want to jot down his details on a piece of paper because he said that wouldn't be professional. He had promised to come by the next day to drop off a card, but never had. It's often hard to get them printed that quickly.

But the strangest visitor that day had been the person from a private mail company who came to leave a packet for Verónica Rosenthal. Marcelo had said she wasn't at home, that the man should leave it with him. The mail delivery person insisted that the terms of their service required the item to be delivered in person. Marcelo thought that sounded ridiculous, so to take him down a peg or two he told him that, if he really wanted to hand it over personally, he was going to have to wait a long time because Verónica Rosenthal was on vacation. The guy asked him if he knew where, and something inside Marcelo clicked. Nobody from a postal service would start asking after the whereabouts of the person receiving a letter or package (which in this case appeared to be some books wrapped in brown paper). At that point he started asking questions and the guy gave a few evasive answers before practically sprinting off.

Now Marcelo was worried. Perhaps the guy was a hired assassin and the package contained a bomb that would go off when Verónica opened it. He must check any delivery that came for her more carefully. And he would try to convince the neighbours of the virtues of installing security cameras. With any luck the ginger lad would return with his card and a budget so they could talk further.

II

Whenever a famous writer or popular artist died, when a politician or party was implicated in a corruption scandal, when Messi won something or another Argentine athlete excelled, she breathed easy: it meant that edition's cover story was not going to be for her. And she was quite sure the editors of Politics, Culture, Entertainment and Sports felt the same when the scales tipped towards some horrific crime, the discovery of a human trafficking gang or narco warfare, because in those cases responsibility for the week's cover fell to her, Patricia Beltrán, editor of Society, the stand-out section of the weekly magazine *Nuestro Tiempo*. The other editors wouldn't admit that Society was the most important section – it just had more pages. But they certainly found their lives complicated when Patricia was away and had to be replaced with the idiot from Culture (who reckoned himself a poet and edited accordingly) or the cretin from Entertainment (who thought journalism meant having famous friends who passed on gossip). Her vacation had passed all too quickly, though, and now here she was, in the weekly editorial meeting, with the editor-in-chief waiting for them to put forward brilliant ideas.

"We've got nothing for the cover this week," was his automatic opening sally, one that no longer alarmed the newsroom veterans. There was always something for the cover of the next issue. No magazine or newspaper had ever come out without a cover for lack of a lead story. That was something the younger editors didn't take into account, so they got anxious when the editor made his catastrophic announcement.

Patricia suggested opening with the fifty-kilo haul of cocaine discovered by Tucumán police on Provincial Route 305 in the vicinity of El Sunchal. The van had been coming from Bolivia on a back road that ran parallel to Route 9. It had already travelled through two provinces (Jujuy and Salta) and it wasn't clear whether the intended final destination was Tucumán or another province. So far, so good: this looked like nothing more than a successful police operation. But the case had other layers. Three people had been travelling in the van: a Bolivian from Santa Cruz de la Sierra wanted by the Drug Enforcement Administration, a Salteño named Arturo Posadas and a Tucumanian, Ignacio Sandoval. Posadas happened to be Chief Superintendent Posadas, head of Criminal Intelligence in Tartagal. And Sandoval was a deputy superintendent in the Tucumán police force, specializing in intelligence. It seemed that Route 25 was to have been kept clear for them but, as luck would have it, officers from the ecological division of the Tucumán police force were patrolling the area that day looking for poachers and animal traffickers. When they stopped the van to search it, they were expecting to find species at risk of extinction, not fifty kilos of cocaine. Posadas, as well as being a chief superintendent, was the son of a retired police officer who had risen to the rank of chief of the Salta provincial police at the beginning of the year 2000. All these links between the provinces looked suspicious to Patricia.

The Télam news agency story didn't have much more, but there was enough, all the same, to suspect a conspiracy of drug traffickers, police and doubtless also politicians.

"We could send Kloster to Tucumán and put something together using agency pics. It would mean revisiting stuff we've already done on Bolivian drug traffickers," Patricia said.

"I see this more as a Politics story," said Álex Vilna, the editor of Politics.

"You mean do the story but run it in Politics rather than as a cover story?" asked the editor.

"No, it could be a cover, but if there are politicians involved and links to high-ranking police, then I don't see this in Society."

"Darling, it's all yours," Patricia said to him. "Send Kloster if you like – he's got nothing to write this week – or send someone from your section."

"No, no. I was correspondent for a Tucumanian newspaper a few years ago and I've got good contacts there. I can go myself."

"Our expenses budget only covers coach trips," the editor reminded him.

"That's fine, I'll fly and pay the difference myself. I'll ask González to give me a bit more travel allowance, and bingo."

"How about we play on the title of that Mercedes Sosa song about Tucumán, 'The Garden of the Republic', and call it 'The Garden of the Narco Police'?" the editor suggested.

Some nodded, while others expressed mild reservations to which nobody paid any attention. Everyone, apart from Vilna, was concentrating on their pitches, safe in the knowledge that they wouldn't have to deliver the cover story, or at least not that week.

Patricia doubted Álex Vilna was going to turn in a good piece. He wasn't the kind of investigative journalist able to convert his findings into a huge news story. But she preferred not to raise any objections. It didn't look good to fight another section for a story and anyway, she had nobody to send there apart from Kloster. He wasn't the world's best writer – not the worst, either – but he would have given the story a bit more bite than Vilna.

If Verónica had been in Buenos Aires, Patricia would have sent her to Tucumán. But her favourite writer was on vacation, and deservedly so. Verónica needed to get her teeth into a good investigative story, an article to lift her out of the apathy into which she had sunk after her work on the train mafia. She didn't want Verónica to become what she was: a journalist who had lost her faith, an atheist of her profession, a respectable editor.

III

A hard day, a harder night. That was how she planned to start the email to Verónica after what should have been an unmemorable Saturday had, regrettably, become unforgettable.

That Saturday had started early, with a call from her ex to say he was down with a bad case of flu (man flu, no doubt) and wasn't going to be able to take Juanfra that weekend. As if *she* had ever sent the kid over to his house because she had so-called flu! At any rate, Juanfra was older now and, even if he didn't know how to cook himself a meal, he did know how to go to the door and pay for a delivery. And it wasn't as if her stupid ex had known about her plans. That Saturday Paula happened to have a lot of things lined up.

Better calm herself down: a restorative shower, an espresso for her and a milky coffee for Juanfra with pastries from La Barcelona. And then start making new arrangements. She was supposed to be meeting Luciano for dinner at 10 p.m. She could bring that forward a couple of hours, take Luciano to a McDonald's and then get down to business. She didn't want to frighten him off. Luciano was so sweet. Practically a boy, only twenty-three. She could even get him in to look after Juanfra some time – although, thinking about it, Juanfra was probably more sensible than Luciano.

She read Verónica's email again. It was the second one she had sent since she went away. Paula didn't fully grasp what had happened with the European girls after Verónica's fling with the Norwegian. If she went solely on what she read, she would think Verónica was having a whale of a time hopping from one bed to the next, from a Norwegian woman to some promising young single from the Argentine north. But Paula had learned years ago not to go on her friend's words alone. Her work as a journalist had taught Vero to disguise her feelings and conceal facts. And, reading between the lines, it looked as though she wasn't having such a good time. Paula should address this in her next email, tell her to relax, let the others go to hell, give her heart a rest. Verónica was like one of those boxers who want to get back in the ring a month after being knocked out, with broken bones and head still spinning.

Writing all that was going to take time. Better put it off until tomorrow. At lunchtime there was a birthday celebration for Pili, their Spanish friend who lived in Buenos Aires now. By rights, Paula and her other friends should hate Pili, who had got herself a husband within six months of arriving from Galicia while the others had been on the romantic battlefield for decades, with mostly unhappy results. In any case, she and the other girls, plus a few friends Paula didn't know, were going to meet at Pili's house to eat *pulpo a feira*, a Galician octopus dish Pili was planning to prepare herself.

How Pili managed to write her blog, tweet every two minutes, go to all the private views, cook, look after a three-year-old and keep herself more or less presentable and reasonably awake, was something Paula could not begin to understand. She understood better when she arrived at her friend's house and discovered that the *pulpo a feira* had passed on to a better place, or rather another day, and been replaced with takeaway empanadas because Pili felt "*fiaca*" at the prospect of cooking. Pili had very quickly absorbed the concept of extreme apathy conveyed by that singularly Argentine word.

The second surprise of the day was that she didn't know, or had forgotten, that the party was a family affair. Pili's husband was there and, even though the women had come without their partners (the few who could boast one), those who had children had brought them, while Paula had left poor little Juanfra on his own, eating two burgers on a plate with mashed potato which he had to warm through in the microwave.

To make things worse, all the mothers had small children, including babies just a few months old, and they were at that stage (which Paula had got past years ago) of talking only about their children, their amazing accomplishments and minor ailments. It was worse for the women there who had no children, not to mention those who didn't want any. What with the hysterical laughter of some woman she didn't know,

Pili's husband's monkey chuckle, the children's shrieking, a baby crying and the sweetcorn empanadas (the only kind left), Paula's best option was to take refuge in her glass of wine, but only after she had called Juanfra and established that he had eaten everything and not set fire to the apartment or anything like that.

But things were about to get even worse: by the time the coffee (filter, not espresso) came out, the women who didn't have children – whether by choice or for want of a partner – had retreated to the sun room, the perfect haven on a breezy day at the end of summer. The women without children began to roll joints. Quietly scandalized, Paula waited for the reaction of the women with children, since the smell of weed was clearly detectable in the living room. To her surprise, some of the mothers left their children running about or in another mother's arms and went off to have a smoke. Paula found such behaviour appalling, more befitting adolescents than a group of women who were all over thirty. When one mother returned, stoned, to the living room and started loudly trumpeting about whatever her baby was doing (nothing, basically), Paula decided it was time to leave. She had the perfect excuse: she had to work. Because that evening, to top it all off, she had to be at a lecture given by a very fashionable French writer published by the imprint for which she did publicity and who'd had the terrible bad manners to come to Buenos Aires only for the weekend, meaning she had to work on a Saturday.

She went back to her apartment. Checked her son was alive. Juanfra told her she smelled horrible. Luckily he was still too young at ten to recognize the smell of marijuana, unlike the idiot taxi driver who had brought her home.

Paula changed clothes and set off to the theatre where the Frenchman was giving his talk, "Eroticism and transgression:

from literature to life". The tickets had been distributed in advance and all the seats were full. A large number had been reserved for the press, all keen to hear from an international speaker. Since she was the one who knew all the journalists, and since everyone from the imprint was chatting with the guests, she had to stay at the door. A man she didn't recognize approached her, claiming to work for an obscure magazine. He didn't have an invitation. Since she was charged with door duty, she explained politely to him that he couldn't come in. The man insisted, brandishing a press pass that looked more fake than a two-dollar bill. Paula said "no" to him in the same tone she used for her son when he was being a pain.

"I'm afraid you can't come in. All the tickets have already been given out."

"You fucking old bitch," the man replied.

If he had just said "fucking bitch", she would have laughed drily. But "old" was going too far. She grabbed the man by the neck, a response that surprised various onlookers, not least the pseudo journalist who couldn't at first push her off. Big mistake. Paula took advantage of that second's doubt to deliver two quick kicks in the style of a Boca Juniors centre back. The man yelped and managed to reach out and yank her hair. Which would prove stronger: the man's neck or a hank of Paula's hair? The answer would never be known because at that moment a couple of people intervened to separate them while Paula, beside herself with rage, started lashing out at the people who were trying to calm her down and shouting, "Let me go so I can kill him." Only then did a policeman who had been standing outside the theatre appear, called in by one of the people present. The police officer took the man outside and called a patrol car, which arrived ten minutes later. The fake journalist was bundled in and driven away. The police officer asked Paula to go with him to the police station to report the incident.

"Will you cover for me at work then, officer? And afterwards will you give my son dinner?" she asked in a voice that may have struck some as on the loud side for addressing a law enforcement officer.

The extraordinary thing about all this was that the intellectual vibe of the successful French writer's lecture had in no way been affected by the fracas. Such was the loftiness of the audience, comprising writers, journalists, readers who wanted to be writers, and maybe a few editors – though not many, because they don't work on Saturdays. Afterwards Paula composed herself, but she didn't go inside to listen to the French writer's talk. She let her boss know she was leaving, as they had agreed, and took a taxi home. On arrival there she found her son, still alive, playing with the PlayStation in almost exactly the same position as she had left him. All that had changed was the state of the kitchen: a pot of dulce de leche had been opened and smeared everywhere, cookies were scattered around, the box of Cepita juice was open and out of the fridge. Nothing unusual there. She took a couple of hot dogs and buns out of the freezer – she always kept some frozen for situations like this – then heated everything up, adding mayonnaise and abundant fries, roughly equivalent to the guilt she felt about serving a Saturday night dinner that would have been more worthy of a Tuesday. She explained to him for the nth time that if he wanted to watch TV he could do it tucked up in bed. Juanfra chewed his hot dog with resignation.

Paula got ready to go out but didn't change her clothes again. She tried to arrange her breasts so they sat higher. She still wasn't too bad in that area. When she got to the bar, Luciano was already there having a beer.

Paula's original plan had been to go a bit further than mere flirtation with this young journalism student who presented a literature programme on a radio station of uncertain audience. The boy used to come and pick up books directly from the publishing house where she worked and he seemed as nice as he was young. She had been very taken aback when it became clear that Luciano was coming on to her and not the receptionist, who was fifteen years younger than Paula. Grateful and emboldened, she had initiated a long campaign of seduction that picked up pace when the boy summoned up the courage to invite her for a drink after work. They were all over each other on that first outing and arranged to meet up the following Saturday to continue getting to know each other more intimately.

The problem was that he lived with his parents and she lived with her son. And her useless ex was incapable of looking after the boy on a weekend that was so crucial to her seduction strategy. She didn't like the idea of going to one of the capital's many love motels. She had a better solution in mind.

Verónica had left the keys of her apartment with Paula so she could water its sad collection of houseplants. There might have been four or five of them, and certainly Verónica had never taken much care of them. They were more dead than alive the first time Paula went to water them. That key was going to be useful to her, though.

After a few beers and snacks, Paula invited the boy to her friend's apartment. Outside the bar they launched into a kissing spree that continued in the taxi. Up to the apartment they went, without encountering the gossipy doorman en route. Paula took her friend straight to the bedroom so as not to waste any time. They weren't even going to have the night together because she had to get back and check on the continued survival of her son. She wanted to create as little mess as possible to avoid any subsequent tidying up: Verónica had left everything immaculate before going off on vacation. And she had done the cleaning herself because she refused to hire a cleaner, arguing, in a way that might strike some as demagogic, "We don't liberate ourselves from domestic work by getting other women to do it for us. The day I find a man prepared to do my sweeping and dusting, I'll give him the job."

Things heated up in the bedroom. Luciano had grown more hands, running them over her body like a frenzied octopus. She unbuttoned his jeans and felt his generous package straining to be released. Without letting go of each other, they fell onto the bed. Her dress was pushed up around her waist; his trousers were round his knees and his boxers round his thighs when he said to her, "You're so pretty, and you have such a great figure." Luciano pressed down on her, his body tense. As their bodies rubbed together, it took Paula a few seconds to notice an unmistakable wetness on her underwear and thighs. Luciano's body went limp and he looked questioningly at her. He was, in fact, mirroring her own expression. Paula moved her hand to her own crotch and encountered a sticky puddle.

"Did you come?" she asked, rhetorically.

The boy apologized, pleading too much excitement or something similar. She wasn't listening any more. She smiled tenderly at him and went to the bathroom, where she dried herself with toilet paper and took off the multicoloured thong she had worn for the first time that day. It was full of semen. She threw it down beside the bidet and returned to the bedroom, where she still managed to have a reasonably good time. Not good enough to dispel the feeling that it had been a really shitty Saturday.

She also felt guilty about having left her thong on the floor in Verónica's bathroom. She had left the bedroom and bathroom tidy but couldn't be bothered to take away the sodden garment.

And now she was worried. She had gone back to the apartment to water the plants and, when she went to the bathroom to get her underwear, found nothing there. Her thong had vanished. She was absolutely sure she had left it on the floor beside the bidet. Somebody had taken it. She planned to write and tell Verónica once she got to the office, but when she checked her inbox she found her friend's latest email. Its contents were so terrible and distressing that it seemed trivial to choose that moment to tell her friend what had happened to her underwear.

IV

Federico remembered very clearly the day he had first met Verónica. It was about a month after he first started working at the Rosenthal law practice. He used to wear oversized suits with too much shoulder padding to seem bigger than he was: a lad of twenty, a star law student. That day he had gone down to the newsagent to buy his lunch: a schnitzel sandwich with everything, one of his food staples along with Ugi's pizza. He had got back to the office and was alone in the kitchen squeezing a sachet of mayonnaise onto the sandwich when she appeared, looking like she owned the place. Without even registering his presence, she searched for a can of Coca-Cola in the fridge. While Federico looked on, she had to move Tupperware boxes and bottles of dressing out of the way to reach the cans. Finally she found what she was looking for, leaned against the counter, opened the can and said:

"So you're the new boy."

"Depends what you mean by 'new'."

"If you can manage to sound that stupid in all your answers, my dad is going to love you."

And she left as she had come, Coke in hand. That was how Federico found out that this girl was one of Doctor Rosenthal's three daughters. Later he learned that she was the youngest, that she wasn't married like Leticia, nor in a steady relationship like Daniela, the other two daughters. As time went on he learned a few more things: that she was – or wanted to be – a journalist, that she lived with her parents in the lavish Recoleta apartment he had visited once in order to deliver some papers; that she had been dating someone, broken it off and was now with someone else. It was like following changes in the weather. Every so often she would appear, say hello to everyone, direct a few words at him and continue on to her father's office. Meanwhile, Federico was consolidating his position in the firm and Aarón Rosenthal was beginning to feel affection, or something like it, for the young man. He got him involved in the important cases handled by the Rosenthal practice and, while he did not let him take decisions, he gradually introduced him into the less visible parts of the judicial apparatus. Once he made a mistake by not first consulting one of the judges of the Federal Appellate Court who was leading a case. Aarón called to reprimand him and he defended himself, claiming that he didn't know he could go directly to the judge to resolve a problem.

"Ignorance is never an excuse. Never," Aarón told him, and it was one of many lessons the veteran lawyer gave the student.

More than a year had passed after that first encounter before he met Verónica in the kitchen again.

"I'm not the new boy any more."

"What?"

"Just that when we met the first time, you asked me if I was the new boy."

"And what did you reply?"

"That it depended on what you meant by 'new'. You said I'd go far in this firm if I kept saying stupid things."

"And from what I hear you are going far, so I guess you're elbowing your way to the top."

"Not elbowing."

"We should ask my dad's other lawyers, see what they think."

"If the subject interests you, we can go to a bar and discuss it over a Coca-Cola one of these days."

"Now that's some serious elbowing. You want to seduce the boss's daughter."

"Boss sounds more appropriate for a ranch than a law firm."

"Look, Federico, I'd be delighted to go and have a Coca-Cola with you, or even a Fanta. But you should know that if my father gets wind of it, he'll kick you out. He's already fired two lawyers before you who tried the same thing."

"I'd run the risk."

"For me?"

And what hadn't he done for her since then? It was a lie that her father had ever fired anyone for going after his daughters. Aarón wasn't a very active participant in family life. There always seemed to be a kind of fog between him, his wife and his daughters. Verónica didn't agree to go out with Federico that day, but the next time he asked, she did. And they drank white wine, not Coke.

Was there anything he *wouldn't* do for her? It was the question he had been asking himself for almost a decade. They had passed through every stage of a relationship apart from engagement. They'd had a fling, been friends with benefits, friends with no benefits. And while Aarón stayed away from family decisions, sisters Leticia and Daniela had adopted him as a brother-in-law, despite Verónica. They invited him to all the Rosenthal events: births, baptisms, Daniela's wedding, Jewish and Christian end-of-year parties. They were eternally grateful to him for looking after Verónica when their mother was dying. The Rosenthal girls longed to see their little sister married to him. And when Aarón gave him a partnership with a ten per cent share in the practice (something he had not done with any of the other lawyers), he realized that he too wanted Federico as part of the family.

Federico had seen Verónica in love with other men, had seen her crying or overjoyed. He had seen her ill with tonsillitis and had once taken her urgently to a clinic with gastroenteritis; he had seen her play with her nephews and nieces, go off to Europe and come back with presents for him: an Italian silk tie, a Swiss watch, a silly toy devil bought in a little Belgian town. Sometimes she gave him presents when there was nothing in particular to celebrate but simply because she had thought of him: a book, some cologne, a CD. It was Verónica's way of showing her presence in his life among her many absences and periods of indifference.

When Verónica had started investigating the train mafia, Federico had been scared for the first time about what could happen. He had helped her on other occasions with journalistic pieces, but had never before had the feeling she was getting involved in something really dangerous and that there was more at stake than a magazine article. And the day she ran over the four criminals, then saw her lover die, Federico resolved that, whatever happened, he was going to protect her. However and against whomever necessary.

That March morning they rang him from the penitentiary service: Danilo Peratta, alias Three, had escaped during an appointment at the hospital they took him to every week. It was obvious there had been a total security breakdown. There must have been accomplices and prison authorities involved. Federico spoke to the acting judge and marvelled at the man's attitude. Aarón Rosenthal had taught him to detest that innocence bordering on stupidity.

Federico had behaved stupidly too. It had always been a possibility Peratta might escape. He should have had someone watching the guy. It wasn't that complicated.

What were Peratta's plans now? Would he go back to working as a hired assassin or try to get revenge? Was Verónica's life at risk? If he'd had an informant inside Villa Devoto he would have a better idea, but he didn't know anyone in the prison. He wasted two days groping in the dark without advancing at all: he didn't know where Peratta was, nor whom he was working for, because it had become clear that it wasn't Juan García who had contracted him (and the other three) to bump off the witness Verónica had been hiding.

Juan García.

He remembered Rodolfo Corso, a journalist he had been helping as an anonymous source in an investigation into a money-laundering operation run by Juan García, the white-collar criminal who had also headed up the train mafia. Federico hadn't liked Corso since hearing him talk lecherously about Verónica, but he decided to put that to one side. He called him, explaining that he needed to know what Peratta had been up to during his months in jail. Corso said he had some good contacts among the prisoners, that he would make some checks and ring him back. Federico worried he would take too long, but the next morning he got a call from Corso.

"I'm told he spent a lot of time with El Gallo Miranda, a nasty piece of work who coordinates a rich variety of crimes from inside. If anyone can tell you anything, he can."

"Can you arrange for me to see him?"

"I can. And I don't think he'll refuse. These guys jump at any chance to socialize."

Two hours later Rodolfo Corso called him again.

"Right then. Rosenthal and Associates obviously commands respect because El Gallo wants you to talk to his lawyer, Rodolfo Mateo, my namesake. I'll give you his number."

"No, that's fine – I have his number. Thanks for all your help."

Mateo was a famous media-friendly lawyer who specialized in getting wealthy criminals out of prison and in showing off his imported cars on TV gossip shows. The advantage of dealing with Mateo was that they spoke the same language. They arranged to meet at a bar on Rodríguez Peña and Lavalle close – but not too close – to the law courts. When Federico arrived, Mateo was sitting at a table at the back, in lively conversation with an older woman. The woman gave him a kiss on the cheek and left.

"If I got paid for every autograph I give, I'd earn more than I make defending idiots."

"And you make a lot."

"I'm not complaining. Your lot aren't doing badly either."

The waiter arrived and they ordered two coffees.

"Is old Pagnini still working for Rosenthal?"

"He retired."

"That bastard knew more tricks than Carlos Bilardo."

Federico didn't want to spend too much time on chit-chat. The person asking the questions controlled the conversation. He should cut to the chase.

"I was going to offer your client money in exchange for information, but I get the feeling he wants something else."

"El Gallo has money to burn. I don't think you'd want to pay him a million dollars for a little bit of info. I'd rather ask you for something that's going to help us and give you the information that's going to help you."

"I'm all ears."

"Among the cases against El Gallo there's one that's completely bananas. El Gallo has a little boat moored in Tigre. It seems the coastguard discovered a speedboat stuffed full of arms. Heavy weapons, military grade. The speedboat got away and docked at the nautical club where El Gallo had his little boat. One of the men in the speedboat jumped into El Gallo's boat and hid inside with some of the arms he had managed to bring from the speedboat. And the coastguard found him there. So now El Gallo, who was already in the slammer at the time, is shitting a brick that they're going to charge him for that too."

"If they were military-grade weapons you know he's fucked."

"Look. The guy in the boat admitted El Gallo had nothing to do with it."

"And does he?"

"They know each other. You know how it is – these guys all know each other. They have some kind of sixth sense for recognizing each other. But he swears and will keep swearing that El Gallo had nothing to do with this."

"So what can *I* do?"

"*You* can't do anything. But Rosenthal can. The federal judge presiding over the case is an old friend of his, Arturo Fader. Simply get him to take a statement from the man who was apprehended on the boat and get him to bear in mind that my client has been in prison for two years and can't control who boards his boat. As you can see, it's simple."

"Not that simple, but I can try."

"Look, my friend, I can't give you anything until there's a formal statement from the court. And I can't even tell you how many lawsuits El Gallo has against him. I'm giving you the most straightforward one. I'm making it easy for you."

Federico didn't want to tell Doctor Rosenthal what was happening. He wasn't above sending the marines in to fetch his daughter and bring her back to Buenos Aires. Not that Federico thought that a terrible idea. He got hold of a copy of the case file relating to El Gallo Miranda's boat, and decided to risk going directly to Judge Fader. He lied to him, saying he needed Miranda not to be tried for a federal crime. He explained that he was making this personal approach because he had started going out with Miranda's sister. The judge chided him, saying he shouldn't get involved in these things, that it was clear the detainee was lying and Miranda was involved in smuggling arms. Federico put on his most forlorn expression.

"You have always been very supportive of the firm."

"Aarón is like my brother, and I know how highly he thinks of you. I'll help you this time, but don't get used to it. You need to pick your battles carefully. This one wasn't worth it."

That afternoon he called Verónica, on an impulse. He wanted to hear her voice, know she was well. It was pointless in a way, because he couldn't talk to her about his suspicions regarding Peratta or help her in any way. He just needed to hear her talking. All the same, she had sensed something was up.

Two days later, Federico called Mateo to let him know his demands had been met. The judge had finally acquitted Miranda on all counts. Half an hour later they met in a bar in Puerto Madero, beneath the building where Mateo lived.

"The guy needed to gather some intelligence. Have someone followed. At no point did he clarify who that was. The work was done for him by two kids, Nick and Bono. I've already spoken to them. I said they had two options: either you'd use a couple of heavies to get the information out of them or they could give it to you for cash. We agreed on fifteen grand. I got you a good price."

Mateo phoned them there and then, said he had the money and arranged a meeting with Federico two hours later in a bar on Dorrego and Córdoba. When he hung up he said:

"I can't do better than that for you. I'll give you time to go and get the money, then you can bring it to me and head off to Colegiales."

Federico went to the office to pick up the money. They always kept a supply of cash for paying informants and he was no longer expected to account for every withdrawal. He took out the money, returned to Puerto Madero, paid Mateo and then went to the bar. There was the redhead and another youth. They looked like two nerds escaped from the ORT Jewish science and technology school. You could tell they were uncomfortable about what they were about to do – breaking professional confidentiality – but that Mateo had convinced them. It was very likely these kids would see only a slice of those fifteen thousand pesos.

Nick told him everything that had happened with Danilo Peratta. How they had got into Verónica's apartment and on which day, what information they had found. He told Federico that Peratta was planning to travel to Tucumán, that he didn't want to wait in Buenos Aires.

Federico went back to the office wondering what excuse he could use to go looking for Peratta in Tucumán. He had to find him before Peratta found Verónica. The guy couldn't have flown there because that would be too risky. It was unlikely that he had driven, either. He must have gone by bus. If Federico flew to Tucumán he could narrow his lead. From what Nick said, Peratta didn't know exactly where Verónica was. Federico could call her and find out. It would look very strange if he turned up where she was for no good reason.

The first flight left at 6 a.m. He had time to drop by his parents' house, and that was what he did. His parents weren't surprised he had come round and invited himself to dinner. Over coffee, Federico told his father he was thinking of going hunting that weekend in the province of La Pampa.

"I wish I could go with you. I haven't been hunting for years."

"Have you got the R8?"

"Take it if you like."

Federico had never liked his father's hobby: hunting large and small game. Almost against his will (or rather, to honour his father's will), he had learned to use a rifle. He wasn't the best shot in the world but he knew what to do, and his father had always made sure Federico had a licence to bear the arms he never used.

His father appeared with the Blaser R8 in its plush case, in which the butt, the muzzle, the magazines, the sight and all the extras pertaining to the German rifle were stored separately. When they got to the airport he would check the rifle in – just like any other hunting enthusiast with a licence to kill animals.

He went back to his apartment to have a shower, shove some clothes in a bag and work out how not to alarm Verónica. He had a few hours in hand but he wasn't tired. There was another problem, though: what he would say to Aarón Rosenthal. As if he had summoned up his boss, Federico's mobile started ringing. *A Ros* appeared on the screen. What was he doing calling at this time of the morning?

"Federico, I have to ask you a favour. It's about Verónica. I need you to go to Tucumán."

Federico felt as though he were falling into a bottomless pit. He couldn't breathe. When he spoke, his words seemed to emanate from the depths of a swimming pool.

"Has something happened to Verónica?"

"No, she's fine. But I've just had a call from Tucumán. Two girls who were travelling with her have been found dead."

"I don't understand, Aarón. I'm sorry – I don't understand what you're telling me."

"My cousin Severo called me. A few hours ago they found the bodies of two foreign girls. Verónica had travelled with them on part of her trip and, from what Severo says, she was one of the last people to see them. Verónica's in Salta now, but they're going to call her back to Yacanto del Valle, which is where the crimes took place. There's already a district attorney there. I need you to go to Yacanto del Valle to be with her, and to accompany her if there's a court order. I also need you to follow the case, because the crime took place after a party that was attended by people our family know. You may need to stay a few days in San Miguel de Tucumán. I don't trust in what Severo may be able to do. All the same, first thing tomorrow morning I'm going to talk to the judge leading the case. There's a flight leaving Tucumán at six o'clock tomorrow morning. Can you go?"

6 *Yacanto del Valle*

I

"If some day we live together, I'd like it to be here," Luca had said to Mariano as they drank coffee in Amigo's bar looking onto the main square in Yacanto del Valle. For him to come out with something like that was quite a gesture, a declaration of love, even. And at that moment it smacked of utopia, because Mariano had just ended a ten-year relationship, because Luca had never been in a relationship for more than a month, and because it would be crazy for a successful architect like Mariano and someone who aspired to be a chef in prestigious restaurants, like Luca, to go and live in small-town Tucumán. And yet what he had said that day on their first trip together had ended up happening, because Mariano had completed a couple of projects that made him a great deal of money and because Luca was never going to triumph in the most fashionable kitchens. He had studied cooking, he could make sushi or a dish of molecular food, but he had learned his art alongside his mother and grandmother, two Italians who worked all their lives in a delicatessen in the Colegiales neighbourhood of Buenos Aires. His strengths (and the things he was most proud of) were pastas, stews, casseroles, shepherd's pie, pickled aubergines, eclairs with crème patissière, and tiramisu. Most importantly, what had begun as an affair – with a bit of travel thrown in – became a lasting love. Besides, they were tired of Buenos Aires.

The second time they travelled to Yacanto del Valle, they discovered a ruined old house that had been on the market for a long time. It was as though it had been waiting for them, and as soon as they saw it, they knew it was perfect for their hotel. They didn't even have to haggle much over the price because the owners, four siblings who were winding up their father's estate, wanted to complete the sale quickly.

They took a short lease on a small farm with two houses. Into one of the houses they moved themselves and into the other Mariano's most trusted employees: a master builder, a painter, gas fitter and an electrician who all regularly worked with him. They hired bricklayers, a plumber and two more painter-decorators. Mariano wanted to recapture the house's colonial spirit while also giving the interiors the look of an international hotel.

The work took six months. Some of the furniture and decorative objects they bought in the town itself. For the rest they had to go to San Miguel de Tucumán and to Salta. Luca took charge of hiring staff: a cook, an assistant, three cleaners, a couple of waitresses and a receptionist to work nights. They had what they wanted: a boutique hotel, a small restaurant and abundant nature, far from the mayhem of Buenos Aires. Once the work was finished, Mariano swapped his job as an architect for hotelier at the Posada de Don Humberto. He didn't miss anything about his previous life.

When they had first opened for business, four years previously, the hotel was not a regular stop on the tourist trail, but every season their numbers increased. The inn was always full in the summer and they took reservations a long time in advance. At this point in March the number of visitors always decreased until the beginning of Holy Week. So when the two foreign tourists and the girl from Buenos Aires turned up, there was no difficulty finding them rooms. These three women seemed no different from the ones who regularly arrived with their rucksacks, chatting in English or another language, cheerful and carefree. It didn't strike Luca and Mariano as particularly odd that one of them, the one from Buenos Aires, left the next day. But when three days went by and nobody went in or out of the foreign girls' room, they began to get concerned.

"Something's happened to them, I'm sure that something's happened to them," Luca said to Mariano, who wanted to wait another day.

They decided to report them missing. It wasn't the first time they had gone to the police station in Yacanto del Valle. There had been thefts, the odd fight between guests, threats made by an ex-employee. They didn't like the police there. And, although nothing had ever been said to them, it was clear the police didn't like them either. They filed a missing person report with Officer Benítez, who got them to sign a statement.

"So what will you do?" Mariano asked.

"We're going to investigate."

"But what, concretely?"

"We'll make some enquiries in town, and if there's no new information we'll inform the headquarters in Tucumán so they can investigate in the rest of the province."

They left the police station with the feeling that nothing was going to get done. Not even the little that had been promised.

"So are we going to sit here with our arms folded?" Luca asked Mariano.

"No, no. Let's wait until tomorrow. We've got the phone number of the girl who arrived with them. Perhaps she knows something or can give some guidance."

It wasn't yet dark. Luca was in the kitchen preparing sauces for the cook to use when making that night's dinner. Mariano was searching the internet for information about the two girls. He had found Petra's Facebook page and some of Frida's academic work, but nothing to suggest where the two tourists might be now. He had their email addresses and phone numbers, so he sent them a message asking where they were. No reply came.

A little before 9 p.m., a police car drew up outside the hotel. Officer Benítez got out.

"The bodies of two women have been found in the hills. They seem to be gringas. You need to come and identify the corpses."

II

She was desperate for a piss. This always happened to her and she was annoyed with herself. She should have gone an hour before leaving, when there was still nobody in the house. The children were at the club, the señora still hadn't returned from having tea with her friends and the señor was somewhere on the estate. But she was so absorbed by her ironing – or rather by the telenovela she was watching while she ironed – that she had lost track of time and, by the time she realized, the whole family was back, running all over the house. And she didn't like to use the bathroom in those circumstances. She felt watched, judged. She was convinced her employers didn't like her using the bathroom either, not even the one at the front of the house, the visitors' one. So whenever they were around she held on as long as she could. And she could, for a long time – but not any longer.

If her grandmother knew about this, she'd give her a clout. One of those slaps on the nape, not very hard, but effective when it came to getting her grandchildren to do as she said. Her grandmother would say: Mechi, you dolt, I'm going to have to talk to your bosses so they make you piss before you leave. The thought of her grandmother talking to the señores terrified her.

To make things worse, it took about fifty minutes to get to her house. Forty if she hurried, like now, legs pressed together and trying to focus on the trees, on the birdsong, on the first shadows of dusk. She had already been walking for half an hour. She was ten minutes from home. Feeling her bladder would burst at any moment, she walked with her toes squeezed, her arms rigid like a wooden doll. What if she ran? She was good at running, and from that part of the mountain to her home she wouldn't come across anyone who might see her sprinting like a person possessed. It was one of the few advantages of living in the middle of nowhere, somewhere overlooked even by the most curious tourists, the ones who came daily to visit the supposed beauty of Yacanto del Valle. She didn't understand why the tourists liked this hilly wilderness full of horrible insects and animals. Nor could she find any appeal in an old town like Yacanto.

Think of something else. She told herself to think of her brothers who had gone to work in the sugar harvest. Of the one brother who had stayed with her grandmother and her because he was working at the ironmonger's in town, although he was almost never at home. Of the chickens her grandmother looked after, of Niebla, who'd had five puppies two months ago, four of which had survived. They would have to give them away – but who to? There weren't many people who liked dachshunds.

She couldn't hold it any longer. She might as well piss right where she was. Not in the road, because, even though by this time the tourists would have gone back to the town to sit at a bar in the square, if she started pissing now some neighbour was sure to appear and then she would have no choice but to commit suicide or move to another town. If she walked a little way into the undergrowth she would be shielded from any locals or disorientated tourists wandering in the area. She stepped away from the road into the vegetation. Not very far, just a few yards. And she saw them.

It wasn't that she saw a foot, or part of a leg, or an arm. She saw their whole bodies, lying in the weeds. One face down and the other side on. The bodies of two women. They looked like abandoned mannequins. They were dead. She knew that straightaway. She wanted to scream, but the howl didn't come out. She felt herself pissing. That warm stream burst out of her bladder and down her jeans, soaking her legs, her tights, her sneakers. Warm piss that seemed to have no end, as suffering would have no end. Because she didn't see the corpses of two strangers. Those two bodies became just one: her sister's. *Bibi,* she thought, or shouted, and ran back to the road, without thinking about her soaked jeans. "Bibi, poor Bibi," she kept repeating, weeping as she ran. Would they never finish killing her sister?

III

That morning Álex Vilna had a meeting with the vice-governor. It was an informal meeting – not an interview – and completely off the record. That much had been made clear to him by Bollini, the Tucumanian congressman who had arranged the meeting from Buenos Aires. It had also been Bollini who had called him when the narco police story jumped from Tucumán to the national news. That time they met at a bar in the Museo Renault in Buenos Aires.

"There's a big power struggle going on within the police," Bollini told him that day as he fiddled with a pack of cigarettes.

He was afraid that everything being reported in the papers could taint the governors, the party, everyone, when the only people genuinely mixed up in this were the Secretary of Justice in Tucumán and the chief of the Salta police, together with the head of the regional police division. Unruly political factions in two provinces. And the governors' hands were tied. If they took disciplinary measures against the conspirators, they looked like accomplices of the police officers already under arrest. But if Vilna was prepared to write a favourable piece, Bollini could pass on to him all the material and contacts he would need in Tucumán.

And how could one say no to Bollini? Not only was he a congressman, but he was a trade unionist too. He was secretary general of the Argentine Union of Sugar Cane Workers, one of the main unions for rural labourers. The AUSCW was the main advertiser for the radio programme Vilna presented on Saturdays. Bollini had also brought in a couple of new advertisers: a sugar company and a private clinic.

Álex promised him he would do everything possible, both on the radio and at the magazine. So when at the editorial meeting Society proposed for the cover a story he had thought of doing as a double-page spread, he had no option but to offer to write it himself. He didn't want to leave what *Nuestro Tiempo* might have to say about this episode in the hands of another staff writer, much less one from Society. When Bollini found out Vilna was travelling to the province, he offered him not only contacts but also a plane ticket and a hire car.

Vilna had already interviewed the head of the departmental police; he had spoken to the father of the detained officer (a retired chief superintendent and former chief of the provincial police); he had spoken to sources inside the police force and a member of the provincial Supreme Court who advanced him, off the record, a rejection of the prosecution ordered by the presiding judge.

He was pretty clear about what had happened. There was obviously a link between the detained police officers and the Bolivian drug trafficker, but he would focus instead on the savage internal battle being waged for leadership of the police in Argentina's north-west. Up until then there hadn't been many cases of drug trafficking, but if the police forces of Salta and Tucumán fell into the hands of factions opposed to the current leadership, it was likely that all the north would be infected by narcos coming from Colombia and Peru.

His meeting with the vice-governor was essentially a formality. Perhaps he would give him the name of a couple of politicians who might have vested interests in all this. And since party loyalties were very labile, it wouldn't surprise Vilna if they were members of the ruling party itself.

He was getting ready for breakfast when his phone rang. It was Patricia Beltrán, the editor of Society. She must be ringing to chivvy him about the piece. The old bag started work early.

"Are you watching the news?" Beltrán asked him, by way of a greeting.

"I was reading the local newspapers."

"Put on the TV. You've got a set in your room, haven't you? Or get it on the internet."

"Has something happened with the police officers? Look, I'm on to some good stuff. I mean I've got some good material."

Beltrán resisted the opportunity to mock him, explaining:

"Two tourists have been found dead in Yacanto del Valle, really close to where you are. An Italian and a Norwegian, both women."

"Do we know who they were?"

"So far we've got nothing. There are all kinds of theories, ranging from that they were at an orgy and overdid the drugs to that they were two girls investigating modern slavery on large estates."

"I'm more persuaded by the first theory. Do you need me to arrange any contacts at this end?"

"No, darling, what I need is for you to go and cover what's happening in Yacanto del Valle."

"Impossible, Pato, I'm working on the cover story."

"Forget the policemen. That's two pages in your section. Now the lead story in the next edition is the tourists' murder. All the magazines will be covering it, and we can't look like we live on Mars. The TV channels have been broadcasting from there with a crappy connection, but I heard they've already sent crews up from Buenos Aires."

"Pato, I don't do crime. Send Kloster or whoever you've got on coffee duty this week."

"Darling, do you think I'm ringing you at this time of day because I suddenly felt an urge to screw up your life? I've just been on the phone to Goicochea. He wants this story on the cover and, given that you're there in Tucumán, he wants you to do it."

"But I've got no contacts in the police."

"My love, you're not an engine that runs on contacts, you're a journalist. Go there, stick your nose in wherever you can, sniff out the shit and tell us what it smells like. Journalism, darling, pure journalism. I'll call you in the afternoon when you're in Yacanto del Valle and I'm in the fucking newsroom."

And the line went dead.

Vilna cancelled his meeting with the vice-governor and revised his notes for the piece that had been going to be the magazine's lead and was now slashed to 1,400 words. And, as if that wasn't bad enough, he had to go and investigate the murder of the two foreign girls. He paid for his room and set off for Yacanto del Valle in his rented car, in a blinding rage.

IV

Verónica was driving with her eyes fixed on the road, her body tense, breathing deeply, mind empty. If she had opened her mouth, relaxed her back or wiped a hand over her face, she might have exploded like a piñata and crashed the car in which she was travelling at eighty miles an hour. In any case, her body had already imploded. Inside, her stomach, her heart, her muscles and arteries were broken.

She had been at the hotel in Cafayate when she got the news that Frida and Petra were dead. She had sent them an email as soon as she arrived in Cafayate, a few hours after leaving Yacanto del Valle. By then she was regretting her impetuous departure and didn't want to let too much time go by without them knowing, somehow or other. In fact, she had sent two emails. One, copied to both of them, read:

> Dear Frida and Petra,
>
> You must be thinking you ran into a madwoman, or worse. Every so often I need to pull off some melodramatic gesture and make a stage exit worthy of Sarah Bernhardt. I needed some space. I've just arrived in Cafayate all on my own and I miss you. If you don't think I'm a hysteric (or at least not a dangerous hysteric) and you would like to continue discovering the glories of Argentina together, I'm here waiting for you.

I'm planning to stay for a few days. I hope we see each other again soon.

Kisses from your mad friend.

And she also sent an email for Frida alone:

Hello, Hello,

When I was twelve years old I went on a school leavers' trip to Córdoba (the province Petra is always talking about). There was a boy from school I loved, and he must have liked me too because on one of the outings he took the opportunity to kiss me on the mouth. My first kiss. So what did I do? Ran off up the mountain, the poor boy running behind me. God knows what he must have thought – that I was going to report him to the teacher, or throw myself off when I got to the top. I don't really know why I was running. Out of fear, out of happiness, out of madness. The theory I find most convincing is that, when desire becomes reality, I tend to run away. I don't entirely understand what happened between us, nor do I think it's really important to be clear about it, but I ran off just as I did at the age of twelve. I don't want you to come running after me. But it might be nice if we saw each other again at some point in our journey (you can take that literally, or as a metaphor for life).

Goodbye, Scandinavian Blonde,

V.

She had also written to Paula with an account of the party. Not a very detailed one, but she felt that it was all she could tell her friend.

Two days later she sent them both another email:

My darlings,

I'm still stranded here in Cafayate. Turns out good wine and a glorious landscape exert a stronger pull than a sadistic lover. If you come this way don't be mean or resentful, but let me know. I want to push on to Salta City, but can't extricate myself alone. Come and liberate me!

That morning, minutes before she got the call from Ramiro, she had switched on the TV and her laptop. She zapped through the channels without stopping on any news programmes. She settled on a music channel that was playing videos from the end of the nineties, bringing back memories from her first job: Alanis Morissette, Jamiroquai, The Cranberries. She decided to write another email to Paula, the third since she had been on vacation. That was when the phone rang and Ramiro's ghostly voice made her feel sure something terrible had happened.

And it had.

Both dead. Petra and Frida. Ramiro wanted to come and fetch her from Cafayate. She refused – she would leave straightaway. After ending the call, Verónica sat staring at the television without seeing it. Then she picked up the remote control and found a news channel where they were talking about the crime. There were still no live images, the screen showing a nocturnal mountain scene. Presumably that was where the bodies had been found. A local journalist came on, speaking down a telephone line. Verónica couldn't understand what was being said, but she clearly heard the girls' names and surnames. She turned off the TV. The silence was absolute. As if split in two, she heard herself say "The bastards killed them." She didn't say "some bastards", but "the", as if part of her mind might already have identified the killers. She thought of calling Paula. Her hands were shaking. She managed to write a few lines. The next image she would remember from the morning was of herself in the car, on the way to Yacanto del Valle.

On reaching the roundabout at the entrance to the town, she turned in and saw Ramiro waiting for her, standing beside his pickup. Verónica pulled alongside, got out of the car and let him hold her. She still felt broken inside, her body tense.

"What happened, Ramiro, what happened?"

He told her the girls had left the party alone, that they appeared to have been accosted by a gang. The bodies had been found only the night before. They had been raped and murdered, but not much else was known. A district attorney was already in Yacanto del Valle, and experts from the police forensics department. The attorney, Ramiro said, wanted to talk to her.

"Where are they? The girls' bodies, where did they take them?"

"They're in the morgue at the hospital in Coronel Berti."

Yacanto del Valle, Los Cercos and Coronel Berti were three neighbouring towns within the same district which shared some facilities, including the Coronel Berti Acute Hospital, about four miles away from Yacanto del Valle. Verónica told him she wanted to see the bodies. Ramiro raised a weak objection before agreeing to take her there in the pickup. They left her car beside the road and went straight to the hospital.

There they found police officers and the district attorney, Raúl Decaux. Ramiro explained to Decaux who Verónica was and the DA nodded, as if he already knew of her. Decaux authorized her to see the bodies and accompanied her himself, along with Officer Benítez, from the station at Yacanto del Valle, and a doctor in charge of the morgue.

Verónica was trembling from the cold. First she studied Petra's face, the sense of calm that initially emanated from it contradicted by a dark mark on her left cheekbone. Then she saw Frida, her blonde hair falling over naked shoulders. There were more bruises here, too, on her neck. In both cases she did the same thing: stroked the girls' heads and kissed their foreheads before the doctor covered them again.

Her body was still shaking.

She left the morgue without hearing what Decaux was saying to her.

From the door of the hospital she saw the silhouette of a person leaning against a car: it was Federico.

Verónica wanted to walk towards him, but she couldn't move. It was Federico who came to her and wrapped her in an embrace. Then her body went limp and the broken mechanism fell apart. It broke into a thousand pieces. Verónica wept in Federico's arms. It was a cry like an animal's howl. A cry combining tears, mucus and words that didn't want to come out, words which were stifled before they could be articulated. She managed to say "They're dead," as if he didn't yet know that. Federico said nothing. He simply held her, to keep her from falling to the ground.

V

Small towns made him uneasy. An outsider always stood out, whereas in the city he could go unnoticed. His chance of success was directly related to his capacity not to be seen. If someone noticed his presence, he was marked. His job was to arrive, kill, leave. The invisible man. In the city, that was easy; he had done it many times without the barest description of him ever coming out. Now he had two problems: nobody was doing intelligence for him, and he was more exposed. He had to operate with a lot of care. Not arouse suspicion.

He didn't get off the bus in Yacanto del Valle but in the next town, Los Cercos, a small place with only a couple of hotels and enough shops to satisfy the needs of the people living there. There were no tourist-friendly bars, just an old store where the men still arrived on horseback and played cards as the sun set.

He thought of asking in the store if they knew of anyone who needed a day labourer, trying to pass himself off as someone looking for work in the town or the surrounding fields, but it wouldn't seem very credible, given his appearance (nothing special, but he was much better dressed than the locals) and his Buenos Aires accent, that he would have ventured so far from the capital to look for work. They would immediately suspect he had come here fleeing justice. And what would on any other occasion have been a wrong assumption was, in this case, the truth.

When he sat down at a table, the few locals present looked him over with a certain indifference. There was little light in the place, the windows were small and the floor seemed to be earth. A man stepped out from behind the bar to take his order. A gin. The man looked at him with greater curiosity than the others. He filled a glass to overflowing and asked him:

"Is everywhere full in Yacanto?"

"I couldn't tell you."

"We were just talking about the little gringas who got murdered. They told me every television station from Buenos Aires is coming here. Are you a journalist?"

"Something like that."

"Do they know yet who killed those women?"

Danilo Peratta shook his head. He was trying to understand what the owner was talking about.

"I bet it was the vagrants you get round here. A lot of seasonal workers from El Chaco, from Santiago."

Peratta was listening out for the names of places in which he might find Verónica. He thought she was in Yacanto del Valle or had perhaps already left for Cafayate. If she was following the itinerary they had reconstructed from her internet searches of hotels and dates, after Cafayate she would go to Salta. The provincial capital might be the ideal place to complete his mission: he could move about with more anonymity, the downside being that it would also be harder to find her.

First, he planned to go to Yacanto del Valle, walk around the town a bit. But before that, he needed to leave his bag in one of the hotels in Los Cercos. He looked for the cheapest one and asked for a room for the night.

There were two ways to get to Yacanto del Valle: taking the provincial highway, or using a back road that was more like a dirt track. He preferred to take the least busy option, even if it meant attracting more attention. He doubted he would run into anyone who might remember him afterwards. And if they did remember him, so what? Sooner or later they would know he was responsible for the murder of Verónica Rosenthal. And he didn't care about that.

He arrived in Yacanto del Valle shortly before midday, found a bar and sat by the window. From there he could watch the square and the people moving through it. Peratta needed to know what was happening in the town. He was used to taking action, so it felt strange to sit drinking coffee, watching and listening. The few people who were in the bar, including the waiter and the barman, were all glued to the news on television. Two foreign tourists had been murdered.

Danilo Peratta wasn't at all happy to see Yacanto del Valle become the focus of national attention. That meant there were bound to be police here, as well as journalists. But if there were journalists around town, they weren't much in evidence. Presumably the outside broadcasting vans had either not yet arrived or were wherever the bodies had been found.

He paid and walked to the only hotel Verónica had looked at on the internet. Unlike Cafayate or Salta, there was just one in Yacanto del Valle, the Posada de Don Humberto. He walked up and down the block a couple of times; stopped for a few minutes on the corner. Finally he went in, walking straight to the reception desk, where there was a man who smiled at him.

"Good morning, how can I help you?"

"Hello, good morning. I'm a journalist from Buenos Aires and I'm looking for a colleague, Verónica Rosenthal. She was going to be staying here for a few days."

The man at the reception desk nodded as though considering something. Finally he said:

"I'm sorry, but I'm afraid we can't give out information about people who are staying or have stayed at the hotel."

So she was staying or had stayed at the hotel. He needed to find a way to get the man to be more specific.

"I understand. It's just that we're working together, and I wanted to give her some information about the crime involving the tourists."

The man at reception gave him a strange look. Why was the bastard so cagey?

"Look, she left here a few days ago. Leave me your number and I promise I'll try to get in touch with her and pass your number on."

"No, that's fine. She must already be in Cafayate," he hazarded to see if the receptionist would bite, but he said nothing further.

Peratta left the hotel with the thought of heading towards that town in Salta. First, he needed to get his bag from the hotel in Los Cercos. He checked the bus times. One was leaving for Cafayate at 3 p.m.

He was hungry. There was a grill opposite the hotel. He'd have some lunch, then go to Los Cercos before returning to Yacanto to get the bus.

Taking a window seat with a view of the street, he could see the hotel entrance perfectly. There wasn't much movement in and out. So he was extremely surprised to see a car arrive and Verónica Rosenthal and a man get out of it, both carrying bags. It looked like they were planning to stay at the hotel. Perhaps, after all, the tourists' murder might come in handy and serve him up the journalist on a plate.

VI

The accumulated tension of the last few days sent Federico to sleep on the plane to Tucumán. It wasn't a restful sleep but one of those states in which noises from the outside world mingle with what's happening in the dream. And it felt less like dreaming than an oneiric elaboration on what he had been thinking. He and Verónica were sitting on a cafe terrace beside the sea. She was carefree, but he was worried because he had to look after her. He felt like a bodyguard but didn't know what to do or how to react. And that was how he felt in real life too: he didn't know how to protect her. Thwarting professional assassins wasn't his speciality. He had put himself in an uncomfortable position – one of failure, in all likelihood. That was something he couldn't allow to happen. Failing meant endangering Verónica's life. Should he ask for help, then? From the local police? Hire a bodyguard?

He was fooling himself. What he really wanted was to be important in Verónica's life, in whatever way he could.

He wanted her to feel safe at his side. To be her personal hero. It was a kind of madness, although this was not the first time he had done something mad for Verónica. He thought of calling her, but he would rather do that once he was in Yacanto del Valle and had a clearer picture of what had happened.

Aarón called Federico while he was arranging the car hire. Verónica's father had already spoken to Judge Arturo Amalfi and to District Attorney Raúl Decaux. He was worried; not only because his daughter had been travelling with the murdered girls, but also because Verónica and the two victims had been invited by a cousin of Severo's wife to a party, and that was where the tourists had last been seen alive.

"Severo was always a bit dopey. He got appointed as a judge in Tucumán partly thanks to Cristina's father and to my friendship with the Hileret family," Aarón told him, adding with a certain weariness or irritation, "and that's not all. The party took place on the estate belonging to Menéndez Berti. Anselmo Menéndez Berti was a colleague of my brother David in the 1980s, on a forestation project in Uruguay. We used to go on fishing trips together in Corrientes a few decades ago. I think these days the estate is run by his son Nicolás, an awkward boy with political aspirations. I'd like you to provide assistance, professional and personal, to all of them."

A minute after the call Federico received a text message from the Rosenthal and Associates secretary with the telephone numbers of Judge Amalfi, District Attorney Decaux, Nicolás Menéndez Berti and Ramiro. He called the DA and told him he was on his way to Yacanto del Valle. There was no need to say much else. Decaux said, almost apologetically, that he wanted to take a statement from Verónica. Federico said that would be fine so long as she was in the right state of mind. "Of course," replied Decaux quickly.

Federico planned to visit Nicolás at home. He wanted to get some idea of what might have happened at the party, see the place. He called Ramiro, cousin of the Witch, as Daniela and Leticia referred to her. He explained that he was from the Rosenthal law firm, that he was ringing to let him know he was on his way to Yacanto del Valle. Ramiro explained that he had been the one to break the news to Verónica that morning, by phone.

"Isn't she in Yacanto?" Federico asked.

"She was in Cafayate and she's coming here now."

Federico asked if he knew when Verónica had last seen the foreign girls.

"I think it was at the party. Verónica spent the night with me. She was tired of the others and decided to continue the journey on her own."

Federico began to understand who it was on the other end of the line.

As he neared Yacanto del Valle he called Decaux again to arrange a meeting. The DA told him that he was en route to the hospital morgue in Coronel Berti. They could meet there in an hour.

He left the road and pulled over in a place the car wouldn't easily be seen. He got out of the car and fished the Blaser R8 out of the back. Then he took it out of its case, assembled it and loaded it. He didn't want to arrive with his rifle in bits if Danilo Peratta might be there. The weapon was too visible to be carried in the front seat, so he put it in the back again, ready to be used.

Arriving ahead of time, he drove around Coronel Berti before parking in front of the hospital, where he waited for the district attorney. He wasn't expecting to see Verónica come out of the building. She wasn't expecting him either and stopped, stock-still. Federico had seen her in all kinds of states, but this was the first time her appearance had scared him. He walked towards her. He thought, when he put his arms around her, that Verónica was going to faint. He tried to soothe her, but she needed to weep and to cling to him.

It wasn't the best moment for introductions; all the same, he made himself known to Decaux, and to Ramiro, who invited them both to his house. Federico postponed his meeting with Decaux until the afternoon. Ramiro himself suggested that Federico take Verónica back to the hotel in his car while he stayed on a for a few minutes to talk to the DA.

"Did my dad send you?" Verónica asked once they were on the road.

"I would have come anyway."

"Thanks."

"Vero, you have to go back to Buenos Aires."

"My dad sent you to fetch me back?"

"No, that's my own opinion."

"I've just seen the girls. They've been beaten, attacked. How could someone do something like that? What kind of animal does this?"

No – Verónica wasn't going to leave until she had found out what kind of person raped and killed women in Yacanto del Valle. Federico didn't want to say anything about Peratta. He didn't want to scare her. Or worse: spur her on to look for Peratta herself.

Verónica showed him how to get to Ramiro's house, where a maid opened the door and led them into the living room. Ramiro arrived about fifteen minutes later. When Verónica asked him what he knew, he gave the same information the news outlets had been repeating since early that morning.

"Between the party, which was the last time they were seen alive, and the appearance of the bodies, three days went by. So why is everyone linking the deaths to the party?" Verónica asked.

"The owners of the hotel reported the girls missing yesterday morning," Ramiro explained.

"I shouldn't have gone. I should never have left them alone."

"Nobody could have imagined something like this would happen."

Verónica remembered she had left her car beside the road into Yacanto del Valle. Ramiro told her not to worry, that he could send someone to pick it up. That they should stay, Federico and her, in the house. To Federico's surprise, Verónica didn't want to stay there. If there were rooms available, she would rather go to the Posada de Don Humberto. Ramiro didn't press the point and called the hotel to reserve two rooms. Verónica asked Federico to drive her to the car she had left at the roadside.

"Fede, I'm really grateful you came," she said, when they were alone, "but it will be better if you go."

"One Rosenthal giving me orders is enough."

"Seriously. I'm going to stay here as long as necessary."

"Necessary for what?"

"You know what."

"Your dad sent me here for other reasons, too. He wants me to follow the case from close quarters. Because of the Elizaldes and the owner of the house."

"And what has my old man got to do with Nicolás?"

"He's a friend of the father."

"All the same, I don't understand what you can contribute."

"Vero, it doesn't matter. Your dad wants me to be here. It's better than being in Buenos Aires. I promise not to be a pain or stick my nose into your business."

When they arrived at the hotel, the man on reception greeted Verónica with a look of concern and told her that a little over an hour ago a journalist had been there asking after her. Verónica brushed the news aside and went straight to her room. Federico took the opportunity to ask more about the supposed journalist and showed the receptionist a photograph of Peratta.

"Yes, that's the man," said the receptionist, adding, with a tone of complicity, "He's not a journalist, is he?"

"No."

"I thought as much. Is he dangerous?"

"Yes. And I'd ask you not to say anything about this to Verónica, Señor…?"

"Please, call me Mariano. And I won't say anything to her. What shall I do if he shows up here again?"

"Let me know, or go straight to the police."

Federico walked out of the front door, looking all around him. Peratta must be nearby. In the bar on the corner, in the grill opposite, crouching behind a tree. They didn't have much intel on Peratta. He had few entries on the police database, and it was likely that he had never been prosecuted for most of his crimes. But Federico knew how professional assassins operated in Argentina: they killed at close range. From a motorbike or a car, or walking alongside the victim. Always firing from inches away. They weren't like Americans. Federico was sure that, wherever Peratta was, he wasn't using a sniper rifle.

The hunt begins, Federico said to himself. He had to catch Peratta before he got too close to Verónica.

7 *A Man of No Importance*

I

Verónica's statement to the district attorney was a fiasco, at least from her point of view. All the DA did was ask a few general questions. He didn't even try to establish why she had left on her own when the women had decided to travel together, why she hadn't checked that they had returned to their room the following morning, why for several days afterwards she had not been at all worried about the girls' fate. She would have been able to provide answers to all those questions and – even if they hadn't contributed anything new – at least she would have felt that the law was in pursuit of the criminals. And if they weren't bothering to give one of the last people who had seen the girls alive a grilling, how many other suspects were being ignored altogether? She hadn't killed them, but the DA shouldn't take that for granted. Then again, if she hadn't taken them to Yacanto del Valle, if she hadn't insisted on going to the party, if she hadn't abandoned them in a place they didn't know, with strangers, exposed to dangers she ought to have foreseen, if she hadn't got everything wrong, Frida and Petra would still be alive.

Verónica didn't say that to the district attorney but to Mariano and Luca, who listened in silence. The DA's interview had taken place in the hotel, in Mariano's office and, when

Decaux left, they appeared. Verónica looked grave, strangely still, and Mariano took her hands, perhaps to check there was still a pulse. That was when Verónica began talking and didn't stop for an hour. She told them how she had met the foreign girls, about the time they had spent together at the house in Cerro San Javier, the back and forth with Frida, their arrival in Yacanto and the party. She told them how she had left the girls on their own.

"Guilt is a very unkind invention," said Luca, quoting an Andrés Calamaro song.

"You're not guilty of anything at all, and that's all there is to it," Mariano added.

"There are other people responsible, love. Murderers, rapists who are right here, in our midst."

"I'm not leaving this town until those bastards pay for what they did."

"Then get ready for a long stay."

They told her how they had worried about the girls' absence, how they had reported them missing and been asked to identify the bodies. How, early that morning, the police had taken the girls' things for analysis. Verónica said she wanted to go to the place where the bodies had been found. Luca offered to take her there.

In Luca's car, a Peugeot that was at least twenty years old, they travelled a few miles along a back road that began after the entrance to the Menéndez Berti estate. As they drove past, Verónica tried to glimpse inside, but could see only the gate, the fence and the trees flashing past.

A police car parked across the road prevented access beyond a certain point. An impromptu car park had sprung up there with several cars already in it. The police officer on duty wouldn't let them through. Verónica searched in her bag for her *Nuestro Tiempo* ID which bore her photograph, the words *Prensa/Press* and a request for the authorities to cooperate.

"Press," said Verónica. The policeman looked at her pass and waved them through.

They had to walk half a mile along a slowly ascending road. The area where the bodies had been found was cordoned off with police tape. Beyond it they could see people working who must be forensics. But there were a lot of other people milling around too, chatting to one another as though waiting for a show to start. There was only one mobile broadcasting unit, from a Tucumanian channel. The Buenos Aires channels would surely arrive any time soon. Luca recognized Officer Benítez and a man in a suit.

"That's Chief Superintendent Suárez, chief of police in Yacanto del Valle."

When Benítez saw them he walked up to Suárez and said something to him. The chief superintendent came over to them.

"You must be the person who was travelling with the young women. My condolences."

"May I have a look at the place where the bodies were found?"

"That won't be possible, unless Judge Amalfi authorizes it." And he pointed to a man talking to three others, all of them wearing suits despite the afternoon heat.

Verónica walked over to the group. "Excuse me, your Excellency," she said, and the judge gave her a stern look, calculated to intimidate. "I'm Verónica Rosenthal."

"Daughter of Aarón?"

"Yes, that's right."

The judge's expression softened; he shook her hand and squeezed her arm in a gesture of condolence. "Let me introduce you, dear. Doctor Ruiz, director of security in the province; Señor Ferro, director of investigations, and retired brigadier Pacenti, director of criminology. This young lady is the daughter of Doctor Rosenthal, an old friend."

Verónica shook hands with the three men. She didn't believe her father and the judge were friends, but she certainly wasn't going to choose that moment to doubt it.

"As well as knowing the victims, I'm a journalist. I'd be interested to see the crime scene."

"Of course, come this way. I'll go with you." The judge took his leave of the other men and called over Chief Superintendent Suárez, who was still standing with Luca. "That man standing further up, as though observing everything from above," said the judge, pointing, "is the secretary for security in the province. As far as they're concerned I should be arresting someone in the next half hour."

Chief Superintendent Suárez caught up with them as they reached the crime scene. They looked at the area without crossing the police tape: two sets of trousers and T-shirts occupied the space left by the bodies.

"We wanted to use mannequins, but there was a technical hitch," the chief superintendent explained.

The scraps of material thrown down among weeds and shrubs gave the impression of clothes tossed about in a storm.

"I don't know if it's a good idea for you to see all this," Judge Amalfi said to her. "It's not a pleasant sight for a young woman, especially not if you knew the victims."

"Doctor, I assure you it doesn't affect me," she lied. "I want to know what happened."

"You journalists..." said the judge, without completing his observation. "Chief Superintendent, please be so kind as to bring my young friend up to date."

"The bodies were found at around 1800 hours by a young girl from the vicinity. They were lying on the ground, one face down and one on her side. Both the deceased were semi-naked, with evidence of blunt force trauma and possible sexual aggression. Both bodies had bullet entry and exit holes. There's evidence that they were killed here. Or rather, that they were brought here alive. There were also some garments scattered around them. The autopsy will confirm whether or not there was a sexual assault and if there are DNA traces from other people, either in the presence of semen or skin under the nails, or hair on victims' bodies."

"Who's going to perform the autopsy?" Verónica asked.

"This morning the director of the medical forensic team was here, with a biochemist. She's the one who'll be carrying out the tests."

"And when will the results be available?"

"Some by tomorrow. We'll know then if there was a sexual assault, and if death occurred as a result of injury caused by a firearm or by blunt force trauma. Also the exact time of death, although the state of the bodies suggests it was at least a day before they were found. Other investigations, like DNA samples, take longer. The forensics are also working towards a confirmation of where they died, if they were brought here dead, and how many assailants there were."

To one side of the area where the clothing lay there were some burned-out candles and a dead animal, perhaps a chicken. There were flies around it and a line of ants leading to the remains.

"What's that?" Verónica asked.

"An Umbanda offering," said the superintendent.

"A what?"

"What's left of some kind of black magic ritual. There were some marks on the body, separate from the contusions. Cuts that appeared to be ritual markings."

Verónica looked at the judge, who shrugged. "We can't rule anything out," he said, without much conviction.

She pictured Petra and Frida's bodies treated like dolls to be mutilated, broken, thrown away. She felt dizzy.

"Are you all right?" Luca had walked over to her and put his hands on her shoulders. Verónica nodded. She felt a cold sweat and cramps in her stomach.

"We should go," said Luca, and Verónica let him lead her away. They had walked just a few yards when a familiar face emerged from a little group that had been chatting as though at a private view. The expressions of surprise were mutual.

Álex Vilna walked over to her with a smile. "What are you doing here?"

"I could ask the same thing."

"I'm here because your boss sent me. Weren't you supposed to be on vacation?"

"Hang on – Patricia sent you here to write a piece?"

"I came to Tucumán to write about the narco police, and I got roped into covering these fucking murders."

"What narco police?"

"Come on, Verónica, are you stoned or something? The narco cops, the police chiefs who were found with fifty kilos of coke."

"Aren't you a political editor? What are you doing covering crime stories?"

"The police story has political aspects that my writers would struggle to explain. Or, if you prefer: I sent my best writer, and that's me. And when I was in Tucumán, your boss had the brilliant idea of turning the murder of two hippie chicks into a cover story. And who was the muggins who happened to be on the spot? Who's going to save *Nuestro Tiempo*'s bacon again? Me."

Álex Vilna had one undeniable talent: he could raise the blood pressure of the most hypotensive person on the planet. If Verónica had thought for a moment she might be about to faint, she now felt more likely to explode. And Álex would take the full force of the blast.

"Don't tell me your boss cut your vacation short and sent you here because she doesn't trust me," said Vilna. "Or did you volunteer your services so you could protect your patch?"

"I'm not covering it."

"Just as well, because I'm all over this. I've already got the title and everything: 'Macumba comes for two Europeans'. The subtitle could be something like 'Sex, tourism and black magic. How a ritual orgy ended in the deaths of a Swedish and an Italian woman'."

"Álex, you're a machine for spouting shit."

"I may not have your way with words, but I get exclusives. Guess what exclusive I've landed? Photos of the girls."

"What photos?"

"Photos of the corpses, sweetheart. The little girlies, lying in the grass half naked. And they're hot, too. Well, they were. We're going to sell a hundred thousand copies."

And she exploded. Something came out of her that was neither a scream nor a wail. It was something she had never done before and, seeing how it left her hand, it was very likely she would never do it again: Verónica closed her right fist and threw it hard straight into the face of Álex Vilna, who didn't see it coming and had no time to put up his guard. Vilna fell back on his ass, his face bleeding while Verónica howled from the pain of the blow. Everyone stopped what they were doing to see what was going on and to try and figure out how a flyweight girl had managed to floor a super middleweight man.

"You mad bitch! You're fucking psychotic!" yelled Álex, still on the ground and trying to staunch the bleeding from his nose and lip.

"And you're a fucking vulture!" By now Luca was trying to move Verónica away while she kept on screaming: "Get up, you fucker, and I'll smash your face in!"

Luca managed to get her into the car, start the engine and drive quickly away. Verónica got out her mobile and immediately sent a text message to Patricia Beltrán: "Publish Vilna's photos and you'll never hear from me again."

"As soon as we get home you need to put ice on that hand. It's going to swell up. I didn't realize you knew how to box."

"Me neither."

Her editor's response appeared on the mobile screen: "I have the photos already. I'm a journalist, not a muckraker. Don't worry. How did you find out? Where are you?"

"I'm in Yacanto del Valle. On vacation."

"Do you want to write the piece?"

"No."

"OK."

"Keep Vilna in line. He'll do anything for a story."

"I know when to crack the whip."

They arrived at the hotel. As he parked the car, Luca asked her, "Who was that guy?"

"Nobody. A man of no importance."

II

"She reminds me of Lucía."

Mariano was already in bed, watching Luca get undressed. He enjoyed this show which Luca put on with feigned indifference every night. And, despite the passing years, Luca's body was still lean, firm, commanding, with an elasticity that came from hours of rowing. He liked the way he slept naked both in winter and summer, how he folded and put away his clothes as he removed them, prolonging the striptease. If there was a place in paradise reserved for him it must be this: the contemplation of Luca's body as he took off his clothes. But paradises didn't exist. Or, as he had read once, only if they were paradises lost.

"She has attitude," said Luca and, coming from him, that was the highest honour to which a woman could aspire.

Lucía was Mariano's older sister. She had been disappeared in 1976, when a military gang had arrived at their house in the middle of the night. Mariano constantly relived the episode. The brutality of the soldiers, their parents' bewilderment, Lucía's terrified face, his own fear. His sister saying goodbye first to their father, then their mother and lastly to him (a kiss on the cheek, a squeeze of the shoulder, two words: "Keep studying."). Nor could he forget the face of the soldier who, wanting to seem polite, had said to his mother, "Don't worry, señora, if she hasn't done anything you'll have her back home in a few hours."

Lucía never appeared again. Their father's heart broke from grief and their mother never stopped hoping her daughter would come home. Mariano had also grown up waiting for that return. And when he started studying architecture – the same degree she had been working towards when she was seized – he tried to find some similarity to his sister in the girls studying alongside him. The memory that stayed with him was of a passionate young woman, a fighter who could not stand injustice.

It was hard for Mariano to accept that architecture had been her vocation, not his. That he had chosen the profession to be close to Lucía, to her world. And perhaps inspired by her (in spite of being an atheist, he was convinced Lucía still had influence over his life), he had done very well in his chosen career. He would have entered old age as a successful architect if he hadn't met Luca.

"What are you thinking about?" Luca asked as he got between the sheets.

"About Verónica, and about the conversation with Federico this morning."

"That guy's in love with her."

"But I got the impression she had something going on with our art dealer."

"A love triangle. I like it. I'd love to see Federico and Ramiro in some Greco-Roman wrestling contest to win her love."

"You know what I think? That we should get that girl out of this town, at least for a few hours. Imagine having to be here all the time, with the memory of what happened still so fresh."

"Taking her on a day trip won't make her feel any better."

"I know, but getting away from Yacanto would at least give her a break from so much suffering. Why don't you invite her to Club Náutico? It's far away, a different atmosphere. It's not the perfect solution, but it's better than hanging out in the town square..."

"Maybe. Ramiro's a member too. I don't think they'll want to go and, to be honest, I don't either."

"A change of scene will be good for us."

III

Federico had managed to find Verónica before Danilo Peratta, but that was no guarantee he could prevent an attack. He felt confused, uncertain how to proceed. Perhaps that was what prompted him to share his concern about Verónica with the owners of the hotel. So when she told him she was going to the place where the bodies had been found and that Luca was accompanying her, he didn't offer to go too. Peratta was professional enough not to try killing someone with so many police around.

He called Nicolás Menéndez Berti and introduced himself. Nicolás suggested coming to pick him up later so they could talk more freely at his country house. When he arrived at the hotel it was in a 4 x 4 similar to Ramiro's, and to many others Federico had seen around town. It seemed a plague worse than locusts.

They settled in a spot on the enormous veranda from which they could watch a spectacular sunset over the fields. A uniformed maid offered them drinks. Federico accepted a coffee and Nicolás asked the maid to prepare him a maté. A few minutes later she reappeared and Federico feared she would stay with them, replenishing the maté gourd with hot water as necessary, but she left a thermos and utensils and went away.

Federico had been closely observing Nicolás. It was something he always did the first time he met a potential client. He had learned how to discern the truth from gestures and movements rather than words. Everybody lied, including those who came to confess a crime or some terrible wrongdoing. At some point they would not tell the truth and, in order to defend them correctly, he needed to know what they were hiding, albeit unconsciously. It was clear to him that Nicolás's apparently calm facade, his disinclination to talk about what had happened, concealed a volcano.

"I don't understand why my father has to go bothering Rosenthal and getting you to come here."

"I'm just here in an informal capacity. I haven't come to offer you the services of the firm because I'm sure you don't need them. But I want you to know you can count on us."

"It's incredible that Rosenthal's daughter was also at the party and was the one who brought the foreign girls."

"Have the police been here? Did they take a statement from you?"

"They took one from me and from a few employees who were working that night. Like the person in charge of security."

"Did they gather any evidence?"

"They took the recordings from the security cameras at the entrance and from another one at the main door into the house."

"Are there any cameras inside? In one of the rooms, or another part of the estate?"

"No."

"Do you know how the girls left that night – were they on their own, or with someone else?"

"No, I didn't even know they were here. I don't really understand why everyone is so sure this was the last place they were seen alive."

"That could change at any moment if we get a new lead. What I do know is that they left the hotel to come to a party here and never returned. We need to find out more about where they may have gone, if they were alone or with other people, if they went willingly or were tricked or threatened."

"And you think that's something they can find out?"

"Going on the legal, police and political activity I've witnessed in the last few hours, I'd say there's a lot of interest in resolving this quickly."

Back at the hotel, Federico thought of something he had overlooked through inexperience. He called the lawyer, Mateo.

"My dear Doctor Córdova, this is beginning to feel like harassment. Are you about to ask me out?"

"I need to speak to Nick again. I want to know if Peratta has a mobile phone and what his number is."

"They'll want another five thousand for that information."

"If there's a number, I'll send you the money tomorrow through someone at the firm. But I need to know right away."

Mateo called him ten minutes later. "Here's the number – write it down. I make life so easy for you."

Federico often worked with the IT specialist who did all the intelligence work required by the Rosenthal practice. He was fat, affable, well into his fifties. Not the typical geek who lived inside computers, he had learned his stuff before the explosion in all things digital. And yet in the 1990s he had been a fearsome hacker, using the nickname La Sombra or Shadow, before he became a consultant in communications and systems. When a multinational company tried to sue him for industrial espionage, he took on Aarón Rosenthal as a lawyer. La Sombra was found not guilty on all charges and started working for the law firm.

"I've got the phone number. Can you trace it?"

"If it's a phone with GPS that'll be a cinch. If not, then it could take some time."

Federico gave him the number, and a few minutes later La Sombra had the information.

"I took the liberty of tracing you, too. Luckily you're both using phones with GPS, so it was easy. You're in Yacanto del Valle and the other guy's in Los Cercos, a town nearby. Not much more than two miles."

"Can you follow his movements? I need someone to let me know if he comes closer. If necessary, get someone to track him round the clock."

"Don't worry. There'll be someone monitoring him twenty-four hours a day. If he gets close, we'll call you. Bear in mind that if he turns his phone off, or it runs out of battery, we'll lose him. The same applies if he leaves it somewhere."

He saw Verónica arrive at the hotel and go straight to the restaurant kitchen. She came out with her hand buried in an ice bucket.

"Don't ask," she said to him.

"Just one question: shall we have dinner?"

"I'm not hungry, Fede."

"Have you eaten anything today?"

"A bit."

"We're having dinner, then. I'll meet you here at nine."

IV

They went to an Italian restaurant called Mamma Giuliana, which looked on to the square. Initially, Federico seemed anxious and distracted by his phone. He took several calls and was careful not to let her hear any of them. Could he be talking to her father? Whatever the case, if he didn't want her listening, she would respect that. Verónica turned her attention to the menu. She wasn't hungry, but she should eat. She ordered gnocchi in *salsa rosa.* All this – the restaurant, sitting at this table, the menu – seemed distant and impersonal to her. This wasn't her, she wasn't here.

"Have you thought about what you're going to do?" Federico asked her.

"No. I don't trust the DA, or the judge, or the police."

They finished dinner and returned to the hotel. He stayed at the bar for a while, talking to Mariano. Verónica went to bed. She was tired, but it was the kind of tiredness that gave her insomnia. She lay on the bed with her eyes open.

Identifying an urgent need for whisky, she got dressed again and went downstairs. The restaurant was closed. She asked the man who was on night duty at reception if he could get her a glass, but he had no access to the bar. Without thinking it over, she rang Ramiro.

Ten minutes later he arrived to pick her up from the hotel. Back at his place, in his living room, he offered her a choice of whiskies.

"Bourbon, anything. And bring the bottle."

"Are you planning to get drunk?"

"No."

Verónica and her friends, in their regular sessions dissecting the male species, had arrived at the undeniable fact that all men hid something: either a wife, or their homosexuality, their impotence, their misogyny, their Oedipal love for their mothers, or their complete absence of adulthood. They concluded that the first thing a woman should ask herself when she met a man was "So what's this one hiding from me?" In Ramiro's case the question was hard to answer. He was one of those people who can be read like an open book, whose lives are predictable: they are born with a silver spoon in their mouths and their lives end in ripe old age, perhaps after playing a round of golf and surrounded by grandchildren. Between beginning and end is a journey that, with some variations and nuances, encompasses a lot of fooling around with girls, marriage to someone with a good surname, a family, lovers, a career or some kind of commercial enterprise, professional triumph, travel to world capitals, relaxing on beaches with all-inclusive hotels, having children and grandchildren who are sure to continue on the same successful path. At that moment, when she felt as though she were walking through the wreckage of her own life (how many loved ones had died in less than a year? How many had suffered through her actions?), Ramiro's story induced a certain envy or admiration, or a combination of both. She felt good there, in his living room, drinking bourbon, listening to the steady voice of Ramiro, the ideal boyfriend, the perfect husband.

"Ramiro, I'm going to need your help."

"Whatever you want."

"I won't rest until I find out who did this to the girls. There's so much apathy and bureaucracy involved, and the system is so fucked, it could be years before they find anything."

"Whatever happens, you can count on me."

"I can't help wondering what would have happened if I'd stayed at the party with them." Verónica pondered this for a moment, Ramiro watching in silence. "Would they have killed all three of us? Did people at the party do it? Or someone else? Where did they find them? Did they take them by force or did the girls leave of their own free will?"

"Nobody knew the girls apart from us, so it's going to be difficult to find someone who remembers seeing them leave. The police have taken away the security cameras from Nicolás's house. Let's see what their investigations turn up."

Verónica yawned. Ramiro suggested she stay the night and she politely turned down the invitation.

On the way back to the hotel, Ramiro told her he wanted to organize a lunch at the Club Náutico restaurant. He and Luca were both members and they thought it would do her good to get out of Yacanto del Valle for a while – the club was a good way out of town. Verónica refused. She had a lot of things to do the next day. Ramiro didn't press the point but told her to think it over and call him if she needed anything.

Verónica barely slept that night. She kept waking up, seized by an anxiety that she ought to be doing something, although she didn't know what she could need to do at that very early hour except think, remember and reproach herself. She got up and sat in the armchair as though waiting for someone to come in and provide the answer, or at least some peace of mind. She slept for a couple of hours sitting there.

When she went down to breakfast, Federico was already in the dining room. Verónica asked him to get her the telephone numbers of the district attorney and the judge, because she needed to speak to them. Since DA Decaux seemed more amenable, she called him first and asked for a copy of the autopsy results. The DA hesitated. Finally he agreed to send her a summary with the most relevant details, but he wouldn't have them until that afternoon. Decaux asked her if she knew any of Petra's next of kin. They had tried in vain to locate relatives through the Italian embassy. Verónica told him that Petra had been in a relationship with an Argentinian man but that she didn't know his name, and that they had split up a few years ago. The DA informed her that the next day the Herlovsens, Frida's mother and father, would be arriving. Verónica felt a lump in her throat. For the first time she thought of Frida as someone's daughter.

The call ended without Verónica having a chance to ask if there were any firm leads in the case so far. She thought of the article Álex Vilna would now be writing. It crossed her mind to ask Patricia to send her the text before publication to see if he'd written anything stupid. Then she realized that meant acting like those interviewees who want to read the article before it comes out. She had always refused to let them. So she should be consistent now and not bother Patricia.

Luca reminded her of the invitation to lunch at Club Náutico. Since the autopsy results weren't arriving until afternoon, they might as well spend those hours doing something. It was all the same to Verónica whether she spent the time in Yacanto or some other place, so she told Luca she would go with them. She invited Federico too, but to her surprise he declined the invitation. He had things to do in town. Was Federico carrying out his own investigation? And if so, why wasn't he sharing his findings with her?

Her phone rang, interrupting these thoughts. It was her friend Paula again; she'd had three missed calls from her the day before. This time she decided to answer. Hearing her friend's voice was like stumbling across an oasis.

"Do you want me to come up there? Look, I can leave Juanfra with his father and be there in a few hours."

"No thanks, Pau. Federico's here."

"That's reassuring."

"Tell me what you're up to. I need to hear about something different from what happened here."

"The other day I nearly beat the shit out of a guy who was trying to sneak into an event with a writer."

"And I punched some dickhead in the face yesterday."

"We're two mean bitches."

"Damn right."

"Ah, and something really strange happened to me. I don't know if I should tell you."

"Details, please."

"I used your apartment for a tryst."

"OK..."

"But something strange happened."

"I hope you haven't left condoms all over the place."

"That's the thing. For reasons we needn't go into, I left my thong on the floor in the bathroom."

"Yes, spare me the details."

"And the next day I went to water your plants and collect my underwear, but it wasn't there."

"Are you sure?"

"A hundred per cent. I left it on the floor by the bidet. It was one of my favourites, with a kind of dotty pattern."

"That figures. You don't think you took it home the same day as the tryst?"

"No, darling. Walking through the streets with no underwear on is not an experience one forgets. I'm a hundred per cent sure I left it in your bathroom and that it disappeared. I reckon the doorman came in and took it."

Verónica ended the call feeling concerned. Marcelo had a key to her apartment. That didn't mean anything, though: he was incapable of doing such a thing. He might have the hots for her, but he had principles too. He would never steal an item of underwear, or spy on her, or lie to her.

She decided to call him. After the usual greetings, and without telling him what had happened in the last few days, she got to the point:

"Hey, Marcelo, have you by any chance been in my apartment in the last few days?"

"Not even once. Why?"

"And you haven't noticed any strange activity?"

"In your apartment? No. Do you want me to go in and check everything's all right?"

"No, don't worry. My friend Paula is going every so often to water the plants."

"Now you mention it, there was something a bit odd: someone came to leave a package for you, but he wouldn't let me take it. And the guy wasn't from any of the usual courier companies. I suppose he could have been from a private messenger service. It's not as if I know them all. Some of the questions he asked … how can I put it … there were just too many of them."

What was going on? Someone had got into her apartment. They were looking for her, going through her things. At least here in Yacanto del Valle she could feel safe. But when she went home she would have to find out what new trouble she had stumbled into without even knowing it.

V

Danilo Peratta took the bus that went from Los Cercos to Coronel Berti. He walked around the town, which was quite a bit bigger than the other two. He was looking for an old car to steal, one you could start by hot-wiring. He wanted to avoid taking out the car's owner because that would attract a lot of attention. In an alleyway leading to a stream, he found a Dodge 1500 that had to be at least thirty years old. He stood there for a while casing the area. There was no house nearby, no neighbours around. After twenty minutes he approached the vehicle. The doors were unlocked. One of the advantages of living in a small town.

He got into the car and looked into the rear-view mirror for a few seconds. Nobody to be seen. He used a screwdriver to unlock the steering wheel and looked for the ignition wires. The dashboard lights came on and the engine purred. Slowly, checking to see if anyone was watching or following him, he drove out of town.

Arriving in Yacanto del Valle, he parked the car two hundred yards from the hotel where his target was staying. There seemed to be some unusual activity in the street leading to the square. He saw an outside broadcast van from Buenos Aires go past. It must be journalists arriving to cover the women's murder. With any luck they'd soon be talking and writing about the murder of one of their colleagues, too.

It suited him to have a lot of outsiders arriving in town. It would make it easier than usual for him to go unnoticed. He walked towards the hotel then stopped a block away and stayed there, watching the entrance. The sun was beating down and he began to feel hot. He thought of going to the grill opposite the hotel, but the receptionist he had spoken to might turn up there and recognize him. He couldn't take that risk.

He didn't have to wait much longer. A 4 × 4 pulled up at the entrance to the hotel. Soon afterwards his target came out of the hotel with two men, one of whom was the receptionist he had spoken to before. They got into the pickup and drove off towards the main road. Peratta quickly turned round and walked back to the Dodge. He saw the pickup turn south on the main road. It wasn't difficult to catch up. They drove for about twelve miles before turning onto a smaller road.

Peratta tried to be inconspicuous, but it was difficult on a road with so little traffic. He let the pickup get as far ahead as possible without losing sight of it. The vehicle turned onto a short road that ended at the entrance to a sailing club. Driving on, he stopped the car a few yards ahead. He couldn't do anything inside the club; he would have to wait for her to come out, ideally on her own, although that seemed very unlikely. Peratta was going to have to take all four of them out. A complication, but not a serious one if none of them was armed.

He made a plan. Driving back past the entrance to the club, he continued, stopping about five hundred yards further on. He positioned the car at the side of the road. When he saw the pickup appear, he'd move the car, blocking their path, and gesture for help. He'd approach the 4 × 4 as though to explain what the problem was and then shoot them. First the driver, then the other two men, and her last. Before he killed her, he'd take the thong out of his pocket and show it to her. He'd tell her that he wasn't just going to kill her, he was going to fuck her too. That seemed fair compensation for what she had put him through.

Not many cars came along this road and all of them were going to the sailing club. Time passed slowly and only the odd person cast him and his old car a half-interested glance. He should have brought a hip flask with some gin in it.

Peratta felt drowsiness gradually overcoming him. Suddenly his phone pinged and the noise struck him as out of place. It was a text message from a number he didn't recognize, containing just one phrase: *Throw it away.*

Who had sent this, and what did they mean? Or had it been sent by mistake? Only Doctor Zero's people, El Gallo Miranda and Nick, knew this number. And throw what away? All at once he understood. He had to get rid of the phone. This fucking gadget could lead them to him.

Peratta looked at it now as though he were eyeing up a traitor. He got out of the Dodge and walked a few yards towards the trees. Further on there was a pond. He hurled the phone in that direction and watched it sink like a stone. When he returned to the road he paid no attention to the car driving towards the sailing club. But the car did not continue. Ten yards beyond the Dodge it came to a stop. Only then did Peratta start paying attention. A man got out of the car and began walking towards him. The man was carrying a rifle. Was it one of the security guards from the club coming to ask what he was doing? Peratta smiled at him to seem friendly. But the man lifted his weapon, pointed at him and fired.

8 *The Mind of Man Is Capable of Anything*

I

In normal circumstances, it would have been a perfect day to spend in the country. The morning was sunny, there was almost no wind. It was perhaps a little too warm for the end of March, but ideal for eating in the shade, as they did, the four of them, on the terrace of the sailing club. Verónica tried to concentrate on the food, on each mouthful, but it was impossible; impossible, too, to follow the others' conversation. If they noticed she wasn't paying attention, they were polite enough not to mention it.

Halfway through lunch, Verónica called Federico. She wanted to run past him the questions she was thinking of asking the judge: what had happened to the girls' phones? Had all their clothes been found or were some items still missing? Had they checked the security cameras at Ramiro's house yet? But Federico wasn't answering his calls.

When they had finished eating, Ramiro invited them to go out sailing for a bit. Verónica wasn't in the mood for a boat trip but she also didn't want to seem unfriendly to Ramiro, who kept insisting on taking her to see his boat (a Bermuda Twentyone, as he was keen to tell them). She agreed to a spin on the lake, on condition they head back to Yacanto afterwards.

They walked to the jetty and Ramiro asked for the boat to be lowered into the water. As the club employees were manoeuvring the vessel, Ramiro's younger brother Nahuel appeared and greeted Verónica with indifference. He was wearing a sleeveless shirt that showed off his muscular arms. Ramiro had mentioned at some point that Nahuel was a rower. The boy seemed rather agitated and drew his brother aside for a quiet word.

Verónica stood watching from the shed as the blue and white boat was lowered into the water. When the Bermuda was ready by the dock, Ramiro came back alone.

"One prize idiot – that's my brother."

"What's happened?"

"I don't know. It seems his girlfriend is pregnant and wants an abortion. He was asking me for some money, so he's going to drop by the gallery later on."

They got on to the boat. Ramiro gently steered it away from the dock.

"I hope you don't get seasick."

"My dad used to have a boat moored in Tigre, so I'm used to it. I used to steer it, in fact."

Ramiro invited her to take the helm. Verónica's father's boat had been much less sophisticated, but it wasn't very different to handle. Ramiro put his arms around her, circling her waist in a subtle embrace. Verónica didn't stop him.

"I've got a confession," Ramiro said. "When I was little I was terrified of water. I didn't know how to swim. By the time I learned, I was quite old – seventeen, eighteen – and I never got to be a good swimmer. I flounder about in the water. Nahuel, on the other hand, can do everything: rowing, jet-skiing, diving – you name it."

"He certainly looks sporty."

"When I was at school, about ten or eleven years old, a teacher mentioned that orangutans never learn how to swim. So from that day onwards they called me Orangutan. Even in secondary school, although they shortened it to Oran. And some bastard just called me Onan."

"Good nickname."

"Yes. Oran stuck for such a long time that there's still the odd friend from my adolescence who calls me that."

They cruised for a few minutes. In the middle of the lake the tranquillity was absolute. Ramiro got her to stop the boat, which rocked gently.

"Whenever I want to get far away from the world, I come here."

It was certainly far away from everything. The shore was barely discernible, just water on every side. Ramiro tried to kiss her but Verónica gently stopped him.

They returned to the shore, where Mariano and Luca were waiting for them, then set off back home. Verónica called Federico, who still wasn't answering his phone. None of the four of them noticed the bloodstains by the side of the road.

11

After talking to Decaux, Verónica's knees were shaking. The district attorney had promised to email her a summary of the report, but he had ended up telling her over the phone instead.

What was known so far was that Frida and Petra had been murdered within twenty-four hours of the party. They had been savagely beaten, both with fists and with a machete. Both showed signs of having been raped. Both had traces of semen in the vagina and anus. Although the DNA analysis was still pending, all the evidence pointed to two or more perpetrators. Frida had been strangled. Once dead, she had been shot in the back of the neck. In Petra's case, the cause of death was a bullet that had perforated her lung and heart and exited below her left nipple. She had died instantly. Both had epithelial cells under their fingernails, which suggested an effort to fight off their attackers. They had died in the place they were found. The forensic biochemist wanted the search widened to include nearby trees whose branches might have scratched the assailants and thus collected some biological material.

The DA told her that they were still searching for genetic fingerprints, that hairs had been found which could belong to the attackers. There were prints left by footwear and tyres too. Everything was being analysed.

Verónica asked Decaux about the girls' mobile phones. He told her they were discovered at the scene of the crime and that so far nothing relevant had been found on them. The same applied to the clothes, which had been torn or destroyed. They were still being analysed.

The security cameras from Nicolás's house had not revealed much. Although the girls were not captured leaving the property, that was not altogether significant because the recording only showed people sitting in the front seats of their cars or leaving the property on foot.

So far the strongest lead was the Umbanda offering left beside the bodies. The hypothesis was that the women had been tricked into leaving the party by someone who had then taken them to the gathering of some kind of sect.

Verónica asked if he had been in contact with the people attending the party and the DA conceded that it was impossible to investigate everyone. There had been a lot of them, and no guest list. He was hoping a witness would come forward who remembered having seen the two young women with someone and that the information would shed some light on their last hours.

After ending the call, Verónica couldn't stand up. The shaking began in her legs and extended up to her jaw. It was a few minutes before she was able to calm herself. She drank some water and called Federico again. This time he answered. He said he was in the hotel dining room. Verónica went downstairs and found him sitting at the back of the room drinking a coffee. He looked like a contented regular, whiling the time away.

"I've been calling you all day," Verónica reproached him.

"I had things to do."

She told him about her conversation with the district attorney. "I have the feeling we're missing something obvious," she added.

"Like when you lose keys that were in your hand a minute earlier."

"Exactly."

"In that case you have to do what I do when I lose mine. I go back and repeat all the movements I made since the last time I had them in my hand."

"So I have to reconstruct everything that's happened since we separated at the party?"

"Ideally."

"That's impossible today. But I do need to go back to the beginning of the investigation. I ought to speak to the person who found the bodies."

"She's a teenager who lives out in the backcountry. The investigating judge told me. The girl lives near to where it happened."

"Do you have her name?"

"I can get it."

Minutes later they set off in Federico's car. The judge had

not only given them the girl's name, Mercedes, but he had instructed Chief Superintendent Suárez to wait for them at the crime scene and direct them to her house. Once they were in the car, Verónica told Federico that someone had gone into her apartment while she was away. He waited a few seconds before replying.

"Yes, that's true."

"You knew?"

Federico concentrated on the road ahead and Verónica said impatiently, "How could you know and not tell me? Who came into my house?"

"Danilo Peratta, the sole survivor from the four guys you ran down in front of the building."

"But wasn't he in prison? Didn't he get a life sentence?"

"He escaped from the hospital where he's been having check-ups."

"What did he want going into my apartment?"

"He wanted to know where you were because he wanted to kill you."

"And you didn't think to tell me?"

"I was going to tell you as soon as it became necessary. I came here for various reasons, but the main one was to make sure he didn't get near you."

"Does he know where I am?"

"It's sorted, Verónica. The guy's not going to be a problem."

"What do you mean? How do you know?"

"Today I waylaid him on the way to Club Náutico. I shot him."

"Are you mad, Federico? The man's an assassin, he could have killed you."

"I was counting on the element of surprise. He didn't kill me. I didn't kill him either. He got away with a gunshot wound."

"So he's still a threat. Why didn't you tell the police?"

"I don't know the police round here and I don't trust police I don't know. Now that I've found him, and he's injured, I've informed the gendarmerie. It's a special body that works with the Penitentiary Service."

"But how will they find him? He escaped, right?"

"Look, it's highly likely he's already dead. He lost a lot of blood. He got into the car he'd stolen and abandoned it six miles further on, in the foothills. If I could find the car – which I can tell you was awash with blood – I imagine the border patrol will get to it in a few hours."

"Fede, you shot him. You're going to have to explain that to the police."

Federico took his eyes off the road for a moment to look at her.

"OK, maybe you won't have to explain. But what you did was still madness. Where did you get the gun, when did you learn how to shoot?"

"Vero, if you paid me more attention, you'd know things about me."

"You can be a real asshole sometimes."

There was a long silence.

"Now I understand why you called me."

"It was also because I wanted to hear your voice."

Federico had managed to throw her off balance. All those days she had been in danger without knowing it while he had been the perfect minder, keeping her safe. It was impossible to imagine him wielding a gun. She couldn't even imagine him confronting someone in any other place than a court of law. He was right: there were things she didn't know, to which she hadn't paid attention. She had never asked herself the question before but now it was compelling. What was Federico capable of? How far would he go for her?

III

If the crime scene had been busy the day before, now it was more crowded than ever. There were radio and television units, broadcasting live. At the centre of it all, standing near the makeshift mannequins, was District Attorney Decaux, surrounded by microphones. He appeared to be giving a press conference.

Verónica went to look for Chief Superintendent Suárez and found him standing alone beside a police car. He had already been informed that they wanted to go to the witness's house and pointed out the way: they had to follow the path up to the second property. Verónica thanked him and, as she was about to leave, Suárez said to her:

"I've been wanting to ask you a question since yesterday. You travelled to Yacanto del Valle with the two deceased, you all went to the party, and that was where you parted company."

"Yes."

"According to the hotel owners' statement, it seemed that the three of you were going to stay several days and that you changed your mind. You were in such a hurry that you left around dawn."

"Early in the morning, yes."

"So the question I want to ask is this: how have you avoided being considered a suspect by either the district attorney or the investigating judge?"

"I'd be asking myself the same question in your shoes."

"Well, I'd like to hear your answer."

"I'm sorry, Chief Superintendent, you'd have to ask them, not me."

"Fair enough. And don't worry, I will."

"I don't know if you've had a chance to look at the autopsy

report, but everything points to more than two men being involved."

"Yes, of course. I don't see you killing anyone. But you should be investigated all the same. You could have been the procurer. You took the girls to the party, left them there and disappeared."

"I imagine it's no use me telling you I didn't do what you think I did."

"Listen, Señorita: don't attempt to intimidate the witnesses or pervert the course of justice. No matter how many friends you have in the court system, I can guarantee you won't succeed in that."

Verónica walked away feeling that, of all the people investigating this crime, Chief Superintendent Suárez was the only one she could trust. She thought of mentioning this to Federico as they walked up the road leading to Mercedes's house, but decided to say nothing.

They arrived at the house, an adobe hut with a straw roof. A wire fence and a broken gate marked the limits of the property, at the back of which was a chicken coop with a vegetable patch to one side, as well as a brick room separate from the house. A black dog you wouldn't want to get on the wrong side of ran out barking, a dachshund waddling behind. Verónica didn't need to clap her hands to get attention, because an older woman had already come out of the house and was walking towards them with a look of suspicion. She asked them what they needed.

"Mechi isn't here. My granddaughter is working." She asked who they were.

"I was a friend of the girls who died," Verónica said.

Mechi would be home in a bit. They asked permission to wait for her outside and the grandmother said they could do as they pleased. Verónica and Federico walked a few yards away and sat under a tree. The dogs quietened down and the big one wandered off, but the dachshund stayed, watching them.

"I think it might be easier if she talks to me on my own. She may be intimidated if there's a man there."

"Whatever you think. I'm happy just to sit and wait for you here."

An hour later the girl arrived. She came walking slowly up the path, as though delaying the moment of arrival. A typical teenager in jeans and a vest, giving them the same wary look as the old lady. Verónica stood up and walked towards her.

"Hello, Mechi, my name is Verónica. I'm ... I was a friend of the girls you found. I'd like to talk to you."

Mechi peered behind Verónica to where Federico was sitting. "I've already told the police and the judge everything I know," she said.

"Yes, I know. But I need you to tell me as well."

"What for?"

"To help with the investigation. As well as being a friend of the girls, I'm a journalist."

"It won't make any difference anyway."

At that moment the old woman reappeared. "Mechi, don't be rude. Come in, Señora, I also saw the bodies of those poor girls. Come in, please." Verónica stepped through the broken gate and Mechi followed, looking sullen.

This time the dogs kept quiet as she entered the property, only approaching to give her a sniff. Inside, the house was dark and smelled of vegetable soup and burning wood. A pot was boiling on an old range. The floor was made of trodden earth. Mechi's grandmother shook a chair, as though to dislodge crumbs, and invited Verónica to sit down. She repeated the action with a rubber-backed tablecloth, although there wasn't a speck of dust anywhere in the room.

As Verónica entered the house, three dachshund puppies launched themselves at her. She sat down but couldn't shake off the puppies, who were biting her sneakers. At least she wasn't wearing sandals. Mechi smiled at the puppies like a mother amused by her children's antics. Or perhaps she smiled because they were mistreating Verónica, as she herself would like to do. Her grandmother told Mechi to get the animals out of the house. Huffily, she picked them up and took them outside.

When she came back in, Mechi sat in the other chair while the older woman remained standing, as though ready to correct her granddaughter if she put a foot wrong. Mechi told Verónica how she had left the path and seen the two bodies lying on the ground. She had been frightened and had run to tell her grandmother.

"I thought she was seeing visions. The girl's had nightmares ever since Bibi died."

"So you also saw the bodies on the ground."

"Poor things, they were all exposed. I tried to cover them up as best I could. I didn't want the police to see them like that."

"I told my grandmother not to touch anything, that we might get the blame, but she ignored me."

"Apart from the bodies, did you see anything else?"

"I didn't want to look," Mechi said.

"There was that awful monstrosity," said the grandmother.

"What monstrosity?"

"The macumba they put together there."

"You think this was to do with witchcraft?"

"Witchcraft? More like mockery."

"Mockery? Why?"

"A white cockerel in macumba? Who's ever seen such a thing?"

"You don't use a white cockerel in macumba?"

"No, Señora, a black cockerel or nothing."

"So…?"

"Some idiot wanted to make a macumba ritual but got it wrong. They're not just murderers, they're ignorant brutes."

Mechi was looking down.

"How old are you, Mechi?"

"Seventeen."

Verónica thought that if her mother had started talking to a stranger when she was seventeen, she too would have bowed her head and asked the earth to swallow her up.

Mechi looked up then, and asked her, "Were they raped? Were the girls raped?"

"Mechi," her grandmother began, reprovingly.

"Yes."

The teenager started to cry. Her grandmother shook her head and turned to the range to stir the contents of the pan. Verónica reached over to touch Mechi's head, to calm her.

"Bibi was, too."

"Who is Bibi?" Verónica asked her.

"My sister. They raped her too, before they killed her. And nobody ever went to prison."

IV

Verónica felt the kind of internal jolt that told her she had made a breakthrough in her investigation. Her pulse quickened and her senses sharpened, like a cat sensing danger.

"What happened to your sister?"

"I just told you: she was raped and murdered."

"When did that happen?"

"I don't know. A long time ago."

"Six years ago," said her grandmother. "Mechi was very little."

"But I remember."

"How did it happen?"

The grandmother went to sit down in a chair.

"Bibi was very pretty. She had lots of suitors, but she was very stubborn. She didn't want to go out with anyone from the town. She wanted to move to San Miguel, but I wouldn't let her. When the girls' mother died, I promised to look after them, and I wasn't going to leave her alone in the city."

Verónica saw how the old woman's body bent further over; she felt guilty, and guilt weighs heavy. Verónica knew that.

"She liked to go dancing. She used to go with friends. That night she got all dressed up and off she went."

"Had she gone out with these friends?"

"Yes, but none of them could say what had happened."

"They lied because they were afraid, or because somebody paid them off," said Mechi.

"I did everything I could, my dear. I even paid for a lawyer, but they couldn't find anything."

"Where was the body found?"

"Just past Coronel Berti. They threw her on the side of the road. A week after they had killed her."

"And nobody was arrested?"

"Nobody."

"We all know who it was. El Gringo Aráoz," said Mechi, and her grandmother nodded.

"But he didn't get arrested?"

"El Gringo Aráoz is from a wealthy local family. They said all kinds of things about my granddaughter. They dragged my poor girl's name through the mud just to save that man."

Verónica left Mechi's house with a list of things she planned to confirm in the coming days: Bibi's full name, along with that of the possible culprit and of the lawyer who had defended the family. She also swapped numbers with Mechi. The girl's attitude had changed during her visit, and now she seemed interested in what Verónica was doing.

"I'm going to need your help," she said to Federico as they were driving back to the hotel. "First of all, what is the statute of limitations for a crime?"

"It depends what crime it is."

"Murder and rape."

"Between twelve and fifteen years, depending on what kind of homicide it is."

"Six years ago Mechi's sister was murdered in circumstances very similar to Petra and Frida. And nobody was ever charged."

"Do you think it could be the same person?"

"Nothing like an unpunished crime to stir up the spirit of recidivism."

"Perhaps."

"And what if there are more crimes? What if, as soon as you start investigating one, you stumble across another? Couldn't there be more?"

V

He hadn't thought the other man would shoot, and that was a mistake. A basic principle of survival is always to assume that, if another person has a weapon, they will use it. He didn't realize until the guy lifted his rifle. He did manage to jump to the side, but the bullet was faster and caught him just below the right nipple. If he hadn't moved, it would have found his heart. The resulting rush of adrenaline helped him reach his car. He was in no state to return fire. A second shot shattered the rear window, but didn't hit him. He started the car and got out of there. The other man was either too slow or decided not to follow him, because he didn't see his assailant's car behind him again. Who was he, though? And who had told him to throw away the phone? They had found him anyway. He had behaved like an amateur.

Peratta took the main highway but, as soon as he could, turned off onto a minor road, drove two hundred yards down it then pulled over, still keeping an eye on the road behind him. He searched in the glove box for some sort of material, found a chamois cloth and pressed it hard against the wound. It was incredibly painful, but he couldn't let his guard down yet. He started the car again and drove on a couple of miles, even though the wound made driving almost impossible. He reached a junction and left the car at the side of the road. It wouldn't take long for them to find it there. He must act fast or it would be game over. Coming towards him down the road was one of those dilapidated old vans you only ever see in small towns. He signalled to it and the driver stopped with the intention of helping him. He surely didn't expect to see a blood-soaked man pointing a gun at him.

Danilo Peratta climbed into the passenger seat.

"Where do you live?" he asked.

The man was a farmhand with weather-beaten skin. He couldn't have been more than forty and he was wearing tattered overalls.

"In Los Altos del Paso."

"Where's that?"

"About six miles from here."

"Who do you live with?"

"My missus."

"Who else?"

"No one else."

"Take me there."

The man turned the van around, retracing his steps.

"You need a doctor, my friend."

"Shut up and drive."

Peratta felt dizzy. He had to fight not to close his eyes and to keep his gun pointing at the farmhand.

Altos del Paso was a village with a few dwellings separated by small fields. The man drove into one of these fields and parked in front of a modest house which was either still under construction or having some new rooms added to it.

They got out of the van and went inside. Peratta was still using the chamois to keep pressure on his wound. In his other hand he held the gun and kept it pointed at the man. His wife, who was in the kitchen, put her head round the door to greet her husband and stifled a scream when she saw the gun pointing at him. Danilo silenced her. The man gestured at her to keep calm, and the three of them went into a small living room.

"Is there a pharmacy near here?"

"The nearest one is twelve miles away."

"You're going to go to the pharmacy and buy what I tell you. Get a pen and some paper."

The man took a pen out of the cupboard and a block of paper.

"You're going to buy two packets of bandages, gauze, some lidocaine spray, tramadol tablets and Celox – starts with a 'c', ends with an 'x'. If you take more than an hour, I'll kill your wife. If you come back with someone, I'll kill your wife. Understood?"

The man hurried off. Peratta asked the woman for a towel. Without removing the chamois, now a ball of blood, he pressed down with the towel, which very soon began to turn red. He asked for some water and the woman poured him a glass. He asked for more. Peratta drank the second glass. He made her sit on a small couch opposite him. The woman obeyed without speaking. Peratta put his gun down beside him. He knew the woman wasn't going to try anything.

It was about fifty minutes before the man returned with all the things he had been asked to get. Peratta wanted to know if they had asked any questions in the pharmacy, but there had been no trouble.

He made the man sit on the same couch as his wife and asked her to open the two sachets of Celox. He made her bring a glass of water, take out two tramadol tablets and open the lidocaine spray. Peratta took the two tablets and removed the towel and chamois from his wound, which was hardly bleeding now but was red and raw. He leaned back, trying to get more comfortable in the chair, then ordered the woman to pour the Celox granules onto his wound and to spray the surrounding area with the lidocaine. She was shaking but still managed to do exactly as he asked. Then Peratta told her how to wrap the bandages around his chest. His shirt, the chamois and towel were left on the floor, all soaked in blood.

Half an hour later Peratta still felt rough, despite the tranquillizers. He needed something stronger, but he wasn't going to be able to get hold of that in a pharmacy without a prescription. Besides, the wound was going to get infected. The precautions he had taken weren't enough. He needed to see a doctor or he would die.

He didn't want to do this, but there was no choice: he asked for a telephone and the man handed over his mobile. He called Five.

"I'm fucked. Here in Tucumán. I've been wounded. Tell Doctor Zero I need his help."

"The Doctor said you were on your own with this one."

"He can let me die and lose one of his men, or I can hand myself in and go back to prison."

Ten minutes later, Five called him.

"Tell me where you are. Tomorrow morning first thing I'll be there."

He had to ask the man to explain how to get to the house. It wasn't an easy place to find.

Peratta started to feel increasingly dizzy and weak. He must have a temperature. He asked if there was any alcohol. The couple had a bottle of red wine and some hard liquor. He asked the woman to bring the bottle of red wine, opened. He shouldn't drink it, he knew that, and yet as the wine slipped down his throat he began to feel calmer.

He wasn't sure if he had done the right thing asking Doctor Zero for help. It wasn't necessarily a good sign that Five was on his way to Tucumán. It meant one of two things: either he was coming to kill him, to put an end to his story and avoid compromising Doctor Zero, or Doctor Zero was taking the trouble to help him get better. If the latter, he wouldn't be able to continue with his revenge plan. His time with Rosenthal would be over and he would have to go back to working for Doctor Zero. And he wasn't prepared to accept that.

And what if they were coming to finish him off? If Five was travelling here just to shoot him in the back of the neck? Peratta could hold off these two peasants, terrified as they were by his wounds and his gun, but he would be powerless against a professional like Five. He must remain alert and, at the first sign that Five was there to kill him, get the upper hand.

The hours until nightfall dragged. He wasn't hungry, but he didn't want to grow even weaker. He asked the couple if they had any bread and cheese. He told them to bring him something and to eat themselves, too. When they had finished, Peratta, with a great effort, stood up. He felt the world spinning around him, and tried to regain his composure to avoid showing how bad a state he was in. He made the couple go into the bathroom and followed them with the gun. Luckily for him, the bathroom was as he had imagined it. The window, there for ventilation, was far too small for anyone to escape through. There was a lock on the door. He locked them in and warned that he would be listening out for their every movement. If they didn't cause him any trouble, then first thing next morning he would leave with his friend and they would be released. They just had to wait.

He returned to the armchair, took two tranquillizers and finished off the bottle of wine. As though on a kind of roller coaster, he dropped off, then woke up again every few minutes, agitated. He was aware of cockerels crowing at dawn, birdsong, a van going by in the distance. He didn't hear Five arriving. When he opened his eyes, there he was.

"Do you think you can make it to San Miguel de Tucumán?" Five asked him.

Peratta tried to speak. His tongue felt thick inside his mouth. He nodded. "They're looking for me," he managed to say with great effort, fighting to breathe. "They know I'm here."

"Don't make trouble for yourself. Tell me, is there anyone else in the house?"

Peratta pointed at the bathroom door. "Two of them."

"Did anyone else see you?"

He shook his head.

Five went to the bathroom, opened the door and shot the couple. His silencer muffled the noise. Next he went to Peratta and helped him stand up. Danilo said to him:

"I thought you were coming to kill me."

"We need you for a job."
"Is it urgent?"
"Yes."
"Where?"
"Here, in Tucumán. We need to kill Verónica Rosenthal. And this time we can't fail."

9 *Forty-two Photos and a Video*

I

Verónica wasn't having a good night. Insomnia was her constant companion. She would have had a drink, but once again she had forgotten to buy a bottle of whisky to keep in the room. To make matters worse, her whole body itched. Her arms, stomach, behind her knees. She had suddenly developed a rash and couldn't stop scratching. Since she couldn't sleep, Verónica went over the conversation with Mechi and her grandmother a thousand and one times. She needed to find out more about Bibi's death. Federico was going to make enquiries in the Tucumán courts to find out more about what had happened in the case. Just as it seemed that the itch was abating and she was drifting off to sleep, an image popped into her mind of the man who had entered her apartment. If he was still alive, he would return.

She got up at 6 a.m. and, without really thinking about what she was doing, put on jogging clothes and went for a run in the town. It was another way to get to know the place. She didn't make a habit of running in Buenos Aires, but she knew that this would be a useful time to think, clear her mind and show herself she wasn't scared.

At that time of day Yacanto del Valle looked like a movie set. The streets were almost empty of people. But there was a flow of trucks taking labourers out to work in the country.

She ran past the entrance to Nicolás's estate and was tempted to go in and see him. Then she circled Ramiro's house and gallery and continued past the police station. As she passed the hotel, she saw two mobile broadcasting units parked outside, one from Tucumán and the other from Buenos Aires. The windows in the houses were still shuttered. This was a quiet town, monotonous, predictable. Jogging through the empty streets, she was a symptom of the disquiet they wanted to drive out. Small towns don't like strangers, dead or alive.

Suddenly a dog ran out of a yard, barking and apparently with every intention of biting her. Verónica shouted and ran faster. The dog didn't follow. She got back to the hotel feeling shaken, tired and breathless. For a few minutes she stood outside, trying to get her breath back.

Mariano was already behind the reception desk and they chatted briefly. Verónica went to take a shower then to have breakfast. In the dining room were a young couple, a family with two children and her. Federico had still not come down.

She needed to see Ramiro, so she called to see if he was up. He told her he had to wait for a buyer who had an early appointment at the gallery, but that she was welcome to join him there if she wanted. As she was leaving the hotel, Mariano offered to give her a lift.

Verónica was struck by a thought: "Mariano, Federico hasn't by any chance asked you and Luca to look after me, has he?"

"The Posada Don Humberto offers a complete service to our clients."

"OK, because if it was on account of a criminal who was looking for me, from what I hear, he's out of circulation now."

"Whatever you say." Mariano winked at her.

Verónica walked to the Galería Arde and, since it wasn't yet open, rang the bell. Ramiro came out and led her to his office.

"Would you like a coffee?"

"I've just had breakfast in the hotel, thanks. And I get the impression you don't know how to use the coffee maker."

"You shouldn't underestimate me. I don't rely on my assistant for absolutely everything. Anyway, we have a very simple stove-top espresso maker that even an orangutan could use."

"Orangutan? I don't think camels know how to swim either."

"Which would be logical, because there's nowhere in the desert to practise."

"Ramiro, I've come here to ask a few questions. Can you help me with something that's come up? Do you know who Gringo Aráoz is?"

"Of course, a great full back in the Universitario Rugby Club until he retired. An agronomist. He got married about two years ago."

"Was he implicated six years ago in a crime involving a young woman?"

"Not that I remember."

"Are you a friend of his?"

"We move in the same circles."

"Was he at Nicolás's party?"

"No … hang on, let me think – actually, I believe he was. He was. Do you think he could have something do with the girls' deaths?"

"I really don't know. Truthfully, I've no idea."

Ramiro walked back with her to the entrance. They were outside saying goodbye when Verónica heard a voice she recognized calling her.

"Verushka!"

She turned round to see her friend María, a crime correspondent from a television channel based in Buenos Aires. They hadn't seen each other for more than a year and greeted one another effusively, both surprised to be meeting again here. Verónica introduced Ramiro and noticed how María looked him up and down. They said goodbye to him and went to Amigo's, the bar on the square, for a chat. On the way there, María asked if she was seeing Ramiro.

"Not exactly."

"You're lucky I arrived late, because I'd have him off you in ten minutes."

"Don't play the femme fatale – we both know you're married."

"Don't remind me."

María had been sent to cover the Tourist Murders, as the crime was being dubbed on TV news banners and in newspaper headlines.

"So are you here for *Nuestro Tiempo* too? I saw that slimy creep Álex yesterday and he didn't mention you."

"He's got the cover story. I happened to be on vacation in the area, but I've decided to stay on and see what I can find out."

"There are lots of theories, luckily. If not, I don't know how I'd fill the time. I'm on-air in an hour and I don't stop until night. So long as the ratings are good, they'll have me singing all day long."

"No rest for the wicked."

"I'm not complaining. Poor girls, imagine coming to this shithole only to get raped and murdered."

"There are vermin everywhere."

"Not just vermin. Evil bastards."

"Meaning?"

"Look, since I started in this line of work I've seen more crimes than the dishy Dexter. And you can tell right away if someone's been murdered in an outburst or an attack of jealousy or to cover something up. Generally, people kill to keep someone or something quiet: witnesses, accusers, cheats. That's not what's happening here. These two murders don't silence anything. It's more like they're screaming."

"Screaming?"

"When someone kills in the way the tourists were murdered, they don't do it to hide a rape. They do it because they want to send a message to a particular audience. That's why they were treated so viciously. It's a *mise en scène.* A piece of mortuary theatre. Or, to put it another way, it's like a text written on the body: if you can read it correctly, you'll understand the message. Because someone is trying to say something here."

"A mafia-style message."

"I'd go much further. These are polysemic deaths. Apologies for using big words, but my years of university have to count for something."

"Polysemic is something that has multiple meanings, right?"

"I had a teacher who used to say that metaphors are an explosion of meanings. Think of it this way: these deaths are an explosion of meanings. If you read them literally, you're only going to see one part."

"The parts have to be put together."

"I'll tell you something else: if you can find out who the message is directed to, which audience they wanted to show those bodies, we'll find out who was responsible."

Verónica was surprised by how much María was telling her. She didn't like to share her theories on stories. She never normally gave up what she had, but on this occasion she wasn't there as a journalist. So she ventured to say to María:

"A few years ago there was a similar crime, involving a girl from round here. They killed and raped her. Nobody went to prison. I'm wondering if there might be other similar cases and if anything links them."

"That wouldn't surprise me."

Just then María's phone rang. She looked to see who it was, then stepped outside to speak alone. She returned exultant.

"A source. Well, DA Decaux. That guy likes cameras more than I like French fries. If you promise not to pass it on to any of the other channels, I've got something that may interest you. Use it in the magazine, if you like, because it'll be old news by the time your piece hits the news stands. This afternoon they're going to arrest a guy and accuse him of these crimes. Come with me if you like, and you can be there when it happens."

II

"Everything will be tied up today."

"Have you spoken to the judge?"

"DA Decaux signed the order. In a few hours they'll arrest the culprit."

"Only one? This is the work of various people."

"Then the suspect will serve up his accomplices."

"I've seen Nicolás and Ramiro."

"Yes, I know. There's a plane leaving for Buenos Aires tonight. Come back, and bring Verónica with you."

"I can't see Verónica wanting to return."

"Talk her into it. There's nothing more for her to do there."

As if the Rosenthals were easily talked into anything. Father and daughter were the most obstinate people you'd care to meet. Federico could try, but Verónica wasn't going to want to go home until the last of the men responsible was locked up. And that afternoon they were only arresting one.

What's more, he knew nothing about what had happened to Peratta. His contact had told him there was no trace of the villain. Had he headed into the backcountry and bled to death? If so, they should have found the body by now. Peratta was clearly operating alone. But when Federico had tracked him down, the guy was throwing away his phone. Somebody had let him know Federico was after him. Why would El Gallo Miranda or Nick do something so stupid? Peratta was nothing more than a lowly hitman. Miranda and Nick wouldn't want to create problems with anyone. Unless Mateo... It must be him. Mateo was a lawyer, so scruple-free. He was prepared to do anything for a bit of money or an iota of power. Mateo defended a lot of powerful criminals. He knew who would want to know about Peratta. If Federico had been in Buenos Aires he'd have had Mateo singing like a canary within twenty-four hours, but it was difficult from Tucumán. He would wait to see what Verónica did. If she decided to return, then he'd go for Mateo.

Federico had arranged to meet the district attorney in a cafe in Coronel Berti. When he arrived, Decaux was finishing a telephone conversation. You could tell he was talking to a woman, because he was trying to sound seductive.

"Case solved, my friend," he said to Federico. "Today we've arrested the main suspect. Justice moves quickly in these parts, eh. You could learn from us in Buenos Aires."

"I'm sure you're right."

"I've got something for you to pass on to Doctor Rosenthal's daughter." Decaux handed him a memory stick.

"What's on it?"

"The photos that were on the Italian girl's camera. I imagine she'd like a copy. She's in quite a few of them."

Federico took the USB stick and considered it for a moment. The DA read his thoughts.

"Don't worry, the police haven't seen these photos. If they got hold of them, they'd be on the cover of all the papers today, making trouble for young Rosenthal. Only the judge and I have seen them."

On the road from Coronel Berti to Yacanto del Valle, Federico wrestled with a moral dilemma. Should he look at the photos on the memory stick or just give it straight to Verónica? There was no security reason for seeing them – he couldn't use that excuse. It would be simple voyeurism. He arrived at the Posada de Don Humberto and asked Mariano for Verónica.

"She hasn't got back yet. Is it true she's no longer in any danger?"

"No, it's not true. We know the guy is wounded, but the gendarmerie still haven't found him."

"Then we need to know where she is. Why don't you call her?"

At that moment, Verónica walked through the door. Federico felt disappointed: if she hadn't appeared, he would have gone to his room to look at the photos. Now he felt obliged to hand over the USB stick straightaway. They went to sit at one of the tables in the dining room.

"The DA gave me this for you. It's the photos Petra had in her camera. You're in some of them."

"Have you seen them?"

"What? Obviously not. They're yours. The DA told me what's in them. Only he and the judge saw them. Is there likely to be any image that could implicate you in the investigation?"

"Fede, everything implicates me. I brought them here, I took them to a party, and I went off while they were slaughtered. If that's not being implicated, I assure you no photo can make things worse for me. They're just vacation snaps. Petra was going to send them to me by email."

"I wanted you to know there's no news of Peratta."

"Meaning?"

"He could have died in the hills, he could be hiding somewhere. In any case, I don't think he stands much chance of getting to you."

Verónica asked him about the Bibi case. Federico had arranged to go to the courts in San Miguel de Tucumán the next day. He said that he still had no information but that he would get hold of some very soon. Then he told her:

"They're going to arrest a suspect today."

"Yes, I know. I ran into a journalist friend who's going to be there when they arrest him. I'm going with her."

"Your father wants you back in Buenos Aires tonight."

"The last time my dad said something like that was when I was sixteen years old and going to a party and he told me not to come home late. Guess how much attention I paid him then."

"If you stay, I stay."

"Tomorrow I'm going to San Miguel de Tucumán. I may need to stay a couple of days there."

"I should go too. To the courts, about the Bibi case."

"Then let's go together."

"Your boyfriend will get jealous."

Verónica didn't answer him.

Federico wrote an email to Doctor Rosenthal's secretary. He said that he feared the case was going to become more complicated in the next few days. Verónica had got hold of some good information in this regard. And since she was staying to investigate, he would rather accompany her, in case of any complications.

He didn't exactly tell the truth in the email, but then he was a lawyer. Truth was not a quality held in high regard by his profession.

III

Verónica locked herself in her room and the first thing she did was connect the memory stick to her laptop. She felt her heart speeding up. There were forty-two saved images. The district attorney had made her a copy of all the photos in the camera. There was Frida and Petra's entire journey, from the moment they had met in the city of San Miguel de Tucumán to their last days in Yacanto del Valle. First she glanced through them quickly. She found the ones in which she appeared, in scenes that were painfully familiar. There were also some photos Petra (or had it been Frida?) had taken of her without her realizing: lying on the lounger sunbathing, sitting reading the Marta Lynch novel on the veranda, preparing something in the kitchen. There was a photo, undoubtedly taken by Petra, in which Frida and she were returning from the swimming pool. The image captured an exchange of glances between the two of them, both oblivious to Petra's lens. She zoomed in until her face and Frida's were in close-up. Placing her fingers on the screen, she caressed Frida's face, traced her cheeks, circled her eyes, delicately touched those lips she had kissed. She did to the image what her gaze had been doing to Frida on that brief walk through the garden.

Afterwards she went back and looked at every photo in detail. She tried to imagine in which circumstances they had been taken, hoping to reconstruct Petra and Frida's story before they had met her. They looked happy, carefree, beautiful. There were various images of Frida that Petra had taken without her realizing, just as she had done a few days later with Verónica. Only now did she appreciate the sensitivity with which Petra had observed them. Through her photos she discovered much more than Verónica – and certainly Frida – had intended to reveal. She also looked at the photos Frida had taken of Petra. In a couple of them the Italian was singing, guitar in hand. There were no photos of anyone else, apart from Verónica. She was the only person to have been incorporated into their story. The last picture was of the three of them sitting in the bar in Yacanto del Valle.

She had been looking at the images on Explorer and only now did she see that there was a video that had surely been recorded with the same camera. Frida appeared holding the camera and focussing it on herself. She said: "I'm sorry, little one, you're too much of a boy for a woman like Petra. But you know what, kid? Your Italian granny has written this song for you."

Then the camera swivelled round to show Petra with her guitar who, starting with her habitual *eh*, began to sing: "*E dimmi quanti anni quanti anni ho / tu dimmi quanti anni quanti anni ho / ho molti anni molti anni più di te / ma quanti anni, quali anni non lo so/ caro bambino, imparerai, / il tempo vola e va, / non te ne accorgi, ma no, lui non ritornerà.*"

At that point Petra stopped singing. "There's been an accident," Frida was saying. They both burst out laughing. The video ended there, with their laughter.

It had got late. She wanted to talk to Chief Superintendent Suárez. Verónica went to the police station, but he wasn't there and they couldn't tell her how to reach him. She returned to the hotel, where her friend María was coming to meet her in a few minutes.

Luca was smoking in the door of the hotel and, accepting his offer of a cigarette, she stood beside him.

"Did you two know anything about the murder of a girl six years ago, here in Yacanto?"

"That was a year before we moved here. I think I heard something about it, but I can't remember anything in particular."

"Do you know El Gringo Aráoz?"

"Impossible not to know him if you live round here. The guy was completely out of control. Tearing up and down the streets in his car like an idiot, getting wasted, getting into fights. He caused all kinds of mayhem, but since his family owns half the region he could misbehave with complete impunity. Notice I said half the region – not half Yacanto, but much more than that. Fields of soya, citrus fruits: the Aráoz family has everything. That's what Argentinian landowners are like: untouchable bastards."

"You said he *was* out of control. Did he change?"

"Oh yes. When he got married he turned into a respectable gentleman. He drives around in his 4 × 4 with his wife and baby. The wife's from a traditional Tucumán family, with links to the media."

"Apparently this guy might have had something to do with the murder of that girl."

"I don't think El Gringo would have deprived himself of any crime in his youth. Anything is possible."

A car and an outside broadcast van came down the road. María was sitting in the back seat of the car and motioned to Verónica to get in beside her. In the front, next to the driver, was a producer from the channel for which María worked.

"Do we know who they're going to arrest?" asked Verónica.

"They've just confirmed it. We're going to Los Cercos. There's a *terreiro* there. Do you know what that is?"

"A kind of temple, right?"

"It's where Umbanda is practised. They're going to arrest Pae Daniel. Decaux has already passed on all the details: Pae Daniel is a Brazilian priest who's been living in Los Cercos for ten years. According to Decaux, the *pae* and his followers carry out black magic ceremonies. Ritual orgies. He and some of his followers – who haven't yet been identified – kidnapped the girls and subjected them to an Umbanda rite."

"I happened to write a piece on some *umbandistas* in Mar del Plata a few years ago and, while I wouldn't say they were all angels, accusing them of carrying out black masses seems like quite a leap."

"There are Catholics who do good works and others who carried out the Inquisition, so I think you have to allow that the gods of Orixás preside over all kinds of behaviour."

They pulled up behind some patrol cars outside the police station. The producer got out, went into the building and returned two minutes later.

"We're leaving right now," he said as he got back into the front seat.

Moments later a number of police officers appeared and climbed into three patrol cars. Chief Superintendent Suárez and DA Decaux travelled in one of them. The police vehicles drove off, the television crews following them.

"Are you going to broadcast the arrest live?" Verónica asked.

"We'd like to," the producer said, "but the DA has asked for discretion. I think he's worried in case something goes wrong. So we'll film the arrest and then get the broadcast truck ready to go out live from there over the next four hours."

"Or more," said María.

"Or more," repeated the producer with resignation.

"It depends on our ratings," María explained. "And I really hope they're good, otherwise next time they'll be sending me to check the price of lettuces in the Mercado de Abasto."

Pae Daniel's *terreiro* was on the edge of town, surrounded by houses, rather than in the country, as Verónica had imagined.

The police got out of their vehicles and so did the cameraman, the sound engineer, gaffer, the producer and María. They were ready in eight seconds, like a Formula One team changing tyres. The police advanced on the order of Chief Superintendent Suárez, the cameraman bringing up the rear. Further behind came María, then other members of the production team, the district attorney and another court official. Verónica went with them. Decaux was surprised to see her there.

There was just a few minutes' wait. Verónica felt strange. She was about to see the face of the man who might be responsible for the deaths of Frida and Petra. Yet something told her this impressive display of force was more for show than anything else.

If the television producer was hoping for a shoot-out, injuries, or at least some shouting and screaming, he must have felt very frustrated. The police emerged almost immediately from the house, with Pae Daniel in handcuffs. He was a man of about fifty, dark-skinned and stocky, verging on fat. A mixed-race Brazilian from Bahía, transplanted to Tucumán. That did seem strange. Verónica was as certain the man was a fall guy as she was that El Gringo Aráoz was somehow involved in the crime. Or was there some connection between Pae Daniel and El Gringo Aráoz? Either of them could have been responsible for the girls' deaths. No: Verónica couldn't be sure of anything.

After the arrested man had been bundled into a patrol car, the camera turned to María, who started to reprise what she had already told Verónica. Her ability to speak without hesitating or getting muddled was incredible. Verónica could never have done it. After wrapping the segment, they started getting the truck ready to broadcast live. The producer was trying to find some member of the priest's family to interview. The neighbours turned up and surrounded the truck, waving to the camera even though it wasn't rolling. Verónica's mobile rang. It was Mariano.

"Frida's parents are here."

When Verónica said nothing, he added:

"They wanted to stay in the hotel where their daughter had been. Tomorrow they're meeting the judge."

"I'm on my way."

"Where are you?"

"I accompanied a police operation in Los Cercos. At the home of an Umbanda priest."

"Pae Daniel?"

"Yes."

"I know him. Once we went there for a *jogo de búzios* ritual. It's when the priest reads the future by casting cowrie shells. Did you drive?"

"Actually, I was driven. Now I have to work out how to get back, because everyone here is busy."

"I'll come and get you."

IV

They were sitting in the armchairs in the lobby, coffee cups in front of them. Luca was with them and speaking in English. Verónica went up to them and introduced herself with a kiss. Mariano stayed a few steps behind.

The father, Karl, was tall and blonde with a prominent bald patch. The mother was called Herbjørg and physically very different from her daughter: small, with silvery hair and very pale skin that was almost translucent. And yet her blue eyes and her gaze were Frida's. The father's physical similarity was less disconcerting than seeing the daughter's gestures in her mother. They didn't know who Verónica was, nor that she had shared the last part of Frida's journey with her, as she explained now in English, a language they understood perfectly. They did, however, know Petra. They spoke quietly and seemed calm, but every so often the father took out a cotton handkerchief and wiped his eyes. The mother sat very upright and tried to smile whenever Luca refilled her water glass. They asked Verónica how they had met, what Frida had talked to her about, if she had seemed to be enjoying herself. Verónica tried to answer their questions, but she found it very hard. Not because it required talking about Frida, but because it also meant talking about herself, her feelings and her pain. And she didn't want Frida's parents to feel compassion for her, especially not when they were managing their own grief with such dignity.

"Frida was always very special," Karl said. "As a teenager she worked with an NGO that supported Bosnian immigrants. Later she helped build schools in Senegal. At some point she discovered Latin America and fell in love with Buenos Aires. We were happy she was coming to Argentina. We thought it would be safer than Honduras or Angola."

"In reality," added Herbjørg, "we were always a little anxious when she was away from home."

Frida's parents wanted to know if anyone had been in touch with Petra's family. Verónica told them what she knew: that Petra had no family, apart from an Argentinian ex-boyfriend the embassy had not yet managed to locate. Karl and Herbjørg were going to meet the judge, with a view to taking Frida's body back to Oslo.

V

Next morning, Verónica called Judge Amalfi. She had spent the whole night thinking of Petra, about how alone she was, even in death. She asked the judge what was going to happen with Petra's body. Amalfi told her that an official from the Italian embassy was on his way to Tucumán to handle the matter. In any case, both Frida's parents and the embassy were going to have to wait two more days before they could take possession of the bodies, since a few more tests needed to be done. The judge reminded her that there were also Petra's belongings to be dealt with.

"Doctor, forgive the indiscretion, but are you going to charge Pae Daniel?"

"In a few hours I'm going to take his statement, and then I'll decide what comes next. What's clear is that he can't have been alone in this. So far we have all the elements of an Umbanda rite, and these are being deciphered by a specialist. DA Decaux has requested his prosecution. Once I have the expert opinion, certain details I've requested from the medical forensic team and a statement from the accused, I'll have a clearer picture."

Later, Verónica went to the police station. This time she found Suárez in his office. He beckoned her in.

"Are you happy we've found the man responsible for the crimes?"

"Do you really believe he's responsible?"

"The DA seems very sure. I don't know if you saw him on all the news programmes last night."

"I didn't watch television. And you – what do you think?"

"The investigation is just beginning."

"Do you remember the Bibiana Ponce case?"

"The name rings a bell, but I don't remember the case."

"She was a girl from Yacanto who was raped and murdered six years ago."

"I've only been at this police station for two. I got sent here as a punishment for not doing as I was told in Tacitas."

"What did they want you to do?"

"Not to arrest the son of a judge, who should have been tried for drug trafficking. I'm always coming up against the child of some lawyer, as you see. Refresh my memory: what happened in the other case?"

"Bibiana Ponce turned up dead at the side of a country road. She had been raped and violently murdered. Nobody has gone to jail for the crime. But everyone knows who did it: Guillermo Aráoz, El Gringo."

"Ah yes, I know the one."

"El Gringo Aráoz was at the party I went to with Frida and Petra. Perhaps he had something to do with this."

Verónica left the police station with the feeling Suárez didn't altogether trust her theories. When it came down to it, he would very likely take some satisfaction from believing someone like her might be guilty. She didn't mind him thinking that, so long as he took seriously any information she gave him.

She returned to the hotel, where she had arranged to meet Federico so they could travel together to San Miguel de Tucumán. Federico was going to look into the Ponce case and she wanted to make a survey of similar crimes committed in the region. To do that, she would need to consult the archive of some provincial newspaper. Neither Yacanto de Valle nor the other cities nearby had their own newspaper, just local FM radio stations. The provincial newspapers only had digital versions of the last few years and so she was going to have to do what she most hated: trawl through the paper archives. She called Patricia Beltrán, hoping her editor could put her in touch with some Tucumanian newspaper that would let her visit their archive.

"Does this mean you're going to write something on the tourists story? Weren't you supposed to be on vacation? Shouldn't you be in Jujuy or some other godforsaken backwater?"

"I probably will write something. But since I'm on vacation, I'm not promising you anything. And Jujuy isn't godforsaken."

"Any place that doesn't have a subway is godforsaken, my dear."

"Could you arrange for me to go to some Tucumanian newsroom with good archives?"

"Tucumán ... let me think. Would you want to see the whole paper, or just crime stories?"

"I'm looking for crimes similar to the ones committed in Yacanto del Valle."

"Then I've got something better. Juan Robson, an old crime correspondent, retired now. They call him El Inglés, the Englishman."

"So I have to trust his memory?"

"Don't be cheeky. El Inglés Robson was – and surely still is – obsessed with crime news. You can trust his memory, and his archive even more so. The guy used to cut out any crime story and keep it, just in case. He retired ten years ago. He worked in Buenos Aires for a time. About a year ago I ran into him at a celebration that had been arranged for a colleague. I have his phone number. I'll call him and let you know if you can visit."

Ten minutes later a text arrived from her editor: *Will be delighted to help you. He has the archive. Call him...* And Patricia attached Juan Robson's phone number. Verónica called him immediately. Robson wasn't all that friendly on the phone, but he did say she could drop by that afternoon.

While waiting to leave for the Tucumanian capital with Federico, she chatted to Mariano. She told him about Petra. Verónica was going to speak to someone from the Italian embassy to see if they would authorize her to take charge of the funeral and Petra's belongings. She thought Petra should be taken back to Córdoba, where she had been happy.

"Leaving aside the complications of moving a body," said Mariano, "and the difficulty of finding a cemetery in Córdoba, I think it would be better to have the funeral here. The Partido cemetery is nearby, on the outskirts of Yacanto."

Not long afterwards Federico and she left Yacanto del Valle.

"I have to meet up with a colleague who's going to give me a copy of the case file. Have you thought where we might stay?"

"At my cousin Severo's house. I still have the key. Any news of Peratta?"

"Nada. But I'm sure he's very far away from your cousin's house."

VI

He couldn't remember anything after Five arrived to get him out of there, just one long dream about his childhood in Quilmes. In it, he saw a coastline he identified as Ensenada. His brothers and sisters were there, all of them very small, and his parents, who were young, but he was an adult and was wounded, as though he had travelled through time from

Tucumán to the Quilmes of thirty years ago. At some points in the dream he stood alone contemplating the immensity of the River Plate. At others, he followed his siblings when they wandered off from their parents. He was worried they would get lost, that they would drown. His siblings took off their clothes and went into the river. He couldn't follow them because he didn't know how to swim; he had never learned. But before the dream could become a nightmare, his siblings emerged from the river, accompanied by his parents. He couldn't understand why they were all naked. It embarrassed him. Was his sister looking lasciviously at him?

He woke up somewhere that looked like a hospital room: iron bed, oxygen tube, a machine to check vital signs, an IV stand. He was on his own. Bright white lights heightened the sensation of being in hospital. Was he actually in one then? Had he been arrested? Where was Five? A man appeared, about sixty, almost bald, well dressed.

"How do you feel?" he asked.

The only answer that came to mind was *weak*, but he didn't say it. He made a gesture of resignation.

"You've lost a lot of blood, but that's all. The bullet didn't hit any vital organs. It could have been much worse."

Three closed his eyes. He didn't feel like talking to the doctor, if that was in fact what this man was. When he opened them again, Five was standing there, watching him.

"You were asleep." The other man settled into a chair.

"Where am I?" Three asked and tried to sit up, but found he couldn't.

"In a safe place, with a doctor and even a nurse. An old one, but you can't have everything."

"Where?"

"In San Miguel de Tucumán."

"When do we have to do the job?"

"Relax. Sometime soon. Doctor Zero doesn't want any mistakes. The longer we wait to do it, the longer we wait to get paid. Same goes for him."

"Who contracted us?"

"You know very well we never get told that."

"I'm curious to know who wants the same thing I want."

"That's what I don't understand: why Doctor Zero wants you to do it. Work and pleasure should never be mixed."

"Doctor Zero knows I'm effective."

Five stood up. He wore a certain derisive smile that annoyed Three, as if Five were a master from whom he had to learn.

"I'll come and get you tomorrow morning. I reckon we're going to have to do the job in Yacanto del Valle, or perhaps here. There's your bag with your things. There's a new set of clothes, too."

He didn't say goodbye when he went, just left. Moments later the nurse appeared, an old woman with indigenous features and a surly expression. She was carrying a tray with food that looked like the kind you get in hospital. She helped him stand up to go to the bathroom. Back in the room, Peratta looked through his bag. There was his gun. There, too, was the thong. He touched it lightly, a gentle caress.

10 *The Robson Archives*

I

"You're a literary character, aren't you?" Juan Robson asked as he welcomed Verónica to his apartment in the centre of San Miguel de Tucumán. Everything was tidy and polished. It didn't look like a man's home: the walls were covered with little paintings, the coffee table laden with ornaments.

"A character? I don't think so… As far as I know, I'm made of flesh and blood."

"You mean nobody's ever told you?" said Robson, addressing her in the formal third person.

"No, nobody. Please let's not be formal, you can use *vos*."

"Baron Rosenthal! The unforgettable villain in Salgari's *The Tigers of Mompracem.* He was Sandokan's enemy. Both of them were in love with Mariana, the Pearl of Labuan. But nobody reads Salgari any more."

"Well actually I did once meet someone who'd read a lot of Salgari, but he never told me about the coincidence of my name and that character's. Perhaps he'd forgotten it."

They sat in the armchairs and chatted for a while: Verónica about what she was investigating, and Robson about how he had assembled his archive.

"I started out in journalism at the end of the 1950s. I've been cutting out and saving crime stories ever since. In the 1980s a newspaper offered to buy the whole archive, but I didn't want to sell. This is my life. Everything is easier now with the digital revolution, but in my day owning the information meant having an advantage."

"Newspapers have their own archives."

"Yes, of course. But they don't always work very well. Anyway, one moves workplace and it's better to have all the information to hand, no? Equally, when a colleague needs something, my doors are open."

"Did you retire a long time ago?"

"Seven years ago, when my wife fell ill. I decided to leave journalism and take care of her. Later, when she died, I no longer felt like going back to writing."

Robson led her to another room, where the walls were covered from ceiling to floor with shelves. There was a table in the middle and a ladder which made it possible to reach the highest shelves. On one side was a wider shelf, bearing a photocopier.

"Someone I worked with gave it to me more than ten years ago. And it's very useful, as you'll soon see. The cases are organized by year. If a crime was committed in 1975 and the trial didn't take place until 1980, you have to go back to the start – 1975. Murders, robbery, fraud: there's every kind of crime in these fifteen thousand envelopes. You don't need to open them to know what's inside. Each one is labelled. So you need to look for 'rape' and 'death'. But once you find it, you'll have to look at the cutting inside to see if it refers to Yacanto del Valle or another part of the country."

"I've got my work cut out."

"I'll help you. I don't have anything better to do."

The first thing Verónica did was search for the case of Bibiana Ponce. She made a note of a few points that interested her, although much of the information was repeated from one article to the next. Only one mentioned Aráoz as a suspect.

Then she began a more systematic search, from the most recently published articles back to the year 2000. After a whole afternoon of this, she had thirty-two rapes followed by femicides. In the environs of Yacanto there had been two: Bibiana Ponce and a girl from Santiago del Estero found on a construction site. According to the news cutting, the men responsible had been two builders who were quickly arrested.

"How curious," said Robson, who had started the other way round: with the earliest cases and going up to the present day. "I've found a case similar to the one you're investigating: in 1962 two young Austrian nurses who had come to do social work with indigenous communities in Quilmes were found dead at the side of Route 307. They hadn't intended to be in Yacanto del Valle – their car had broken down and they were planning to continue their journey the next day. They were raped and murdered. The perpetrators were never identified."

Robson handled the paper cuttings with the delicacy and precision of someone who had spent a lot of time ordering them.

"It says something else: the person who wrote the article – which has no byline – recommends that women not travel alone on country roads. That this could, and I quote, 'awaken the base instincts of confused men'."

"Confused?"

"In another case I've found, from 1965, concerning a girl who was raped and stabbed to death, the writer wonders if this might not be a classic case of *crime passionnel.* I'll read you the end: 'What must the girl have done to provoke such fury and savagery in a man?'"

"That's disgraceful. In the first case, is there any other useful information?"

"Nothing that seems relevant. I'll make a copy for you."

Robson photocopied the articles and made them both coffee. It was dark by the time Verónica called Federico. He was in a bar near Robson's home.

"What are you doing there? I mean, I gave you the key to my cousin's house and the GPS coordinates."

"I get bored on my own in a weekend house. After I dropped you at the journalist's place I met a guy who works in the courts and photocopied the Ponce case file for me. So I looked for a nice little bar and sat down to read it. The time flew by."

Federico came to collect her and they went for dinner. They picked a pizzeria with pretensions of something better – a lot of plants, a lot of light and food that tasted of nothing. They arrived at Severo's house a little after ten o'clock. Only then did Verónica realize there were too many memories there. They should have gone to a hotel. She poured herself a triple measure of Johnnie Walker and hid herself away in the room she had used on the previous visit. After drinking the whisky she spent much of the night staring at the ceiling, fighting her insomnia and the itchiness that persisted in her legs and arms.

II

She got up before Federico. On the coffee table were two enormous folders of photocopies, a block of notepaper and a glass of wine. Federico must have stayed up reading.

Just as she was making coffee, he appeared, greeting her with a kiss on the cheek. He was fresh from the shower and smelled of shampoo and aftershave.

"I see you got stuck into the Bibiana Ponce case," Verónica said, handing him a cup of coffee. Federico went to the fridge and took out some cheese.

"Yes, I read the whole dossier. Fortunately – or unfortunately, depending on how you look at it – it wasn't very long."

"Two whole folders' worth?"

"Four hundred sheets aren't much, bearing in mind that the case was six years ago, that nobody has yet been charged and that half of Yacanto del Valle gave evidence."

"Draw any conclusions?"

"I've got bad news for you: nobody names El Gringo Aráoz. And obviously he doesn't appear giving evidence. Are you sure the sister wasn't mistaken?"

"She was very clear, quite emphatic. And, going on what Mariano told me, this guy has a history of violence and taking things too far."

"Well, society itself allows the children of the elite to go wild as long as they don't kill anyone. It's a tacit agreement. Drive fast, get drunk, get together with your buddies to beat the shit out of some poor unsuspecting person, grope a girl. No member of the privileged classes is going to do time for something like that. They only draw a line at premeditated murder. If you knock down five children because you're drunk and high on drugs, you're forgiven. If you deliberately kill someone, justice stirs."

"Not always."

"Of course, because then all kinds of other variables come into play: power, corruption, the ability of a good lawyer to extricate you from your predicament. But the system is predicated on your not killing. If Aráoz committed a homicide and you pushed hard enough, he could go to prison."

"Thanks for your optimism."

"I'm beginning to doubt that the guy could be guilty of killing the Ponce girl. Is it just me, or is this breakfast the closest you and I have come to married life?"

"Given that we don't have sex ... yes, it's the closest."

"In spite of everything, there are a couple of interesting witness statements in the dossier which, either through neglect or intention, nobody considered worthy of further investigation."

"And there's the lawyer the grandmother hired. What about him?"

"Waste of space. He must have scraped through his law exams. I called him yesterday because he doesn't live in Yacanto del Valle any more. I asked him about Aráoz – he didn't know him. According to him, they put together a great case."

"Just with no convictions."

"Let me talk you through the stuff I found. A friend of Bibiana, Roxana Lombardo, testifies that she used to go out dancing with the victim. That the previous week they had been invited to a party and that she, Roxana, had persuaded Bibiana not to go. The reason? Because you shouldn't get together with people who don't even say hello if you see them in the street afterwards. Who doesn't say hello?"

"Rich kids to poor kids, married men to single girls."

"The Saturday they kill Bibiana, Roxana meets her early and they can't decide where to go, so they split up. Roxana goes to a dance in Coronel Berti, and she doesn't know where Bibiana went."

"To a party like the one Nicolás had. But that party wasn't exactly an orgy. There were guys ranging from twenty-something to forty-something and girls who looked pretty young. I must have been the oldest. But the same applies to a lot of places where women don't get killed or murdered."

After breakfast they headed towards the centre of town. Federico planned to go to the courts. He wanted to see if there were any outstanding criminal charges against Aráoz, and also wanted to meet Severo Rosenthal on business connected to Rosenthal and Associates. Verónica was going to continue combing the archive at Juan Robson's apartment.

On the way, they bought the most recent edition of *Nuestro Tiempo*, with the tourist murders on the cover. Verónica quickly flicked through it to check they hadn't published photos of the corpses, and thankfully Patricia had kept her word. The central piece, by Álex Vilna, was flanked by two columns – by a psychologist and a criminologist – and an interview with a forensic scientist based in Buenos Aires who answered some technical questions.

She read the main piece. Vilna was taking at face value the theory of a double crime committed in the context of a black magic ritual. The girls had been selected at random, kidnapped and taken to an unknown place to be abused and murdered. The magazine had gone to press before Vilna had a chance to include confirmation of Pae Daniel's arrest; it didn't even give his name, although it did mention a Brazilian "Umbanda chief" who lived in the area being accused of the crime. It seemed that the district attorney or someone from his office had passed him information, albeit partial. TV channel beats weekly magazine, thought Verónica. It wasn't the first time something like this had happened. The article wasn't bad, it just didn't contribute anything new, and certainly nothing different to the story currently being told on television. She was also struck that the article described the murders as "femicides". That wasn't Vilna. She detected Patricia's hand in that.

Glancing through the rest of the magazine, she saw there was another article by Vilna, a double-page spread from San Miguel de Tucumán. A "narco police" case. Álex must have had to work harder this week than in the rest of the year put together, Verónica said to herself.

III

Robson was waiting for her with maté. Verónica hadn't drunk it for a long time. She hated the ritual – the gourd passed around the partakers and refilled with hot water each time – so in the office she only occasionally joined in.

"Do you like it bitter?"

"However it comes is fine by me."

Robson had worked late into the night and managed to reach the beginning of the 1980s. In those twenty years he had found seven cases in the area around Yacanto del Valle. As well as the Austrian nurses, there was a twenty-four-year-old woman, a teacher in a rural school who had been found raped, strangled and partially scalped in 1968. In 1971, the body of a thirty-one-year-old woman, married with two children, was discovered on waste ground; she had also been raped and strangled, her face disfigured. In 1973 a woman's body, burned and with evidence of sexual assault, was found in a ditch. Confirming her identity had proved impossible. The case that had got the most attention was that of a fifteen-year-old girl who went missing on an outing in 1975. She was raped and found dead in a gully. She seemed to have fallen in and hit her head while trying to escape. In 1977 a body was found lying behind a church. It belonged to a woman aged twenty. She had been burned with cigarettes, one eye gouged out, her jaw smashed. As she was said to be a guerrilla in the ERP, the People's Republican Army, this was described as an "act of war" (on whose part? Against whom?) and the news quickly disappeared from the media.

"The cases from 1968, 1971 and 1975 were solved. Nothing links the people responsible for those three crimes: they're from different social, cultural and age groups. Given how many years have passed, one imagines that the guilty parties have already been freed or died. If they are free, they may have reoffended."

"I've noted down six cases, and you said there were seven."

"I was keeping this one until last. It's the most interesting of all. Claudia Rinaldi, a girl of twenty-one, raped and killed with a lethal dose of cocaine in 1982. She turns up at the side of a country road. News reports from that time talk about an orgy. Argentines are still living in a dictatorship at this point and in the framework of a Catholic society that puts the blame on women. So everyone wanted to think of this woman as a prostitute. Never mind that the autopsy said she had been raped. Nobody was found guilty. One article talks about a rich kids' party. Two days later, an editorial in the same newspaper points the finger at fantasists who invent stories and see conspiracies, besmirching a generation of wholesome and patriotic youths."

"Using patriotism as a defence already sounds nasty."

"It's the language of the time. As I said, nobody went on trial. Now, skip to 1984: a Tucumanian human rights association tries to bring a case against some members of the military involved in the kidnap and disappearance of eight workers from a factory on the outskirts of San Miguel de Tucumán. There's evidence from a political prisoner stating that one of those soldiers had been torturing and raping female detainees since the time of Operation Independencia. The witness adds that the same soldier raped and murdered a young woman in 1982, and that politics and ideology played no part whatsoever in that incident. That's the girl whose body turned up on the outskirts of Yacanto del Valle. The girl the press pretended was a hooker, thus justifying their indifference towards the crime. The man accused of those crimes was Guillermo Aráoz."

"Impossible. Aráoz must be in his early thirties."

"His father. He had the rank of captain in the army."

Robson passed the cuttings over to Verónica, who studied them with amazement. There was the article from 1984 that linked Aráoz's father with the murdered girl.

"There are no other articles about this case?"

"Aráoz is still being tried. The disappearance of the factory workers is part of a 'mega case' and no sentences have been handed down. But the girl's murder wasn't an act carried out as part of the repression of the dictatorship. Therefore, it is not considered a crime against humanity. In other words: it expired."

"So he could still be sentenced for the other deaths, but not for the femicide."

"Exactly."

IV

That day, Verónica found four more incidents that had taken place in the last fifteen years. In most of the cases she and Robson separated out, the essential elements were the same: young women between fifteen and thirty-four whose bodies were left exposed to the elements – on the side of the road, on wasteland, in the undergrowth. Sexual assault was always the motive and the murders appeared to be *criminis causae*, murders committed to conceal the rape. There was definitely some improvement in the attitude of the press – and perhaps of the courts – in their treatment of these crimes. Coverage of the earlier cases included some tutting about the temerity of these young women in walking on their own or stirring the base instincts of men. More recent articles mentioned male aggression, although the word *femicide* was not yet used. In every case where the murderers had been found, the culprits were men.

But there was something else that linked these cases which Verónica couldn't quite put her finger on. Reading over them all again she still couldn't find the common denominator. Apart from the coincidence of the Aráozes, father and son. She could hear Patricia Beltrán's voice saying *You'll know it when you see it.* And that's how she felt: that something obvious was right in front of her and she couldn't see it.

She spent the whole day with Robson. When Federico came to get her in the evening, Robson invited him in. Federico told them that Aráoz was not the subject of any criminal proceedings, but he was facing a commercial suit: the fraudulent bankruptcy of a company exporting citrus fruits.

"You have to be pretty inept to sink an export company like that," Robson observed.

"From what I could find out, he carried on trading but put everything in his wife's name. So … nothing that the average Argentine with a bit of money doesn't get up to."

Just then Federico's phone rang. Somebody was calling from the law courts to let him know Pae Daniel had been released on the grounds of lack of evidence.

"Pae Daniel suffers from severe lumbago. Luckily for him, on the night of the party he had to be taken urgently to hospital. What with all the waiting and his ongoing pain, he ended up spending the whole night in the emergency room. He didn't go home until five o'clock in the morning. As you can imagine, there are lots of witnesses for all this. And there's something else: according to the autopsy report, the marks on the girls' bodies – which are part of a purification ritual in Umbanda – were made after their deaths."

It made no sense that the DA didn't know this about the marks, except in the context of a long-held antipathy between him and the judge, something Federico had learned about in the corridors of the Tucumán courts. Somebody had planted this false evidence to divert attention from the real culprits. What Federico couldn't yet understand was why the people responsible had made the marks after the girls' deaths and not before.

"Unless it wasn't the murderers but someone else who had an interest in muddying the waters. Or who wanted to pin the crime on Pae Daniel."

V

Once they were back at the house in Cerro San Javier, Verónica called Chief Superintendent Suárez. She wanted to know if he had been able to interview Guillermo Aráoz.

"Señorita, I'm a bit too old to be treated like a nincompoop."

It wasn't the answer Verónica had expected.

"I don't understand —"

"Look, I've already said it would be helpful if you explained things better. And now you're telling me that someone at the party was responsible for a similar crime committed a few years ago."

"That's exactly it. Guillermo Aráoz is suspected of having committed the rape and murder of Bibiana Ponce six years ago."

"And he was at the party."

"Yes."

"You saw him there?"

"No, I don't know him personally."

"But you were at the party."

"I wasn't introduced to every single person there and I didn't see Aráoz. But reliable sources have told me he was there."

"He has a very strong alibi that refutes your assertion."

"Alibis can be arranged, Chief Superintendent."

"Don't tell me how to do my job. Aráoz went on vacation to Europe with his wife and child a month ago. Unless he slipped back into the country without passing through Immigration, I think he has a very good alibi."

Verónica was totally confused. She called Ramiro but his phone was either switched off or out of range. Several times she dialled the number again without reaching him. When she tried the gallery, the call went straight to voicemail. Verónica left him a message anyway, asking him to call her. Meanwhile, Federico was taking care of dinner: spaghetti with tomato and basil sauce. He had opened a bottle of wine and was stirring the pan where the sauce was cooking.

"Your cousin even has chopped onion in his freezer," he said when he saw her come in. He poured a glass of wine, passed it to her and resumed his stirring.

"I didn't know you could cook."

"Only someone like you could think that making this sauce and boiling some spaghetti constitutes cooking. Have you spoken to the chief superintendent?"

"Aráoz is in Europe and Suárez thinks I'm full of shit."

They ate at the kitchen table. When they had finished, Federico poured himself another glass of wine and walked out onto the veranda. Verónica tried Ramiro again, but the phone was still switched off. She washed the plates and tidied the kitchen before ringing him again. This time Ramiro picked up.

"You told me El Gringo Aráoz was at the party."

"I told you that he could have been there. I don't remember every guest."

"But you knew this was too important to say the first thing that popped into your head."

"Verónica, I told you what I thought. I didn't realize it was so important."

"Did you know El Gringo Aráoz's father is also suspected of having raped and killed a girl?"

"People say a lot of things. I think you're getting everything mixed up."

Verónica hung up. She didn't feel like speaking to him any longer. Ramiro called her back a couple of times, but she didn't answer.

Walking out onto the veranda, she didn't see Federico and turned round to go back inside. Then she heard steps behind her coming from the garden and spun round to see Federico appear, a glass of wine in hand.

"You bastard, you scared the life out of me."

"Didn't mean to."

"I thought I was about to get shot. Look, my hands are still shaking."

"Calm down and look at the sky. Tell me, which is your favourite moon?"

"Favourite? I don't know – none of them. Isn't there only one moon?"

"Phases of the moon. Mine is this one: the waxing crescent. Everyone loves a full moon, but I like the phase after the new moon when the curved sliver appears – the waxing crescent."

"Fede, you wouldn't be trying to seduce me by talking about the moon, would you? As a strategy, that's roughly two hundred years out of date."

"Did you know there's a moon called the black moon?"

"Forgive me for changing the subject. Why did Ramiro lie?"

"In what respect?"

"He obviously knew Aráoz wasn't at the party. They're friends, and he must have known Aráoz was on vacation in Europe. I appreciate he might not know if his friend had hopped over to Salta, but to Europe?"

"He might have lied to tell you what you wanted to hear."

"I'm not convinced."

"Maybe he lied because he wanted to send you in another direction. So you'd waste time and, bearing in mind what happened with the chief superintendent, so you'd lose credibility. Although he doesn't strike me as someone who's capable of planning anything much."

"I obviously can't trust him."

"You sure know how to pick 'em."

"Hey, Fede, there's something I didn't tell you."

"When someone like you says that to me, I get butterflies."

"Me too," said Verónica, and fell silent. A few seconds passed before Federico asked:

"Weren't you going to tell me something?"

"I had a thing with Frida."

"What do you mean, a thing?"

"I liked her, we liked each other. What can I say. You know I'm not all that good when it comes to matters of the heart. Frida was an amazing girl. You would have loved her."

"Aha."

"I don't know where things might have ended up if we'd had more time. All I know is what happened was like a lightning bolt."

"So you like girls now? What about Ramiro?"

"Falling in love with a man is complicated enough, so imagine the shock to my supposedly heterosexual heart. As for Ramiro … in another time and context – if I was already thirty-five and about to turn thirty-six, for example – perhaps we would have gone out for a time."

"I'm actually lost for words."

They stood for a while looking at the sky.

"There's something I haven't told you," Federico added.

"Go on then."

"I watch lawyer shows."

"You're a fool."

"It's relevant. There's a series from a few years back, *Ally McBeal*, about a thirty-something single lawyer. In one episode they're talking about a guy, and her friend tells her three questions you should ask yourself to work out if a man is the one for you: could you have children with him, can you imagine yourselves growing old together, and would you pluck a strawberry dipped in cream out of his navel with your mouth and eat it? Can you see yourself doing those three things with Ramiro?"

"You shouldn't watch so much TV. I'm going to sleep. We have to leave early for Yacanto del Valle tomorrow."

Before bed, she put on some mentholated talc she found in the bathroom cabinet. It wasn't a cure, but at least it soothed the itching a bit. She had a rash on her stomach and arms now, but it had gone down on her legs and luckily had not spread to other parts of her body.

VI

They were in the car, driving without talking. On the radio an FM station was playing eighties music. They were relaxed but alert, staying within the speed limit and respecting all the traffic regulations so as not to attract the attention of any passing police car. They had put the guns underneath the seats. Three had a false ID and a new mobile phone given to him by Five. Doctor Zero hated his men to mess up through foolishness or carelessness. While they were on the road, the phone rang. Only one person could be calling him.

"I hope you've learned your lesson."

"Yes, Doctor."

"Do you know Chipi Barijho?"

"Is he a soccer player?"

"He was. I think he's retired. When he was playing at Boca, the idiot used to sneak out of training camp to go and play soccer with his friends in the shanty town. And what happened? He went and injured himself, the prick. That's what happened to you. Don't bring your home life to work. Understand?"

"Yes, Doctor."

"Find the money and pay someone else to do the job for you, end of story."

"Whatever you say."

"You're lucky, because this job is to do exactly what you wanted."

"There won't be any mistakes this time."

"Let the pro beat the amateur."

"That's how it will be."

"It had better be. I didn't get you out of this fix so you can follow your dreams, but so you can work."

Five told him that this time they weren't going to stay in the area. They didn't know how hard the gendarmerie and federal penitential service were looking for them in Yacanto. It would be better to stay in Tafí del Valle, a larger town with a lot of tourism. Their presence there wouldn't attract any attention.

When they arrived at the hotel, Five left him in the room and went out. It was more than an hour before he returned. Now Three knew exactly what bothered him about Five: he acted as though he were the boss. True enough, Five had saved his life – but only on the orders of Doctor Zero. At no point had Doctor Zero said Five was in charge of this operation, and yet he acted as though he was the one taking all the decisions. Moreover, he had kept him away from the people doing intelligence. Three was going to let Five do things his way, but if he spoke again to Doctor Zero, he'd make his thoughts clear.

"I hope there's a nightclub in this shithole, because if not we're going to die of boredom."

"There are nightclubs everywhere."

Five beckoned him over to the table in the room. He had spread out a sheet of paper with hand-drawn plans.

"We're going to be here a few nights. We're going to do the job around daybreak, at the hotel where the chick's staying. We go into the room and shoot her in the head. Nothing else. No talking, no nothing. A clean, simple job. Get it?"

"Do you think I'm a moron?"

"Not at all, pal. But I don't want you suddenly thinking you're the hero, or the boyfriend. There's no talking, no contact with her. Is that clear?"

Three didn't answer but stared hard at the sheet of paper with the drawings on it.

"There are two ways to do it: taking out a bunch of people, or the bare minimum. Option two is always preferable."

Why was Five explaining all this to him? He didn't need a lecture on how to do his job. Nor to be told why he should do it in a particular way. Before Five continued with his beginners' course for hitmen, Three interrupted.

"Just tell me what you've got planned."

"The hotel has two entrances, one for guests and a gate at the back. The back entrance is locked with a key at night until six o'clock in the morning, which is when one of the kitchen staff comes in and the suppliers start to arrive: soda water man, the butcher, the grocer. They arrive, dump their stuff and go. As soon as the hotel employee is back in the kitchen, we have to go in and make our way over here, to the area where the bedrooms are. Our little bird flew away, but she's back in the hotel today and they gave her the same room she had before: number twenty-four. We shoot the lock off. Going in and out shouldn't take more than two minutes. From there we head to Salta. A van will be waiting there to take us back to Buenos Aires."

Not long to go now. Soon he would be face to face with the woman who had tried to kill him. He would do everything Five said. He wouldn't speak to her, wouldn't touch her, but he wanted to look her in the eye. He wanted her to know he was the one who was going to shoot her. He wanted Verónica Rosenthal to see him smiling before he squeezed the trigger.

11 *A Silent Funeral*

I

Federico and Verónica returned to Yacanto del Valle and found everything the same as two days ago: the television and radio mobile broadcast units were still in town, and there was still speculation about who had killed the tourists and how. Meanwhile, the police and DA seemed as lost as they had on the first day of the investigation.

Verónica was in her room writing up her investigations and the most recent developments. Had she been wrong about a possible link between El Gringo Aráoz and the new crimes? Pae Daniel had been released without charge, but somebody had planted the evidence of black magic. Could it have been someone known to the Brazilian? Another priest, another practitioner of Umbanda rites? One of his followers? What could the motive have been? Mechi's grandmother had known immediately that it was a fake macumba rite. She must speak to her again. Besides, she wanted to speak to Mechi about her sister. Verónica called her and they arranged to meet at quarter past six in Bar Amigo. The telephone in her room rang. It was Luca, to say Frida's parents were about to leave.

Verónica went down to the hotel lobby and found Herbjørg and Karl ready to depart. They stood holding their little suitcases, their shoulders hunched. They were also taking the rucksack Frida had used during her travels. Verónica walked over to them and bid each a tender farewell. They had taken possession of Frida's body, and that night a plane was leaving that would take them all home to Oslo.

"I never imagined I would be taking my daughter home like this," said Herbjørg, struggling to contain her grief. Her eyes filled with tears. Verónica embraced her and, feeling that contact with Frida's mother, began to weep herself. Herbjørg pulled away, looked at her and spoke with a mother's firmness:

"Go away from here, don't stay. This place is cursed."

Karl took out his business card and gave it to Verónica.

"We'd like you to come and visit us."

Moments later they were gone, and Luca brought her something that tasted like ginger tea. Verónica didn't like teas, especially not the exotic kind, but she took it from him without demur. At no point had she felt she ought to return Frida's MP3 player. She considered it hers, as if her friend had left it to remain present in her life.

She called María and suggested they have lunch together, since her friend had no live broadcasts at that time of day. They went to the Italian restaurant and found various journalists from Buenos Aires already there. They said hello, chatted about the case. They discussed the release of Pae Daniel and everyone expressed disappointment that the Brazilian had refused to speak to the press. Some of them had offered him good money to do so and he had angrily rejected it. While they discussed the crime, Verónica kept up a professional front. Nobody seemed to suspect she had known the victims.

"In cases like this," María said while surveying the menu, "I always ask myself what was in the mind of the killer."

"Rape, murder."

"It's the torture part I don't get. Because you can kill, rape or abuse someone while in a state of hatred, arousal, perversion, whatever. But the time between the beginning of the rape and the moment when the girls were finished off must have been between twenty and forty minutes. Time for the guy to regret his decision or try to hasten the ending or change his mind. But he doesn't do that, he keeps to the plan. There's no sign of arousal, or violent emotion, or the murder being intended to cover another crime."

"What is there, then?"

"Evil. Evil exists."

"Evil is causing torment. Torture is evil in its purest form."

"To torture someone is to think the crime through. A murder or a rape can be unmeditated crimes. Impulsive. Let me be clear – I don't mean in legal terms, because I don't consider that an extenuating factor. But when you see the degree of violence visited on these girls, you realize some thought went into their deaths."

The waiter came to take their order, but María's eyes were fixed on Verónica. When the waiter had moved away, María asked her:

"Did you know those girls?"

Verónica took a few seconds to answer.

"Yes."

"I won't ask you anything about it. But I want you to know that, when you say their names, something in you seems to break. Bear it in mind."

Verónica smiled and drank some water.

"Thanks," she said, and María changed the subject. They didn't discuss the murders again during the rest of the meal.

II

A town is like a cage. At least that was how Verónica saw Yacanto del Valle. She felt stuck in a back and forth between the hotel and the square, between the square and the police station, or between the hotel and Ramiro's gallery. She couldn't imagine living in an environment where everyone seemed like a character in a play repeated until the end of days. She felt out of place. Luca and Mariano, on the other hand, seemed very comfortable in that world. When she arrived at the hotel, Mariano was waiting for her with news.

"The attaché from the Italian embassy is in Coronel Berti. I took the liberty of talking to him and explaining your intention to take charge of Petra's funeral. He seemed pleased. Apparently it's very expensive to send a body from here to Italy. He's waiting for us in Coronel Berti with some papers for you to sign, and you can collect Petra's belongings at the same time."

They went together. On the way there Verónica realized she hadn't driven for days. If it wasn't Federico driving her, it was Mariano or Luca. She didn't mind the company. On the contrary; she felt as though she wasn't really up to doing anything much, even driving a car. It was soothing to travel as a passenger and take in the views on either side of the road.

"One day we're going to get drunk together and I'm going to tell you a lot of things about myself," Mariano told her.

"Such as?"

"That you remind me of my sister."

"Your sister."

"She was disappeared. They took her in 1976. I was twelve years old."

"Oh, Mariano."

"I don't want to get dramatic or anything. I just wanted to tell you it makes me happy you're so like her."

Verónica squeezed his arm.

The diplomat from the Italian embassy was waiting for them at the entrance to the Coronel Berti hospital. He explained how they had tried to find some relation of Petra's and kept drawing a blank. From the way he acted, though, it seemed they probably hadn't tried all that hard. His eagerness to pass on the responsibility for Petra's body was further evidence of that.

After signing all the paperwork the judge had sent so she could take charge of Petra's body and effects, Verónica was given the rucksack and the guitar. Outside the hospital, Mariano said:

"I've arranged for an undertaker to take the body straight to the cemetery tomorrow morning at eleven."

Back at the hotel, Verónica went up to her room. She put the guitar and rucksack down on one side of the room. She didn't feel ready to look through Petra's belongings. She left the rucksack untouched.

She walked over to Amigo's shortly before the time she had agreed to meet Mechi there. Since she knew they had Wi-Fi, Verónica took her laptop and ran a search on Guillermo Aráoz senior. She found quite a lot of information about his activity before and after the military dictatorship. There were various allegations of human rights abuses. In 1975 he had been transferred from Córdoba to Tucumán and moved into the provincial capital with his wife and children. In 1980 he bought a ranch in the area of Yacanto del Valle with money derived from "the spoils of war", according to various allegations. In 1981, he took early retirement. The soldier turned rancher. During the last years of the dictatorship he made good contacts among the Tucumán movers and shakers and, in 1983, he supported the candidate who later became mayor of Coronel Berti. As for the rape and murder of a twenty-one-year-old girl in 1982, there was no information at all. Verónica had only the published article Robson had copied for her. The last activity she could find for Aráoz senior was from midway through the year 2000: he appeared as a member of the steering committee of the province's Rural Society.

She stopped reading when she saw Mechi arrive. The girl looked taller and more relaxed than the last time she had seen her, perhaps because on that occasion Mechi had been arriving home after a long walk and this time she was a young woman breezing into a bar. She was still just as serious, though. She wasn't a girl much given to smiling.

Mechi ordered a Coca-Cola. Verónica asked about her work. The girl explained that she was one of two maids working for the Arregui family. She went there Monday to Friday, 9 a.m. to 6 p.m. She also worked some Saturday nights, when the Arreguis had visitors. Verónica asked if she was studying. She had some subjects pending, but she wasn't currently studying because she had started working full-time. Then Verónica told her what she had managed to find out.

"Your sister's case isn't closed and hasn't expired. So we still have time to find the people responsible. You told me it was El Gringo Aráoz. How can you be sure? You were little when it happened."

"My sister was very pretty. And El Gringo was after her. I heard her say that more than once. I was always eavesdropping on what she talked about with her friends."

"So did they go out together?"

"Bibi was playing hard to get. El Gringo had an official girlfriend. A stuck-up posh girl who ended up getting married to the youngest child of the Arteagas, a family from round here. Anyway, her best friend told me."

"Roxana?"

"How did you know?" asked Mechi, surprised.

"In the witness statements, Roxana mentions parties with rich kids, but she doesn't name Aráoz."

"She told me Bibi and El Gringo had had a fight because my sister didn't want to go back to his house. And that that Saturday Bibi said to Roxana they should go to the party but Roxana didn't want to know. They went for a beer in Gorriti's bar and El Gringo went to find her there. Bibi tried to make her stay but Roxana didn't want to know. Even Gorriti told her that those boys were jerks and she shouldn't hang out with them."

"Gorriti was the owner of the bar? He said that to Roxana?"

"Yes."

"And where can I find this Gorriti?"

"He sold up and left."

"When?"

"Right after they killed my sister."

"What about Roxana, does she live here?"

"She went to San Miguel."

"Are you in touch with her? I'd like to talk to her."

"No, but I can ask some of my sister's other friends. I'm sure they'll know how to find her."

They talked about Pae Daniel's release. Verónica told Mechi that she'd like to speak to her grandmother again, and they decided to go and find her straightaway. As they walked back to the hotel, where the car was parked, Verónica asked her if she liked living in Yacanto del Valle.

"No," she said, without elaborating.

They were driving when Federico called, wanting to know where Verónica was. When she told him she was on her way to Mechi's, he lost his temper, saying she mustn't move around on her own, that Peratta was still at large and they had to be on their guard. Federico told her he would go to Mechi's house too and wait for her outside.

The two dogs barked on their arrival there but, as Verónica walked through the gate, they merely sniffed her. Mechi's grandmother opened the kitchen door and the dachshund puppies rushed out in a gaggle.

The grandmother prepared coffee.

"I don't believe you told me your name the last time we were here."

"Ramona Ortiz."

"Ramona, do you know Pae Daniel?"

"Of course I do. When he moved here I used to go to his house. He came from the Amazon straight to Tucumán."

"Do you practise Umbanda?"

"My dear, at this age it's hard to take on anything new. But I thought perhaps I could learn to do hexes. I won't lie to you: I wanted to make a doll of the man who killed my granddaughter, but Pae Daniel explained to me that it wasn't Umbanda."

"And so you stopped going."

"No, I kept going because I'm stubborn. I thought the *pae* was lying and that one day he would teach us. I only wanted to hurt that miserable swine, mind you, not anyone else."

"And do you get on well with Pae Daniel?"

"I take him a black cockerel every now and then. And he talks to me about the Orisha, who connect human beings with the spirit world, and things like that."

"I need to speak to him, because I think he may be able to help us find the people responsible for the girls' deaths. Since he doesn't want to speak to people he doesn't know, I thought I might have more luck if I went with you."

Ramona couldn't go the following afternoon, but they agreed that Verónica would pick her up the day after and they would go together to see the *pae.* She left the house expecting to be accosted by all the puppies, but only one approached her.

"They're being weaned," Mechi explained. "Niebla doesn't want to feed them any more but the puppies keep trying. Apart from this one, who's already got used to Grandma's rice."

Verónica squatted down, more than anything to prise the little dog from her shoe. The puppy immediately licked her hand. Verónica stroked her head. She was an ugly little mutt, like all dachshunds.

"What's her name?"

"She hasn't got one. We're giving them all away. If you put El Gringo behind bars, you can have her."

Verónica laughed nervously. "Just what I need. A dachshund. I'd settle for seeing him prosecuted. I don't think he'll go to prison right away."

"Well, if you make it happen, I'll give you the puppy."

Outside Federico was waiting for her; he smiled and waved.

"Listen, Bruce Willis, we're going to have to go in separate cars."

"Lead the way and I'll follow you."

III

As a teenager she had been drawn to cemeteries and when, at twenty-two, she went backpacking round Europe on her own, she took a list of graveyards to visit, as well as one of museums. She had been to Père Lachaise in Paris, to Highgate in London, to the Jewish cemetery in Prague and the one for Protestants in Rome. But now she was the other side of thirty, graveyards repelled her more than anything else. The aversion had in fact begun at her mother's burial. Although she had gone to the funeral, she never returned to La Tablada cemetery. She knew her father went, that her sisters even took their children there. She couldn't go. Or rather, she didn't believe. She didn't believe there was anything there connected to her mother. Verónica had arrived at the conclusion that the place where you get buried is an irrelevance. And to think she had become emotional beside the tombs of Jim Morrison and Karl Marx.

Petra's funeral was attended by Luca, Mariano and Federico, as well as herself. The graveyard in Yacanto del Valle was a plot of land with simple graves, topped by headstones and crosses. They parked the car at the entrance and walked towards the area indicated by the undertaker. There were a few trees dotted around between the rows of graves.

Some cemetery workers were finishing digging the pit for Petra's grave. Seeing the mourners approach, they asked them if there was going to be a headstone. That was a question none of them had thought about and which Mariano promised to address in the coming days. The hearse couldn't reach that part of the graveyard, so they had to carry the coffin there themselves. Since there were only four of them, the undertakers helped them. Of the six people carrying Petra's body, Verónica was the only one who had known her. Such solitude, even in death, seemed unjust. Petra was someone who deserved to have family, friends and loved ones everywhere.

Verónica cried. But now she was crying because Petra didn't deserve that solitary and silent end, that meagre band of strangers. She closed her eyes when the gravediggers started to throw earth onto the coffin and tried to remember a prayer, a supplication like "El Malei Rachamim", but she couldn't. Instead she repeated Petra's name to herself.

Federico put his hand on her shoulder and led her away. They returned to the car. Before he started the engine, Mariano said:

"I couldn't say this before, but I want to now. God or nature or murderers can put an end to your life, but nobody can take away the life you have lived. That life is part of the cosmos. Petra is every moment she lived, including those days she shared with you. Your lives will always be intertwined, and nobody, not murderers, or nature, or God, can prevent that. That's what I wanted to say."

IV

Mariano believed in order – not in the military sense or the kind loudly espoused by retrograde sectors of society, but in an order where everything had its place in the world. Life, for him, was like a symphony he could hear throughout the day and night: the rhythm of travellers who arrived at his hotel, the staff busy with their tasks, the children who ran shouting past the door, the leaves that fell in autumn, the cloudbursts, his hands on Luca's body, their breathing in the early morning. If ever there was a discordant note in the melody, he noticed it before anyone else. The symphony fell out of tune, life lost its order if something had gone awry.

And his fine ear for daily life was alerting him now to a strange noise around him. Although it would be more correct to say that it was around the hotel. He thought he knew the source of that dissonant murmur: he intuited that Verónica was in danger. He needed to take immediate measures.

When they returned from the graveyard, he told Verónica he had to change her room. She didn't complain, only asked which room he was moving her to.

"Not to any of them. You're coming to our house. We have a guest room there that's going to be for you."

In reality their house was simply a wing of the hotel, reached by crossing a patio and a veranda that started at the end of the run of rooms on the south side. It wasn't very big but it had the benefit of a spare room, the one Mariano now offered to Verónica. Luca looked questioningly at him; Mariano avoided his eyes.

There was something else he wanted to do, too. Mariano went to the police station and spoke to Officer Benítez. He asked him if he wouldn't like to earn a few extra pesos working as a security guard during the night. It wouldn't be for very long. Mariano explained that he would have to stay in a room that served as a wine cellar and was midway between the hotel and their house.

Back at home, he went to the wine cellar and installed a computer there, connecting it to another one in the house. If anyone so much as touched a key or clicked the mouse, a sound would be made in the cellar. A home-made panic button, which Mariano tested and found to work perfectly.

With those preparations made, Mariano felt that the symphony was back in tune, although he was conscious that maintaining order was no simple matter and that the unexpected could always happen.

V

Ramona got into the car and pointed out to Verónica the road that led to Pae Daniel's house. Federico had surrendered the passenger seat to Mechi's grandmother. Ramona liked talking, or perhaps she simply felt calmer when conversation was flowing. She told them about the five grandchildren she had been looking after since her daughter died. That two of the boys had gone to work in the sugar harvest, on the other side of the province. That the other boy lived with Mechi and herself, but that he wasn't often around. She also told them that she had three other children, all living in the Yacanto area. Ramona asked them if they were romantically involved or just worked together.

"We're friends," Verónica answered.

They stopped the car in front of the *pae*'s house. Federico stayed in the car. Ramona clapped her hands and a woman appeared, greeted her by name and signalled that she should come in. As they walked across the garden, Ramona explained that she needed to speak to the *pae*.

A minute later Pae Daniel appeared. He looked taller from close up. He must be about fifty years old, with abundant hair that was almost entirely grey. He greeted Ramona with some surprise, remarking that it had been several months since they had last seen each other. Ramona explained that she was here on very important business. Gesturing towards Verónica, she added that she needed him to speak to her. Only then did the *pae* seem to see the other woman.

"It's a pleasure to meet you. I'm Verónica Rosenthal."

"What do you need?"

"It's about your arrest."

"I don't want to talk about that. It was a police error."

"This lady was a friend of the murdered girls," Ramona said.

"I don't think I can help her."

Pae Daniel was nothing if not intransigent. He had decided not to talk and seemed determined to stick to his guns.

"Somebody wanted to make you look guilty of the double homicide. They not only attacked you but also insulted your beliefs. And that person is connected with the deaths of my friends."

"I can't think how I can help you."

"That person planted false evidence to incriminate you. It's clear that person knows something about Umbanda, and perhaps even practises it. And if they practise Umbanda, you must know them."

The *pae* considered this for a few minutes. Finally, he invited them in.

The room was full of candles, but only a few were lit. Verónica was surprised to see an enormous image of Jesus Christ. There were other smaller images too, both of Christian saints and of Afro-Brazilian gods. The room smelled pungently of a sweet perfume.

"If they had asked me," Ramona said, "I would have told them you didn't do it. You would never use a white cockerel."

"Perhaps the person deliberately did the ritual wrong to avoid annoying Ogum."

"The district attorney didn't ask who, other than you, could have assembled the elements that linked the deaths with Umbanda?" Verónica asked.

"No. He was too busy asking about the orgies we organize. All I did was try to prove my innocence."

The *pae* walked over to a sideboard and took out a photo album.

"There are twelve children of Ile who visit me every week. You might think it could have been any of them, but no. I know each one of them. I know their spiritual quality and I know it's impossible it was an initiate. But just over a year ago a woman used to come who wasn't interested in Umbanda but in the *kimbanda* rituals that would allow her to harm someone. And that negative attitude was transmitted to the group. She contaminated it. I had to throw her out. Since we always take photographs of our ceremonies, I have some of her."

Pae Daniel showed them a picture of a woman dressed in red, surrounded by men in red and black who seemed to be dancing. There were other photos of her. She was a woman of about fifty, thin and with hair dyed light brown.

"And you believe it's her?"

"I believe in Zambí. It's very possible that this is her work."

"Do you know her name?"

"Adriana Vázquez. She lives on the way out of Los Cercos, on the road with the roses. It must be the second or third house."

VI

When they returned to the hotel, Federico said he would look into Vázquez. Verónica, meanwhile, returned to the material she had gathered at Robson's house. Once more she was drawn to the case of Aráoz senior. The only article linking him to the military quoted the Tucumán Association of Human Rights as a source. She looked up their telephone number, rang it and was put through to the secretary of the association. He had been active in the group since the late 1980s and was well aware of Aráoz, who was at that time one of the defendants in the "mega case" trial for violation of human rights during the dictatorship, but he didn't remember the case of the girl who was raped and murdered. He asked if he could take Verónica's number and get back to her after he had looked at Aráoz's file. Twenty minutes later he called to say he hadn't found any information to link Aráoz to a crime like that. He clarified that it was very probable the information had not been kept if it hadn't been a crime committed as part of state repression in that era.

Verónica had to make an effort not to say something rude. The man was undoubtedly working for a noble cause. Fighting certain battles meant leaving aside other, equally valid ones. A feminist association would surely have taken the girl's death into account but not that of an adolescent male, victim of a police death squad. Verónica didn't question just causes, but the indifference that certain activists or social warriors showed towards crusades other than their own was no less annoying. And she was certainly in no position to throw the first stone. After all, she had passed over hundreds of other crimes that did not fit the profile of her own investigation. She hadn't paused to consider cases of people missing through trafficking, or of young casualties of the drugs war, or victims of police abuse.

Yes, she was in a very bad mood. She called Federico to ask him to see what he could find both on the woman Vázquez and the current circumstances of Aráoz senior. Federico called her back within the hour.

"Guillermo Aráoz, retired captain of the Argentine army. Civilian life hasn't treated him badly. He has land – not only here, but in Salta and Córdoba. He's a member of the Rural Society of Tucumán. At one point he was treasurer, but now he's retired from all administrative roles. He also dabbled in politics in the nineties and got as far as provincial congressman for the Fuerza Republicana party."

"A man of conviction."

"You bet. These days he spends his time on outings with the grandchildren and taking his wife to Miami to refresh her wardrobe."

"How can I find him?"

"I've got phone numbers, addresses and an up-to-date photo. I'll send you everything right now. But I warn you that the guy doesn't give interviews, he doesn't speak to anyone from outside his circle. That's on the advice of his lawyers from the Rivelli practice, which specializes in defending military men who've been prosecuted for crimes against humanity. That's the crime Aráoz is being tried for. And here's the icing on the cake —"

"Don't talk to me about cake."

"Everything's connected. Captain Aráoz is a member of the sailing club your young man frequents. Plus, every Saturday he has lunch there with the same group of people. All old farts like him. Tomorrow is Saturday. Get lover boy to invite you to his exclusive club and we'll be laughing."

"You'd be perfect if you weren't such an idiot."

"That's what my mother says when she hears me talking to you."

Before ending the call, Verónica asked if he had found out anything about Adriana Vázquez. Federico said he was still looking into it, but that it would probably be a few hours before he came up with anything.

She called Ramiro, who sounded quite defensive on the line. She suggested meeting up and he invited her to dinner that night. Verónica proposed lunch the next day at Club Náutico. Ramiro thought that was a good idea, because he had been thinking of taking the boat out. They agreed that he would pick her up at the hotel shortly before lunch the following day.

VII

The old-school investigator was a thing of the past: these days the same work could be done by hackers. It was no longer necessary to hire an ex-police officer to get the information you needed; you just handed over the coordinates and the hacker did the rest. Federico was grateful for the services of La Sombra: not only could he break into a computer network system, but he also knew the right places to look for information. He used his initiative, analysing scenarios, evaluating the scant material given him and working miracles with it.

Once more, Federico called La Sombra. He asked him to find out everything he could on Adriana Vázquez. All he had to go on was the woman's name and the place she lived.

It wasn't long before La Sombra called back with what he needed: a complete report that culminated in a revelation:

"Vázquez has two sons: Sebastián and Álvaro. They're labourers. They're currently working in the area, on land belonging to Menéndez Berti."

Federico didn't need to ask for the brothers' work address. If Adriana Vázquez's sons had something to do with the death of the two girls, then Nicolás Menéndez Berti could be involved. He really didn't like the way the pieces of this story were coming together. He called Aarón Rosenthal and told him the latest.

"What did Menéndez Berti tell you?"

"He seemed innocent enough, although he was nervous. Which is understandable given that the two women had been at his party."

"Perhaps he was nervous because he knew more than he was letting on. Go and see him, tell him about this Vázquez woman and see if this time he tells you what he knows."

He went to Nicolás's house without calling first. Better not to give him time to prepare his answers. Nicolás showed him into the same room as before. Federico told him what he had learned about Vázquez and her sons.

"If they're responsible for these deaths, your situation looks more complicated."

"There's no reason why it should, because I'm absolutely innocent. I don't have, nor did I have, anything to do with those girls. They came to my party along with dozens of other people, many of whom I don't even know. As for my employees, I'm obviously not putting my neck on the line for them. I know those lads. They don't seem like bad sorts, but I wouldn't be all that surprised if they were the ones who'd done it."

"Are they still working for you? Are they here?"

"They stopped coming. The foreman told me. I thought they had quit. That's quite common."

"And when did they stop coming?"

"I think it was the day after the party. Yes, of course, the day after the party some of the labourers had the day off, and those two never came back."

"Were they the only ones?"

"No, there was another one who didn't return. Javier Reyes."

It was evening by the time he left, and he called Judge Amalfi. The judge was surprised to hear about all they had found out while the district attorney was still empty-handed. He told Federico that Decaux wasn't a man you could trust. The judge was thinking of sending Chief Superintendent Suárez to Vázquez's house with a summons and informing the DA of the fact. Decaux would be annoyed, but he didn't care about that.

"Call me tomorrow and I'll let you know what's happening," said the judge, sounding friendly.

When Federico spoke to Amalfi again, he had already made some decisions.

"We're going to search the homes of Vázquez and Reyes. The three men haven't been back home since the women were killed. Reyes is married and his wife is pregnant, which makes his absence even more suspicious. I want to compare DNA samples from these three with the semen traces found on the victims."

"What about Adriana Vázquez?"

"I'm going to take a statement from her and, if she's responsible for the black magic nonsense, I'll put her in prison. I've already given instructions to the Chief Superintendent and the DA. I hope we may be close to solving this case."

VIII

Five started from a reassuring premise: if he was ever arrested before killing someone, the only thing he could be charged with was attempted murder. There were no warrants out against him, and he was not the suspect in any crime. All his jobs had been carried out with the discretion, rigour and speed required by a profession that allowed no margin for error. The price of a mistake was prison or death. Prison wasn't forever, but it took its toll. You were no longer so effective. The big jobs went to other people, the money went down.

Five and Three stopped the car a hundred yards from the back entrance to the Posada de Don Humberto and waited. The arrival of the cook signalled the start of the day's activity. The cook left the gate unlocked, so that suppliers could come in and out freely. One of the advantages of living in a small town.

They got out of the car and strode towards the property. There was no need to talk. They knew exactly what they had to do. Three quietly opened the gate and they entered the internal courtyard. There was no one to be seen, no movement anywhere. The dawn chorus was under way and a cockerel crowed in the distance. They walked towards the door leading to the rooms on the first floor.

The corridor lights came on automatically. Room twenty-four was the second one along. They would need to break the lock with a single shot, then shoot the target. No more than ten seconds could pass between the first and second shots. Five took out his gun and shot at the door. Even with the silencer, the blast echoed down the hall. Three also had his Glock in his hand. He went in first, with Five behind him.

There was nobody in the bed. It wasn't even unmade,

nor were there any suitcases, or any sign that the room was occupied. They opened the bathroom door knowing they weren't going to find anyone there.

"They fucked us over," said Three.

"Let's abort, go back to the car and wait for instructions," said Five.

"No."

Three took the lead and Five followed him. He had been given no instructions on what to do if Three reacted in this way. Five had hesitated and Three had seized the initiative. By the time Five realized what was happening, they were on their way to the reception area, weapons in hand.

The receptionist saw them arrive but froze on the spot, unable to react. Three grabbed him by the neck and pointed the gun at his forehead.

"Where is Verónica Rosenthal?"

Stammering and almost crying, the employee said:

"I don't know, I only work at night. The owners are the ones who will know."

"Where are they?"

"They live in the house at the back of the hotel."

In normal circumstances, they would have had to kill him. Never leave a witness alive. But Five saw things weren't going well and thought that killing the man might make it worse. So he grabbed hold of the receptionist and told him to lead them to the house.

Together, the men walked the length of the hotel. Five and Three had both concealed their guns in case they ran into anyone. At that moment a fruit and vegetable delivery van drove in through the back gate, but its occupants paid no heed to the three men. The receptionist pointed out a door to them. Five directed Three to open it. Three shot at it and the lock gave way.

They entered the living room and, as they walked towards a bedroom, a man appeared with another behind him.

"Where's Verónica Rosenthal?" Three asked again.

The man who had appeared first said he didn't know what they were talking about. Three walked over to him and smacked him in the face with the butt of the pistol. The man gave a howl of pain and fell onto the floor.

"She's in room number eight, on the ground floor," the other man said.

"Where is that?" asked Five, not realizing someone had come into the house and was pointing a gun at Three.

"Put down the Glock or I'll spray your brains all over the floor."

There was a good chance Five would be quick enough to shoot the man before he killed him. The man would probably hit Three but not manage to fire a second shot. Suddenly everything was out of control. He had been wrong to follow Three in his mania. Things could get much worse if they resisted. Five laid his weapon on the ground and shouted at Three.

"Put the gun down, don't be stupid."

Three put his pistol on the table. The man must be a cop. He made them lie on the floor with their hands behind their heads. They did as he said.

They waited there for five minutes without anyone moving, until they heard the sound of police sirens. They were going to prison. Three already had several charges against him, but he himself could only be charged with aggravated assault. They hadn't even tried to kill anyone. That wasn't entirely reassuring, though. When Doctor Zero found out, he was going to be furious.

12 *Family Matters*

I

Everyone was angry. Luca was annoyed with Mariano because he refused to go to hospital, despite the cut to his lip. Mariano was indignant because Luca let everyone else apart from him be right. Federico was livid with both Luca and Mariano because they hadn't told him about their newly implemented security system. Verónica was furious with Luca, with Mariano and with Federico because nobody had told her about anything and they treated her like someone with a weak heart, someone who couldn't be exposed to any kind of upset lest she keel over and die.

The police had taken Three and Five to the police station in Yacanto del Valle. Chief Superintendent Suárez was furious because he had the feeling these people (who had even hired one of his men) did whatever they felt like without him knowing what was happening in his own town. He had asked the witnesses to come to the station and make a statement.

"I'm not eight years old, you can't treat me like a little girl who needs protecting. I have a right to know what people are saying behind my back. I know you mean well, but share what you know with me. I'm not going to go out with a sign that says 'shoot me'."

"Verónica," said Federico, "we do what we can and however we can. Obviously I needed to be in the loop," he added, looking at Mariano, while Luca nodded and applied ice to his partner's lip.

"I didn't say anything because I wasn't sure. I didn't want to seem paranoid or alarmist."

"You should see a doctor. To be sure there are no internal injuries."

"All the same, I want to tell you all that I'm very grateful to you for looking after me," Verónica said. "If not for you, I'd be dead."

"This is where we all hug one another and exchange high fives," said Mariano. "But I suggest we go to the hotel dining room and have breakfast instead. It's a bit early, but I don't think anyone feels like going back to sleep."

After breakfast, Verónica went out alone for a walk in the town. It was a hot day, but she had heard somewhere that rain was on its way. She hadn't seen rain since first arriving in Tucumán. Around mid-morning, Mechi rang.

"I spoke to Bibi's friends and got hold of Roxana's number. She's living in San Miguel. I phoned her and she told me you should call her. I asked the other friends if they knew anything about El Gringo and they clammed up. They don't want to talk."

"And Roxana?"

"I don't think she wants to either. Call her, go and see her."

Verónica lit a cigarette and sat down in the square, observing the town's growing hubbub. To one side, a little market of food and artisanal products was just beginning to open up, even though there were no potential customers yet. Her phone rang. It was Federico.

"I have news of Adriana Vázquez. Two of her sons work for Nicolás Menéndez Berti. As labourers."

"Whoa."

"They're two boys in their twenties who live with their parents. The dad is also a farm labourer in the area. But the boys haven't been home since the day before the bodies were found."

"We have to go and see that woman."

"No, we don't have to go anywhere. I called Judge Amalfi and brought him up to speed. He told me he would bring her in to make a statement."

"And how do we know the sons aren't at home and that they've been missing since that day?"

"That comes from the judge, who's a bit pissed off because he has to investigate the DA alongside these boys."

"Is he Superman or what? When did he find that out?"

"I spoke to him a while ago. I gave him the lowdown about the woman yesterday."

"And you're only telling me now?"

"Vero, this isn't a race for a journalistic scoop – which you have anyway. It's to see justice done. And that's what the judge is there for. I was going to tell you this morning but, what with everything that happened at the hotel, I didn't get the opportunity and I wanted to press on."

"The judge will screw it up. He'll ruin everything."

"Of course, whereas we'll solve everything without a hitch."

"And the DA?"

"Judicial infighting. If one says black, the other says white."

"And Nicolás? Two of his workers could be implicated. What about him?"

"Good question. I don't know the answer."

Leaving aside the fact that Federico had gone to the judge first, Verónica felt for the first time that the case was beginning to move forward. They had found the loose thread in a ball of wool and now they just needed to pull it.

II

The relief of the last few hours evaporated when Federico heard what was happening with Peratta and his accomplice. They weren't going to be moved to San Miguel until Monday. From there Peratta would be transferred to Buenos Aires to serve out the rest of his sentence, with more time added for his latest misdeeds. Until then the two criminals would be kept in the police station in Coronel Berti which, although a bit bigger than the one in Yacanto, was hardly a maximum-security prison.

While giving his statement about what had happened at the hotel, he took the opportunity to talk to the chief superintendent about the danger posed by the two criminals. Suárez insisted that every precaution had been taken to ensure the prisoners did not escape. On Monday he would hand them over to the National Guard to be transferred. There was no danger.

Even so, Federico was worried. A criminal fugitive, shot and gravely wounded, had reappeared with precise intelligence and an accomplice. This wasn't a simple case of personal revenge. It looked like organized crime. And when one professional assassin fails, another is sent in their place. Who had ordered the murder of Verónica, and why?

III

Ramiro surprised her by arriving a few minutes before their date, looking happy. He told her that he had been taken aback by her call, that he had been planning to get in touch but was frightened she would reject him. That he thought they should pick up where they had left off and proceed slowly but implacably.

"Implacably," Verónica repeated, trying to understand what the word meant in the context of what Ramiro was saying.

They arrived at the club. Verónica suggested they drop by the restaurant, where they had a gin and tonic because it was still early for lunch. She observed the other members of the club. None of them was the Captain Aráoz from the photos Federico had shown her the previous night. Ramiro asked how the investigation was going, but Verónica told him nothing. She was beginning to regard Ramiro as someone not to be trusted.

They went to the boathouse and had the boat brought out. On the lake, Ramiro let Verónica take the wheel. They didn't stay out long because Verónica wanted to have lunch.

They returned to shore and went to the restaurant. Ramiro was hungry and she a little uneasy. They ordered a plate of Gruyère and prosciutto, followed by *cannelloni alla rossini* and a bottle of Navarro Correas red. Verónica picked at her food while looking round the restaurant: no sign of Aráoz. Perhaps this time he wouldn't come? Had Federico been misinformed? She was asking herself these questions when Aráoz walked in with three other older men. They greeted the occupants of some of the other tables as they passed, then sat down at one beside a large window looking onto the lake. She had expected him to be taller, more imposing. But Aráoz was of average height, slim but with a belly. He was wearing a light blue sweater tucked into brown trousers and boat shoes a shade darker than the trousers.

At that moment the waiter brought their coffee. Ramiro started telling her something about the gallery. Verónica interrupted him:

"That's El Gringo Aráoz's father, right?" She pointed out the man in the blue jumper.

"Yes, do you know him?"

"I still haven't had the pleasure."

Verónica put the napkin that had been lying across her lap beside her plate. She stood up and walked over to the table beside the window.

"Excuse me, are you Captain Guillermo Aráoz?" she asked.

"Retired Captain," he confirmed with a smile. His four companions watched her.

"My name is Verónica Rosenthal."

"Rosenthal," Aráoz repeated.

"Yes. I'm a journalist for *Nuestro Tiempo* magazine."

Aráoz's smile became a rictus. It was clear he was making an effort to appear calm.

"You're wasting your time, Señorita. I'm not going to talk about a case that unfairly persecutes men who fought for their country."

"Forgive me, Captain, that's not the case I wanted to ask you about."

"Ah, very well. Then tell me how I can help you." Aráoz looked at her with a mixture of paternalism and a certain lascivious intent. The other three watched expectantly.

"I hope you can help. Do you remember Claudia Rinaldi?"

For a few seconds Aráoz seemed to be searching his memory.

"I don't know the name."

"That's understandable. A lot of years have passed. What was your relationship with Claudia Rinaldi?"

"I've just told you I don't know who that person is."

"What I'm not sure about is whether you knew her as a child or a little before Claudia was found, raped and murdered, on the outskirts of Yacanto del Valle in 1982. Do you remember?"

"Please leave us now."

"Did you take her to a party? Were some of these gentlemen also there?"

"Leave now, Señora," said one of the other men in a voice loud enough to draw attention from diners at other tables.

"Did you rape her alone or were other men involved? Does your wife know that you used to rape women?"

Aráoz stood up, his fists clenched. Ramiro had also got to his feet but stayed standing beside his chair, not daring to approach the table. The restaurant had fallen completely silent.

"One last question, Captain Aráoz: how did you manage to avoid an investigation?"

"Go away immediately. I'm going to call security to have you removed from the club," said one of the other men at the table and tried to take her arm, but Verónica briskly shrugged him off.

"Don't bother, I'm already leaving. I recommend the cannelloni. They're very good."

IV

Ramiro and Verónica had never seemed more like a couple than on the journey home from lunch at Club Náutico. Ramiro was furious and Verónica, her mind racing, was trying to fend off his attacks.

"You're out of your mind."

"Ramiro, it's OK. We left."

"That isn't El Gringo, that's his father."

"I know. Do you think I'm stupid?"

"So why did you pick a fight with him?"

"Because he probably killed and raped a girl in 1982. And if that's not enough, he's a royal bastard who's only now facing justice."

"What are you, a communist?"

"Ha ha. Everything's fine, Ramiro."

"So now you're laughing at me on top of everything else."

"No. I'm definitely not laughing. The other girls were killed the same way Frida and Petra were. If there's no investigation, all these crimes will go unpunished."

"I don't understand you. You spent barely a week with those girls and now you won't let it go. I understand that you're upset, but you've been way out of line with what you're doing from day one."

"What am I doing?"

"Digging in the shit. As though you enjoyed it."

"I'm not going to argue with you. I apologize if I made you look bad at the club."

"You need to find a calmer way of dealing with all this."

"Perhaps, but I'm not going to stop until I see the men responsible behind bars."

Verónica was thinking of ringing Patricia. She had an article in mind. In fact, she was so focussed on the idea that when she got out of the car she gave Ramiro a kiss on the mouth. A short kiss, a peck, but enough to leave him confused as he watched Verónica disappear into the hotel.

Walking past the reception desk, she saw Luca.

"Since I'm no longer in any danger, can I go back to the room I had before?"

"As you wish. You're welcome both in our house and in the hotel."

Luca passed her the key to her old room and Verónica moved her things over, along with Petra's rucksack and guitar. She still hadn't decided what to do with her friend's belongings. Once she had settled into the room, she called Patricia Beltrán.

"You'd better be ringing about something important, because you're interrupting my day off."

"God, of course, it's a Saturday. That's the problem with being on vacation – you lose track of the days."

"I spent ten years working Saturdays or Sundays at the newspaper. I can assure you nobody in their right mind would do it willingly."

"Look, do you have a double or a triple free? I have a piece that might fill it nicely."

"I can pull the article on famous people's pets."

"What's your opinion on dachshunds?"

"Dachshunds?"

"Yes."

"Is that your piece?"

"Seriously, what do you think of them?"

"That they're horrible."

"OK. Anyway. I'm in Yacanto del Valle. My investigation has thrown up at least twelve similar crimes in the area in the last fifty years. Almost all of them seem calculated: a young woman between fifteen and thirty-five, sexually assaulted then murdered, her body discovered later lying in an open space: roads, wasteland, etc."

"They're all unsolved femicides?"

"In some cases the men responsible went to prison, in others people were arrested but it was never clear if they were the actual criminals or stooges, and half of them walked free."

"OK, it sounds good, but I imagine there's more to this than the body count."

"Imagine a town divided by a dangerous road that has to be crossed every day. What's the statistical probability of being hit by a car?"

"Well … high."

"However careful you are, however many times you look both ways, there's a chance you'll get hit and, in fact, there will always be someone who gets run over. So what probability is there of being raped and murdered in a place like Yacanto del Valle if you're a woman moving around on her own?"

"I don't know, but it's certainly much higher than if you're a man."

"Exactly. Do you know what the most dangerous road a woman has to cross is? Impunity. The social impunity that sees these crimes as a fact of life, accepted by everyone."

Patricia liked the pitch.

"Oh, and I've also got material for a sidebar. There's an ex-military man here who's being prosecuted for crimes against humanity during the dictatorship."

"In the Tucumán mega-trial?"

"Yes. The same man was identified as being responsible for the rape and murder of a girl. But since that had nothing to do with his criminal activity in the military, nobody investigated it. There's nothing to go on."

"Let's give him the benefit of the doubt."

"He tortured, raped and murdered political activists. Let's just say there's a pattern of behaviour that could have spilled over into his civilian life."

"Write your sidebar, but end it with what you said: his previous history, the possibility he may have reoffended outside the political sphere."

"How long?"

"Nineteen hundred words. Including the sidebar. Are there any pictures?"

"Robson has copies of the original articles."

"That won't work. Leave this with me. Send me the list of cases on Monday morning. And the piece first thing Tuesday."

There were days when Verónica thanked her lucky stars she had Patricia Beltrán as an editor. With Beltrán it was always yes or no. She hated hesitant editors, the kind who accepted an idea for a piece then started changing it. Another editor might recast this article she was proposing to Patricia as a piece on the insecurity of life in small towns, or fifty years of rapists loose in Tucumán, or Argentina's ten most horrific crimes. Hesitant editors cast doubt on the journalist's ability to write the article, the editor-in-chief's capacity to understand it and the public's desire to read it. They ended up asking for the same piece that had been published a year ago in the same magazine, or the previous week in a rival publication, or that morning in the Spanish newspaper they read to signal their cosmopolitanism. Patricia, on the other hand, was clear about what she wanted and what she could get out of her writers. And she always had something to contribute. She really listened to the pitch and, even at the ideas stage, was beginning to edit the article. Verónica, knowing that her editor always made useful suggestions, noted down some of her thoughts.

She called Roxana, who had been a friend of Bibiana's. It wasn't hard to arrange a meeting, doubtless because Mechi had already used her powers of persuasion. But she couldn't meet Verónica until Tuesday. She lived in Banda del Río Salí, on the outskirts of San Miguel de Tucumán. Verónica thought that perhaps she shouldn't put too many details about the Bibiana Ponce case in her article. She didn't want to reveal too much for fear that someone would start leaning on Roxana. Better not to show all her cards.

V

Saturday afternoons and Sundays were just for her. Mechi might help her grandmother around the house and with the animals, but the rest of the time she could do as she pleased. That Sunday, around midday, she found a corner at the back of the property where she wouldn't be seen by her grandmother. She had bought a packet of cigarettes and was thinking of smoking. It was the first time she had done it. Mechi lit the cigarette with some difficulty and drew on it. She coughed, pulled on the cigarette again and, even though the smoke went in her face, it was better than the first time. The taste wasn't that great, but she didn't hate it. When she had finished the first cigarette, she lit another one. Now she tried to imitate the style of Verónica when lighting it. She put the end in her mouth, lowered her head a little, glanced up and tried to speak with the cigarette between her lips as she lit it.

"Tell me, Mechi, how do you manage to be so intelligent and beautiful at the same time?"

And removing the cigarette she answered herself:

"I was born like that, Verónica. It's a pity no one in this shithole has noticed."

She took a long drag and this time managed to blow the smoke out and up almost as well as Verónica.

"They haven't noticed that you're beautiful, or that you're intelligent?"

Mechi began to feel slightly nauseous and put out the cigarette with her shoe. When she got paid she was going to buy some sandals like the ones Verónica wore, although she probably wouldn't be able to get them in Yacanto del Valle. She wondered if Verónica had a boyfriend and what a boyfriend from Buenos Aires would be like. One day she would leave this town for the capital and she too would have a Buenos Aires boyfriend, handsome and with a wild beard.

Her grandmother had told her that Pae Daniel had said the person behind the cockerel sacrifice was a crazy old woman who lived on the road to Los Cercos. There were a lot of weirdos round here. She needed to get out.

Mechi hid the cigarettes and matches under some bricks. If it rained, as forecast, they might get wet, but she didn't want to take them inside the house. On the way to her room, she remembered the crazy old woman who had made Rosalía's life impossible. Her friend was going out with a very handsome boy called Sebastián. Rosalía was striking and seductive, with lots of men in her past and now Sebastián under her spell, and the boy's mother didn't like her one bit. The old bat started putting lots of hexes on her. She threw salt in the doorway to her house and left her a doll with broken legs and no head. Once, as Rosalía was coming out of school, the woman threw a strange dust over her. Rosalía ran after her that time. If she had caught the old woman, she would have killed her. But the truth was that Rosalía did start to feel unwell. She kept getting diarrhoea. Her head hurt. There were days she thought she might be going blind. And one day she confessed to Mechi that her body had started to smell really bad. That she had to use masses of deodorant, loads of soap. When she finished with Sebastián, all her problems disappeared. Never mind how handsome he was, she wasn't going to go out with the son of a madwoman for all the gold in the world.

And what if it was the same old madwoman?

She felt her heart beating faster. She called Verónica and asked her what the old woman's name was.

"Adriana Vázquez. Why?"

"I... I know her. Yes, I do know her." She struggled to get the words out.

"Seriously?"

"Yes, her son was my friend Rosalía's boyfriend."

"You know the sons?"

"Yes, of course, Sebastián and Rulo. Pretty and Ugly."

"Mechi, you're a genius."

"For real?"

"I want you to tell me everything you know about those boys."

They arranged to meet that afternoon in the same bar as before. Mechi went back to fetch her cigarettes. She would take them with her and light one in front of Verónica. She was a genius.

VI

After speaking to Mechi, Verónica started on the article she planned to deliver that Monday. The telephone in her room rang. It was Mariano.

"Someone's asking for you at reception."

"Who?"

"Your father."

For a moment she thought Mariano was joking. That perhaps by "father" he meant Federico.

"Federico?"

"No, your father."

It couldn't be true. It must be a trap. An assassin masquerading as her father in order to kill her or send her a message, mafia-style.

"Aarón Rosenthal?"

"Your father, Verónica," said Mariano, in the same even tone.

Anxiously, she went down the stairs. Could something have happened to one of her sisters? Or one of their children? Her concern must have shown because the first thing Aarón said was, "Don't worry, everyone's fine," adding, "We need to talk."

Verónica offered to take him up to her room or to the hotel dining room. But her father said he would rather go somewhere else.

They left the hotel. Outside was a car with a driver who made as if to get out, but her father gestured to him to stay put and to wait there.

"You've got a chauffeur?"

"I came with one of the interns from the office. I don't like driving cars that aren't mine."

They walked from the hotel to the bar without speaking, both smoking. Her father seemed preoccupied. To break the tension, Verónica asked after her sisters. He told her that Daniela and Leticia were both fine, that he'd had lunch with them the day before at Leticia's house. He told her with a smile that Benjamín, Daniela's son, wanted to be a drummer.

"That's given me an idea for his birthday. It's coming up soon."

"Daniela will kill you."

They went to Amigo's, where the waitress greeted Verónica like a regular. They ordered coffee and Verónica looked at her father expectantly.

"What a good lawyer you'd have been if you'd wanted to," Aarón said.

"I'd get mixed up between laws, codes and courts. There are too many numbers and sections in law."

"It's much simpler than that. Someone – an injured party, an entity or the state – is the victim of another person or institution and you have to do everything possible to defend your client. Basic law is common sense."

"Yes, you've told me that before. But I didn't believe you. And I was right."

"Vero, darling, as I'm sure you realize, I didn't come all this way to persuade you to study law."

"Something tells me that in a minute I'm going to wish you had."

"You're not wrong. I want you to come back to Buenos Aires."

"I'm going to go back, Dad."

"I want you to come back right now. To stop what you're doing up here."

"Dad, two of my friends have been killed. They were killed and violated. The people responsible are still out there and the law hasn't caught up with them."

"And what has Aráoz got to do with any of this?"

"Aráoz?"

"Captain Aráoz and his son."

"They're suspects in two other crimes that took place in this town."

"I'm not going to get into an argument about whether or not you have proof of that."

"I should hope not."

"The captain and his son don't concern me. I care about friends, or the children of friends having problems. Here in Tucumán I've done business and had dealings with the Menéndez Bertis, with the Posadas and with a lot of other people I hold dear, who have helped me and whom I'll help in whatever way I can. And you are part of this family."

"Which family? My family consists of you, my sisters, their children and husbands."

"You're wrong. A lot of what the Rosenthals have we owe to people who gave us help when we needed it."

"Those people didn't give me anything. They must have given it to you. That's nothing to do with me."

"The Menéndez Berti boy and Elizalde's sons probably think the same thing about their fathers. It's easy to say that."

"Dad, you're turning this into a tragedy when the real tragedy is the death of two girls."

"A dog has better conduct than you."

"What are you saying?"

"You should never bite the hand that once fed you. Never."

"I don't understand you."

"Yes you do. And that's why you have to come back."

There was a silence during which Verónica avoided her father's gaze. What she couldn't understand was something deeper: how was her father not going to allow her to get to the truth? She was his daughter. She thought of saying that – *I'm your daughter* – but it seemed redundant and pathetic.

"I'm not going back."

"As you wish. But don't count on Federico or the practice to help with your investigation. If you care anything about that boy at all, don't ruin his life."

VII

Federico and Verónica saw each other at lunch that Sunday. Mariano and Luca had invited them to eat in the hotel restaurant. It was the first time the four of them had been together since the events of the previous morning. Verónica wondered what it would be like to be in a relationship like the one Mariano and Luca had. They seemed so contented, so interested in one another (she didn't want to say "in love" because that sounded too adolescent or nineteenth-century), their union impossible to break. Her own relationships broke like Bohemian glass in the hands of someone with Huntington's disease. It must be impossible for a relationship like the one they had to last a very long time. At some point all couples foundered.

"How was the meeting with your father?" Mariano asked her.

"Difficult."

Verónica looked at Federico, who was still finishing off the contents of his plate. He didn't acknowledge the look. He seemed to know she had been with her father.

After coffee, when they were alone, Verónica said, "Did my dad really do a number on you?"

"Nothing too bad. I could handle it."

Federico told her there was another possible suspect as well as the Vázquez brothers. He was called Javier Reyes. Raids had been carried out the day before on both the Vázquez and Reyes houses. The judge wanted to bring in the brothers' mother. But there were still no new developments.

Later, Verónica returned to her room to continue writing her article. When she checked her watch, it was already time to go and meet Mechi. As she walked to the bar, she thought over the events of the last few days, when one – in fact two – men had been looking for an opportunity to kill her. Now she could walk in peace.

At any moment it would start raining. The wind was getting stronger, lifting eddies of dust on the crossroads. Far away there was a rumble of thunder. It was getting dark earlier.

Mechi was already waiting in the bar. Verónica liked the girl. She was bright. If she wanted to, she would go far. And she was pretty, with that straight black hair she always wore tied back. She must be very popular with the boys.

The girl told Verónica what she knew about the Vázquez brothers. The younger one, Sebastián, had been Rosalía's boyfriend. The mother was crazy and had put various hexes on her friend to make her give up the son. And she had achieved her aim. She had become famous as a witch, at least among Mechi's friends.

"Actually, all mothers-in-law are like that," Verónica said.

Sebastián must be about twenty now because he had been three years ahead of her in primary school. He had always been good-looking and all the girls swooned over him, but it was Rosalía who landed him. Sebastián was quite shy and a bit of a loner. Rulo was a few years older than Sebastián and she didn't know him as well. Only that he was a troublemaker, always getting into scrapes.

"What kind of scrapes?"

"He crossed the line. In clubs he'd go up to women and say obscenities or even grope them. He got into fights with the men. Nobody likes someone hitting on their girlfriend."

"And do you know Javier Reyes?"

Mechi thought for a moment. "The name doesn't ring any bells. They have a friend they call Oso and I think his name's Javier, but I'm not sure."

"None of them have been back home since the night of the party. Do you have any idea where they might be hiding?"

"No, but I can find out." Mechi took out her packet of cigarettes and went to light one.

"I don't think they let you smoke inside here."

"True, I always forget."

"If you like, we can leave our things here and go and smoke by the door."

They stood by the wall outside. It was very windy and they struggled to light their cigarettes. Mechi didn't seem all that expert in these matters.

"Verónica, I wanted to ask you something. I'd like to go and live in Buenos Aires."

"When?"

"I don't know – now, in a year, any time really. I can work as a maid in someone's house."

Verónica drew deeply on her cigarette. "I don't think it's a good idea. Yes, you should come to Buenos Aires, but not to be a maid."

"It's the work I do here. There, it's bound to be better pay and everything."

"If you come to Buenos Aires I can help you, but not to work in a house. It's the worst job. If you start working as a maid, it's very likely you'll be doing that for the rest of your days. Thirty, forty years cleaning other people's toilets, looking after their kids, then their children's children. And for just a few pesos."

"So what do you think I should do?"

"There are some crappy jobs which are better than that. I don't know, stacking shelves or working on the till in a supermarket. They mistreat you, underpay you – although maybe less than in a house – but at least you have prospects. Slim ones, but prospects all the same. You could end up being chief cashier or, I don't know, floor manager. You could have a career within the limits of the supermarket. But not in a house. They won't even reward long service."

"But I don't think anyone would hire me."

"Well, of course they won't hire you. How can they hire you if you haven't even finished secondary school? Do you want to have a good life, a decent job and to grow as a person?"

Mechi was cowed by Verónica's emphatic tone. "Yes, I'd like that."

"Then let me give you two bits of advice. One: study, get through secondary school however you can but stick it out. Even better if you carry on studying afterwards, but you must at least finish school. The second piece of advice is key: don't get pregnant. Life is too hard for a girl without having a baby to look after too. And above all, don't have a child because you didn't take precautions. If you do that, you'll ruin your life. However much your boyfriend tells you he's going to help you look after it, don't believe him. It's never true."

"But one day I'm going to want to have children."

"Think about it when you already have a stable job and no more plans to study. Let's just say you shouldn't even think of becoming a mother for the next ten years."

The rain had arrived. Verónica offered to give Mechi a lift home. She paid the bill and they went outside, running through the downpour. The town felt strange, and not only because of the storm: there was more movement and traffic than on previous days. Everyone seemed to be going in the same direction, towards Coronel Berti.

"What's happened to bring so many people out onto the road?"

"It must be something to do with the murdered boy."

VIII

That morning, Mechi told her, the Coronel Berti police had gone to carry out an operation at one of the houses on the outskirts of town. It was in a poor neighbourhood which, while not yet quite a shanty town, was expanding by the day. In circumstances that remained unclear, a police officer had killed a teenager in his home. When the news came out, fury quickly spread among the neighbours.

"There's a protest happening now outside the police station in Coronel Berti."

She dropped Mechi at her house and decided to go to Coronel Berti to see what was happening. Like a doctor running towards an emergency, Verónica's journalistic instincts led her straight to the public protest.

The scene that greeted her in the town's main square was like a vision of hell. Some two hundred people were rampaging in the rain, destroying everything in their path, while the sound of gunshots could be heard. Several fires had been started and even a car overturned. Verónica left her own car outside the area of conflagration and continued on foot. People were very angry, shouting and demanding justice for the dead teenager. Some boys who couldn't have been more than eighteen were throwing Molotov cocktails at the shops. Thunder and lightning made the atmosphere seem all the more hellish. Verónica had to run a few yards to avoid being caught in the middle of a mob escaping from a group of police who seemed as fired up as the protesters. She stopped under the eaves of a building. Her body was soaking and she was trembling. She thought she could hear her telephone ringing, but when she looked at it the caller had already rung off. There were five missed calls from Federico, who called back at that very moment.

"Where are you?" he asked sharply, almost shouting.

"At a protest that's happening in the square at Coronel Berti."

"Get out of there now. Have you got the car?"

"Yes."

"You need to leave. Come here now. Right now."

"What's happened?"

"They smashed up the police station at Coronel Berti, and Peratta and the other guy have escaped. Come now."

Verónica's legs were shaking. She looked all around her, certain she was about to come face to face with the assassins. She wanted to run towards her car but, as in nightmares, her legs refused to cooperate. She had to make a great effort to impel herself forward then, having finally picked up some speed, she had the misfortune to slip and fall in the mud. Somebody helped her up, but she neither looked at them nor said thank you. She kept running, reached the car and locked herself inside it. Frantically she turned round, expecting to find one of her assailants in the back seat. Nobody was there. She started the car and sped away. There was a cramp in her left leg and an uncomfortable chill swept over her body. She kept driving with her eyes on the rear-view mirror. Nobody seemed to be following her. At the entrance to Yacanto del Valle she spotted Federico's car and slowed down without stopping. Federico followed behind her and they drove to the hotel.

Mariano was waiting at the door. Also there was Officer Benítez, the man who had disarmed Peratta and his accomplice. She felt her soul returning to her body. But her heart was still racing. Someone (Mariano?) said she should have a hot shower and change her clothes. Verónica looked at them one by one. Their voices seemed muffled compared to the noise of the rain. Molotov cocktails were still exploding in her head. Streaks of lightning were still blinding her. Someone (who?) told her to relax, that the hotel was safe. Verónica nodded.

13 *On Love*

I

His concern for Verónica had given way to a general irritation with her: what was she doing in Coronel Berti? Why had she ended up in the middle of a riot? Verónica answered him as best she could.

Now Federico had a new reason to be worried: if Peratta was free, it was likely he would return to kill her. He spoke to Chief Superintendent Suárez and asked him to send a police car to the hotel. Suárez refused, saying that too many of his men were tied up in Coronel Berti.

"Imagine the problems you'll have if these escaped criminals kill a woman in your jurisdiction," Federico pointed out.

The chief superintendent agreed to send a patrol car. With the presence of Officer Benítez and the deterrent effect of the patrol car circling the hotel, Federico thought they could have a quiet night. All the same, he couldn't sleep a wink.

At dawn he went down to the lobby and found Mariano drinking a brandy. They talked for an hour about the fugitive hitmen. Federico told him what he was most worried about at that moment:

"Could Peratta have hired an assistant? Would you contract a second architect for a job you've already done dozens of times?"

"Not unless it was a very big job."

"Or unless someone hired two architects to make sure the job was done right. And I think that's what happening. Somebody hired them to get Verónica out of the way."

"And why would they want to do that?"

"Because of her investigation into the murdered girls. So that's the key to finding out who's behind this. The same person responsible for the murders must have ordered Verónica's execution."

Federico didn't mention it to Mariano, but he was also worried by the interest shown by Verónica's father in this whole affair. Why was he so protective of Ramiro, of Nicolás and their families? The truth was that Aarón had sent him to shield the same people Verónica was investigating, to erase any incriminating evidence on them. Verónica had not realized Federico was striving for exactly the opposite outcome to her. To eliminate the evidence, though, he needed to find it first.

II

Doctor Zero bit into a slice of Gruyère. Slowly chewed it. He tended to take a ceremonious and methodical approach to all things, neither hurrying nor lingering over them. Then he drank from his glass of white wine. He studied the ripples on the River Plate. A fresh breeze swept the area.

Failure was a possibility. Distant, tiny, but always present. It would be childish – or, as he preferred to say, amateur – not to be aware of that. Professionals are not permitted to fail, but if they do, they know there are consequences that must be considered, measured, calibrated, so failure doesn't turn into a path of no return.

The Verónica Rosenthal case was something out of the ordinary. The year before, that woman had managed to pull off something the police had never managed, taking out four men in one strike – three wiped out for good and one sent to hospital. Even so, that could have been the end of it. He wouldn't have retaliated against Verónica. You had to keep your eyes on the business. And his men must work with a surgeon's precision. He couldn't distract himself or waste time on settling scores.

For that reason, when they hired him to liquidate Rosenthal, he felt no personal satisfaction. Only a slight disquiet, the feeling that he would have preferred a different assignment. But he didn't choose; he simply assessed the risks and challenges, selected the right men and charged a sum commensurate with the effort. Had it been a mistake to put Three on this job? Perhaps. Then again, Three had been successful on missions where another man would have failed. How could he not trust such a man?

Three times he had saved Three, as if his *nom de guerre* were a kind of premonition. He had got him out of prison, got his bullet wound seen to and now, once again, he had sprung him from prison. None of this had been easy or without cost. He knew how to reward his men, but he needed them to be effective. Neither Three nor Five had been effective. He must think about how to resolve this situation.

The task had been made easier by a fortuitous telephone call. Apparently the person who had hired him wanted to talk. Doctor Zero could already imagine the complaints. They confused contract killing with a delivery service arriving late with the sushi. To his surprise, the call wasn't to reproach him.

"It's lucky, Doctor, that the lads haven't done the job yet."

"What do you mean?"

"She's more useful alive now."

"I don't understand."

"Listen, Doctor, I know details don't interest you. Basically, the journalist is on the wrong track, and that's useful to me and my people. Let her cluck in someone else's chicken coop."

"Should I take it that the operation is suspended, then?"

"No, Doctor, just postponed for a few days until she does what we're hoping she'll do. A Rosenthal is always persuasive in legal circles."

"When, then?"

"Not today, not tomorrow or the day after. In two days' time I'll ring you and confirm the date."

"I've got people working on this."

"And I'll cover your costs."

"I'm going to need you to send the money now."

"Doctor, I'll send you the first half. You know that I guarantee payment."

"And if you go to prison, who's paying?"

"Before I go to prison or die of a heart attack, Rosenthal will be out of the race. And that depends on you."

After the call, Doctor Zero felt annoyed. He didn't like working for people who changed their plans on the fly, rich people who didn't weigh up the actual consequences of liquidating someone. That imbecile had no idea what he was doing. Neither him nor his people – if those people even existed. Just look at what they had done with the women tourists.

On the other hand, this postponement of the job came just at the right time. Rosenthal and her entourage were doubtless braced for an attack in the next few days. As time passed, they would let down their guard. Surprise was the best weapon.

Plus, the extra time meant he could give more thought to what to do with Three. Should he keep him on the job?

Should he get him out of there? How would Three take it if he were no longer part of the team that was going to end the life of his personal nemesis? Now Doctor Zero had a few days to come up with answers to those questions.

III

Verónica was driving while Federico slept in the passenger seat. He had asked her to drive to San Miguel de Tucumán. As far as the Cerro San Javier, in fact. They had both agreed that it was better to keep on the move, not to stay in Yacanto del Valle. Federico had suggested they stay at Severo's house in the city itself, but Verónica dug in her heels. She said she'd rather be shot than spend the evenings with the Witch.

They were playing music from Frida's MP3 player. The road was quiet, albeit rather slippery after the previous day's downpour. Verónica kept an eye on the rear-view mirror. At one point, a white Audi appeared behind them and trailed along about a hundred yards behind their vehicle. It was strange that a car should appear so suddenly but not drive up and overtake them. The Audi kept the same distance. Fifteen minutes had gone by now and it was still there, behind their car. Verónica turned off the music, as if that would allow her to concentrate better on the other vehicle. She thought of waking Federico, but it wouldn't be helpful. Unless he got out his gun and started firing at them, like in the movies. No, better not go there. And certainly not if he was going to make her feel nervous by back-seat driving. She accelerated slightly and the Audi fell behind a little, but not for long. Now, in fact, it came up even closer behind them. Verónica saw that further along there was a YPF service station, one of those big, busy ones. She swerved into the lane for the service station with almost no drop in speed, raising dust and the eyebrows of several onlookers. She drove past the cars queuing for fuel and made for the service area. The Audi had also entered the station, but it didn't advance beyond the pumps. Verónica woke Federico. At that moment the passenger door of the Audi opened and out stepped a woman in her thirties. The back doors also opened and two people came out, crouching down. No, they weren't crouching after all. They were children who ran towards the woman and held her outstretched hands.

"Are we there?" asked Federico, stretching.

"I stopped to get fuel. Want a coffee?"

In the bar they crossed paths with the woman and her two children, who were pestering her to buy chewing gum and Coca-Cola.

"I hate the nuclear family," said Verónica and Federico pretended not to hear her. He was used to her antisocial outbursts, particularly at Hanukkah and New Year's Eve parties when she got together with her sisters.

The rest of the journey was uneventful. Once more they settled into the house at San Javier, where Verónica noticed a few changes. She rang her cousin who, as well as confirming that a cleaner had been in, insisted she stay as long as she needed. Later, Verónica discovered Severo had also restocked the alcohol. There were two new bottles of Johnnie Walker. For a very brief moment she felt rather ashamed.

Each returned to the room they had occupied on the previous visit; in her case, the same one she had used the first time she came. Federico checked that the alarm was working.

As the hours passed, a kind of calmness began to overtake her. The chance of their being attacked seemed negligible. Somehow, Federico had managed to make her feel safe in his company. She spent much of the day ensconced in her room writing her article. In the afternoon the sun came out, but it was cool. She could see Federico walking in the garden and talking on the phone. She was surprised to find herself gazing at him.

Federico called her when he had made coffee, and took the cups out to the veranda together with a little tin of Austrian biscuits he had found somewhere. He asked her how the piece was going, then brought her up to speed with the latest developments.

"There's a match between the semen traces and the DNA samples from Vázquez and Reyes that the judge took from their clothes. So they *are* responsible for the girls' deaths."

"Pieces of shit. The mother cobbled together that monstrosity to cover for them."

"The mother hasn't said a word. They charged her with obstruction of justice, but she's been released. It's possible the brothers will try to make contact with her."

"Those bastards must be out of the country by now."

"I don't think so. As I said, the three men are responsible for the rapes and murder, but DNA from another person was found under Petra's fingernails."

"So there were three rapists, but at least four murderers."

"Exactly."

"Nicolás Menéndez Berti," Verónica declared.

"That's what the judge thinks. I'm not so sure."

"It was at the guy's house. The others are his employees. Oddly, the security cameras didn't record the girls leaving. Did they leave by some other exit with no cameras?"

"The judge is going to take his statement. And if he consents, they'll take a DNA sample."

Verónica took off her glasses, rubbed her eyes and sat with her hands over her face. Looking up, she said:

"He'll have an alibi. He's bound to."

"The DNA test is important."

"It must not be his."

"Wait, Verónica, don't go so fast. It's possible he didn't do it."

"These people always get away with it."

Verónica went back to her room to finish her article. She was annoyed with Federico for defending Nicolás. She called Patricia and told her the latest news on the case. Her editor asked her to write it up as an article.

"No, Pato. It's hard to explain, but I'd rather not write this one. If you like, speak to Christian or whoever you think best and I'll pass the details on to them. But I will send the piece I promised you in ten minutes."

Patricia passed the telephone to Christian, who had been following the case through the media. Verónica told him the names of the three fugitive suspects and asked him to emphasize the fact that they were employees of Nicolás Menéndez Berti. And to put that court sources thought he might soon be tried as an accomplice to the double crime.

"Are you sure about that?" asked Christian, who was nobody's fool.

"Totally. Put it in. My sources assure me that this is the guy who set everything up."

"To what end?"

"I don't have the motive. Because he's a pervert? A guy who uses women to the point of actually killing them? There's a piece by me in this edition in which I talk precisely about this, about the impunity surrounding these crimes. Ask Pato to show you it."

Verónica ended the call, finished checking her piece, sent it to Patricia and lay staring at the ceiling. She needed to be on her own.

IV

Someone was banging on her bedroom door. It was Federico calling her to dinner. The room was dark. She had fallen asleep and now it was evening. Verónica washed her face to wake herself up and looked in the mirror: the woman looking back had bags under her eyes, messed-up hair and an angry expression. A depressing image, enough to alarm anyone. If she left her room looking like that, Federico would run a mile. She brushed her hair, put on deodorant and tried to exchange her baleful expression for a light and steady smile.

Verónica went to the kitchen, where Federico was wielding a frying pan and watching a pot full of boiling water.

"What a vision."

"Risotto *all'uso*, Federico-style. Nothing fancy. The provolone on the table is for grating on top, but if you cut it into little pieces it could be an antipasto. I've just opened a bottle of wine. Get me a couple of glasses, *por favor*."

They sat down to eat there, at the kitchen table. She asked him if she looked a fright.

"You're not at your best."

"No, I know. But I look forty or fifty."

"Cut it out, narcissist. You want me to say that you look fantastic and that anyone would take you for twenty."

"No, idiot, seriously. I've just looked in the mirror and I seem to have aged ten years in ten days."

"Let's just say that a week ago you'd aged twenty years. So now you look better."

Federico served himself more rice, but Verónica didn't want seconds. They stayed in the kitchen until they had finished the bottle of wine.

"Your cousin has quite the DVD collection."

"Yes, the first time I was here I watched a different movie every night."

"Do you want to watch something now?"

"Go on then."

They moved into the living area and Federico began looking through the DVDs.

"What would you like to watch?" he asked her.

"What sort of thing do you like?"

"Movies that don't have a ten-minute shot focussing on a pot plant."

"I don't mind what we watch."

"Woody Allen or Almodóvar?"

"Almodóvar."

"*Talk to Her* or *Broken Embraces*?"

"I've seen *Talk to Her*. Wait while I go and get some whisky. Do you want something?"

Federico wanted a whisky too, so Verónica brought one of the new bottles of Johnnie Walker and they made themselves comfortable on the sofa. It was the first time they had watched a movie together. In fact, before staying in this house the first time, they had never shared daily life together. Federico might seem part of the Rosenthal family furniture, but he had never been on vacation with them or stayed the night at her father's place or either of her sisters' homes. The few times they'd had sex, they hadn't shared much more than their bodies. To eat together, watch a movie, nestle on a sofa without the tension of trying to seduce one another, was something new to them both. Federico seemed to be enjoying the experience. Verónica would have liked to rest her head on his shoulder, but that would be going too far. One shouldn't tempt fate. She watched the whole movie without venturing over the imaginary border in the middle of the sofa.

The next day they had the television on while eating breakfast. On every channel the news was that the killers of the foreign tourists had been identified and were on the run. Photos of the three men were shown. Verónica looked steadily at them. For the first time she was seeing the faces of those animals. Trying to identify some trace of their cruelty, she found nothing. They were very average, the kind of men you'd pass in the street or see in a bar anywhere.

She saw her friend María reporting on the case from Yacanto, and other reporters too, but nobody was linking the three murders with Nicolás. Verónica sent a text message to María saying: *The three men worked for Nicolás Menéndez Berti, owner of the house where the party was held. The judge is going to take a DNA sample from him.* Half an hour later, María called her.

"Are you sure? Because I heard something about that from the courts, but the DA here refuted it."

"I don't know what Decaux's game is, but I assure you that the judge has Menéndez Berti in his sights. And if you put two and two together you get four."

"Can I use this?"

"Obviously."

Shortly afterwards, María was live to camera again and this time added to her previous dispatch the details Verónica had given her. The other channels were still not saying anything, but in a few minutes they were sure to be reporting the same. Federico had gone outside to make a call and Verónica phoned Roxana to confirm their meeting again. Roxana was waiting at her house in Banda del Río Salí, a few miles from the provincial capital. Verónica set off to meet her, Federico going too. The shadow of Peratta forced them to take all possible precautions.

*

La Banda was a town of low houses and wide avenues. Away from the avenues, the residential streets were reminiscent of a humble district on the outskirts of Buenos Aires.

Roxana's house had a paved area in front and a carport. Toys were lying around on the patio. Verónica rang the bell and a pregnant woman about her age came to the door. She had blonde hair and blue eyes. She was quite short, and with the pregnancy her already ample bust looked fit to burst out of her clothes. She showed Verónica into a living room full of photographs, many of them of a little boy.

"How many children do you have?" Verónica asked.

"I'm expecting my second. The eldest is four and he's playing out the back at the moment. Do you have children?"

"No, I'm single. But my sisters have three children between them, and I see how much they put into being mothers. Children are a lot of work."

Roxana offered her a coffee and Verónica accepted. Soon she came back with cups, sugar, sweetener and some little cookies.

"You were a close friend of Bibi's."

"We were like sisters. Since primary school. We were always together."

"I'm a journalist, I don't work in the judiciary and I'm not a lawyer. But I want to get the case reopened and for there to be an investigation into who killed Bibi."

"I can't see that happening."

"You gave evidence in court at one point."

"Yes, but neither Bibi's family's lawyer nor the district attorney nor the judge wanted to hear what I had to say. When I started talking about that man, they told me it wasn't a good idea to bring him into it. That I could end up going to prison for giving false evidence."

"And who was 'that man'?"

"El Gringo Aráoz. Guillermo Aráoz."

"So what did you do?"

"The first time, I named him. I did it once more, but not again after that. One day some guys shouted at me from a car that what happened to Bibi would happen to me too if I didn't shut my mouth. I was scared."

"And what is it that you knew?"

"That Bibi had had a thing with El Gringo. The guy had a girlfriend, but he also went out with other girls, just like all the other rich boys round there. Bibi was in love with El Gringo, but the guy just wanted her for his own amusement. Bibi got tired of the situation and left him. And that's when El Gringo got heavy, always looking for her, following her and making scenes if he saw her with another guy. And Bibi liked that. It made her feel that El Gringo was in love with her, just not ready to leave his girlfriend. I told her to forget the guy, that nothing good was going to come of it. But she wouldn't listen. The Saturday before she was killed, I persuaded her not to go to a party El Gringo was having in his house, because his girlfriend was away in Buenos Aires. I didn't want to go because there was a guy who had treated me badly, who had been with me then pretended not to see me in the street, as if I were a whore. I persuaded Bibi not to go. We don't have to be anybody's plaything."

"But the following Saturday you couldn't persuade her."

"She was in too deep. Plus El Gringo had said he wanted to invite her to another party at his house. But I'd seen his girlfriend that morning in the square. She wasn't in Buenos Aires and I didn't believe he would have people round to his house with his girlfriend in town. That night we went to Gorriti's first to have some beers. I wanted to take her to a dance hall which was opening that day, but she wasn't interested. She was excited because El Gringo had sworn he loved her, that he was leaving the girlfriend, that that night would be their first one together as a couple."

"That's what she told you?"

"I saw it with my own eyes! El Gringo was sending her these little messages every ten minutes. There was nothing I could do about that. At midnight, El Gringo came to pick her up in his car."

"Was he alone?"

"Yes. I still remember how excited Bibi was. She gave me a big smacker of a kiss when she went. I remember it really well."

Roxana took a sip of coffee. Verónica said nothing.

"I wanted El Gringo to pay for what he did, but nobody cared. And I was scared. I was looking all around me when I walked down the street. So when I met the man who's now my husband, I told him I wanted to move here."

"Would you be prepared to say all this in front of a judge?"

"What's the point? Nothing will happen, just like nothing happened to the men who killed the tourists."

"Three men have already been identified."

"I've seen the photos. Now they're saying that the great-great-grandson of Colonel Berti is guilty too. But there's no way he'll ever go to prison."

"He will, just you wait and see. If he's responsible for the girls' deaths, he's going to pay for what he did."

"OK, well, when that guy gets locked away, come back to me and we'll go to court. And I'll tell them everything I know. I don't want any trouble."

"Are you still frightened?"

"Frightened? No, not any more. I'm going to have a baby girl and I don't want her to run into guys like that one day. But is there any point if everything comes out, my own life gets dragged through the mud, I get treated like a slut and then nobody pays? Put the men who killed the tourists behind bars and I swear I'll give evidence, even though my husband doesn't want me to."

Roxana stood up and went to the kitchen. She poured herself a glass of water from the tap and drank it in one go. Then she went into an adjoining room. Verónica heard a drawer being opened. Roxana reappeared a few minutes later.

"I've been thinking about this a lot in the last few days and I want to confide in you. So I'm going to give you something nobody knows I have."

She placed a mobile phone, quite an old model, on the table.

"That day Bibi was anxious, and when El Gringo turned up she left her phone on the table. I realized straightaway, but when I went out to give it to her she'd already gone. All the phone calls and the texts El Gringo was sending from his phone are there. You just have to find a charger for it, because I've had it put away for years."

Verónica couldn't believe it. Something like this would make it much easier to get them to bring Aráoz to trial. She picked up the phone as if it were a rare treasure.

As they were saying goodbye, she remembered something Roxana had said to her and which she had been turning over in her mind.

"Why do you think they're going to drag your name through the mud?"

"That's what the lawyer for Bibi's family said to me. Since I also hung around with rich guys who had girlfriends, they might think I was a prostitute. We wanted to have fun, to dream that those boys could fall in love with us. And then the idiot I was with looked away from me when I went to say hello to him in a bar. He may have been all brilliant smiles like a toothpaste ad, but he was a jerk, a nasty piece of work, just like his best friend, El Gringo Aráoz."

"A toothpaste ad? What was the name of this guy you were seeing?"

"Ramiro Elizalde."

V

Things were getting complicated. Federico had called Nicolás several times without reaching him. Meanwhile, Aarón was pressuring Federico to do everything possible to remove Nicolás from the investigation – but that was going to be difficult if he couldn't manage to speak to him. To top it all off, Verónica had broadcast Nicolás's possible involvement to the four winds. There were already cameras trained on the entrance to the Menéndez Berti estate and journalists declaring that the brains behind the double murder lived there. He knew Nicolás had voluntarily presented himself to give a DNA sample. In Federico's mind, even with the results not back, that ruled him out as the fourth man. Could it be another of Nicolás's employees?

Verónica emerged exultant from Roxana's house. It was the first time since arriving in Tucumán he had seen her so happy.

They stopped at a bar in San Miguel to have a coffee and Verónica told him about her conversation with Bibi's friend.

"First the girls' deaths have to be resolved," said Verónica. "Only then will she feel safe enough to give evidence."

After leaving the bar they looked for a phone shop and were lucky enough to find a charger compatible with the phone Roxana had given her.

Back at the house, Verónica plugged in the charger. The phone was working, and she was able to see the texts straightaway: there were loads from a certain Guille. A quick check to confirm that it was Aráoz's phone number at the time could be enough to land him in serious trouble. There were love messages and veiled threats, too. And a few from that night confirming that he had promised to take her to a party. Verónica made a note of all the messages. It wouldn't be difficult to reopen the case, especially if Roxana came forward to testify.

Federico had to make an effort not to forget that danger lurked outside the house: Peratta. He felt safe in this place. Every so often he checked the alarm, and he had his gun case to hand and was alert to any call from his contacts who had links to Peratta.

"Let me take care of supper tonight," Verónica said to Federico that night, to his surprise.

That was very unexpected, coming from her. Federico went out into the garden. He liked looking at the sky from there. It wasn't like the sky in Buenos Aires. The one over Tucumán was darker, with more stars. Soon Verónica appeared with two glasses of wine.

"If you like, I'll teach you how to spot the satellites," she said.

Sure enough, if he concentrated, he could see celestial bodies which looked like stars except that they were moving in the sky. He hadn't realized Verónica knew about this kind of thing.

"I didn't actually know about it. Petra told me one night. We were standing right about here."

"Look at the moon. It's almost full. There's only a little way to go. Everyone loves a full moon. But it makes me feel a bit sad knowing that the next day – or rather, the next night – it's going to start getting smaller, until it disappears."

"That's life, Fede: we're born, we grow, we shrink and die. The bitch is when you die too soon. Frida and Petra had loads of plans. They were people who did good in the world. And evil bastards caused their deaths. I think about this all the time."

Federico would have held her, would have told her this pain would pass. It wouldn't disappear, but she would get used to it, as people get used to a scar.

"Hey, what about dinner?"

"It's in hand. Let's go to the kitchen."

Inside there was a delicious smell of melted cheese.

"What have you made?"

And Verónica, as though she were sliding out of the oven a dish made by Paul Bocuse himself, exclaimed, "Pizza Sibarita."

"Ah, you're shameless. You put a frozen pizza in the oven and call that cooking?"

"First of all, I didn't say I was going to cook, but that I would take care of supper. I could have called for a takeaway, you know. And secondly, these pizzas are really good. Don't be a spoilsport."

"And thirdly, you don't know how to cook."

"I know the basics: how to make coffee, boil noodles – though admittedly I usually do them too long – and rice, I can do steak but don't like to because the kitchen fills up with smoke and smells, and my star turn: roast pumpkin with mozzarella."

After washing up, they repeated the previous night's line-up. Verónica went in search of the bottle of Johnnie Walker and two glasses; he looked through the movie options.

"Have you seen *Buffalo '66*?"

"No, who directed it?" asked Verónica as she filled their glasses.

"Vincent Gallo. He directed it, stars in it, composed the soundtrack."

Federico put on the movie and they settled back into the same places as the night before. At times, it was quite painful to watch the story of the ex-convict who kidnaps a girl in order to pass her off as his wife to his parents. The viewer wants things to go well for these two losers in life.

"If it ends badly I'll kill you," Verónica told him.

Federico didn't want a tragic ending either, or even a sad one. To his surprise, Verónica moved towards him and leaned her head on his shoulder. He sat still, frozen, not knowing what to do. Thousands of thoughts flitted through his head, not least how short their sexual relationship had been compared to their lengthy platonic one. Verónica knew that in all the intervening years, he had never stopped carrying a torch for her. He had learned to tolerate the boyfriends and lovers. He had hooked up with other girls, girls who were nicer, younger and even prettier than Verónica (scratch that: she was still the prettiest), but he had never been able to get her out of his head. And now *her* head was resting on his shoulder. Because she was tired? Was she sad about the movie, or still traumatized by everything she was going through? What did she want from him? Federico dared only move his body a little so she could rest her head more comfortably. He could feel the warmth of her body close to his. What to do? If he made a wrong move he could ruin this time together, destroy the trust she had built in him. She might even think he was trying to take advantage of her vulnerability. Better, he thought, if the decision were not left to him. Let the movie make it. If it ended badly – and all signs were that it would – he would say *See you tomorrow* and go to his room. No harm done. If the movie ended well, he'd kiss her.

The movie finished, to all intents and purposes with a happy ending. He shuffled down a bit to be on a level with Verónica's face, both of them leaning against the sofa. She smiled at him.

And he kissed her.

It was a series of short kisses, like the sound of an engine turning over until it engages. Then the short kisses became one long, warm kiss. Verónica moved closer, until she was almost facing him, and he put his arms around her. He had waited years for that embrace and now it was happening. At any moment it might be interrupted or change into something else, like in a bad dream.

Verónica drew lightly away and said, "This is madness, Fede. It's the closest to incest we can get."

"I'm not your brother, or your lover either. I love you more than I would love you if I were part of your family, or just some guy you sleep with every now and then."

"I still like you, even though you say 'sleep with'." Verónica gave him a kiss. A few kisses.

Federico moved his hand under her T-shirt, stroked her back and unclasped her bra. Verónica's eyes were half closed and her mouth open as he squeezed her breasts.

"Let's go to my room," said Verónica.

He followed her to the room where she threw herself across the bed, face down, to reach the bedside table.

"I've got two condoms," she said, taking them and turning her head. Her ass looked devastating in jeans. "I hope that's enough."

"One's more than enough, if you ask me."

"You're kidding me," she said, laughing.

"No," he said, climbing on top of her and kissing her neck.

Verónica turned over, leaving the condoms to one side. Federico was kissing her, but he wanted to eat her, bite her, chew her, taste her whole body. He pulled off her T-shirt and the bra which was already undone, and unbuttoned her jeans. She was wearing black lace underwear that matched her bra. He turned her over again and Verónica let herself be turned. Before Federico's eyes were her naked back, her ass accentuated by the underwear. He bit her nape and kissed all the way down her spine. When he reached her underwear he began to pull it down with his teeth and she turned over. Federico buried his face between her legs. Eating her, biting her, chewing her, tasting her, hearing Verónica's moans. She sat up and asked him to stop, and took off his clothes. Now she was the one throwing herself voraciously on his body. She sucked with dedication, every so often smiling up at him. She groped for a condom, opened it with her mouth and put it on him, then climbed on top and started to move. He caressed her breasts, waist, legs. She leaned on his chest, then moved her hands towards his neck, circling it with her slim fingers and starting to press down, slowly at first then harder as she came closer to orgasm. Federico began to feel that he couldn't breathe and tried to tilt his head back, but the pressure of her hands made that impossible. He saw that she was climaxing and didn't want to interrupt her by removing her hands from his throat, but he was getting increasingly short of breath. She was crying out and he was practically passing out. With what remained of his strength he did something he wouldn't remember moments later: he pushed her backwards, without even thinking about it. A second later he was coughing wildly and Verónica was next to him looking on with horror. He couldn't talk, even though she was asking if he was all right. What he wanted was to gulp down all the air in the room.

"You almost killed me," he finally gasped, his breathing still broken but a little more oxygen in his lungs.

"I'm sorry, I didn't mean to, I swear."

"I imagine! If I'd thought you wanted to kill me I would have got the hell out!"

"I'm sorry." Verónica stroked his face, his chest.

"You really are crazy. Certifiable."

“I’m sorry,” she said again as she removed the condom and went down on him again.

VI

When he woke up, Verónica was still there. He looked at the time: half past twelve. The last time he had been aware of being awake was around seven o’clock in the morning. Now Verónica was sleeping, breathing deeply. Her hair all over her face. Gently he pushed it back. He wanted to see her properly. He would have liked to pull off the covers and gaze at her body. Run his hands over her. Daylight was filtering between the slats in the blinds. If, before going to sleep, he had thought that she wouldn’t be beside him in the morning, now he feared that when she woke up she would tell him everything had been a mistake, that they should go back to acting like siblings.

Verónica half-opened her eyes.

He braced himself for any reaction, knowing he needed to behave like a gentleman and not make any pathetic scenes about being used for sex.

“What time is it?” she asked, forming the words with some difficulty.

“Half past twelve.”

“What day?”

“Wednesday.”

Verónica opened her eyes more fully. “For a moment I was scared it might already be Thursday or Friday.” She noticed him looking at her. “What’s up?” she asked.

“Nothing. I’m just waiting for the moment when you say it was all a mistake, a rampant case of incest and other awful things I don’t feel like hearing. You may think I’m a fool, or a mother’s boy, or your father’s son, or some other thing that gives you an excuse to back away. But you're wrong. I'm the man who can make you happy. The only one, I think. And anything you might say to the contrary is madness. Just another example of your madness. And don't start going on about how there are other men, or that intimacy could ruin our friendship or anything else like that, because I don't want to hear it. Do you understand?"

"I think so. You've been awake for a while, haven't you?"

"A little while – why?"

"I don't know, you've clearly been thinking a lot."

"And what do you have to say?"

"About what? About the night we spent together? About you? The night: spectacular. You: a delight."

"Nothing else? And what about you? What have you got to say?"

"That I'm divine. That none of your other women, past or present, can fuck you better than me. I don't know what else to say. Now be a good boy and go and make some really good coffee."

It was one of those rare days when everything seems to go perfectly. They had a late breakfast and then Federico said that it would be a great day for an asado. Not at a grill, but at home, made by him. Verónica asked him several times if he was sure he knew how to do one. He said that, given the magnificent outdoor barbecue area the house had, it would be crazy not to use it. They should go to the city to buy meat, and also condoms.

They took the car to San Miguel, where Verónica bought condoms and a couple of packets of cigarettes in a newsagent. They found a butcher that looked trustworthy and parked outside. Federico asked her if she ate offal.

"Obviously: chorizo, black pudding, sweetbreads, kidneys."

"Wow."

"Wow what? I bet I've had more pre-match chorizo hot dogs than you."

In the butcher they bought a chunk of flank steak, two chorizos, a black pudding and half a kilo of offal. At a grocery store they bought tomatoes and lettuce, as well as a bag of charcoal just in case, because Federico was hoping to use dry branches. It was past four by the time they started lunch, and past six when they finished it. Federico ignored a couple of calls from the office. If it was very important, Aarón himself would call. Verónica went to her room.

That night they ate what remained of the steak – which was almost all of it – then went out to the garden. It was the first time he had held her like this. They sat on the same lounger and stared at the sky while he gently stroked her stomach and breasts. Afterwards they didn't watch a movie but went to his room. Since their timetables were still off-kilter, they chatted and fucked until dawn. Later he fell asleep. He woke up at about ten o'clock in the morning, had a shower and got dressed. Glancing at his phone, he saw that he had four missed calls from Nicolás Menéndez Berti, and went to the kitchen to call him.

"I didn't have anything to do with the murder of those girls," said Nicolás without preamble.

"I'm sure you didn't."

"But everywhere they're saying I'm responsible. I even saw it on the website of the magazine that Rosenthal girl works for."

"The real culprits have to be found so everything can be cleared up. Did you do the DNA test?"

"Yes, yes, I didn't have any contact with either of the girls."

"Were you calling to tell me that?"

"No. But they're playing a dirty game. They pushed those corpses onto me."

"What do you mean?"

"I didn't give all the recordings to the police. I want you to see the one I've kept back and tell me what to do."

VII

When she opened her eyes, Verónica found herself alone in Federico's bed. She looked at her watch. It was eleven o'clock. For a moment she thought of going back to sleep, but she ought to get on with things. What was she doing, though? Had she gone mad? If she wrote to Paula, she'd get called every name under the sun. All her friends would shake their heads disapprovingly. Even her sisters, who wanted nothing more in the world than to see her marry Federico, would eye her suspiciously.

But what did they know? For years she and Federico had shared more than would be usual even in an average marriage. And if it was so common for a couple to realize after several years that they were no longer united by either love or passion, why couldn't the opposite happen? Why not believe that, after sharing so much else in their lives, love and desire could burst forth between two people who already had affection for one another? Had she really said love and desire could "burst forth"? Had she turned into a character in a romantic novel without anyone alerting her to the fact?

This silliness must be a sign that what she had with Federico was serious. When she had come out of the morgue, completely broken, there he had been, waiting for her outside. The way he'd held her had kept her from going completely to pieces. And he had been with her every moment since then, looking after her and accompanying her. When they found out Peratta and his accomplice were on the loose, Federico had suggested going to San Javier and for the first time in ages she had felt something approaching the anxiety of desire. Yes, she wanted to go, wanted to be with him, alone and far away from everything. He was angry with her for going to Coronel Berti alone and she was thinking that tomorrow they'd be on their own and together. It was strange, because she had always preferred him not to be around when awful things happened in her life: her mother's funeral, Lucio's death, her grief afterwards. She had always sought out solitude or the company of other people, even people she loved less. Now, though, she wouldn't want to be with anyone other than him. On more than one occasion she had caught herself gazing at him in silence. Because the Federico capable of so many things (even killing for her) wasn't the nice, attentive boy she used to see in her father's office, the one she'd fucked. He was much more than that. *Passion burst forth,* she said to herself, and imagined the words scrolling along the bottom of some sensationalist news report.

Verónica got up and went to her room without seeing Federico, who must be in the kitchen or the garden. The asado was lying heavy in her stomach. There were some charcoal tablets in her pouch of remedies, and she took two with a glass of water. Better not tell Federico about this or he'd make fun of her. She looked for her cigarettes and lit one.

She sat on the lavatory, thinking that she should call Robson to see if he had any news. Beside the toilet was a copy of *Nuestro Tiempo.* The latest edition was already out in Buenos Aires, but it wouldn't reach Tucumán until the next morning. Verónica picked up this old copy and flicked through it absent-mindedly. There was Vilna's piece on the crimes. How quickly that black magic angle had dated. Verónica skipped through the sections and other articles to get to Vilna's other piece, which she hadn't yet read. She was curious to see what the Politics editor had to say about drug traffickers. Police from the forces in Salta and Tucumán were implicated, but it was clear Vilna was trying to save their necks.

Suddenly something caught her attention. The secretary of justice in Tucumán was Menéndez Berti. The alleged narco cop in Salta was called Posadas and was the son of Eusebio Posadas, one-time chief of the Salta police force. Posadas was the second surname of her cousin's wife. It wasn't an altogether unusual name, of course. There must be lots of people called Posadas in the country – even in Salta, from where the Witch hailed. But Verónica remembered that, a few years ago, when she was writing an article about the suppression of a protest, the Witch's father had put her in touch with Alberto Posadas, an uncle of Severo's wife and at that time chief of the Salta police. The Posadas currently in custody was his son.

A long time ago she had worked on several articles with a photographer called El Tano, who could come across as gruff at first but was actually very kind and a mentor to young journalists like herself. On one occasion, Verónica had told him she was writing an article on a fight between *barra bravas*, notorious soccer hooligans at the Boca ground. El Tano told her to look into the violent suppression of a teachers' protest that had taken place a few days previously at the city legislature building.

"Why? What's that got to do with it?"

"Listen, love, a journalist's basic job – and don't let anyone tell you otherwise – is to find a link between two apparently separate events that are in fact connected. Find out who the leaders of the *barra bravas* are, who beat up the teachers and what political affiliations the two groups have. I bet you find out it's all part of the same thing."

"In other words, they have two jobs. Hired thugs and professional fans. Violent in either case."

"Violence is the language they use to show their power or to intimidate. You don't just need to connect people but also events: the fight between the *barras* wouldn't have happened if the teachers' protest hadn't been suppressed."

Menéndez Berti in two news stories, a cousin of the Witch on one side and another cousin in Yacanto del Valle. Would the girls have been murdered if the narco cop hadn't been arrested? And there was the father of Posadas, perhaps the father of Menéndez Berti, the father of Aráoz, perhaps the father of Elizalde? And so much interest from her own father in what was happening there. What game was being played out through Petra and Frida's deaths? She had to get back to Yacanto straightaway to find the missing pieces.

When she came out of her room, she saw Federico in the living room. She was about to tell him she had to go back when he said:

"Pack your things. We're going to Yacanto del Valle."

14 *Working the Land*

I

Nothing was worse than delays. They were dead time when you wanted to get the job done. It was better when they told him who and where the target was so he could go there and eliminate them. This job was already taking too much time. First he'd had to rescue Three, wait for him to recover, stay hidden. And now Doctor Zero was telling them to wait for new orders. In the meantime, they had to lie low in this shitty barrio on the outskirts of San Miguel de Tucumán.

Five had learned to be obedient, though. If they told him to spend a month in one room, he would do it. He didn't get frustrated or rebel, much less make the mistake of disobeying orders and walking out. So when Doctor Zero had ordered them to hang fire, they complied. There was nothing for it but to wait, putting their lives on hold until new instructions arrived.

But Three didn't seem to agree. No sooner had they escaped from the police station in Coronel Berti than he wanted to go back to the hotel where the chick was staying. He'd had to grab Three by the neck and tell him very clearly to his face that they had escaped thanks to Doctor Zero, that they worked for him and must obey his command. Without relaxing his grip on Three's neck, Five had used his free hand to call the Doctor, who had told them to leave town immediately for San Miguel de Tucumán and to wait there. The other man had looked on angrily, realizing he had no option but to fall into line. He repeated that the surprise factor was crucial, which was why they should go the same day. Five had explained to him that the first thing the police would do on discovering their escape would certainly be to send cops to the hotel. Not only to protect the chick, but to catch them.

Five realized it also bothered Three that all Doctor Zero's instructions came through him. Three still believed himself to be the most important of the Doctor's men. He was wrong. The Doctor's right-hand man now was him, Five.

"How about this: I go alone, do what I have to do and don't charge. It's on me," Three said again.

Five was struggling to keep Three cooped up in the hideout. He had no option but to call Doctor Zero and explain the situation, using the excuse of going out to buy cigarettes so they could speak privately. After a ten-minute conversation – much longer than usual – Five had new instructions.

"Doctor Zero says the wait is over. We're leaving for Yacanto del Valle."

Three took a deep breath. Finally his moment had come.

"I was on the verge of going anyway," he confessed to Five.

They set off early for Yacanto del Valle. Five drove all the way in silence. He was in a terrible mood. He didn't like any of this. But he was following orders.

A few miles outside Coronel Berti, Five turned the car off the road and drove it towards some trees where he could observe the road without being seen.

"What are we doing here?" Three asked.

"Watching the road and waiting."

After a quarter of an hour, Five said:

"I'm getting out for a piss."

Five walked towards the trees behind the car, unzipped his flies and unleashed a long stream of urine. He walked slowly back, approaching on the side of the passenger window. He could see Three fiddling with the radio dial. When Five was half a yard from the window, he took out his gun and shot Three in the head. Instantly Three slumped forward. He hadn't even had time to realize he was about to be killed. A quick shot without any of the terror that comes before death. It was the best he could do for his partner in crime.

He pulled Three out of the car and left him lying in a spot that was more visible from the road. The police should find the body quickly. If the journalist saw Three's corpse, she and her entourage would let down their guard. That would make his work easier.

It was true Three's death made things simpler. But it was also true that the Doctor was doing this because Three had become too visible and could end up compromising him. The Doctor could get someone else tomorrow to kill Five. Rules were there to be followed.

What a fucking terrible day, Five thought as he returned to Tucumán to await new orders.

II

Federico decided it was better not to tell Verónica the reason for their return to Yacanto del Valle. He didn't want her to know he was meeting Nicolás. Verónica, for her part, spent some of the journey developing her theory on a possible link between the narco cops scandal and the girls' murders. It couldn't be coincidental that the murders had taken place the same week as prominent members of the Salta and Tucumán police forces were arrested.

"There are now at least three suspects," said Federico.

"There are three guilty of rape and murder. But it must go further than that."

"The fourth man, whose DNA was under one of the girls' nails."

"But what if there are more? How far can the long arm of the law reach? Obviously you're the perpetrator if you commit rape, murder or assault, but who gave the order?"

"Well, there's a crime of 'intellectual author', which is like an accessory before the fact."

"I'd love to know how often these intellectual authors actually go to prison, though. Especially when they're powerful people." Verónica considered her theories for a moment before adding: "Intellectual author – and who's the intellectual author of *Popul Vuh*? Who's the intellectual author of Carnaval? Who's the intellectual author of the circumcision of babies or female genital mutilation?"

"I don't quite follow."

"With femicide there's an intellectual author who will never be condemned: the very society which tolerates and normalizes it."

"I can imagine that line might sound good in an article, or in the closing arguments of a criminal defence lawyer, but with murder someone's always physically responsible, whether as a direct author or an intellectual one. And I'll tell you something else, not that I want to start an argument. It's true that the majority of murders of women are committed by men. But so too are the majority of murders of men."

"I suppose they taught you that at law school. And you repeat it like parrots. Male chauvinist parrots."

Fortunately for Federico, they had arrived at Yacanto del Valle. They parked the car outside the Posada de Don Humberto and found Mariano at reception. He said they had dispensed with the security guard after Federico and

Verónica left, but that they would arrange for Officer Benítez or whoever else was available to return that night. Mariano asked Verónica if she would rather stay in the hotel's main building or in their house.

"We're going to stay together in a double room."

"Ah," said Mariano, registering Federico's poker face.

In fact it would be the first time they had shared a room, because at Severo's house they had each had their own. It was strange to share so much intimacy.

Federico lay on the bed and watched her unpack. "Are you sure you want us to be in the same room? Because if it's just to have sex, I can make myself available all the same. I can visit you in your room for a few minutes."

"To have sex. I think my first mission in your life is to improve your language."

"OK – fuck, screw. Is that better?"

"And what's this about a few minutes? Why a few minutes? No, darling, I want to go to sleep watching TV with you beside me. It's better if you learn to put up with my ways quickly. If you don't like them, you can take off whenever you like."

Verónica put her suitcase on the floor and lay down beside Federico. She hugged and kissed him. "I think I'm losing my mind," she said.

"I, on the other hand, think this is the sanest I've ever seen you."

Federico had to go and meet Nicolás and then bring Aarón up to speed with everything that was happening in the case, but Verónica had started to take her clothes off and he thought it would be very rude to interrupt her merely to attend to work. Verónica climbed on top of him, completely naked, before he had a chance even to unbutton his shirt. Federico grabbed her ass and pulled her towards his face while sliding further down the bed. It was a new perspective of her body, seeing her from underneath while he sucked her and she leaned against the wall, her breasts seen from below, her navel up close, her moans coming from above.

III

Ever since his wife had died and he decided to retire, Juan Robson liked every now and then to make an audit of his life, especially his working life. His family life was easier to evaluate: he hadn't been the best father, but nobody (himself included) would hesitate to call him an excellent husband. He had always been by his wife's side. He had loved her more than anyone, more than his two children, who always seemed distant to him.

When his wife fell ill, cancer attacked her slowly but inexorably. There were two years of treatments, of trips back and forth during which he never left her, just as he hadn't in the last forty years. The children were worried, they came to visit, but they didn't belong there any more, not even in the house. One lived in Mendoza and the other in Buenos Aires. Robson looked after his wife and would never have dreamed of reproaching the children for not doing more. He loved them in his way, and he knew they loved their mother.

When he ended up alone he didn't seek refuge in journalism, as many had thought he would. There was no longer any sense in looking for a story, writing it, nosing out the truth and putting it in an article. He asked for voluntary retirement and went home to wait for his pension. He liked to spend hours cloistered away in those rooms that his wife had decorated and filled with what were now memories. If he closed his eyes he could imagine his wife was in another room, in the bedroom, or the bathroom, and that made him happy.

Every so often this routine was interrupted by a visit from some colleague who wanted to consult his famous archive. He took advantage of these opportunities to socialize a little and to revisit his own professional life. He liked to compare himself with whichever journalist was visiting and to think how he had been at their age, what things had interested him, at what stage of his career he had been.

When Verónica Rosenthal arrived on the trail of murdered women, he wondered if he had at any point been interested in such a case. And it was true that on more than one occasion he had been obsessed with discovering the perpetrators of some crime or other. He had turned up evidence that had eluded investigators. But when he started helping her to search the archive, Robson had a strange sensation, as though he had been found out. He couldn't explain this feeling until he came across the case of Claudia Rinaldi, the girl murdered in Yacanto del Valle in 1982. There were two short articles about the crime. The one he showed to Verónica. And the other one, which he had written himself.

Robson had managed to expunge from his memory everything about the case, until now. These last thirty years he had not lost sleep, not even once, thinking about the crime against that girl. But his memory must have salted the story away in some dark recess of his mind. Now he remembered perfectly what had happened.

The story had reached his paper's newsroom via the police at Yacanto del Valle. It was one of those crimes that move the public: a young girl was raped, murdered and thrown out of a vehicle on the side of a road in a small town. Robson wrote a short report with the information available at that point and set off for Yacanto the next day. He spoke to the girl's family, her friends and even a witness who had seen a Ford van dropping off a bundle which later proved to be the body. The witness had taken a licence plate number. All the evidence, the observations of family and friends, and a simple check on the national vehicle register led to the same person: army captain Guillermo Aráoz. Even the chief superintendent at Yacanto, Roberto Gatti, had confirmed to him that Aráoz was deeply involved.

At that time the dictatorship still had a year left to run, but it had entered its final phase and it was no longer impossible to accuse a military man of a common crime. And yet Tucumán was a difficult province; the transition to democracy would not be simple there. When Robson returned to the newsroom with all the material he needed to write the article, his editor stopped him short. He told him that the piece was not going to appear in the newspaper. There was an argument which ultimately Robson lost. He had one card left – that Chief Superintendent Gatti or the investigating judge might themselves move towards arresting Aráoz – but that day never came. And gradually he forgot about it, other cases came along, other murders, robberies and scams. A time came when he no longer remembered it. Until now.

He still saw Gatti because the chief superintendent had been promoted soon afterwards and had to move to San Miguel de Tucumán. They never talked about the case. Gatti had retired a few years before him, but Robson had his home phone number. After Verónica Rosenthal's visit, he had called him and asked if they could meet for a chat. They had arranged to meet in a bar on Calle San Martín. They hadn't seen each other for nearly five years.

Gatti was the same as ever, as vigorous and bad-tempered as when he was chief superintendent. Robson didn't beat around the bush but immediately brought up the case neither of them had investigated, expecting Gatti to have a convenient memory lapse. He was sure the ex-cop would claim not to remember the crime – but that wasn't what happened.

"The Rinaldi girl. I remember it very well."

"Captain Aráoz did it."

"Yes, of course. A nasty piece of work, that Aráoz. He didn't want me in Yacanto del Valle. That's why they sent me to San Miguel."

"I thought they'd rewarded you for keeping your mouth shut."

"It was a kind of reward, but it was also because Aráoz didn't want me there. I'd found out too much about the Rinaldi murder and the old soldier couldn't forgive me."

"So what was it you'd found out?"

"Bear with me, pal. I already have a touch of Alzheimer's and I don't remember everything."

That wasn't true. Over the following hour Gatti recounted all the details of his investigation and the conclusions to which he had come.

It seemed Aráoz saw it as his right, his *droit de seigneur*, to do whatever he wanted with the girls working on his land. Claudia had refused to go with him on more than one occasion, as her family had testified. One afternoon, Claudia was returning to the place where she lived with her parents and siblings, and she met Aráoz on the way. He forced her to get into his pickup. A maid who worked at the Aráoz house – a friend of Rinaldi's mother – saw how he locked the girl in an old shed they didn't use any more. She also heard the girl shouting. Aráoz ordered that no one go near the shed. The maid, who lived in quarters connected to the main house, heard Aráoz setting off in his pickup at dawn. Soon afterwards he dumped the body at the side of the road, not realizing that a local man who knew the area had seen him and memorized the licence plate.

"Listen, Gatti, if everything you've told me had to be legally corroborated because it's going to appear in an article, would you be willing to do that?"

"Are you going back to journalism?"

"No, I'm not, but there's a person who's interested in revisiting the case."

"I'm going to look like a piece of crap, but never mind. I'm old now and I've been washed up for a while. Yes, I'll happily repeat all this to whoever you like."

Back home, Robson wrote the Rosenthal girl a long email with all the information Gatti had supplied him. It was everything she would need. He wasn't brave enough to confess to her that he could have written that article thirty years ago.

IV

It was already starting to get dark by the time Federico arrived at Nicolás's house. He had called him before setting off and found him still as jittery as he had been that morning. Federico didn't tell Verónica where he was going or why. He still wasn't entirely sure what his next steps would be or how to proceed.

This time, the maid led him to a kind of studio. Nicolás was sitting looking at a laptop screen but stood up when he saw Federico and came forward to shake his hand, then directed him to a chair on the other side of the desk. He returned to his own seat and they sat face to face, with the Apple logo in Federico's eyeline.

"I can't stand this any longer," Nicolás said.

Federico remained silent.

"I've got all the TV stations talking about me, my house, my party. They're treating me as though I were the murderer."

"That was always a possibility once it became known that the guilty parties worked here."

"Even that Rosenthal girl's rag said it was me."

Federico thought it unnecessary to explain that the magazine didn't actually belong to Verónica.

"They're trying to pin those murders on me. On my family. Do you understand?"

"But why would they do that?"

"My dad's involved with some sensitive material and they wanted to send him a message."

"Because of the narco police case?"

"They've been wanting to get him for a long time. And now, with all this mayhem, they've managed to get the governor to withdraw his support and ask for my father's resignation."

"Because of the girls' deaths?"

"What else do you expect the governor to do if the Secretary of Justice's son is implicated in a double murder?"

Nicolás opened a drawer in his desk, took out a memory stick and passed it to Federico.

"But I'm not going to just sit here and take it. We know very well who gave the order for this shitshow."

He paused for a few seconds then continued:

"When the police came, they demanded the security cameras. They took the ones from the entrance by the security booth, plus the ones that were inside the house on the landing and another from the back patio."

"From what I've heard, there's nothing significant on any of the tapes."

"There are things that are hard to explain."

"Nicolás, it doesn't make sense at this stage to keep anything you know secret."

"I'm aware of that. That's why I'm giving you the memory stick. There's a copy there of recordings from other cameras."

"Which the police didn't see?"

"They're not out in the open. They're not security cameras. They're – how can I put this? – concealed."

"You mean they're for spying?"

"Something like that. They're all over the house. The ones of interest here are in the men's changing room and in my room. I've saved the relevant frames on the memory stick."

Nicolás turned the screen of his laptop to face Federico and opened up the video player. Images appeared from a changing room. The resolution was much higher than with a security camera.

"The first images are from the night of the party. There are a few frames before and after that prove the recording is from that day. I haven't copied them for you because I'm not interested in giving you legal proof. This is something else."

The footage also had sound, although loud music obscured everything. On the screen two men appeared, recognizable from photos Federico had seen: they were the brothers Vázquez. They didn't speak to each other but seemed to be waiting for something. Presently a third man, Reyes, appeared, greeted them and stayed in the frame. Then a few minutes later a fourth man arrived, a young guy Federico didn't recognize. Nicolás paused the video.

"Nahuel Elizalde. Ramiro's younger brother."

"So...?"

"What follows is a conversation with Nahuel. A day before the party."

The screen no longer showed the changing rooms, but a bedroom. The scene could be from a decadent theatre play: a lavish room; a man sitting in his underwear on the edge of a bed, holding his head in an apparent gesture of worry or pain. On the other side of it, a man came out of the bathroom wearing nothing but boxer shorts. The seated man was Nicolás. The standing one, Nahuel. Unlike the previous video, this one had perfect sound. Putting on his jeans and white T-shirt, Nahuel said:

"You have to see that your dad's fucking all of us over, not only my cousin in prison. I don't give a fuck about the Posadas. There's a lot of money at stake here and other people who need to be handled. This is a total clusterfuck."

"You know there's nothing I can do."

"Either you stop him, or we stop him."

"Don't threaten me."

"Your dad is getting to be a pain."

Nicolás stopped the video.

"So Nahuel was the one who organized everything?" Federico asked, and Nicolás laughed.

"Nahuel? No, Nahuel couldn't organize a dolls' tea party. As a friend of mine says, he's all brawn and no brain."

"Ramiro Elizalde?"

"Ramiro's had it in for me for years. He thinks I perverted his brother. He actually used that word to me once: perverted. And he likes conspiracy theories, orchestrating manoeuvres that make him feel like a Machiavelli or a political genius. He's just some dickhead who thinks he's important because he can name three artists off the top of his head."

"When Nahuel said they were going to do something about your father, they didn't know anything about the existence of the tourists at that stage."

"I imagine the original plan was to pick one of the girls at the party. The Europeans were probably chosen at the last moment. They must have thought that would get more coverage in the papers and on television. There's another video that shows how Ramiro separated the tourists from Rosenthal's daughter."

Nicolás clicked Play and there was Verónica, wearing a short white dress, kissing Ramiro in the same room where Nicolás and Nahuel had been before. The same music as in the first video could be heard but seemed to be coming from further away. They kissed, she tried to steer him towards the bed. He resisted and suggested going to his house. She hesitated because she didn't want to leave the girls alone at the party, but finally agreed.

"They wrecked my life," said Nicolás in the same pitiable tone he had used when talking to Nahuel in the other video. "They've ruined me for ever."

Federico nodded, but he wasn't listening any more.

V

Federico came out of Nicolás's house reeling like a drunkard, his mind befuddled, his step uncertain, overcome by a sensation of not being entirely sure where he was, nor where he had to go or what he had to do. He got into his car and sat for a few minutes, gripping the steering wheel without starting the engine. As he finally drove away, he decided not to go to the hotel. Instead he parked near the square and started to walk. It was already dark and there weren't many people in the street. He had the memory stick in his coat pocket and kept feeling it to be sure it was still there.

Seeing Verónica so beautiful, so dressed up, so into another man, had left him devastated. He mustn't be weak. He must focus on what was important. The memory stick was Nicolás's last chance both to extricate himself from the maelstrom of accusations and to save his father – although that would be difficult. The videos weren't for him but for Aarón. Even the one with Verónica. It was almost a mafioso message: *I have more videos of your daughter. Either you help me, or I'll make them public.*

Federico walked to the square and leaned against a tree. He called Aarón and told him he had the videos. He explained what was in the first two, but decided to say nothing about the video with Verónica in it.

"What idiots they are," said Aarón, clearly furious. "Posadas senior and Menéndez Berti senior should have been able to reach an agreement without all this nonsense."

"Aarón, the nonsense includes the rape and murder of two women."

"Yes, of course. They're completely useless. If I weren't friends with their fathers, I'd see to it they rot in jail."

Federico made a mental note of Aarón's decision: the Elizalde brothers weren't going to prison. Aarón was still talking.

"On top of everything, Judge Amalfi is obsessed with screwing over Menéndez Berti and locking up his son. But with the evidence we have in these videos, he's going to have to back off if he doesn't want the Elizaldes to go down."

"He won't want that."

"Of course not, Amalfi isn't an idiot. I'm worried about the DA. He's one of those types who like to build their careers on media exposure. I don't like people like that."

Federico walked over to an empty bench and sat down. He felt weary.

"This is what we're going to do, Federico. The murder of the young women can't go unpunished. We've got rapists and murderers here and they must go to prison. Justice must find the three fugitives. The name of Menéndez Berti must be cleared."

"Menéndez Berti senior."

"The idiot son who keeps having parties."

"Would you like me to speak to the judge, and to the DA?"

"No, I'll do that first thing tomorrow. What I want from you is to ensure that nobody, but nobody, gets hold of those videos. There must be nothing that incriminates the Elizaldes, understood?"

"Yes, Aarón."

"When I say 'nobody', I mean Verónica. She doesn't even need to know these videos exist. Bring them to the office and we'll keep them safe."

It wouldn't be the first time Aarón had stored compromising evidence. His safe was like a Pandora's box: many people feared it and the success of Rosenthal and Associates was partly built on it. Aarón knew when to bring his paperwork out of the dark vault. It was a collection of aces, giving him a winning hand in courtroom poker.

"Come back to Buenos Aires tomorrow. Bring the memory stick and take a few days off. Try to persuade Verónica to come back too. There's nothing more to investigate now."

And before hanging up, Aarón said for the third time:

"Verónica mustn't find out about any of this."

Federico didn't return to his car but walked instead to the hotel. He had to think hard what to do. But however much he tried to get his ideas straight, he couldn't get away from the fact that he stood between Verónica and Aarón. There was no solution that didn't involve betraying one of them. *Conflict of interests*, he thought.

Verónica was in the hotel restaurant. It was already dinner time and she was waiting for him.

"Where have you been? Mariano and Luca want us to eat with them."

He invented an excuse about the firm (after all, what he had been doing for the last few hours did have something to do with Rosenthal and Associates). It was lucky they were with Mariano and Luca; that way the conversation could be steered in a less awkward direction. At any rate, Verónica seemed very happy, because she had received a long email from Robson. She was thinking of writing an article about Aráoz senior and his part in a case that had been long forgotten and would now never be brought to justice. It wouldn't be the same, but at least she could ensure nobody forgot who was guilty of the death of a young woman murdered in the early 1980s.

"See?" Verónica said to Federico. "There are some things the law does badly that journalism can do well."

"I'm not your daddy, don't start on that with me," he answered, mentally kicking himself for being the one to bring up Aarón and his fights with his daughter.

Luca went back and forth between dining room and kitchen. He himself had prepared the dishes they chose from the menu: pâté with cognac, braised lamb and chocolate meringue profiteroles – not exactly a light meal. They spent a long time at the table afterwards, their conversation accompanied by plenty of wine.

Back in their room, Verónica collapsed onto the bed while Federico had a shower. When he came out, she was asleep. Federico tried to make no noise. He turned out the light and got into bed. A moment later she got up and went to the bathroom then asked him very quietly, on her return, if he was asleep. Federico was awake but said nothing. Soon afterwards he heard Verónica's steady breathing.

He had to make a decision and act on it. He wasn't going to go home the next day, as he had promised Aarón. He would stay on until he could be sure Verónica was safe from Peratta. He wouldn't tell Verónica about the memory stick. The Elizaldes could breathe easy.

VI

Mechi had made a few decisions. She would go to night school in Coronel Berti. The deadline for registration was still a few days off and she had already found out there were spaces. For now she would keep working for the Arregui family, but she would look for another job. Not in a private house, but in a shop in Yacanto del Valle. In three years' time she would go to Buenos Aires. She wouldn't have children until she was thirty or thirty-five.

For now, however, there were more pressing questions for Mechi. One was how to help Verónica get El Gringo Aráoz convicted. She had seen him strolling around town with his wife and little son. They had all looked very happy, even the baby in its little stroller. El Gringo must not even remember he had raped and killed her sister. If she had asked him why he'd done it, he would have replied: *I don't know any Bibi, I've never met anyone called Bibi.*

Mechi had watched them for a while and followed them as they looked in shop windows, bought ice cream and sat at a table outside a bar to have coffee and for El Gringo's wife to breastfeed the baby. For two hours she walked behind the family without their realizing. The advantages of being invisible. During that time she thought of doing lots of things: stealing the baby and tossing it into the air, like a bag of French fries, in the middle of the square; finding an iron bar and smashing it over El Gringo's head, shouting *Murderer*, shouting *You're a bastard and a murderer*, spitting on him. But she didn't do any of those things. When they left the bar, El Gringo and his wife walked a block then climbed into their 4 × 4. She stood watching as the pickup drove off, as it went further, grew smaller, disappeared.

Mechi knew Verónica wouldn't act the same way, wouldn't follow him or imagine doing horrible things. She would simply make sure he ended up in prison, getting raped by the other prisoners every night.

There was something else she had to do for Verónica: find out where the Vázquez brothers were – Pretty and Ugly. That was what Rosalía and her other friends called them. But she had never liked Sebastián and didn't find him pretty, much less a good person: when his mother had put the hex on Rosalía, Mechi suspected that he knew about it and found it amusing; in fact he'd probably helped to make the little voodoo dolls.

She had to ask Rosalía if she knew anything about the brothers, but it would be better not to do this on the phone. She was more likely to tell the truth face to face. They were friends. All the same, she didn't know if she would tell Rosalía why the search was on for the boys.

Rosalía and the other girls used to meet in a club called La Pulpería, a kind of run-down bar where they sold beer at a reasonable price and didn't add a surcharge for underage drinkers. When she finished work, Mechi told her grandmother she was going to meet some friends, that she wouldn't be home until dinner time. She sent a text to Rosalía that said *Going to Pulpe – R U?* A minute later she got a reply from her friend: *Here alrdy.*

She needed to be careful with Rosalía. If she found out Mechi was asking questions in order to pass information on to the journalist, she'd get angry and not say anything. Mechi would need to bring the subject up subtly, unhurriedly, to get her to talk.

When she arrived at La Pulpería, she saw that Rosalía was with some other kids: La Chaqueña, Andrea, Cuqui, Toño and Pablo. They were sitting against the wall outside, drinking a beer which they passed around. They shouted at her to come over.

Mechi drained the last bit of beer from their bottle. Toño asked her to buy another, so she went in and asked for a litre bottle of Quilmes. She took a swig first, then passed it on to the others.

Rosalía stood up, grabbed Mechi's arm and led her away from the others. She seemed happy, animated. "I was going to call and say we should see each other," she said.

Mechi took out her packet of cigarettes and lit one. She was getting better at this.

"Have you started smoking?" Rosalía asked her.

"Yes, got a problem with that?"

She needed to bring up the subject somehow, but first she would let Rosalía tell her whatever it was she wanted to say. Her friend seemed anxious to say it. She must have hooked up with Cuqui – she'd liked him for a long time. Mechi blew out smoke.

"I've got something to tell you."

"So tell me, hon."

"I got back with Seb."

"You're back with Seb? Are you serious?" Mechi stared at her.

"Yes, but his mother doesn't know."

"You're kidding me."

"No, babe, I mean it."

"But Seb and Rulo are wanted by the police."

"So what? Anyway, they're innocent – he said so."

"Who said so?"

"Seb – are you even listening to me? We're going out again, but it's a secret. From his mother and the police."

Mechi struggled to absorb what Rosalía was telling her. How could her friend have gone back to her ex-boyfriend if everyone was looking for him?

"So how did this happen? How did you get back together?"

"He called me. Without telling the others, because he didn't want them calling anyone on account of him being accused of murdering those girls."

"So have you been to wherever Seb is?"

"Yes, they're hiding out in a house in the country, past the Monte de los Ríos. He came here, to Pulpe, to fetch me. On a motorbike, wearing a helmet, and in clothes that were too big for him. To make himself look different. When he called, he asked me to buy cigarettes, as many as I could. I had to get the money off my old man."

"I can't believe it."

"I always get money off him."

"I mean I can't believe you met up with Seb."

"He took me to the place where he's hiding with the other two. He took me into a room and it was really sweet. We did everything."

"Girl, this is incredible."

"He told me that when all this is over and people realize they're innocent, he's going to talk to his mother and tell her not to bother us any more."

"So you've only seen him once?"

"No, I've been loads of times. I had to learn the route because Seb can't always come and get me. It's dangerous with all these fucking cops around."

They fell silent.

Rosalía smiled. "I left you speechless, babe."

Mechi nodded.

"The last time the guys kept hassling me. Bring some of your friends, they said. They're obviously tired of spying on me and Seb."

"Seriously? They said that?"

"Well … they're on their own, poor things. There's no way you'd come with me, is there?"

Rosalía had her brother's moped. She'd been using it since getting back together with Seb, to travel to the house where the three men were hiding. Mechi got on the back and hugged her friend tightly. She hadn't thought twice before saying yes, that she was willing to go and visit the guys. It was her chance to find out where they were hiding and to pass the information on to Verónica. The journalist wouldn't believe it when Mechi told her how lucky she'd been.

In Mechi's rucksack, the girls took three bottles of beer which they had bought in the club, splitting the cost.

It wasn't easy to get to the house. They had to ride through the hills on dirt roads that were like a labyrinth of zigzags, carefully negotiating the uneven ground that was scattered with fallen branches and stones. After passing through a grove of trees, they arrived: it was an old neglected house. One of those abandoned country houses you see in horror movies. Rosalía left her moped beside two others parked outside the door.

Someone – not one of the Vázquez brothers – leaned out of a window. He went back inside and Sèbastián opened the door shortly afterwards. Rosalía ran into his arms and they kissed. When they drew apart, she said:

"I've brought Mechi."

15 *The Call*

I

The men brightened at the sight of the beers Rosalía produced from the rucksack. They asked if the girls had brought cigarettes, and Mechi gave them what remained of her pack. Rulo and Javier looked her up and down and smiled. Mechi's biggest worry until then had been keeping a map of the route in her head. There had been many twists and turns, but if she memorized it well, with any luck she would be able to tell Verónica how to get there.

"You look very serious," Rulo told her.

He really was ugly. He had a kind of twisted nose and a grimace that made you think he was about to cry even when he was trying to smile, as at that moment. He had long, dirty hair that looked as though it had been drawn with a thick, brown pencil.

"That's just the way I am."

"She's a bit of a buzzkill," said Rosalía, who was sitting next to Seb.

Javier, who was next to Mechi, put a hand on her leg. "She seems very sweet to me."

Mechi removed his hand. "Stop. Don't even think about it."

Sebastián and Rulo laughed.

"The dark girl's prickly," said Sebastián.

"Don't rub her up the wrong way," said Rosalía, and drank some beer from the bottle.

It wasn't Mechi's first time dealing with unwanted advances. She was used to handling tiresome men and defending herself physically if necessary. When guys got drunk on the dance floor, they thought that grabbing a woman's ass was a form of seduction. Mechi had managed to win respect for herself by dishing out the odd slap. But it wasn't the same here. At a dance, if she slapped someone, she could get other guys or girls to come to her defence. Out here, in this ranch house, she could only hope Rosalía would defend her. And there were three guys against her. Or two, if Sebastián took the girls' side.

"OK, I'm going to have to leave," Mechi said.

"Boo!" shouted Sebastián and Rosalía.

"Hey, we've only just started getting to know each other," said Rulo.

What if Rosalía didn't want to come back with her? Mechi had to leave before nightfall. She wouldn't be able to find the way back to the main road in the dark. Anyway, it must be at least an hour on foot, even walking fast. She needed to persuade Rosalía to leave with her, but her friend was busy kissing her boyfriend. It wasn't going to be easy getting her out of there.

"Rosalía, shall we go? My grandmother's waiting for me."

"I'm sure Granny won't mind you staying a bit longer," Rulo said.

"How about before you go the three of us have a little fun? It's been a long time since Rulo and I ate fresh meat."

"And you look fresh and tasty."

"I know you're going to like it," said Javier and put his hand back on Mechi's leg, but this time he squeezed it harder.

"Stop, dickhead, what do you think you're doing?" Mechi removed his hand even more firmly.

"Why did you come here, then? To turn us on then change your mind? Listen, darkie, don't play hard to get because —"

He broke off at the sound of an approaching motorbike. Nobody spoke and Javier went to look out of the window, just as he had when Mechi and Rosalía had arrived.

"It's Nahuel," he said, and didn't sit back down next to Mechi but stayed standing.

A young man came in and surveyed the scene. "What are these girls doing here?" he asked, annoyed, without saying hello.

"We're just having some fun," said Sebastián.

Nahuel went to the kitchen, looked in the bedroom and opened the door to the bathroom. He seemed to be checking there was no one else there.

"Are you fucking retards or what? Do you think this is a joke? There's a million cops looking for us and instead of jerking off you bring these sluts here?"

"Rosalía is my girlfriend," said Sebastián, defensively.

Mechi began to need a piss. She remembered having that same feeling the day she found the dead girls' bodies. Now she was with the men who had killed them. She shouldn't have come with Rosalía. She shouldn't be there now. She should go. Make a run for it. Get out. Wake up and discover all of this was nothing more than a bad dream.

Nahuel sat on the counter of a wooden sideboard. Without speaking, he looked at all of them, as though thinking. He jutted his chin at Mechi. "And who's this one?"

"She's a friend of my girlfriend," said Sebastián.

Rulo and Javier remained silent.

"Let's see if you can grasp this. You're going to have to stay here a good while. Until the police lose interest. If you start bringing people here, do you know how long you'll last? Not even a day. You'll all go down."

Nobody answered.

"Get this bitch out of here." Nahuel stood up and shook out his trousers, which had got covered in dust. "I'll take her," said Rosalía, quietly.

"Are you morons? The bitch opens her mouth and in two hours we've got everyone turning up here, even helicopters."

"I swear I won't say anything," Mechi said quickly, in the thread of voice left to her.

Nahuel didn't deign to look at her when she spoke. He gestured to Rulo and Javier. "You know what to do."

Rosalía stood up, walked over to her friend and took her by the shoulder. Mechi felt her vision clouding over. Without realizing, she started to cry.

"Nahuel, I'll take her away. She's a really good person. She won't tell a soul. I know her."

"You get to walk because you're this halfwit's girlfriend, but don't push your luck or you'll end up face down in the mud."

Sebastián tried to shuffle Rosalía out of the house. She pushed him off, turned around and shouted, "Let me go – can't you see they're going to kill her?"

Javier and Rulo went towards Mechi, who had made herself very small in the chair and was sobbing quietly, not daring to move.

"Nahuel," said Rulo, "the bitch is hot. Can we have some fun first?"

"Do whatever you like, but bury her behind the house afterwards."

Rosalía burst out crying. Javier stood over Mechi, who resisted being pulled from the chair. With Rulo's help, he lifted her out of it. Mechi screamed and Javier slapped her.

"Don't do anything to me," shouted Mechi. "If I don't go home, the police will come looking for me."

Everyone, apart from Rosalía, laughed.

"Really?" Nahuel asked sarcastically. "Next you'll tell me there are a thousand police surrounding the house and that they'll kill us if we don't let you go."

"I have to meet a journalist, and if I don't arrive she'll realize I'm in danger."

Rulo grabbed her by the hair and pulled it. Mechi let out another scream as they pushed her towards the bedroom. Still crying and shouting, she insisted, "I mean it. Verónica is waiting for me. She'll go looking for me if I don't show up."

"Stop, stop, for fuck's sake, all of you!" ordered Nahuel, and, at the door of the room, Rulo and Javier released their grip on Mechi. "What did you say the journalist was called?"

"Verónica."

"Verónica what."

"Verónica Rosenthal."

"For real?" Nahuel said and laughed loudly. "Today is my lucky day. Stop, leave the bitch. I think I'm going to save my brother a bit of money."

The others looked at him, baffled.

"Have you got the journalist's number?"

"Yes," said Mechi.

II

It was a few seconds before she realized that the person kissing her was Federico. Verónica opened her eyes and slowly returned to the real world. It was an effort to leave the dream, in which her mother had been making onion soup. Federico looked triumphant. Would he be like that every morning they woke up together? Truth be told, she'd prefer someone who went to make coffee straightaway and brought it to her in bed, without speaking.

"I have news," said Federico, and she was grateful to be the woman in the relationship and not have to worry what her partner would say next. "They've just called me from the prison service. Peratta has been found dead. Right here. At the entrance to Coronel Berti."

So the hitman nightmare was finally over? She couldn't believe it.

"It's absolutely true. I rang Chief Superintendent Suárez and he grudgingly confirmed it: the corpse is already in the morgue. Danilo Peratta has a bullet in the brain."

"But who killed him?"

"Looks like score-settling. He died as he lived."

"Federico, my dad didn't arrange for him to be killed, did he?"

"Your dad doesn't even know Peratta was looking for you, so it would have been difficult for him to send someone to kill him. I expect the guy kept some colourful company. At any rate, someone has done us a favour."

"Incredible."

"Get dressed – we're going to have breakfast and then go for a walk. I feel like breathing country air."

While they were having breakfast, Mariano recommended a good place for a walk. The Ventoso creek ran behind Yacanto and could be reached on foot in forty minutes via a wood higher up in the sierra. There were trees, flowers, birds – a little paradise almost unvisited by tourists. Luca had made them a picnic with schnitzel sandwiches, grapes, cashew nuts and several bottles of water. They set off early on their excursion.

They reached the creek out of breath and with aching legs. The hike had taken almost an hour, but it was worth it. The magnificent landscape transmitted a special calm, a feeling that everything in the world was in perfect order.

"These places will be wonderful once they can be reached by subway," said Federico, collapsing onto a log. Verónica walked to the stream and washed her burning face. The water was very cold, which felt good on her skin. Federico took a towel out of the rucksack and passed it to her. Verónica dried her face and threw herself on top of him, kissing him.

"I'm all sweaty," he protested, trying to get her off him.

"I love sweaty men."

"Sweaty *men*?"

"Well, sweaty you, then."

They kissed and she remained sitting on top of him as he tried to arrange himself more comfortably against the tree. For more than twenty minutes they sat like this together.

"Fede, do you mind if I ask my dad to fire the receptionist?"

"Camila?"

"Yes, that hussy you used to go out with."

"Vero, are you out of your mind?"

"It was a joke. As if I would ask my father to do such a thing. Why did you and Camila break up, anyway?"

"I don't know... She had some strange tastes."

"Strange tastes?"

"Yes. She was twenty-one and acted as though she were fifteen. I act like a forty-year-old, so there wasn't much chemistry. She liked dancing, taking ecstasy, taking selfies of herself in the mirror. And I'm too old to have a jealous tiff with my girlfriend because she puts up half-naked photos of herself on Facebook."

"Did the little hussy actually do that? I never thought she was right for you."

"Just as well you don't have Facebook."

"What do you mean?"

"Nothing."

They ate the cashews and then the schnitzel sandwiches. Then they walked along the river, stopping at one point to eat the apples.

"A thermos of coffee would have been nice," said Verónica, lighting a cigarette when she had finished her apple.

"Vero, tomorrow I'm going back to Buenos Aires."

"Why?"

"Your dad needs me there. With Peratta off the scene, it doesn't make sense for me to be your minder. You're going to stay on, right?"

"I can't leave."

They walked back to the town slowly, as though trying to prolong the excursion. Back at the hotel, Verónica called Patricia and offered her the piece on Claudia Rinaldi's murder at the hands of Captain Aráoz. Her editor accepted immediately, and suggested she also write a piece on new developments in the tourists case, but once again Verónica refused. Whatever happened, she would never feel able to write about the case. Before ending the call, she clarified that the article she was sending Patricia was written together with Juan Robson.

"El Inglés is writing again?"

"After a fashion."

She wasn't going to consult Juan Robson on this because she knew what those stubborn old hacks were like: he would refuse. But she wasn't prepared to take sole credit for the investigation, or to publish the article under her own byline with *Reporting by Juan Robson* underneath, in smaller print, as the magazine's editor liked to do. Robson's email constituted an impeccable piece of journalism. All she'd really had to do was cut and paste. And she was sure Robson would be happy to see his name attached to the piece.

Federico was in the bedroom, so she took her laptop to the hotel bar. She could work there without interruption. At that time of day, there was nobody at any of the tables. On her way there, she saw Mariano in the reception area with one of the tourists who had recently arrived.

Verónica switched on her computer and started rereading the material Robson had sent her. She hadn't got halfway through the email when her phone rang and she looked to see who was calling. Mechi's name came up on the screen. She answered immediately.

III

It hadn't been an easy decision. In fact, it was the first time he'd had to neutralize someone from his own team. But now he knew Three would neither ruin his career nor his business: he was still the only person providing hitmen who worked with the precision of surgeons.

His phone rang. It was the client who had contracted him to assassinate Verónica Rosenthal.

"We're back in business," he said.

"Just as well – I don't like delay. Plus, every day that passes, the job gets more expensive."

"Yes, I'm aware of that."

"Are we going to have to put a new tail on her?"

"That shouldn't be necessary. If everything goes the way I think it will, I know where she's going to be tomorrow or the next day. Three days max. We just have to be ready to strike."

"In Yacanto?"

"My idea is to take her to Club Náutico, which is quite far away from here."

"I don't like closed clubs. It's harder to get out."

"It's going to be the ideal place, I assure you."

"I'm thinking of sending just one man."

"That's your call, not mine."

"Two in a club would be a crowd."

"Then I'll get you just one member ID."

"I'm going to need more funds."

"I'll send you twenty per cent. The other thirty when the job's done."

"Sounds good. I'll need a map of the club, with alternative exits marked and the coordinates of where our man should wait."

"I can send all that and the movements will follow in a couple of hours. All I ask is that this time you don't fail."

Doctor Zero was used to dealing with all kinds of clients. Guys who thought they were heroes in a movie, others who had a change of heart five minutes before the job was supposed to take place, some who got an attack of post-mortem guilt and called him in hopes of shifting the guilt onto him. There were also some who understood exactly what his work entailed: they hired him, gave him the coordinates and paid him. But he'd had a funny feeling about this guy right from the start. Doctor Zero sensed – and he was never wrong when it came to reading people – that this guy didn't really understand what was involved in sending one person to kill another. That he was acting like a capricious child who'd had his toys taken away.

IV

Mechi was crying. She was talking too, but Verónica couldn't understand her because the sobs prevented her from speaking clearly. She asked Mechi to calm down, to repeat what she was saying. The weeping was silenced then, and replaced by the voice of a man:

"Listen, don't hang up, don't shout, don't call anyone. Speak normally to me."

Verónica glanced around her as though looking for whoever was speaking to her, or for support from some quarter, although there was nobody else in the dining room.

"Who's speaking?" she managed to say.

"Did you hear your friend crying?"

"Where's Mechi?"

"Mechi's here, with us."

"What's happening? Don't hurt her. What's going on?"

"Calm down and listen carefully. Do you want to see your friend alive?"

"You'd better not do anything to her, because —"

"Listen to me. If you want to see Mechi alive, you're going to do as I say. Or would you rather listen to her die? Do you understand what I'm telling you? Answer me."

"Yes, I understand."

"Then you're going to do what I say and you'll see her alive. Don't talk to anyone and don't hang up on me, understand?"

"Yes."

"Where are you and who are you with?"

"I'm in the dining room at the hotel, on my own."

"Without hanging up, while you're still talking to me, you're going to go to your car and drive on your own to the place I tell you to go."

"Yes."

"Are you going to the car?"

"I have to find my keys."

"Where are they?"

"Here in my bag."

"Get them out and walk to the car."

Verónica searched in the bag with her free hand, but it

was shaking too much for her to find anything. She turned the bag over and tipped its contents onto the table. She saw the key, picked it up and made to leave. She wanted to take her glasses, but they were hidden under her bag and she couldn't see them.

"Have you got it?"

"Yes."

"Now walk calmly to the car."

"OK."

She left everything scattered over the table, her laptop switched on, her upturned bag emptied of its contents.

"While you walk, tell me, what were you doing?"

"I was writing an article."

"For the magazine?"

"Yes."

"What's the magazine called?"

"*Nuestro Tiempo.*"

Verónica walked through the reception area. Mariano was still talking to some tourists. She didn't look at him but opened the door and stepped into the street.

"Is your boyfriend there?"

"I'm alone."

"Are you outside?"

"Yes."

"Walk to the car. And don't hang up. If you do, or if we get cut off, we'll shoot your friend."

"I'm on my way. Don't do anything to her."

"That depends on you. Understand?"

"Yes."

"Have you reached the car now?"

"I'm getting in."

"Put the phone on hands-free. Have you done that?"

"Yes, it's on."

"Now you're going to drive. You have to take the main road to Los Cercos. Do you know where Los Cercos is?"

"Yes."

"But you have to keep talking to me, so tell me about everything you see."

Like an automaton, Verónica described everything she saw as she drove: a white car, trees on either side, a gate. Every so often the voice made some observation or asked for more detail: was the gate open? What model was the white car? Verónica gripped the steering wheel, not leaning back against the seat. It had started to get dark and she couldn't see all that well without her glasses. She kept talking, telling the man what he wanted to know but not hearing the words herself. If she had been asked to repeat what she had said two sentences ago, she wouldn't have been able to do it.

As she entered Los Cercos, the voice ordered her to take the first turning on the left, then to park and finally to get out of the car.

"Wait there for a few minutes. He'll be there soon."

"Who'll be there?"

"The person who's going to bring you here, to where Mechi is."

A motorbike drew up ten yards from where she was standing. The rider wore a helmet. He didn't get off the motorbike or remove his helmet, but he looked towards where she was standing.

"Is the motorbike there now?"

"Yes."

"You're going to come with him. I'll take this moment to say goodbye. I have to go. I'm not going to get to see you. *Chau.* You can hang up now."

Verónica tried to ask him where they were taking her, why they hadn't brought Mechi to her there, what they wanted from her. But the man had already hung up and the motorcyclist was revving his engine. Verónica walked towards him. The man made no gesture. She climbed on the back and the motorbike accelerated away. Verónica gripped the sides of the pillion, but the road had too many bends and potholes for her to keep her balance without holding onto the driver. The thought that she might be touching one of the men who had murdered Petra and Frida filled her with revulsion.

They arrived at a ranch sheltered by a grove of trees. A moped and another motorbike were parked there. The motorcyclist stood up and took off his helmet. Getting off the bike, she recognized him immediately: it was Rulo, the older brother of Sebastián Vázquez. Another man leaned out of the window. Verónica walked towards the front door, which opened at her approach. She was vaguely aware of someone pushing her from behind. Ever since Mechi had called, she had been trying to imagine what state the girl might be in. The image that greeted her was much worse than what she had pictured: Mechi was in the middle of the room, naked and on her knees. Her face was swollen from crying.

Verónica went over to Mechi and put her arms around her, trying to cover the girl with her body. Mechi, crying unceasingly, could not move. She was a statue. Sebastián was holding a gun while Reyes, standing with his hand on his hips, had no weapon. The two were smiling at each other. One of the men said something, but Verónica was focussed on comforting Mechi. "We'll be leaving soon, don't cry, we're leaving," she told her. Verónica thought she could hear another woman crying in an adjoining room. The younger Vázquez moved to the door that led to the other room, satisfied himself that it was locked and ordered in a loud voice:

"That's enough, Rosalía, stop whining. If you fuck about, the same thing will happen to you."

"This is the bitch who was looking for us," Reyes said.

Verónica didn't notice him touching her hair as he spoke. When she didn't react, he pulled her hair to get her attention. "You were a friend of the other two, weren't you? Small world."

"That was a good time, right?" said Rulo, as if seeking the approval of his accomplices.

"Take your clothes off, bitch," Reyes ordered Verónica.

The first thing she thought was: *They're going to kill me.* She didn't comply because she was waiting to be shot. Along with Mechi. Only when Rulo roughly pulled off the top buttons of her shirt did she take in what they were saying. Rulo's violent gesture had disoriented her.

"Come on, bitch, we don't have all day."

Verónica could hear Mechi wailing, and the sound of a stifled sob reached her from the other room. She finished unbuttoning her shirt and took it off together with her bra; she took off her shoes, her trousers and her underwear. She didn't realize she was naked because it wasn't her standing there without clothes at that moment. Not Mechi either. At that moment Petra and Frida were the ones taking off their clothes, the ones trembling, the ones begging not to be hurt. *Poor girls, poor girls,* Verónica repeated to herself quietly.

"On your knees, bitch," one of them (Sebastián, Reyes, Rulo?) yelled at her.

She felt the earth floor scraping her knees. Someone grabbed her breasts from behind and squeezed them hard. The other two laughed. She thought of Frida, of Petra, their fragile bodies, so easy to hurt, to abuse.

"These girls are dying to suck cock."

"A little respect for the journalist. She went straight for the boss and left us with the two sluts."

"We're gonna make these ones scream, too, the little whores."

"Look at the ass on it."

"She's gonna love getting it pounded. Look, how d'you like my dick? Makes your mouth water, right, bitch?"

At no point had Verónica cried. The grief she felt for her murdered friends was yielding to an ever greater fury. She didn't care if they raped her or if afterwards they killed her, as they had Petra and Frida. Before that she was going to do everything possible to defend herself. She thought of headbutting Sebastián, who had the weapon, in the balls. He might shoot her in the process, but she would still hit him hard. She didn't care what happened afterwards. She tensed her body ready to hurl herself on him, then heard an explosion. Like gunfire.

If it had come from the front door, the noise might have made more sense. But the sound came from the room where the other girl was locked up. Somebody had shot off the lock and was opening the door, to the astonishment of everyone. It wasn't Rosalía who appeared, however, but Federico, with a rifle aimed right at Sebastián's face.

"Drop the gun!" he shouted.

"I'll shoot her, I'm gonna shoot!" Sebastián shouted back, pointing his gun at Verónica.

Behind Federico were Mariano and Luca. Both had kitchen knives in their hands. Rulo had moved out of range towards a chair. Verónica realized he planned to throw it at Federico to knock the gun out of his hand. She had to risk getting shot by Sebastián and lunge at his balls. Federico and Sebastián were shouting at each other. Verónica had begun to move towards Sebastián when Reyes' voice, raised above the others, cut through the commotion:

"Fuck's sake, the cops are here. Outside. The cops."

Verónica made a headlong dive for Sebastián a second before Rulo threw the chair at Federico, whose shot went towards the ceiling. Sebastián let out a howl of pain and fired in the direction of the girls, missing them both. Verónica was lying splayed on the floor. Sebastián wasn't going to miss a second time, but then Luca slashed his arm with the knife, making him drop the gun. At that moment the police came in, a lot of them. Mariano had helped Mechi up and Federico pushed Verónica to one side as the officers threw the three men to the ground. Luca picked up the girls' clothing and passed it to them. Mechi, who was still crying, started screaming when she saw them make her friend lie face down along with the others. Rosalía screamed too. Chief Superintendent Suárez ordered them into the kitchen. Verónica put her arms around Mechi and walked her into the other room. She helped her dress, wiped her face and said several times, "It's over, Mechi, it's all over. We're all right."

"Rosalía," said Mechi.

"I'll go and see. You stay here."

She finished dressing as best she could and walked out of the kitchen. The three men were still on the floor. So too was, Rosalía, sobbing endlessly. Verónica walked towards the chief superintendent, who was at the other end of the room standing beside Federico, but as she passed one of the three men she couldn't contain herself and kicked him in the ribs.

"Fucking bastard," she shouted at him and kicked him again.

Federico made to move towards her, but the chief superintendent placed a restraining hand on his arm.

Verónica walked to one of the other men and repeated the gesture.

"You evil son of a bitch."

She kicked him several times.

Her legs hurt and she didn't have the strength to kick any more.

"Fucking monster."

With the little energy she still had she placed her foot on the third man's face and pressed down with all her weight. The man screamed. Verónica wished she was wearing heels. Stiletto heels, to sink into the eyes of those three evil bastards.

16 *Truth or Dare*

I

Luca liked to say that Mariano was a serial conversationalist. That he could chat to anyone, no matter who. Spending hours on the reception desk of a hotel every day, he got his fix. So it wasn't unusual for him to have struck up a conversation with those two tourists who were looking for somewhere to spend the next few days. While he was still describing the merits of the different rooms and the complimentary breakfast, and before he had offered to show them a room, he saw Verónica pass by like a streak. She was talking on the phone and her face was contorted, like someone hearing bad news. He looked over to where she had been sitting in the bar and noticed that she had left everything lying there, including her handbag and laptop. Mariano abandoned the tourists mid-sentence and called Federico's room.

"Get down here. Verónica's in danger," was all he said. It might be an exaggeration, but he would rather be alarmist than regret not having taken action, later.

He went outside and saw Verónica walking towards her car. Mariano ran to the kitchen and luckily found Luca there. He said to him:

"Verónica's going somewhere. Something bad's happening."

Luca picked up two large knives and without needing to say anything else, they walked round to the front entrance in time to see Verónica driving towards the main road. At that moment Federico arrived with his gun case and Mariano told him Verónica had left. They all got into Luca's car and caught up with her at the junction with the main road.

"Keep back. I don't want her to think we're following her," said Mariano.

Out of the corner of his eye he could see Federico had opened the case. He turned round to see what he was doing and found the young lawyer assembling a rifle.

"Do you know how to use that?"

"I certainly do," said Federico.

Mariano called the police station and asked to speak to Chief Superintendent Suárez. He explained that Verónica was investigating the double crime, that she had gone running out to meet someone, that they were at that moment following her and heading towards Los Cercos. The chief superintendent said that he had officers available but couldn't send them off into the unknown. At best they could wait at Los Cercos. He gave Mariano his mobile phone number so he could call him directly.

Arriving in the town, they saw Verónica take the first turn right. They followed at a distance, driving around a block. It was a small town with not much chance of getting lost. Soon they were back behind her car. They saw her get out, still speaking on the phone. Then they saw the motorbike waiting for her. She climbed on and the bike drove off. Mariano called Suárez again.

"She arrived in Los Cercos, got out of the car and onto a motorbike. We'll follow her, but I'm worried we'll be spotted."

Luca was trying to keep his distance, but it was such a winding road that the motorcyclist seemed bound to spot them at some point. When they had been driving for about fifteen minutes, Luca suddenly braked.

"What's up?" asked Mariano.

"I know where they're going now. Get Suárez for me."

Mariano dialled the number and listened in astonishment as Luca gave him directions. He ended the call and started the car, advancing slowly, trying not to get too close to the motorbike. Luca must have felt Mariano's gaze heavy upon him, because without lifting his eyes from the road ahead, he said, "Nahuel."

"That jerk," said Mariano furiously.

"There's no other property for miles."

Two years ago, Luca had had an affair with Nahuel. Luca had told Mariano himself and, even though they had never talked about fidelity and initially had a very free relationship, in the last few years there had been nobody else, for either of them. When Mariano found out, he tried to put it out of his mind, but that didn't last long. Unable to contain himself, there had been reproaches, accusations and deeply hurtful insults. It had been harder for them to recover from the things they had said to one another than from the affair itself. Mariano knew Nahuel used to take Luca to a ranch house he owned on land belonging to a relation of the Elizaldes. And that episode, which had been buried under other bad memories, now resurfaced with absolute clarity. It took him a few minutes to realize that if they were going to Nahuel's bolthole, then the younger Elizalde was probably linked to the deaths of the tourists.

Luca parked the car about two hundred yards before the entrance to the house. He guided them to a path that led to the back of the property. The area was covered by vegetation and the distance between it and the house was shorter;

besides, it was less likely anyone would be monitoring that part of the property. They crept towards the window of a back room. The sound of crying came from inside: a girl was shut in there. Mariano let him see her at the window, indicating with a gesture that she should keep quiet, but the girl started screaming instead. She stopped when Federico pointed his rifle at her. There was no need to break the glass, because the window was unlocked. Once more they told the girl to keep quiet. From the other side of the door they heard men's voices, laughter, someone crying. Federico tried to open the door, but it had been locked with a key the other side. Without saying a word, he shot off the lock. He opened the door and found the men and the girls kneeling on the floor.

II

Chief Superintendent Suárez had insisted that, as a minor, Mechi must be taken to the police station, where she could wait for a responsible adult to collect her. Federico explained that she lived with her grandmother and that it would be more traumatic for the elderly woman to have to go all the way there to get her. Much better if Verónica and the others took her home. The chief superintendent was so pleased by the arrest of the three convicts that he decided to overlook protocol: he let Mechi go with them and made no mention in his report of Federico's rifle or Luca's knife. That was partly to keep them out of trouble, but surely also to keep more glory for himself once the success of the operation became known.

Suárez approached Verónica to ask if she was all right. With a few little pats on the shoulder, he told her she had been very brave. The tone he used to speak to her was quite different from the one he had used in the past. For once, there was no aggression or suspicion.

Mechi was better, but still worried about her friend Rosalía. The police had taken her away with the three criminals. Verónica asked Suárez about this, explaining that the girl had nothing to do with the crimes.

"I have to take her all the same. Unless one of the three implicates her, the district attorney's sure to let her go."

"And does DA Decaux already know what happened?"

"He's going to give a press conference within the hour at the police station. I'm sure he'll call the girl's parents and let her go then."

As soon as the chief superintendent allowed it, they left. Stopping off in Los Cercos, Luca went to La Pulpería and bought water for them all. They needed this break, especially Mechi, whose face was still swollen from crying. Mariano and Luca chatted to keep her distracted.

"Are you studying anything?"

"I'm going to go back to night school over there." She pointed to the other side of the square, where a flagpole was flying the Argentine flag.

"So you work."

"Yes."

"What do you do?"

"I'm a cleaner for the Arreguis."

"And are you happy with that work?"

"Yes, but I'm going to look for something else."

"Do you know how to cook?"

"My grandmother's a really good cook. And I help her."

"Grandmothers are always good cooks," said Luca.

"Not mine," Mariano objected.

There were a few seconds' silence, then Luca made Mechi an offer:

"We have a hotel in Yacanto, the Posada de Don Humberto. You've probably seen it. I need a kitchen assistant. If you're interested in learning to cook..."

They parted ways in Los Cercos. Luca and Mariano continued by car to Yacanto; the others got into Verónica's car, which she had left parked there, and drove to Mechi's house. Verónica travelled in the back with her and held her hand. Mechi squeezed it tightly. They travelled the rest of the way like that, the contact more intense than a hug or stroking. They only let go when they reached Mechi's house, by which time Verónica's arm had pins and needles.

"Mechi, I don't want to bombard you with questions just now, but the person who spoke to me on the phone wasn't one of the three arrested."

"No. There was another one, who left."

"Did you see him? What was he like?"

"Tall, muscly, a pretty boy. They called him Nahuel. He was speaking on the phone with a handkerchief over his mouth. When I told them I knew you, he said he was going to save his brother something."

"Did he say anything else about his brother?"

"I don't think so."

III

Verónica let the hot water run over her. She closed her eyes and tried not to think of anything, to empty her mind, to detach herself from the physical sensations that still persisted, to let the water wash everything away once and for all. For half an hour she stood under the shower. She didn't want to cry or feel afraid, nor to remember anything that had happened; she just wanted to think of it as an accident: she had suffered no broken bones, no injuries, just shock and a feeling that she was going to die, that they were going to rape and kill her. Like Frida and Petra had died. It was only when she thought of the girls that her body began to shake. And no, she couldn't allow that. Those men didn't deserve her fear. It was an accident, she was alive, there were no visible injuries.

A few minutes earlier, in the car, after dropping off Mechi, Verónica had said to Federico:

"Nahuel, Ramiro's brother. He's the one behind all this. And surely Ramiro too. I can't believe it. I can't believe —"

"Nobody's going to put Nahuel or Ramiro in jail. Three arrests have been made now. Tomorrow everyone will consider the case closed."

"Are you fucking kidding me?"

"No. I know how the judges, politicians and prominent families operate in this province. Only a few days ago we had an Umbanda priest looking at twenty years in the clink despite having nothing to do with the crime. At least we know that these three delinquents are guilty."

"But they're not the only ones."

"They're never the only ones."

For a few minutes neither of them spoke.

"Vero, we have to go back to Buenos Aires."

"You know what I feel? That ever since you arrived in Tucumán your main objective has been to get me to go back home."

"You're being unfair."

"There's another man, or two others, who are also guilty of this crime, who are free and who may kill someone else."

"These aren't serial killers."

"How do you know? It's easy for you to say they won't do it again. Say that to Mechi, who was almost raped and murdered. Say it to me."

"I am saying it to you."

"Besides, I promised Roxana they were all going to jail. So she could give her evidence and see justice done for Bibi. And six years ago Ramiro was abusing Roxana. What do you know about what this guy and his brother are capable of?"

"Do whatever you like. But I'll tell you what happens at the end. The judge doesn't want to try anyone else. He's a friend of the Elizaldes. The Minister of Justice is going to resign and the person who replaces him is going to be grateful for this crime because it landed him a job as minister. However much this new minister says otherwise, he's not going to get to the bottom of anything."

"Were you always so cynical? Were you always so like my father?"

"Don't be ridiculous."

They had arrived at the hotel. As soon as the car stopped, Verónica jumped out and went to their room. She stood under the shower for as long as it took to feel that she was recovering her own body.

When she came out, Federico was not in the room. Nor did he appear in the following hour. He must be in the bar or sleeping in another room. It was now after midnight and Verónica decided to go to bed. She didn't sleep well, waking up several times. She had cramps and cold sweats. She dreamed of the squashed rodent she had seen at the house in San Javier. Only now it was alive and crawling all over her, her stomach, breasts and neck, leaving a trail of sticky blood wherever it went.

Finally, as dawn was breaking, she fell into a deep sleep, undisturbed for two or three hours.

When she opened her eyes, Federico was sitting in the armchair, watching her.

"Have you been there long?" she asked.

"A while. I couldn't sleep all night. I couldn't settle into the room Mariano and Luca kindly gave me. I asked them for the bill for our stay and they sent me packing."

"I'm going to stay a few more days."

"We need to have a conversation about that."

"Don't start that again."

"I'm going to have a shower, then let's have breakfast and talk afterwards."

IV

It had been a long and uncomfortable night. Federico hadn't even gone to bed. Seeing that he and Verónica had argued, Mariano had found him alternative accommodation. In the new room, he turned on his computer, looked at his emails, answered a few and then copied the three files from the memory stick. He didn't watch them again; he remembered each of them perfectly.

Federico had to make a decision that couldn't be put off any longer. Whatever he decided would have enormous consequences for his life. Aarón would never forgive him if he handed the videos to Verónica. He was quite sure that, if any other lawyer at the firm did something similar, they would never practise law again. Aarón wouldn't be so hard on him, but there would still be consequences.

Verónica was right. The system of legal protections that the Elizaldes and even the Menéndez Bertis enjoyed would not allow them to go to prison. However much they hated one another, they knew not to rock the boat. Nicolás would do nothing to push for the brothers' conviction. He would settle for clearing his name. An article in the local paper, something in the national press and a slap on the back from the governor would be gestures enough.

It wasn't the first time Rosenthal and Associates had covered up a crime. Federico couldn't remember their having concealed a murder, though, at least not in the time he had been there. They had saved money launderers, the odd corrupt businessman, they had eliminated all trace of an inconvenient lover for a politician (without doing anything to her, of course, just buying her silence) and lobbied particular judges. Nothing Federico needed to lose sleep over. And after so many years with Aarón, he had managed to grow a thicker skin that allowed him to set aside a few just causes. Cynicism is very catching.

And perhaps he would have done the same in this case, if Verónica had not been caught up in it. Perhaps he had less of a vocation for justice than a desire to feel useful to her. Then again, perhaps he really was guided by conviction, by the same beliefs that had motivated him to study law in the first place.

Once more Federico ran the case of the murdered tourists through his head. A power struggle within the judiciary and the Tucumán and Salta police forces, involving the Menéndez Berti and Elizalde families, had played out in a small Tucumanian town. The Elizalde brothers had wanted to divert attention from what was happening in San Miguel de Tucumán by getting other men to assault and kill the girls. To rape and then kill them: a small matter for the brothers and a clear message to the Menéndez Bertis, who also had no interest in the truth being revealed.

The third video on the memory stick he deleted. Dawn was breaking. He went to Verónica's room and found her fast asleep. She was so beautiful he could have spent hours watching her breathing. And that is what he did, staying beside her until she woke up. He invited her to breakfast. In the dining room, Federico passed her the memory stick with all the discretion of someone handing over drugs. Verónica asked him what it was.

"There were cameras in the Menéndez Berti house. There are two recordings here that compromise Nahuel Elizalde."

"How did you get hold of them?"

"Nicolás gave them to me."

"And he gave them to you personally?"

"He gave them to Rosenthal and Associates to put pressure on the Elizalde brothers and to get the authorities off his back."

"But my father —"

"Vero – let's concentrate on doing what we can with what we have. If I give these videos to Judge Amalfi, he'll throw them in the trash. It won't be the first time a judge has dismissed incriminating evidence. DA Decaux has fallen out with the judge, and that plays in our favour. He wouldn't dare go against the judge in every case, but if there's media pressure, the guy is going to jump on the bandwagon. And we should give a copy to Superintendent Suarez, too, just in case."

"If María says it on television, you can guarantee there will be reverberations everywhere. Although you run the risk of it seeming anecdotal. What we need is a piece explaining all the details, the links between the murder of the girls and the narco police."

"You can do that."

"No, I'm not going to write about it. And is there any evidence connected to Ramiro?"

"Nothing in these videos. But Nicolás has no doubt he's the main culprit. Nahuel wouldn't have been bold enough to do anything without the approval of his older brother. Besides, there's what Mechi heard."

"That he could save his brother something? What things can you save someone? Time or money. So if it wasn't time, it must have been money. Did Ramiro hire someone to kill me?"

"It's possible. For that reason, once you've given your colleagues all the information, we're going back to Buenos Aires. You're going to be safer there than if you stay here."

"So there's no way to prove Ramiro's involvement?"

"I suppose we'll have to resign ourselves to seeing only one of the Elizaldes locked up."

Verónica headed to her room to talk to Patricia Beltrán and to read over her article about the murder committed by Captain Aráoz. Meanwhile, Federico went out for a walk. He had taken a giant step, one that would be confirmed once he arrived back in Buenos Aires and handed in his resignation to Aarón Rosenthal. An important chapter in his life was coming to an end.

V

Verónica called Patricia and described the material she had. She didn't even have to explain that she wasn't going to write the piece. Patricia told her that she had no available writers, but that she could get a freelance writer on it. She was going to suggest it to Rodolfo Corso. Shortly afterwards, she rang back to confirm that Corso had said yes, that he would arrive by bus the next day and that Verónica should wait to give him her notes and contacts.

"I told him to put 'reportage' on the invoice, rather than 'investigative report'. That way they'll pay him better."

Verónica copied the videos from the memory stick onto her laptop and watched Nahuel plotting with the other criminals. She was surprised to see him with Nicolás.

Federico was right. Her life would no longer be in danger if she returned to Buenos Aires. Moreover, when the story broke, she would no longer be the only person investigating the case. She called Federico.

"Fede, Rodolfo Corso is arriving tomorrow afternoon. I'm going to meet him and hand over all my material. If you like, we can leave for San Miguel de Tucumán in the evening and then go from there to Buenos Aires."

Verónica would only give the videos to María once Corso had touched base with all the contacts. It wouldn't be right if the television reporters knew more than he did.

For a couple of hours she continued working on the article that was going to appear jointly under her and Juan Robson's names. Then her phone rang. It was Ramiro.

She hesitated before answering. Should she curse him, tell him he was a shit, that she knew he had masterminded the crimes, that he had wanted to kill her? If she did all that, she would only succeed in frightening him off. On the fifth ring she answered, trying to make her voice sound as normal as possible.

"I heard they caught the men responsible."

"That's right."

"Are you OK?"

"Just about."

"Listen, Verónica, we've seemed to end up at loggerheads the last few times we've met. I don't want something that started so well to end on a sour note."

"No, of course not."

"I'd like to invite you to lunch tomorrow at Club Náutico. Just the two of us. Can I come and pick you up at eleven o'clock?"

"That sounds great."

"Just one thing, though: don't swear at any of the members."

After the call, Verónica felt a strange sensation. Neither anger, nor fear, nor doubt. She felt cheerfully surprised. Even if she had planned it herself, she couldn't have organized this any better. It was exactly what she needed.

She wouldn't say anything to Federico. She couldn't tell him. Because she already had a plan, and he wasn't part of it.

VI

It had turned out easier than expected. Ramiro called Doctor Zero and told him that the next day the hitman would need to be at Club Náutico before midday. He explained that they would go sailing first. When they got back, he would find an excuse to stay behind in the boathouse while she walked on along a path to the restaurant. That would be the ideal moment for the professional to do his job.

He stressed that this was the last opportunity. That this time they must not fail.

17 *The Killing of Verónica Rosenthal*

I

If somebody had asked Verónica Rosenthal that morning how long she had been in Yacanto del Valle, she wouldn't have had a ready answer. She remembered all the things that had happened and the places she had been to, but her temporal awareness had compressed everything into one long day: from the moment Ramiro had waited for her beside the road until now, as she prepared for their final meeting, time had contracted and it seemed as though only a few hours had passed. Certain days she recalled only through a kind of haze, containing the unreal shapes of a dream. And, as in dreams, familiar faces appeared out of context: her father walking through Yacanto del Valle, her friend María drinking coffee in the town bar, Robson with his infinite brown envelopes, Federico's naked body underneath her. All those things couldn't really have happened. She must have fallen asleep beside the road that first day and be waking up now, a few hours later. But no: she really was waiting for Ramiro. And only he seemed real to her, solid. She saw now exactly what had happened. There were no doubts. She knew who had done what. And so she waited for Ramiro, thinking of nothing apart from their meeting, her mind working at an unusual speed. She could foresee every situation, every movement that might happen in the hours ahead. Her brain ran through the scenes over and over again, clarifying them with each pass, putting every sentence in its place. She was waiting for Ramiro. And Ramiro came to pick her up, to take her to Club Náutico.

Federico wasn't with her. Perhaps he was in the hotel bar. If so – and if she happened to run into him – she would be obliged to invent an excuse that was bound to seem as implausible to him as it was unacceptable.

Mariano had been waiting for her on the landing. He had taken her arm with an unusual firmness and asked her what she was doing.

"I'm going to meet Ramiro."

"Verónica, you're about to do something disastrous. You're putting yourself in danger. He's Nahuel's brother."

Verónica released her arm.

"I don't need advice. We're grown-ups, right?"

"Don't do this."

Mariano didn't understand anything, couldn't understand. Nobody, apart from her, could feel what she felt at that moment.

She reached the reception area. There was Ramiro in chinos, a brown polo shirt with pink trim, and boat shoes. He kissed her on the cheek and they walked together to the pickup.

II

They didn't talk much in the car. The radio was tuned to an FM station playing syrupy music. As soon as they left Yacanto, the signal died and Ramiro tried to tune into another station. But they couldn't get any programme for long and they ended up listening to a show about aromatherapy and runes. Their conversation was mostly confined to observations about the plight of a local radio presenter.

A brilliant sun picked out the colours of the landscape, the trees, the limpid pond. They parked in the shade and got out, stretching their legs and breathing in the scent of nature. It was a perfect day for a country jaunt or a boat trip. A light autumnal breeze took the edge off the sun's heat.

Verónica's phone rang. Federico's name appeared on the screen. She didn't answer, switching the ringtone to vibrate. Seconds later the screen registered another missed call from Federico.

On weekdays the club was almost empty, with just a few members moving lazily around the facilities. Some sunbathed on the bar terrace, while others supervised repairs to their boats. The rowers who trained in the morning had already finished their session and the second group wouldn't arrive until dusk. It was still a long time until lunch.

They strolled through the grounds to the boathouse. Ramiro wanted to go out on the lake before lunch, and that seemed like a good idea to Verónica.

One of the boys who worked there took the boat to the lake. Ramiro got on first then gave his hand to help Verónica. She registered his warm skin, soft, a little damp, like the pelt of a trained seal. Instinctively she wiped her hand on the linen trousers she was wearing. He asked her if she would like to take the helm. Verónica settled into the driver's seat, started the engine and narrowly avoided the last of the rowers arriving at the shoreline. She glanced at her phone: five missed calls from Federico.

"I practically hit a rower," she said, as the boat moved away from the jetty. "Your brother's into rowing, isn't he?"

"That's right," said Ramiro, standing beside her, his eyes closed and his face tilted towards the sun.

"To think it could have been him. How awful if I'd hit him."

Ramiro didn't answer, silently basking in the sun while she struggled to control the boat. He seemed relaxed, calm, even happy.

"Hey, did your brother manage to arrange that abortion?" Veronica asked him after a few minutes.

"Which abortion?"

"The last time we came to the club you told me he'd asked you for some money so his girlfriend could get an abortion."

Ramiro seemed to search his memory before answering. "True, I did say that." He opened his eyes and looked at her. "Actually, I lied. He asked me for money, but not for that. He needed to help some friends."

From where they were, the shore was a line in the distance. There was no noise apart from the boat's engine. They could see no other vessel around them. Verónica made a little circle and turned off the engine. Now the only sound was of waves lapping against the side of the boat.

She had a text message from Federico that read *Where are you? Please reply.*

"I wouldn't call them friends," said Verónica, stepping out of the driver's seat to sit at the back of the boat. Ramiro, standing against the sun, was almost a shadow.

"Call them whatever you like. Friends, lackeys, accomplices."

Verónica stretched her legs. She looked at her toes in their sandals and thought that it had been a very long time since she'd painted her toenails. She should do it again.

"Did Nahuel come up with the idea of raping and killing them, or was it your idea?"

Ramiro looked at her with amusement. He produced a brief, guttural laugh. "I always said you were crazy."

"Nahuel doesn't have the head for this kind of thing, does he? It was you."

"Tourists from Buenos Aires or from abroad were bound to get more attention than a couple of girls from round here."

"And you didn't worry that Nicolás might report you and you could end up in jail?"

"In jail? On account of Nicolás and his old cocksucker dad? No."

"The foreign girls were a guarantee of success."

"Nahuel wanted them to take you. I saved you."

"I should be thanking you then."

"I thought it would be good to have a journalist to put pressure on the rest of the media. I imagined you crying on all the TV shows. I didn't think you were going to go sticking your nose in everywhere once you were back in Yacanto."

"You thought wrongly."

"You should have cried more, stayed at home, made love to me. Today we'd be planning our wedding party."

To make love. That expression had always seemed ridiculous to her, but on Ramiro's lips it disgusted her.

"Do you remember Roxana Lombardo?"

"Who's she?"

"She's a girl you were seeing six years ago, when El Gringo Aráoz killed Bibiana Ponce. Roxana was her best friend and used to make love to you."

"Ah, the little dark-skinned one. I remember."

"Roxana's going to testify against El Gringo. And we have a recording of calls your friend made to Bibiana before he killed her. He's going to wind up in jail."

"El Gringo is an idiot, but I doubt he'll go to prison."

"And we have video of your brother with his three chums. There's even a video of the same room you took me to. Nicolás is in it with Nahuel, and your brother announces what he's going to do. I didn't know your brother was a hustler."

Ramiro sketched a cold smile loaded with violence. His brother's homosexuality must be a touchy subject. How long now until he tried to hit her? Verónica tried to appear relaxed, but all her senses were alert.

Answer me. I'm looking for you. Pick up your phone.

"I bet the fact your brother was making love to Nicolás fed your desire to destroy the son of the Minister of Justice, didn't it? You wanted revenge on a faggot like Nicolás for perverting your brother. Such a handsome boy. Seemed like a waste."

"Are you a psychologist too now?"

"You planned everything, and you sent Nahuel to be present during the rape. I'm still not sure whether you did that as a punishment or because you wanted to re-educate him sexually."

"I should have let them rape and murder you, too."

"You met Federico, right? Do you know what he's going to do? He's going to offer Nahuel's three friends a chance to testify to your or your brother's participation in the crime, in exchange for better treatment. Obviously he can't offer them a lighter sentence, because that doesn't exist here. But there are ways to ensure that their prison conditions are improved and their families supported. I don't know what you can offer them, but he'll go one better."

"Do you think I'm stupid enough to have shown my face to those three? They don't even know I exist. The most they can do is make trouble for my brother, but not me."

"If you were that smart, you'd have realized a long time ago that your brother was a pansy."

"You know what makes me happy?" Ramiro asked her as he stood up. He was a shadow with no face, a silhouette without features. "It makes me happy knowing that soon you won't be able to fuck me around any more. Anyway, it's time we went back."

All the time they were speaking, her body had been tense. Waiting for Ramiro's reaction, for him to lose his temper, lunge at her, hit her. But he had stayed calm, controlling his hatred with the restraint of a man who knows something the other person doesn't. Ramiro had all the composure of a man used to going through life without ever having to face the consequences of his actions. How involved had he been in Bibiana's death? Had there been other women murdered like Frida and Petra? Other rapes? How many women had he humiliated the way he'd humiliated Roxana? Ramiro kept his composure because he felt untouchable, above the law. No, he wasn't going to attack her on this boat. A wave of fury swept from her unvarnished toenails and up through her entire body. Then Verónica acted. She did what she had known she was going to do since the night before. With the agility of a threatened feline, she stood up and threw herself at him. The surprise knocked Ramiro off balance as he prepared to intercept Verónica's blows. But she wasn't planning to hit him – that wasn't why she had lunged at him. As though pressing forward in a rugby scrum, she pushed him a few feet and made him lose his balance. Stumbling, he tried to grab something, but with her remaining strength, Verónica pushed a little more and Ramiro fell into the water.

The accompanying noise broke the peaceful silence of the lake. Water splashed Verónica, who was kneeling, her hands on the edge of the boat. One of Ramiro's shoes had got caught on the side. It was the only thing of his left on board. Verónica went to the driver's seat, started up the engine and drove forward a few feet.

"What are you doing, bitch?" Ramiro shouted at her from the water.

Verónica turned the boat round and steered it towards Ramiro, who was still splashing about, more calmly now he could see she was coming back. But when it reached him, the boat continued onwards, again distancing itself a few feet in the opposite direction.

"Help me get in!" he shouted at her.

Verónica reversed a little, enough to bring her very close to Ramiro's position.

"You're not getting in," she told him.

"What do you mean, you whore?"

"You're a fucking low life. You deserve everything bad."

Ramiro watched her, still moving his arms. "Come on, Verónica, this isn't funny."

Ramiro swam towards the boat; Verónica drove it a few feet further on.

"Are you crazy?"

"You're a murderer, like your brother, like the other three. You're all bastards."

"If you don't let me get in, I'm going to drown."

"You don't deserve to live."

"OK, we fucked up." Ramiro's voice was sounding panicky. He stretched his body out on the lake's surface as though trying to lift more of it out of the water.

"No, you didn't fuck up. You killed two women. You fucking scumbags, you low-life pieces of shit."

"You've won. Let me get in and I'll give myself up. I'll go to the judge and take full responsibility."

"Piece of shit."

Ramiro made an effort to close the gap between himself and the boat. Verónica waited for him and, as he touched the side of the boat, she drove forward again, keeping the same distance between them.

"I can't hold on any longer. Let me get in!"

"You deserve to be impaled, to have your dick and your balls cut off and stuffed in your mouth."

"Come on, please, my arms are dropping off."

Verónica looked around: a speedboat or some other vessel had left the boathouse but was travelling in the opposite direction. They were a spot in the distance, a boat that had stopped to enjoy the stillness of the lake and the glorious sunshine. Slowly Verónica circled Ramiro, like a shark that knows its prey cannot escape. Ramiro tried to follow her with his eyes.

"Verónica," he said in a broken voice, "you're not a murderer."

"They were two beautiful, sweet, good, intelligent girls. Two girls who would still be alive if it weren't for scum like you."

"You're right! I can't last much longer. Please…"

Verónica steered the boat a bit closer and turned off the engine. This wasn't like shooting him or running him over – not even poisoning someone would be like this. In those cases, the act of killing lasted a second: the time it took to shoot, to drive a car over someone's body, for poison to start taking its course. But this way she could change her mind. There was time. There he was, begging her. She could reach out and help him to climb in. She could simply throw him a life jacket.

"Please," Ramiro sobbed.

"Murderer, fucking piece of shit."

"I can't feel my legs," he said, terrified.

"You're going to die because you're a nasty piece of work."

"No, don't do this, no, help me, please, someone help me!" he tried to scream, but his voice was a thin falsetto.

Mid-wail, Ramiro swallowed water and began to splutter. He started to wave his arms wildly about, the worst course of action for someone hoping to stay afloat. He went under, then resurfaced. No shouting; he no longer said anything. He went under again. He tried to lift up his head and with one last effort managed to stretch out his body, as though to swim a few yards. He advanced a little, but couldn't lift his head high enough to breathe. He sank again, silently.

Little waves lapped against the side of the boat.

III

Verónica sat for a few minutes, watching how Ramiro's body sank until it was lost in the depths of the lake.

She looked at her phone. The last missed call from Federico had been a quarter of an hour earlier. She put it away again in her bag, took off her shoes and dived into the water. She should at least look as if she had tried to save him. But she hadn't taken into account the fact that it would be difficult to move once in the water, despite her light clothing. Verónica swam nervously back to the boat, which appeared to be moving on its own and away from her. Those little waves were playing dirty. She felt – or thought she felt – Ramiro's body floating back to the surface and touching her back. After swimming as fast as she could towards the boat, she felt exhausted, unable to climb back on board. Gripping the edge, she tried to pull herself up, but her arms seemed to have lost their strength. She should have taken off her clothes, or not jumped in. Verónica was terrified Ramiro's body might be pushed by the current towards her, that it might touch her, embrace her, pull her down into the water. With her remaining energy, she made one last effort and managed to haul half her body over the edge of the boat. Then, with a final heave, she thrust herself forward and, once on board, let out a long and desolate wail.

Verónica threw the shoe overboard that Ramiro had left behind. So too the life ring. Then she started up the engine and motored towards the shore at full speed, sounding the horn. She saw some people emerge from the boathouse. As she got closer, she started shouting for help. On reaching the jetty, it was all she could do to stop the boat, carrying forward several others that were tied up there. Without getting out, she quickly told the assembled group that Ramiro had fallen into the water, that she had tried to rescue him but he was very heavy, that they had shouted but nobody had heard them, that by the time she'd managed to get out of the water and thrown him a life ring, it was too late. Some men got into another boat and went off in the direction she indicated. There were now a lot of people – employees, a few club members. She saw a security guard on the phone calling for an ambulance. They were asking her what had happened. She cried and shivered. Somebody wrapped a large towel around her. Verónica repeated that Ramiro had tripped and fallen into the water, that he didn't know how to swim very well and she had only made the decision to jump in and help him when she saw that the life ring was deflated, that it had not occurred to her to launch a distress flare. Verónica saw two other boats heading towards the site of the accident. She couldn't stop crying. She felt empty, exhausted. She thought of Frida, of Petra, of how unfair it was that they were dead.

The wail of an ambulance could be heard as it arrived, parting the crowds. A doctor came towards Verónica, asking how she felt. They gave her a tranquillizer. A woman offered to go with her to the changing room so she could put on different clothes. The tranquillizer quickly began to take effect.

Somebody passed Verónica her handbag so she could get out her phone and call someone from her family. She thought of calling Federico, but it was a bit late for that. Instead she called Mariano and told him to come and fetch her from the club, that Ramiro was dead. She hung up and remained sitting, oblivious to the brouhaha around her. She didn't fall asleep, but a kind of calm took possession of her whole body.

18 *Girl Seeks Girl*

I

It hadn't been difficult to gain access to the club. The security guards barely looked at his membership card and didn't give him a second glance. They raised the barrier and let him through. He left the car, which he had rented with fake ID, in the members' parking area. If anything went wrong, he could abandon it there and leave the club by a back door that led to a road.

Five had his gun on him, loaded and fitted with a silencer. He walked calmly through the wooded grounds. Lighting a cigarette, he went towards where he was supposed to intercept Verónica Rosenthal. He wasn't intending to stay there, just to familiarize himself with the area. There was still time in hand. Five walked towards the boathouse, strolling around the place like any other club member, and sat on one of the benches that looked onto the lake. He saw Rosenthal and the man who had hired them setting off in a boat. Usually he didn't know exactly who had ordered a job, but this one had been plagued by so many problems that Doctor Zero had been explicit: nothing can happen to Rosenthal's companion. He's the one paying.

Noticing the boat stop in the distance, he thought it would be a good moment to start taking up his position. He walked back along the path and picked a spot about a hundred yards from the boathouse, where a thicket would hide him from sight. From this vantage point he also had a good view of the lake.

He noticed the boat make some odd, almost spasmodic movements. It went forwards, slowed, reversed, drifted to one side, advanced again, turned in small circles, stopped again. It was like some strange and indecipherable dance.

As he was trying to make sense of what was happening in the distance, he saw the boat pick up speed and head dangerously fast towards the dock. Only Rosenthal was on the deck. The man was nowhere to be seen. She was shouting, but he couldn't make out what she was saying. People started running towards the jetty. The boat had collided with other vessels. Rosenthal got out, shaking. She had to be supported to stop her from falling.

In normal circumstances, Five would not have abandoned his position. But nothing about this could be described as normal. He made for the jetty along with all the other people at the club, got as close as he could and heard something incredible: the guy had drowned. If Five had been a good citizen, a respectable person who paid his taxes and strove for justice, he would have started shouting *She killed him, you idiots, can't you see?* But he was none of those things. He moved far enough away to be able to make a phone call to Doctor Zero.

"There's a problem. The companion drowned."

"The companion?"

"Yes."

"Is he dead?"

"I don't know what she did, but she came back alone in the boat."

"Did she do it?"

"It seems so. What do we do?"

"The guy still owed me money. No pay, no work. Abort."

"OK, Doctor."

"I've never liked this job anyway."

"Me neither."

They hung up. He began to wonder if he hadn't perhaps been lucky. Seeing how the job had gone, he could easily have ended up dead and Rosenthal alive. The girl had more lives than a cat.

He put on his jacket, lit another cigarette and walked slowly towards his car, enjoying the fine afternoon weather.

II

Mariano didn't arrive alone. Federico was with him, walking a few steps behind, but he didn't approach her. It was Mariano who asked how she was and spoke to the ambulance crew. The police also arrived. They asked Verónica what had happened, and she explained how Ramiro had tripped and fallen off the boat. She had to tell her story twice. Federico saved her from telling it a third time by calling the district attorney, who then spoke to the chief superintendent: given that what had happened was an accident, Verónica could present herself that afternoon at the courthouse in San Miguel and make her statement there.

She got into the car still wrapped in the club towel. Mariano drove, with Federico in the passenger seat and Verónica behind. Federico didn't speak to her, other than to relay some details about what she had to do that afternoon. When they reached Yacanto, he said that he needed to go to the courts in San Miguel, that she could change and then follow on. He didn't offer to wait for her.

Verónica had a quick shower, then called her friend María. She told her that she had two videos for her which incriminated a rich young man from Yacanto del Valle.

Federico sent her two texts. In the first he said: *Sent copy of videos to DA and Suárez. Arrest warrant soon for NE.* The second told her where she would shortly need to go to give her statement.

Mariano offered to take her, but Verónica thought she would rather go alone. In the car she listened again to Frida's MP3 player. She felt the selection of music to be a gift that would always be with her. It was going to be difficult to go back to listening to other music.

When she reached the courthouse, it wasn't easy to find the district attorney's office. She called Federico but he didn't answer. Finally, after much traipsing back and forth, she found the right place. The DA dealt with her fairly quickly. There were no awkward questions.

Are you coming back to Yacanto? she texted Federico.

Later on, he wrote back.

Shall I wait for you?

No.

Verónica returned alone to Yacanto to find someone waiting for her in the hotel bar: Rodolfo Corso.

"I've done my homework," he said, showing her a pile of photocopied articles on the girls' case.

"That's not going to be necessary. I'll give you all the material you need."

"Darling, I didn't come to the back of beyond to be your stenographer."

"OK, OK. I'll give you everything I have and then do whatever else you want. The owners of the hotel are friends. You can stay here for as long as you need. Within reason."

"Your boss asked me to send the piece by Tuesday. I don't plan to stay any longer. Small towns depress me."

They chatted for two hours, during which time Verónica told him everything that had happened, the connection with the narco police case, the judicial power struggles and the repetition of the same crime in the town over a period of years. Rodolfo noted everything down. He knew an ex-chief of the Tucumán police force who could pass on information about feuding in the ranks. And he was also in touch with a journalist from Salta who had been fired from a local newspaper when it occurred to him to make a link between the massacre of workers at a sugar mill in the 1970s and some of the region's powerful families. Surely the Elizaldes, the Menéndez Bertis and the Posadas also featured somewhere in that picture.

"The landowners, the wealthy political leaders, the upper-class señores who claim to be so horrified these days by corruption, they're all the grandchildren or great-grandchildren of murderers who made their fortunes by killing indigenous people, workers and activists. It's easy for them to preach from the pulpit."

Verónica found it hard to accept that a colleague might do a better job on a story than her. But on this occasion she was delighted to know that Corso was going to turn in a much better article than she could ever have written.

She went back to her room and started packing, her plan being to catch the next morning's flight. Verónica had hoped to return to Buenos Aires with Federico but had heard nothing from him for hours. She was beginning to worry when he walked into the room. He looked exhausted. Verónica sat on the edge of the bed and Federico in the armchair, opposite her. He said:

"First things first: they're going to reopen the Bibiana Ponce case. Her friend will have to give evidence and, if Aráoz doesn't return soon from his vacation in Europe, they will use Interpol to make him come back. That guy's not getting away."

"And Nahuel Elizalde?"

"There's a warrant for his arrest. It's very likely he's still in the province. These types feel safer on their own territory than outside it. Given the media pressure, I wouldn't be surprised if he hands himself in accompanied by an army of lawyers. I'm going to talk to Frida's parents. It would be good if they could come forward as injured parties. I can represent them, or help them to find competent lawyers."

"They don't come much more competent than Rosenthal and Associates."

"I don't work for the firm any more."

"What do you mean?"

"I've resigned. Well, officially I'm resigning tomorrow when I get back to Buenos Aires, but the decision's already made."

"Are you mad? The firm is your life."

"No, my life is what you're looking at. It's not the firm, not a case, not you, not anything that can be reduced to one part of me."

"Fede, my father adores you."

"Your father knows, as I do, that I can't continue there. Let's say that I didn't meet the standards of quality, fidelity and effectiveness that the company requires."

"What do you mean?"

"Look, Verónica, just to be absolutely clear about this: I'm sick of the Rosenthals, of you and your dad. You're a demanding machine that imposes rules and then does whatever it wants."

"But what's happened?"

"It's over, Vero. A few days ago, in your cousin's house, I dared to think we might be at the start of something."

"We were! We are!"

"Not any more. You know what I was doing all this afternoon? Desperately looking for you. I went to Ramiro's house, his gallery, I ran all over town not knowing what to do or where to go. I was convinced Ramiro had set some trap to kill you. When Mariano called me and asked me to go with him to Club Náutico, I felt as if I were dying. I thought he was going to tell me you'd been killed."

"I'm sorry, Fede."

"And nobody made you go. You went there because you wanted to. You didn't give a shit what the consequences might be. For me, for Mariano, for all of us behind you. You couldn't give a fuck."

"You're very important to me."

"We'd agreed your work here was over. That you weren't going to do anything else. Yet again you lied to me."

"I didn't lie to you. I couldn't tell you where I was going."

"I can't live thinking you don't trust me. It's not fair for you to put yourself in danger and for me to be desperately wondering where you are. I'm sick of following you around like a dog, of hanging on your every decision."

"Fede … it's not like that."

"It makes no difference, you lied to me once more, you did what you felt like. Just as you always have done, ever since I first met you. I've had enough."

"I'm sorry. I couldn't have told you, you wouldn't have understood."

"How do you expect me to understand your lack of consideration towards me? You're a loner, Verónica. You exist only for yourself. You're an egotist."

"I was blind for years. I didn't see that the person who mattered most to me was right beside me. I had to go through this hell to realize something very simple: I love you, Fede. Suddenly it all became clear. There's one person I want to spend my life with, and that person is you. Nothing matters more than that. It's so easy. Our love is so easy."

He sat forward, face covered; she put her hands on his knees. Federico pushed her hands away and looked at her. What he was about to say was already in his eyes. She didn't need to hear the words to know Federico was leaving her.

"Goodbye, Verónica."

He stood up and walked away.

Verónica threw herself back on the bed. Staring at the ceiling, she watched it gradually disappear behind a fog of tears.

Next day, she woke up at dawn and finished getting her things together. She had hoped to run into Federico at the hotel reception but there was still nobody about, only the night receptionist. Verónica waited until Mariano came and confirmed that Federico had left during the night. He said nothing else to her.

Verónica went up to her room and into the bathroom for a piss. She stayed sitting on the lavatory for a while, thinking over the last few weeks. The events of the previous afternoon. About how she had driven out of her life the only person she really wanted by her side. Was it the price she had to pay for that bastard Ramiro never to hurt anyone else? Was Federico right to say that everything she did was motivated by egotism?

She stood up, arranged her clothes and washed her hands. In the mirror she looked haggard, dishevelled, grey. She didn't mind looking old or like shit. What she really hated was not recognizing herself. Not even knowing who that person was on the other side of the glass. She moved her face close to her own reflection and started repeating, like a mantra, "Stupid, stupid, stupid, stupid bitch." She touched her head to the glass, rested her forehead against it.

"Stupid, stupid, stupid, stupid bitch." She wanted to punch that idiot. Clenching her fist, she aimed at the face. The mirror smashed and she let out a shriek. She had blood on her knuckles. "Stupid, stupid, stupid, stupid bitch." Verónica sat on the edge of the bathtub, lost her balance and fell into it, crying and kicking the air as she struggled to get out. She picked out the broken glass that had fallen into the sink and turned on the tap, running water over her cut hand. The blood was washed away, the wounds were exposed, the damage was there to see. Would she always be like this, for the rest of her life?

She used an old T-shirt to keep pressure on her hand and, when she could see it was no longer bleeding, took her things down to the reception area along with Petra's guitar and rucksack. Mariano was still there. Verónica tried to insist on paying her bill, but he would have none of it.

Mariano hugged her tightly and told her to come back. From inside the kitchen Luca appeared with Mechi. She looked happy.

"Let me introduce you to my new kitchen assistant," said Luca.

Verónica took both Mechi's hands.

The four of them walked out of the hotel, Mariano carrying the suitcase and Petra's rucksack while Verónica carried her handbag and the guitar. She offered to drop Mechi off at her house. Verónica wanted to be alone with the girl for a while and tell her about the latest developments in her sister's case. She said goodbye to Mariano and Luca. She was leaving the Posada de Don Humberto for the last time.

III

Luca didn't regret anything. He never had. He had learned mistakes were as important as successes. His affair with Nahuel had awoken in him feelings of surprise, excitement and heightened libido that he hadn't felt for a long time. At no point, not even in those moments of greatest excitement or arousal, had he thought his relationship with Mariano could be imperilled. He had never expected that Mariano would take it so badly and – to a certain extent – not even get over it. Could it be the start of a crisis in their relationship? Or had the trouble started before then? Had they needed to risk their lives to work this out? He should speak to Mariano face to face, not let the bad feeling turn into something chronic. In time, this state of mind could grow into the kind of aggressive indifference that was a feature of so many marriages.

While Mariano was handling some admin in his office, Luca was in charge of the reception desk. A young, attractive man came into the hotel. He had slightly tousled black hair, high shoulders, long legs and a look of being lost not only at that moment, but in life and the world generally. The boy possessed a beauty common to many young people: completely unconscious. He wanted a room. Luca asked him for how many nights.

"Two nights, perhaps three. It depends how long my search takes."

"And what are you looking for?"

"It sounds strange, but I'm trying to find out what happened to the body of a murdered girl."

"One of the two foreign girls?"

"Yes. I knew one of them."

Luca stood looking at him, trying to comprehend what the boy was saying to him.

"Which one did you know? Petra or Frida?"

"Petra."

"Were you a friend of hers?"

The boy smiled with a certain resignation.

"Well, maybe a bit more than friends. Her boyfriend, practically."

"What's your name?"

"Gonzalo."

The boy placed his rucksack on the floor. With his foot he nudged it towards the counter.

"I actually thought we had a relationship, but one day she ran off. I never heard anything more, until I saw the news."

He looked down and seemed to be thinking about what he was going to say. A confession, a declaration of principles, something for a stranger like Luca to understand, but also for him to understand himself.

"I liked her very much. I loved her."

IV

On the way to Mechi's house, Verónica told her that her sister's case had been reopened, that with Roxana's testimony, plus the mobile phone evidence, it was very likely the culprit would go to prison.

"I knew you wouldn't let me down," Mechi said, and flung her arms around Verónica's neck, jeopardizing the car's stability. Verónica smiled, then she said that she would like Mechi to keep the rucksack with Petra's things in it.

Mechi was dying to tell her grandmother that Bibi's case was going to be reopened. When they arrived at the house, she leaped out of the car and ran to the door, forgetting Verónica, who was walking slowly behind with Petra's rucksack and trying to work out whether or not the dogs planned to attack her. But both the big one and the mother dachshund were content just to sniff her. Inside the house, Ramona appeared with the puppies. Mechi repeated, word for word, what Verónica had just told her. Her grandmother was happy at first, then began to cry. Mechi squeezed her tightly and told her not to be so soft.

Ramona was so happy she insisted on giving Verónica a lemon sponge cake she had baked that morning. Verónica put up a weak resistance. Mechi's grandmother wrapped it up for her with no further word.

"I promised you something," said Mechi.

"That you were going to study."

"Something else. That if you managed to get the man who killed my sister sent to prison, I'd give you one of the little puppies."

"In principle, they're only going to reopen the investigation. They're going to charge the guy and there could be a long time between that and him going to prison."

"It doesn't matter. I'm going to keep my word."

"That's really kind, but I'm not very good around animals."

"I don't know if you noticed, but the last time you were here, and today, the same puppy came to see you."

It was true: the same little dog as last time had come to nibble at her sneaker. Verónica had tried to shoo her away with light movements of her leg which could be interpreted as incipient kicks. She was a brown dachshund, ugly, clumsy and persistent. She seemed determined to stay at Verónica's side.

"I can't take her."

"Take her. She hasn't got a name yet. What are you going to call her?"

What would she call a dog in the hypothetical case that she had one? She thought of Paula, but her friend would definitely be annoyed if Verónica called the puppy Paulita.

"Well, she looks like a sausage, so I think I'll call her Chicha, short for *salchicha.*"

Verónica said goodbye to Ramona and walked with Mechi to the car. She had found a box to put Chicha in. On an impulse, Verónica decided to ring the company that had rented her the car to say she would return it in Buenos Aires.

She didn't want to check in the puppy at the airport. Instead, she would take Chicha with her in the car, even though that meant driving nine hundred miles home. She would spend the night in some hotel on the way that allowed pets. In San Miguel de Tucumán, she'd stop at a vet's surgery, get the puppy vaccinated and buy her some pet food. And perhaps some kind of coat. Verónica thought Chicha looked cold.

Mechi saw Verónica off with a heartfelt embrace, one she would always remember. She got into her car and drove away. The cake was beside her on the passenger seat, behind Chicha in her box and Petra's guitar. Once they were on the main road, she plugged in Frida's MP3 player. She selected "Random Play" and the voice of Anna Ternheim singing "Bring Down Like I" filled the air. Chicha climbed out of her box and settled down on the seat. Soon she fell asleep. With her right hand, Verónica opened the package containing the sponge cake. She shouldn't do it, but she was going to anyway. As she broke off a chunk, crumbs scattered in the car. She bit into the sponge: it tasted amazing. She decided to eat all of it before leaving the province of Tucumán. A road sign announced BUENOS AIRES – 856 MILES. She was going home.

19 *Black Moon*

I

This guy was the perfect package. Handsome, witty, sweet and attentive. There was only one problem: he was nineteen.

"He's a child," said Petra.

"But he's over the age of consent. At least they won't lock you up," Frida replied. He was called Gonzalo, came from Tucumán and studied Performing Arts. He wanted to be an actor. Petra had met him on the coach that took her from Córdoba to San Miguel de Tucumán. He had the seat next to hers. Petra had been staring out of the window when the boy said:

"I saw you putting a guitar in the hold. Are you a musician?"

They started talking and she told him she was going to meet a Norwegian friend, someone she had travelled with several times, and that now they were planning a trip through northern Argentina, Bolivia and Peru. Gonzalo kept up a stream of questions and she gave considered answers: she told him about the journey through the fjords in western Norway and the time she and her friend had met in Prague then driven together to Budapest. He asked her about her music, how she had come to speak Argentine Spanish so well, why she had separated from her partner. It amused Petra to see how dazed Gonzalo was by such simple things as a person having lived in more than one country. He was a boy who had not been out in the world, and he was eager to live.

When Gonzalo got up to rearrange something that was about to fall out of his rucksack Petra was able to study him from a better angle: he was very strong. His T-shirt had ridden up, exposing the downy hair around his navel. He had a flat stomach. The bulge in his jeans made her think it might not be a bad idea to keep chatting. When he sat down again she asked him how old he was. "Nineteen," he replied. Petra feared she might be about to do something crazy.

Gonzalo lived with his parents, a doctor and a psychologist. He was the oldest of three children and had been a champion volleyball player with his school team: his greatest achievement thus far and one he talked about with pride.

Petra asked if anyone would be waiting for him at the coach station. No, he said, he would be travelling on to Villa Nougués, on another bus that was leaving later. That was where his family lived. Petra had heard of Villa Nougués and wanted to see it. They arrived at the coach station. Petra asked if he could help carry her things to the hotel, which was a few blocks away. Her friend Frida wasn't arriving until the next day.

Either he was very innocent or knew how to play dumb; either way, he happily accepted. And off they went, she with her rucksack and he carrying the guitar.

He was innocent, as it turned out. When they got to the door of the hotel, Gonzalo made as if to say goodbye and leave. She had to order him: "Wait." And he waited while she checked in. Petra gestured to him to go with her up to the room. In the elevator, while Gonzalo avoided eye contact, she wondered if the boy might be a virgin, or gay. In the bedroom she confirmed that he was neither of those things. Just a shy boy. And quite indefatigable, his physical fitness evident in a brown body of pure muscle and long bones and in the way that, once he saw the way things were going, he didn't stop. Petra felt exhausted and happy, and she didn't mind that the only interruption Gonzalo made was to call his mother to say he would be arriving a bit later.

II

"He's a child," Petra insisted, in answer to Frida's indulgent expression.

They had arrived at Villa Nougués the day before. They were staying in a little hotel, a refurbished house with just a few bedrooms, a garden with ancient trees which gave the place a bucolic feel, and a pool that wasn't very big, just big enough to make the most of the summer's last warm days. Frida was surprised by her friend's attack of saintliness. If the boy was so gorgeous, why not make the most of him? She didn't have to fall in love with him or make a commitment. They were on vacation.

Petra had met up with Gonzalo the same day they arrived in Villa Nougués. Shortly afterwards, Frida received a text that read: *I'm going to need the room. His family's at home.* So Frida took her MP3 player and went to sunbathe on the terrace by the pool. Five minutes later someone from the reception desk explained very politely that she couldn't go topless. Frida put her bikini top on and carried on sunbathing, swearing under her breath. Two hours later Petra appeared.

"Well, you look freshly fucked," she said, in her old-world Spanish.

Before travelling together in Europe, they had always used English to communicate. But on that same trip, Spanish became the common language that both united them and kept other travellers at arm's length. Since then they had continued to speak in Spanish, no matter where they were.

"That boy made me feel old very quickly. Happy too, though."

"How were things with the little lad?"

"You know when you go to a patisserie and you eat a spectacular chocolate cake and you think it's just the most amazing thing in the universe and then you go back the following week and ask for the same cake and it's still delicious, just not quite as much as the first time? Well, that."

"Cloying."

"A bit, but still delicious. What about you?"

"Oh, I'm fine. Except these Mormons won't let me get my tits out in the pool."

In the following days, Petra holed up with Gonzalo a couple more times in the hotel room. She didn't want to abuse her friend's patience. Frida was obliging all the same: she liked walking around that town of beautiful houses and winding roads.

"Gonzalo told me he wants to travel with me. He wants to take a gap year to see Europe and for me to go with him."

"Not a bad idea."

"I couldn't stand him travelling on the train as a Young Person, and me as an old person."

"A responsible adult. You'd be there to look after him."

"That's what I thought. I couldn't take him to half the places I'd like to visit. He's too healthy, too sporty. Admittedly that makes him a fucking machine. But is that what one wants, a fucking machine?"

"Well ... yes."

"Yes, of course you would."

"OK, sweetheart, keep out of my life, eh. And go and fuck your little machine."

Petra decided to arrange a double date and asked Gonzalo to find a friend for Frida. One thing, though: if possible, he shouldn't be quite as young.

They met in a pub close to the hotel. Gonzalo arrived with a young man who looked about twenty-five. He was called Juan and had recently qualified as an engineer. For Frida there was no spark right from the start, so the poor boy kept rowing and rowing without ever arriving at port. Frida, in an effort to combat the boredom which she felt creeping upwards from her feet, set to drinking one mojito after another. Since Petra never lagged behind when it came to drinking cocktails, they ended up very drunk, and the guys did too. Petra went to the hotel room. Frida stayed with Juan, who kept insisting on taking her somewhere. He tried to kiss her. She let him kiss her and laughed. She told him he was moving very fast. Outside the bar, Juan tried to kiss her again and she stopped him, saying that he was a lovely guy but that she had just broken up with someone and wanted nothing to do with men. That undoubtedly in different circumstances they would have had a great time, just not that day. Juan kept trying, almost as a reflex. In the end, he grumbled a bit and went off, leaving her alone at the door of the pub. The young engineer had not been very gallant.

Frida walked to the hotel. Other young people were coming out of the bars and there was a lot of movement in the streets. She didn't want to interrupt her friend, so she walked on to the park and sat on one of the deckchairs. There was no one there, just the sound of crickets singing. The sky was dark blue. She could have spent the whole night there.

An hour later, Petra appeared.

"I thought I'd find you here."

"Perhaps I should be sucking off your boy's older friend in a car. And shouldn't you be in the room, screwing?"

"Alcohol wreaks havoc on the young. I sent him home. What were you thinking about?"

"That when I was trying to think of a lie to extricate myself from the engineer, I actually told him the truth."

"Which truth was that?"

"That love has caused me a lot of suffering and I no longer want anything to do with men."

"And where does that leave me?"

"You know how when you try a chocolate cake it seems like the best taste in the world, and then you try vanilla cakes and coconut ones but they don't taste the same? Well, that's how I feel about you."

Petra sat down beside her and took her hand. Petra's face in the darkness looked like the portrait of some actress from silent movies. They looked into each other's eyes. She had always liked Petra's dark eyes, that expression that seemed always to be seeking something more.

"Do you know what the black moon is?" Petra asked her.

"I'd like to know."

"When the moon gets closer to the sun, we can't see it from Earth. The solar glare is so strong it stops the moon from appearing in the sky."

"And am I the sun or the moon?"

"You're the sun. I'm the moon."

Frida looked in her little bag for her MP3 player and placed the earphones on Petra. "Listen to this song."

Petra sat listening.

"It's beautiful, but I don't understand much Portuguese."

"It says something like nobody noticed the moon, that life goes on and I can't stop looking at you."

Petra kissed her hand. "I think it's time we went to sleep."

It was after midday when they woke up. Feeling hungry, they went to a bar and ordered sandwiches. They were still a little hung-over from the night before and neither of them mentioned their conversation in the park.

When they got back to the hotel, Frida asked what was going to happen to the boy.

"I think he's in love. Or something like it. I'd better end it now. I don't think I'll see him again."

"You should meet him and tell him."

"Responsibility isn't my strong suit."

"Write him a song."

They laughed.

"OK then, I'll write him a song, video it and send it to him."

Petra picked up the guitar, while Frida turned on the camera and looked for the function that allowed you to shoot video. Then she trained it on herself and said:

"I'm sorry, little one, you're too much of a boy for a woman like Petra. But you know what, kid? Your Italian granny has written this song for you."

Petra started singing in Italian. It was a song about the age difference between a woman and a boy. Halfway through the song, a string broke.

"There's been an accident," said Frida, and they both burst out laughing. Frida switched off the camera.

They decided to go and buy a new guitar string.

"I don't think they'll sell them here," said Petra.

"In the pub we went to yesterday bands play live. Perhaps they'll be able to tell us where we can get one."

They set off for the bar.

"You know what I'm thinking, Frida? That we should carry on with our journey. Head to Cafayate. What do you think?"

"Maybe."

They arrived at the pub. It looked different by day. It had a slightly dingy atmosphere, like a bar for single men. But there was a girl sitting alone at one of the tables.

"Good afternoon, do you know where we can buy a string?" Frida asked the man behind the bar.

The barman explained that they would have to go to San Miguel de Tucumán. He told them how to get there. They would need to take a taxi. At that moment the solitary girl offered to take them. Frida looked at her properly for the first time. Just looking at her, she felt her body respond. She had that feeling of being at the start of a story. Of a love story, of a tragedy. Of something that can only happen when one is fully alive.

February–December 2013